DO NOT REMOVE
CARDS FROM POCKET

I've travelled the world twice over,
Met the famous: saints and sinners,
Poets and artists, kings and queens,
Old stars and hopeful beginners,
I've been where no-one's been before,
Learned secrets from writers and cooks
All with one library ticket
To the wonderful world of books.

A WREATH FOR JENNY'S GRAVE

Three months after her marriage to wealthy designer Lars Sven, beautiful Jenny Midnight died mysteriously. Her friend Ruth, grief-stricken, wanted to know why. In Sven's forbidding castle overlooking the Mediterranean, bizarre and near fatal accidents began to befall Ruth and she became even more suspicious about the manner of Jenny's death. Trapped in a castle that might harbour her friend's murderer, Ruth sought the key to the mystery—only to find that in the past lay the evil seeds of her destruction . . .

CHARLOTTE HUNT

A WREATH FOR JENNY'S GRAVE

Complete and Unabridged

ULVERSCROFT
Leicester

First published in New York in 1975 by
Ace Books,
New York

First Large Print Edition
published July 1988

Copyright © 1975 by Ace Books

British Library CIP Data

Hunt, Charlotte
    A wreath for Jenny's grave.—Large print ed.—
Ulverscroft large print series: romance, suspense
I. Title
823′.914[F]

ISBN 0-7089-1836-0

Published by
F. A. Thorpe (Publishing) Ltd.
Anstey, Leicestershire
Set by Rowland Phototypesetting Ltd.
Bury St. Edmunds, Suffolk
Printed and bound in Great Britain by
T. J. Press (Padstow) Ltd., Padstow, Cornwall

1

IT was after the bottom fell out of my
world that I decided to go to Majorca
to lay a wreath on my dear friend
Jenny Midnight's grave.

Ralph Wandsworth was my world then,
or so I thought. We were living together,
without benefit of marriage, in a cottage
on the Mendip Hills within sight of what
they still call, down there, the Severn Sea.

Beginning to make my way as a sculp-
tress, and doing a bit on the side with
homemade pottery, jams, and tweed
woven on an old hand loom, I was shat-
tered when Ralph jilted me.

Oh, there'd been signs and signals for
anybody with eyes to see them, but I had
foolishly ignored them all. Afterwards, of
course, I'd sorted them out like so many
clues in a detective story. But by then it
was much too late.

Some of Ralph's pictures were on sale
in the studio. He painted landscapes—
abstracts—in dark, gloomy colours. All

the avant-garde critics raved about them, but only a few art galleries ever bought any, and even then they'd hang about unsold—sometimes for months.

He'd been away, in London, for a few days. He went, or so he told me, to arrange for a private showing of his pictures in a friend's Mayfair gallery. That was in the third week of August.

I remember that the sun was blazing into the stone-paved courtyard so that the scarlet geraniums, roses, and phlox in the truncated apple barrels blazed with a brightness that put me in mind of the hotel garden on the Costa Brava where we'd gone for our last year's holiday.

I'd come down, before breakfast, to pick up a white pottery horse from the studio that a London client had ordered by telephone a few days before.

Humming to myself, catching a glimpse, a mile or two away, of the sea, lying like grey silk between the great, gaunt hills that are Mendip, nothing warned me . . . or did it?

As sometimes happens before a crisis—does the subconscious have some sort of prescience?—my mind annihilated time. It unreeled before me like pictures on a screen. So perhaps coming events do cast their shadows before them, or maybe the mind itself sees into the future, if only dimly.

Crossing the courtyard, horse in hand, I felt, all at once, chilled to the bone. For I suddenly saw Jenny! Her baby fine ash-blonde hair was pulled into two tight pigtails. She wore the pink calico dress with white collar and cuffs that had been our uniform in the state orphanage. Time, then, rocked . . . I saw her, as if I looked through field-glasses, and she was at the end of the tunnel vision.

She was eleven years old, and sitting on the edge of the dormitory bed.

"Now, Ruth, just look!"

Jenny dragged the white counterpane from the bed, and draped it, with superb grace and panache, around her already developing form.

"I'm going to be a model girl when I grow up, Ruth! I'll make lots and lots of money and marry a rich man. I won't be beholden to anybody for anything! No more, 'Yes ma'am' and 'thank you kindly, ma'am.' I won't help anybody at all—'cept you, darling Ruth! And when I want help, I'll ask nobody but you!"

Oh, they were very kind to us in that orphanage, but to a fiercely independent soul like Jenny, even the kindness was a soreness on the mind.

She'd been left on the orphanage doorstep at six months of age at midnight on a Christmas Eve in the Fifties. Nobody ever found out who her parents were, for although she was warmly dressed and her clothing good, there wasn't the smallest clue to their identity or background.

The nurses called her "Jenny Midnight" because of the time she was found, and the fact that the one who picked her up had an aunt Jenny with eyes her colour. Jenny herself found the curious appellation strikingly helpful when she achieved her ambition and started modeling.

Now, looking down at the base of the white horse, it occurred to me that the words *Ruth Foundling* had at least given the same slightly bizarre distinction to my own career. I'd been left on the orphanage porch too, but there was a note pinned to my shawl: "This is Ruth. Please look after her." I was six months old, too, and I arrived the day after Jenny.

Nobody ever traced my parents, either, but at least I'd started off with my own Christian name, as Jenny was quick to point out. It was the only advantage over her I ever did have, or wanted. I gave her the love I might have given to a parent or sister. She loved me too, but less possessively. For Jenny's real love was life, and the whole business of living. Her vitality was extraordinary.

Of course the fact that we were both left on the orphanage steps, as abandoned infants, and that we grew up together there, in that grim-faced soot-covered building in East London, made a bond between us.

Yet, somehow, I think that even if we'd been reared in quite different circumstances, that sense of affinity would always have been there. Physically and psychologically we were totally dissimilar, but that didn't matter either. Accepting the strong differences between us, all we knew was that, from babyhood on, something had fused us.

Jenny kept her word about never

helping anybody but me, and she'd never had to ask me for help. It was calculated she was probably the older of us, and protected me through the orphanage years with a detached but tender love.

I had light brown hair and grey eyes and totally undistinguished features and personality. I did have a good figure, as Jenny was forever telling me, in an attempt to bolster up my lack of self-confidence.

Jenny was a beauty. Her hair was that fine, ash-gold which looks like spun silk. Her eyes were huge, dark blue, and shaded with thick black lashes. Her face was heart-shaped, and her complexion cameo-fine. The only thing that saved her from being dubbed a chocolate-box beauty was the seductive lure of her own figure, which took her into the top grouping of world models within three years of our leaving the orphanage.

A bit more of the film unwound itself, more pictures came. Six months after the Matron, not unsympathetically, placed us, at sixteen years of age, in sensible employment in offices, Jenny had become the youngest model in a famous dress designing establishment in Bond Street.

And I sat at the reception desk in the sales room. A few months after that, Jenny met and seduced aging Courtney Grafton, head of the business. She told him she was seventeen, and whether he believed her or not I've never known.

But that's how we got our respective positions at Grafton's, and climbed, as you might put it, to our twin ambitions from there. Jenny was Grafton's top model in a year, and I became chief receptionist.

But when I'd got enough money saved and was qualified for a grant, I went to art school, met Ralph, and together, we started the studio.

Jenny left Grafton—the Boutique, not Grafton himself. The two stayed good friends although after that, she was the mistress of many important men, young, middle-aged and old, in her chosen world of fashion and fashion designing.

But now she was dead—had been dead for nearly three months. She died in a nursing home in Majorca, on the Balearic Islands. I got a telegram from the British Consul which said, simply: "Regret Miss Jennifer Midnight died here today.

Appendicitis followed by complications. Please wire funeral instructions."

Abruptly, as grief tore at my heart again, the film stopped unrolling. I turned blindly towards the dark arch of the kitchen door, outlined against the white-wash of the cottage.

In the kitchen I was sipping at tea, wondering just why I'd thought of Jenny so keenly, even imagining I saw her orphanage image, when I noticed, through the open kitchen door, that there was a letter on the wooden flooring of the tiny hall.

In the same second, I heard the Parkets' bassett hound—they have the cottage at the top of the lane—barking his usual deep, baying protest to the bicycling postman.

Cup in hand, I wandered into the hall. Ralph's handwriting on the envelope set up, at first, only a puzzled reaction: he practically never wrote to me.

I took the letter back into the kitchen, set down the cup, and tore it open.

Ruth,

This is a hell of a way to break the news. But we both agreed, when we started, there'd be no strings attached. I've got no exhibition in London, my dear. I'm going to Canada. There's a girl there I owe a year or two. I've enjoyed it, Ruth. Good luck. I won't be back, ever.

Ralph

PS. Sell my stuff for what you can get. I'm afraid it won't bring much.

On the third day I stopped crying, and looked out of the window, and "saw" Jenny again. She was wearing that ghastly pink orphanage pinafore. She stood in the cottage garden, just staring in at me. And she clasped, this time, a posy of red roses in her hand, done up in that immaculate fashion, plastic-sheathed and ribbon tied, that is customary for weddings—and funerals. And, remembering, I caught my breath. Red roses!

Through the cocoon of misery, fury, disbelief, and heartbreak that cut me off from reality, Jenny "spoke" again. I suppose it was the state I was in—either an hallucination, or a vivid imaginative recall. Perhaps I wanted to see her so badly, subconsciously, I just built her up there.

But all she said was, as in the orphanage,

And when I want help, I'll ask nobody but you!

Not, mind you, that in the past, whenever Jenny hurt herself or was ill, I knew about it unless she told me. She kept her troubles fiercely to herself, and was only too anxious to share the happy times, for that, again, was her fiercely independent way.

So we'd never been like twins, or even some husbands or wives, or brothers and sisters, who communicate at a distance mentally. But we did, sometimes, have odd telepathic flashes, so that she might ring me, or write, and say she'd had flu, or been feeling depressed, or, on the other hand, landed a good modeling contract or backed a winner (she loved gambling in any shape or form), and I'd realise I'd been sharing her feelings, because at the time of the acute depression or happiness, I'd have been thinking of her—

10

not able, in fact, to get her out of my thoughts. But since I'd been living with Ralph, these feelings had grown less and less frequent. I was infatuated with Ralph, and I'm very sure he had never liked Jenny. She returned the feeling, always urging me to leave him. And I think, therefore, that his masculine vanity was outraged, for he was a very egotistic individual.

And when I want help, Ruth, darling, I'll ask nobody but you!

Again it came, that small, husky, taut whisper, just as in life she'd always spoken, with laughter always very close. Only now, the laughter was missing . . .

Shaking my head to clear it, I went to the window again. The little figure in the pink pinafore was gone. But that little whisper kept repeating itself in my head . . . and wouldn't go away.

The cottage was rented, furnished. Ralph's paintings, my bits and pieces in the studio, were all I owned. As for the paintings, they could stay there till they rotted. I scorned to do anything with them. Jenny left no money, successful

11

though she'd been. But then, who expects, after all, to die at twenty-four?

She'd spent every penny she earned, and I never blamed her. I think we both thought that one day she'd marry a rich man. I certainly couldn't imagine her marrying a poor one. It wasn't that she was a gold-digger, or even a materialist, but those years in the orphanage had left a much deeper mark on her than on me. I could always do without material possessions, so long as I had someone to love . . . and look where that got you, I thought now, in searing, angry bitterness! Jenny's honest way was better!

A Dr. Max Gertae wrote from Majorca, and the nursing home where they took her from Castello Minerva. He said the operation was successful, but peritonitis set in, and the antibiotics they injected couldn't do their work in time. According to him, Jenny must have had the appendicitis pain for days, and said nothing.

And, unlike me, who was physically very tough, she never had much resistance. Although she always liked to hide all signs of hurt, physical and emotional, a bug or a virus left her depressed and devitalized for weeks on end.

Financially, neither of us took any thought for the morrow, and Jenny, lately, hadn't needed to. Still, I thought, the man in London had sent a cheque only that morning for the white horse.

The rest of the studio furniture, which was mine, I would sell to an art school I knew would buy it, if not offering much. But, altogether, it would be enough to take me to Majorca, pay for my stay for a week or two in some modest pensione.

Oh, I don't think, then, I put Jenny's phantom figure, and voice, down to anything but nerves, and, of course, the deep, sickening emotional shock of Ralph's betrayal. But I knew I must put as much space as I could between me and that Mendip cottage, or go mad. Majorca seemed as good a place in which to take refuge as anywhere considering that, in my absorption with Ralph, I'd never even seen where they laid her. And I would put a wreath on Jenny's grave.

Jenny would never blame me for that neglect. She loathed funerals, all the ritual of death, and never attended memorial services or anything of that kind. Only once, in a sentimental mood, did she say that, if she died before me, I was to send red roses.

"And I'll have pink carnations," I'd told her grinning and we both burst out laughing. Till now, I'd forgotten the incident, even when she died, and I'd wired the British Consul to bury her in the English cemetery on the Island, and lay a floral tribute on her grave with a card: "From Ruth, in Loving Memory."

Ralph, I thought bitterly. While I wasted love on him, I'd forgotten Jenny, forgotten even the very flowers she'd asked for.

But if I sold out and went to Majorca, how should I go? I loathed flying: every second I was airborne terrified me. Another picture flashed itself off in my mind—a leaflet, with a cover showing a smart new coach loading up at Dover on one of the British Railways Ferries.

ESMERALDO COACH AGENCY said the leaflet. "Go overland to Spain and Italy. Come with us to the Costa Brava."

And when I remembered how, when Jenny stayed one weekend with Ralph and me, she toyed with the idea of joining an overland coach tour to Spain, and picking up the Palma ferry at Barcelona, where the coach stopped.

She'd gone to Palma to join Lars Sven, the Norwegian dress designer, who had a villa on the Island.

"I find flying so boring, Ruth. This way might be fun . . ."

In the end, however, Lars Sven sent her the money for the flight, telling her his top model must travel in style. Jenny was staying with him for the rest of the summer, the culmination of the visit being the Autumn Fashion Show, to be held at Castello Minerva, where Jenny would model his most recent gowns for all the elite of the world.

"Ruth," Jenny had gone on, "I'm very excited. Oh, not only about the autumn show. But I think Lars might soon ask me to marry him. And, when he does, I shall say yes. Jetting around the world is very exciting, but I'm beginning to feel I'd like to settle down, even bring up a family."

Remembering her own philosophy, I'd said quietly: "And Lars Sven? Do you love him, Jenny dear?"

Jenny shrugged: those midnight-blue eyes which I always flattered myself only I could truthfully read were suddenly totally enigmatic, even to me.

"He's been honest, like dear old Courtney Grafton." Her first employer, and lover, had died the previous month, leaving her a hundred pounds with which to buy a memento of him. "And he's very rich, Ruthie."

And Jenny looked at me in tender mockery, knowing my own romantic concept that, so long as you had real love, nothing else mattered. At that time, you see, I fondly believed Ralph, in time, would marry me.

Jenny hugged me.

"You're my only true love, Ruth," she said, and we both laughed.

But, still remembering, I went upstairs to the tiny oak-beamed room we'd called, ironically, our guest room. Nobody but Jenny had ever slept there.

All the friends I'd made at college (and there had been quite a few), now seemed to be in limbo. Oh, I got the occasional postcard or photograph at Christmas, and the casual, vague invitation to visit, that one suspected mustn't be taken too seriously.

Ralph's friends never came. Perhaps, I thought, with savage irony, they all lived in Canada?

Jenny had left a few of her belongings in a suitcase. She'd given up her smart service flat in town, and seemed uncertain about what she was going to do after that Majorcan summer. From that, I'd realised how strong were those hopes of marriage with Lars Sven.

Still, she'd had a marvellous life, packing into it more than people three times her age ever achieve. It's true that love makes you selfish, though. Ralph, then, had filled my days and nights. And bitter shame again overwhelmed me when it seemed I only had time to weep for Jenny when my emotional life was in ruins!

But no, that wasn't quite true. I'd wept plenty of tears at the time, or tried to, but Ralph had shut me up.

"She's dead and gone. Okay, you loved her. Now forget her," he'd commanded.

And so strong was my infatuation for him, I'd even tried to obey, as if the suppression of this entirely natural grief was something I even owed him!

Yet the tears came, all the same, at night, and often—as I thought curiously—after Ralph's lovemaking, and he'd turned away with a grunt of contempt, or disgust, or perhaps, a mixture of both.

And once he muttered: "Still thinking of her, aren't you? She was nothing but a refined sort of prostitute!"

And, though he never put it into open words, there was something in his attitude, and his tone, which suggested there was also a word for the relationship between Jenny and me.

Only that wasn't true, And had never been, and our lovemaking must have shown it, as well as Jenny's own relationships with men. But I knew he never believed it himself, but hinted at it out of spite, because Jenny had never liked him and, sexually, stayed completely cold towards him.

In the guest room, turning over the contents of the case, remembering suddenly that ugly, selfish mutter, I think what was left of my love for Ralph died. Or, at any rate, began a merciful, cathartic withering. A man who could talk so callously of a young and lovely girl dying at the height of her career was pretty worthless.

Yes, Ralph's exorcism was painful. Yet, as it worked, my preoccupation with Jenny's fate grew more powerful, the one probably compensating the other.

"I must get away," I muttered, "and once I'm gone, Ralph, at least, will stop haunting me!"

I opened Jenny's case with shaking hands. A few books, mostly poetry, which Jenny loved, the birth certificate the orphanage had discreetly provided us with, and an old address book, scribbled up with telephone numbers.

A leaflet was in with a lot of other junk, old theatre programmes, odd recipes, (she loved experimenting with those) and beauty hints torn from magazines. Beauty hints! Jenny, my beautiful, lovely Jenny, would have looked alluring in an old sack!

There lay the leaflet, then, with its heading: ESMERALDO COACH AGENCY. Next to it was a stout manila envelope, stamped with the British Consul's seal from

Majorca. The envelope held Jenny's passport, the telegram from the British Consul announcing her death, the letter from Dr. Max Gertae, the death certificate, and finally, a letter from Lars Sven.

Dear Miss Foundling:

Jenny talked about you with true tenderness. You were, she assured me, her only true friend—apart from me, she was good enough to add. I am, of course, deeply grieved about her death. But she had the best of medical care and attention. Dr. Max Gertae is a very able surgeon. He did all that could possibly be done.

If it is any consolation, she was taken out of life when still young and lovely. Perhaps, in this rather sick and unhappy old world, that's best—who really knows?

I shall be here, at Castello Minerva, till the late autumn. Although Jenny is no more, I am still hoping to put on my Autumn Fashion Show. She would have wanted that, I know. If you should decide to make a pilgrimage here, to

20

visit your friend Jenny's grave, please let me know. I should be glad to extend the hospitality of the Castello.

Yours in sympathy,
Lars Sven

PS. The bulk of the jewelery and gowns she was wearing here belong to my collection. I'm sending on her own things which Marie, my maid, has packed. Remember, if there is ever anything I can do, I am your servant.

The expensive smaller pigskin case lay in the wardrobe. It had come a month after Jenny died. I'd pushed it there, hating the very sight of it. And, of course, Ralph was at the cottage.

I tried to remember what I knew of Lars Sven, even then disliking the formality, insincere as it struck me, of that last phrase in the postscript.

It wasn't much. He was, of course, Norwegian, and about twice Jenny's age. He wore a Vandyke beard, long brown hair, and had sharply-delineated features.

He was tall, and thin, too thin for his near six-feet, I believed. He spoke English with a very slight accent, wore immaculate tweeds which he ordered, so Jenny told me, through the mail from Savile Row, not much liking to come to England now; they had his measurements from former days. His eyes were very dark, almost black.

He was amongst the best half-dozen dress designers in Europe, and reported to be immensely wealthy.

I saw Lars Sven the day he called for Jenny to drive her to Heathrow Airport. He sent her the air fare and then decided, on impulse, to make one of his rare trips to England. He motored down to pick up Jenny at the cottage.

To me, at the time, that act seemed a bit overpossessive, although I'd not said so to Jenny. I gave them lunch, alfresco, in the courtyard. He expressed himself as charmed. But I felt he viewed Ralph, myself, our pied-à-terre, and insignificant careers, with tolerant, scarcely-veiled contempt. We were not, like him, at the top of the tree.

"Oh I liked the fellow," Ralph protested, when they'd gone—Jenny, as it turned out, to her death. "You're so bloody ultra-sensitive, Ruth. Always too ready to assume somebody or other's patronising you. It's just self-pity. After all, Jenny Midnight was raised in the same orphanage. And look what she's done with her life!"

But that was before Jenny died, before he was forced to accept, and reject, my grief, that interfered with his necessary sex life.

He went on, idly, as he picked up a canvas in which he'd rather too blatantly tried to influence Sven and failed dismally. "I'd cultivate Sven. Might give you a leg up or two in your career!"

My mind, now, curled in contempt at that! Ralph wasn't remotely interested in my career and never had been. He had the bad artist's true egotism, though. If I cultivated Sven, he, Ralph, might get some benefit.

Turning over exquisitely fine under-wear, shoes, suits, dresses, I thought, no longer drearily but with hardening spirit, there was hint enough there for anybody with sense enough to see it.

Ralph had lost interest in me. Plainly, I got on his nerves. Finally, when even lovemaking, where at least I'd imagined he'd had no complaints, palled, he'd gone. And wouldn't be back, ever.

Even as I told myself I didn't care, and even, as with every second that passed, this became more and more the truth, the emptiness I felt was still appalling.

The clothes were all good, and they fitted me, as I could see when I tried some of the underwear on. Well, I'd keep the case and the clothes. There was little sense in getting rid of them, because I needed both if I was to get myself to Majorca. I'd no money to buy new ones, and the others, that Jenny brought and left, were no good for that kind of journey.

Next, I rang up the Esmeraldo Coach Agency. They had a vacant seat on a coach that was leaving for Barcelona in seven days' time. I hesitated only for a second then told them to reserve it, that I'd send on a cheque that day.

And I killed all the time in between by going for long walks over Mendips, and drugging myself with sleeping tablets at night. I'd not got a hotel booked in Palma, but the girl at the Esmeraldo Agency recommended one, and said they'd book me a single room through their tour representative in Palma. Lars Sven's invitation was altogether too grand. I supposed I might call on him.

So that was all right, and in the end, it was a bitter-sweet relief to turn the key in the front door, pile my suitcase (that had been Jenny's suitcase) into the front seat of the taxi that was waiting, and turn my back on the past.

2

I'D deliberately planned the journey so that I need not spend any extra time in London. For that was where I'd met Ralph, and although the memories of the city that also belonged to Jenny made my heart ache, but did not turn my thoughts to bitterness, I'd decided the less time I actually spent there, the better.

The fast train I took from Bristol got me to Paddington well before noon; the Esmeraldo coach didn't start till four o'clock. I took another taxi to Victoria, deposited my suitcase in the left luggage department, and then, for want of anything else to do, wandered into Westminster Cathedral.

Jenny and I had both been baptized and confirmed in the Protestant Church of England religion, for that had been the custom of the orphange. Jenny liked going to church; the ritual, particularly, delighted her. She had often slipped into Westminster Cathedral to be utterly enchanted and captivated by the ritual of the Mass, the candles, the fragrance of the incense, the solemnity and peace.

I had never professed any faith.

"Ruth, you're wrong," Jenny said to me once when, in one of of our rare intervals of serious talk, we discussed life, death, and a possible hereafter. "There must be something, somewhere, into which we go! Otherwise, our lives, here, would make no sense . . ."

The High Mass, in all its colour and splendour, was proceeding at the High Altar, with scarlet-robed priests visible amidst the drifting incense smoke. Slipping into a side chapel, I pushed some coins into the slit in the wall, and took up two white candles. Lighting them from those already burning on the stand, I said no prayers. But I remembered Jenny, and the curious pilgrimage upon which I was bound.

When I came out I had tea at an old-fashioned bun shop. By then I was getting stupidly tense, full of panic-stricken fears about the journey. There were all those strangers I should have to meet on the way, and the tedium of exchanging

27

commonplaces with them, talking to people I'd no desire to know. I was very tired. Even with the sleeping tablet I'd taken the night before, I'd slept scarcely at all.

I wandered off Victoria Street into one of the side streets. Then I remembered I'd not got any cigarettes, and went into a little shop where they sold coffee. Because I only had a five pound note, I bought a packet of cigarettes, some matches, and ordered coffee.

It would kill time, I thought, and sat down at a dark little alcove at the back, and lighted a cigarette, the pigskin case at my feet.

It occurred to me I ought to make a last check of my documents: passport, Spanish currency, and so on. These were zipped up in the outside compartment of the case. I got them out, putting the case on a chair beside the table, checked them, thrust them back into the wallet provided by the Esmeraldo Agency.

As I did so, my fingers encountered some other piece of paper that seemed to be trapped there. I thrust my hand further into the space to draw out a single sheet of heavy blue bond paper.

The handwriting was square, thick, very masculine and strong. It was headed from some address in London, in Mayfair, a street I vaguely remembered.

My dear Miss Midnight,

I would very much like to make your acquaintance.

I have seen your modeling work, and greatly admire your style and technique.

I would like to offer you some work, and perhaps we could meet somewhere in London to discuss this? Would you be so kind as to telephone me at the above number sometime?

Sincerely,
Lars Sven

That was odd! Why had Lars Sven sought Jenny out, when the natural thing would surely have been for him to contact her through one of the modeling agencies? And I'd always thought, from what Jenny told me about him, that this was what he'd done! Instead, it seemed he'd made this personal approach . . .

There was something else in the outside compartment of the smart pigskin case too. As I thrust back the note, I felt against my fingers something softer, more yielding.

Drawing this out, too, I found I was looking down at a sheet of newspaper, the front page of a London daily. And in the centre of the page there was a photograph of Jenny—Jenny, lovely figure sheathed in a sleeveless dress that came only to the top part of her thighs, revealing her beautiful legs and shapely ankles.

Jenny was smiling, holding a big hamper of Christmas toys in her arms: teddy bears, dolls, golliwogs, miniature cars and aeroplanes. Jenny, mink coat over the sleeveless dress, stood on the orphanage steps, poised, and under the photograph, this short article.

FAMOUS MODEL VISITS HOME ORPHANAGE

Jenny Midnight, top model, came back, this Christmas Eve, to take toys and gifts to the children of the orphanage where she was herself reared and educated.

Left on these orphanage steps when she was six months old, Jenny Midnight told our reporter she hoped, one day, to come back again, and begin an investigation into her own life history. "I'd like to search Parish Registers and places," said Jenny Midnight wistfully, "to get some clue about my parents—who they were, where they came from, why they left me abandoned, on these steps . . ."

She explained that, like every child in the orphanage, she had a proper birth certificate issued through a local Registrar, but that she yearned to know her real name and history.

Smiling, I thrust back the cutting. I'd seen that newspaper report last Christmas, and wondered why Jenny bothered to keep it. For I knew she had no real intention of undertaking any such investigation. She liked to romance, but in fact, she now— or when alive—had had a horror that she might find out something it would be better not to know!

There was a flow of customers into the

cafe, much chatter, giggling, demands for coffee, sandwiches, cakes. With a hasty glance at my watch, I realised I'd dawdled too long. I got outside, hailed another taxi, and was transported to Victoria Station.

I knew I must go to the rear to find the Esmeraldo coach and its courier. It was there already but, to my relief, only half-full.

Two Spanish middle-aged couples, loaded down with salami and brandy, took the front seats. A young Spanish boy who'd been spending a holiday with a brother in Hampstead sat across the aisle from me. Then there was a honeymoon couple in the back seat, so fringed with hair and dressed so identically it was hard to tell who was the bridegroom and who was the bride. A middle-aged English couple sat between me and the Spanish boy. School teachers, they were already absorbed in maps and guide books, the wife dutifully making a log of the journey.

Pepi, the French courier, whose Greek-shaped head, plastered with curls, I longed to sculpt, had breezily introduced us all to each other.

"At Calais we pick up the Spanish

coach," he said. "And we sleep at Lyon tomorrow night."

"We have waited for Mr. Hamilton, our only other passenger too long, I think. Bad luck, but now, we go . . ."

We were already turning out of the station yard when a tall chap with long red hair, beard, side-whiskers, and wearing shabby green velvet jeans and an anorak with a torn hood, practically threw his bursting haversack under the coach's wheels.

"What the bloody hell!" yelled the driver. Pepi, eversmiling, curls dancing in the breeze, opened the door and hauled red-hair aboard.

"You just make it, after all. It is Mr. Hamilton, yes?" cried Pepi.

"Yes, it is," growled Hamilton, unshedding, at Pepi's request, his passport, hotel reservation, coach ticket and, horror of horrors, Esmeraldo tour button!—

"Shoulda come on an earlier train, mate!" he added.

"Oui," said Pepi, aggravatingly, "it is not wise to cut things too fine!"

Hamilton, seething, flung himself and his knapsack into the seat directly behind

33

me. I caught the flash of hazel eyes, deeply-set, and really rather fine.

"Ruddy lectures!" I heard him mutter. "Not my fault! Everybody should be made to keep to a proper time table . . ."

Pepi's face—he had a little seat of his own beside the driver—maintained the imperturbable look no doubt assumed especially for the more irritating of his passengers. That veiled glance, to me, concealed an infinite contempt, albeit diplomatically hidden.

Juan, the boy across the aisle, grinned then shrugged, and the English male teacher said, deliberately loud, "Decadent lot, all of them! Always blaming everybody else for their own shortcomings! Disgraceful!"

Behind me I heard Hamilton's weight shift, then he yelled back, "I tell you the ruddy train was late. It wasn't my fault! And anyway, why can't you mind your own ruddy business!"

Every eye on the coach now seemed to be on Hamilton. From deciding he was boorish, I now started to admire his courage.

"What language! Really! Ignore him, Harold dear—much the best way!"

"And go to hell!" muttered Hamilton, under his breath, as if recollecting he must, perforce, share the coach area for the next three days with the rest of us.

I slept in a reclining chair on the Dover-Calais run, and on the journey to Lyon in the big, over-heated French coach into which we filed, like sheep, as we disembarked at the French port.

The rest of the passengers slept as well. This suited me. Never much of a girl for cosy chats with strangers, my mood, if not quite as anti-social as Mr. Hamilton's, was of the kind best described as withdrawn.

Now that I had the time to think, I was asking myself what I was going to do when my money ran out. The visit, or pilgrimage, for that seemed the better word, embarked upon so impulsively, now began to have slightly sinister overtones. My traveller's cheques amounted to one hundred pounds. They would have to cover my hotel bill on Majorca. My fare home was paid but, when I did get back, I should land in England again without a farthing.

I'd elected to return by air, although still loathing it, but I could get a cheap flight from Palma Airport and I fancied the one journey out, by coach, would be enough.

Well, I'd have, of course, to get a job teaching in Art School. Or, if worst came to worst, I supposed, vaguely, that I could work in an office or even become a tea-lady.

We left Lyon on the second morning. I'd slipped upstairs, after the usual breakfast of rolls and coffee, to escape the hurtful jollity of the crowd in the dining room.

The truth was that I felt a complete outcast. Well, wasn't that what I'd wanted, I asked myself as I wasted time before the coach started piling my brown hair up in to a French knot, and thrusting pins into my scalp with clumsy fingers?

If not, exactly, an outcast, at least a solitary traveller, a pilgrim, come to lay a wreath on Jenny's grave. The others on the coach were all ardent holiday-makers. Naturally, sensing the difference that must be plain in me, I was being avoided.

Well, if I ever wanted to get to Majorca,

I'd best start out for the coach. I could always take refuge from the rest of the passengers by pretending to be asleep.

The country had been interesting, but I'd not allowed for nostalgia. Ralph, when we'd motored from Calais to Spain last summer, drove down through this part of France to the Spanish frontier at Port Bou. He'd been so attentive, so charming then, finding a wonderful little inn where we were the only guests, and arranging for us to dine in the stone courtyard, with candles fixed into bottle tops, and Madame and her husband running to and fro with the dishes as if we were very honoured guests.

Ralph, I thought dizzily, when I heard a man shouting. I picked up my bag, hurried down the stairs, there to be confronted by a polite, but obviously irritated Pepi.

"So, there you are, Mees Foundling! The coach—she is waiting! You come quickly, if you please!"

Now I couldn't have kept it waiting more than a minute or two. The previous day, at a lunch-time halt, two of the younger girls held us up for thirty minutes, while they hunted for a side street shop where a particular kind of perfume might be bought. Then, Pepi had shaken his head, as a matter of form, but his smile had been almost indulgent.

Now, one firm tough young hand under my elbow, he hurried me to the side of the gleaming blue and white coach in the cobblestoned yard which, to my fevered imagination, seemed also to be quivering with resentful impatience.

I climbed the two steps aboard to find myself the recipient of darting, indignant glances. The male teacher said, spitefully audible, "Disgraceful; older people ought to know better—not as if she was a slip of a girl. Serve her right if we'd left her behind."

Furthermore, I saw that the passengers had been playing "musical chairs," changing seats, and in some cases, places. Two young girls in jeans and bright blouses sprawled defiantly, in the fourth seat from the front which, till then, I'd had all to myself.

"That's my seat," I said angrily.

"'Tisn't now," said the tougher looking of the girls. Her companion smirked.

Casting a glance at Pepi, I found him ostentatiously writing something in his file.

The schoolmaster's wife's smile made me feel sick. A young couple behind them stared coldly.

"What's she doing, all on her own, the poor Senorita?" murmured the stout Spanish lady, but with something of their condescension.

My colour mounting, my breathing turning to agitated gasps, I pushed my way to the very back of the coach. There, alone in a welter of discarded mackintoshes, guide books, and general clutter sat Mr. Hamilton, looking, I suspected, no more delighted at my tardy appearance than the other passengers, despite their own ungracious, earlier reception of him.

Shoving a knapsack to one side, I squeezed into the other corner seat, leaving him loosely and disjointedly sprawled in the other.

He stared, noncommittal, red bushy eyebrows upraised.

"This particular seat," I said icily—or as icily as I could physically manage, for the temperature, I suspected, was already up in the eighties—"is supposed to accommodate six persons."

"Pardon me, Miss Foundling," I supposed he must have heard Pepi so addressing me, "but the number, actually, is four—on long journeys." His voice, now that he wasn't in a temper, proved to be naturally rather deep and musical, with a hint of Highland Scots and dry humour in it.

"Baggage—all baggage, including knapsacks and overnight bags—are supposed to go into the boot," I snapped, "not clutter up the seats where other passengers elect to sit."

Actually, there was nowhere else left for me to sit as he could see for himself. Those people travelling alone had deliberately spread coats, newspapers, or carrier bags stuffed with food on to the exterior seats beside them.

Feeling like some naughty schoolchild come late to the outing, I glowered at the unfortunate Mr. Hamilton.

"You have very attractive grey eyes," he said reflectively. "Especially when you're mad. They glow."

Suddenly, I found I was giggling, but

40

my laughter had an edge to it, and I cut it off prematurely, suddenly terrified I would, in another minute, either be in tears or hysterics. That would be sure entertainment for the rest of my fellow passengers, already, I suspected, growing bored with the journey.

"Now, now, Miss Foundling," said Hamilton, "you should really eat more. I noticed at breakfast you only swallowed a half-cup of coffee, and you didn't make much of a stab at dinner last night either."

"Mr. Sherlock Holmes of Baker Street, I presume." It was a feeble retort, but now that the sun was full on me, I was already feeling tired before the day had begun, and I knew that if I didn't snap out of it, I should surely burst into tears.

Hamilton merely grinned. "I prefer Agatha Christie."

He then offered me an apple from his knapsack. I declined it. Undeterred, he then proferred an orange, and when that, too, was refused, a cigarette.

I'd run out of the latter, and the aroma, when he lighted his, was suddenly over-powering. I nearly weakened.

Something else overpowered me before

I could accept, however. My stomach contracted violently, my eyes felt as if they were crossing themselves behind their lids and Hamilton's loosely-knit form began to waver about in front of me in the most alarming fashion.

"I say, you're going green!" he said.

I fumbled to my feet and down the gangway. The driver and Pepi seemed a long way off.

"Here! Come on!" said Hamilton firmly. "Hang on to Daddy's hand like a good little girl, and follow me."

Half pulling, half dragging me up the gangway, knocking off the schoolmistress's hat in the process, and sending the man's guide book on to the floor, Hamilton plunged heedlessly on, to summarily tap Pepi on the shoulder.

"Passenger—motion sickness!" I heard him announce, so importantly that even in my physical distress, I wanted to giggle. "Kindly halt the vehicle, s'il vous plaît, yes?"

"Oui!" groaned Pepi, taking one totally disgusted glance at me.

He called something in French to the big, burly driver, and the vehicle halted.

Hamilton swung open the door and grabbed me.

Mercifully, there was a small wood not ten yards back. Into its cool green depths I took my ignominy, and what little breakfast I had consumed.

"Better?" said Hamilton, proferring a huge soft white handkerchief which smelled deliciously of oranges. He stood back, staring.

"Now, you're just wan," he went on critically, "not green. Suits you better, especially under this sun."

It seemed to me a particularly tactless remark.

"And not having had much food inside you, of course, just made it worse!"

I muttered something about wiseacres.

"Not altogether. Used to be a medical student," Hamilton announced bossily. "Before I took up my present job."

I had no energy left even to wonder what that might be. Hamilton peered down the road. Pepi could now be seen, dancing up the sunlighted highway towards us, sculptured curls lifting slightly in what breeze there was.

"O Lord!" groaned Hamilton. "Here

comes the great white hope of the Bolshoi Ballet! Come on, before we get treated to another of those pretty but damn-awful smiles!"

3

MY hand was seized in Hamilton's great paw, and I was hustled down towards Pepi and the chrome-trimmed coach behind him. As we went, I found I was now shaking with suppressed giggles, the product of my fatigue and embarrassment and something in Hamilton himself, a kind of splendid irony which he seemed able, and ready, to extract from the most painful of situations.

Pepi's eye now thoughtfully rested on the pair of us. We climbed back, and proceeded defiantly to our places amidst the combined stares of the coach passengers. I suppose out of human decency, most of them now had managed to fix a commiserating smile on their faces. Even the schoolteachers looked less formidable.

"What's your name—your first name?" Hamilton asked, as we subsided amidst our clutter of possessions again.

"Ruth," I said shortly.

"Amid the alien corn," he smiled. Then

he plunged his hand into the rucksack and produced a phial of Alka-Seltzer tablets, and a small bottle of mineral water of the kind that had a screw cap and a plastic beaker. "I'm Ian. My last name you already know. I'm domiciled in the Isle of Skye; professional address is Mayfair, London. Try that," he said, and put the beaker of fizzing seltzer in my hand.

"Nasty thing, motion sickness. Too much fat, probably. French butter can be very hard on the liver. Add to that the swaying of the coach, and your sleepness night . . ."

I wasn't going to ask how he knew I had had a sleepless night, but that, I thought wryly, seemed only too obvious!

"And you're very edgy," he said critically. "Not at all like a young female going on holiday. Why didn't you go by air?"

"Why didn't you?" I countered.

"Reasons," Hamilton said evenly. "Somebody told me about this Esmeraldo tour. So I thought I'd try it . . ."

Somebody told me too, I thought bleakly.

By then the torpor that often follows such sickness was creeping over me. I began to nod; my eyes were only half in focus. Soon the fields and the poplar-lined roads were left behind us. We halted at some sort of checkpoint, where the coach driver handed Pepi some documents which Pepi, in turn, handed through the coach window for an official to inspect.

We stopped for lunch at an inn set in the sun-baked road. The driver went off for water. In the inn the *cantinero* sold strong coffee in thick, chipped cups at a table set up in the courtyard.

The younger coach members ordered strong red and yellow wine in the three-handled glass holders, and amused themselves as well as the few Spanish onlookers at the other tables, by tipping back their heads and pouring the liquid straight down their throats in the local manner.

Ian Hamilton sat me down at a table by the window, and produced ripe watermelon in cool red slices.

"I—you're very kind," I said again, half-resenting what was now growing into an intense proprietorship, but too languid to reject it. My mind, too, struggled with the feeling that Hamilton was keeping me under some sort of surveillance, and although this seemed absurd, I couldn't quite throw off the sensation.

He drank Spanish wine expertly, from one of the three-spouted bottles, pronouncing it excellent. Despite his bonhomie, there was something enigmatic about him. I couldn't think, too, why he so patently ignored the smiles of several of the girls who were our fellow coach passengers, as if he was deliberately cultivating my society.

Soon I staggered away to the "Dames," a concrete hut at the roadside crowded with other passengers, including the acid schoolmistress. She was trying to wash her hands in a tiny trickle of water in the far-from-clean hand basin.

"I hope you're feeling better," she said piously. "But as I always tell my husband, it's such a mistake to come on these tours when you haven't the stomach for it."

Eyes half-shut, leaning back against the blazing whitewashed wall, waiting for whoever was inside the lavatory to emerge, I fought off an entirely primitive desire to hit her.

The lavatory door opened; one of the

girls, handkerchief to mouth, emerged, and fled, significantly, into the courtyard.

The schoolmistress marched into the inner compartment, slammed the door. Within seconds, she'd flung it open again, to totter out, hands upraised, gasping and white-faced, to double herself up over the basin and vomit.

Needs must, I thought, and went myself into what seemed to be a Spanish Black Hole of Calcutta.

"Drought in all this part of Spain," explained the gregarious Hamilton later, "for nearly three months now. You get any anti-cholera injections before you left?"

I shook my head. Tut-tutting, he shook his.

We re-entered the coach, and soon were off the concrete highway, and bowling on through dried-up mesa, where donkeys with ribs poking through their skins pulled carts full of melons, avocadoes, grapes, and pears. Olive trees with huge gnarled roots grew in groves, and men and women with sticks were harvesting them.

A primitive land, I thought; antique, too, and holding strange, even sinister undercurrents.

"I wonder," I said, not really talking to Hamilton, but thinking aloud, "I wonder how Jenny liked it."

"Jenny?"

"A friend," I explained. And, strangely, but now as if impelled to it, I found myself adding "A very dear friend. She died, in Palma, just a few months ago. Suddenly. Appendicitis with complications."

"Young?" said the quiet voice beside me.

"A few hours, you might say, older than I."

"How come you know the hour of her birth?"

Well, it was just a little like talking to a casual stranger aboard ship. Once we got to Barcelona, I should probably never see him again. I owed him something for his kindness—and anyway, I felt like talking. It was very clear no one else on the coach took the remotest interest in me, or my travels.

So I explained how we were brought up in the London orphanage, adding an outline of Jenny's modeling career, leaving him to guess just how she climbed so quickly, so soon.

"Are you, as it might be, going out to lay a wreath on Jenny's grave?"

His use of the same phrase that had been haunting my mind since I saw that hallucinaton of Jenny in the courtyard of the Mendip cottage, startled me. Again, his questions seemed superficial, wholly idle, but I began to feel a hardness behind the curiosity.

"Why—why do you say that, Mr. Hamilton?"

"Ian," he suggested in that gently ironic way that, to me, went incongruously with the long red hair, the red beard, and the rather hard hazel eyes. "About your question—is there any reason why I shouldn't have asked it?"

I looked out at the flat, hard-baked landscape of a village. The country, the landscape, the olive and walnut trees, even the people, had a steel-like, hard-outlined look, brazen as the sun and the atmosphere. By now, the temperature was up in the nineties. The aridity of the landscape began to depress me, and Ian Hamilton's presence was becoming an annoyance.

"You must forgive me," I found myself murmuring. "I'm just a bit on edge.

I—I've been working hard, before this holiday . . ."

"That, I should guess, is the understatement of the year, my dear girl!"

The coach swerved suddenly to avoid a bunch of attenuated chickens running, squawking, from a farm. The movement threw me against Ian Hamilton.

His hand grasped my waist to steady me as the vehicle swerved back, righting itself. His hand would, I fancied, have happily stayed there, but I moved further over to my side of the back seat.

"You going to Majorca—or Barcelona— or further down on the Costa Brava?" he asked.

"I'm catching the ferry to Majorca. To Palma. I'm staying at Casa Saint Paul, which is where the girl from the Esmeraldo Agency booked me."

"Oh, you booked through them, did you?"

"What about you?"

He grinned and waved a hand at his rucksack.

"Where the fancy takes me. I'll put up at little pensions and bed-and-breakfast places. I understand they are to be found, with a little searching. But I'll be crossing tonight to Palma. I'm going to Majorca, too."

"Oh," I said, and idly wondered if he was married, or if he'd left a girl back home?

He was a complete contrast to fastidious, introspective Ralph. But that, to me, was both a relief and a challenge. He found my company diverting, but, I felt, no more. Indeed, his attitude was slightly irritating in that I fancied he patronised me a bit, if kindly, indulging me like some child who threatened to get lost on her journey. It also seemed to me that there was a touch of pity in this humorous concern, almost as if he felt it a duty to come to my aid, although that duty was, at times, an irritation.

Maturity, no doubt, would grow on me, I told myself. Ralph, too, had always been irritated by my emotional dependence, as he called it. Perhaps Hamilton concealed his exasperation with more skill than Ralph had.

My clothes stuck to me like damp rags. Most of the men had taken off their shirts. Even the schoolmaster relaxed, though still with an air of slight defiance, in his shirt sleeves.

Fast reaching that stage of travel weariness when I longed for a nice cool shower, clean sheets, and a bed, my immediate discomfort was an enormous thirst, which would be quenched only by China tea, pale, hot, and perfumed.

Ahead, the sun glittered on the steel and concrete structure of a frontier post. "Le Perthus," grunted Hamilton. In a few minutes the coach halted. Spanish Customs officials climbed aboard, stared at us, comparing us, most unfavourably it seemed from their expressions, with the passports Pepi handed over by each seat.

I was for staying put in the coach, but Ian Hamilton made me get out, and took me into the splendid new restaurant at the top of the Pass. It had a glass-enclosed balcony looking out on a complex of shops, where the bright Spanish rugs and shawls and wooden bowls and tables were spread in the sunshine.

I recognised the schoolmistress and her husband, critically examining an iron stand on which maps and guide books were set out, beside a line of postcards showing the frontier station.

Hamilton had brought a pot of coffee and two enormous ham rolls for us both. We carried these to a table in the shade of some walnut trees, and as he bit hungrily into the rolls, I was glad to gulp, greedily, at the strong black coffee.

"Feeling better?" inquired Hamilton.

"Yes, thanks. I'll be glad when we get to Barcelona, though. I suppose there'll be time for a meal, and a general tidy-up before we get the evening ferry?"

Ian took a blue and white leaflet from his pocket, lighted a cigarette, began to consult it. I saw that it was headed COMPANIA TRASMEDITERRANEAN, that there was a map of the islands of Mallorca, Ibiza, and Minorca on the top, with a drawing of a ferry boat underneath it, and motorcars coming out of the opened-up hull. *Servicios de Baleares, Junioe, Julio-Agosto Y Septembre, 1973* was printed in a separate caption on the bottom.

"Now, let's see, Ruth. I've booked on the '*Ciudad de Barcelona*,' due to leave Barcelona for Palma at 24.00 hours on Thursday, August 15th—that's to-day. I suppose your booking must be on the same boat? Did you manage to get a *camarote*, in the language of the country!"

The coffee was delicious. A lizard ran across the white tablecloth and regarded me with bright, friendly eyes. The sun, discreetly screened here, was pleasantly lulling. What was Ian Hamilton saying?

"I haven't booked anything," I said, lazily, unperturbed.

"But you said the Esmeraldo Agency . . ."

"No, only the room, at the Casa Saint Paul. I did enquire about a ferry passage. They said they didn't book them, that I'd have to do that myself when I got to Barcelona."

"Hmm. Well, I hope you're lucky; it *is* August, my dear girl!"

A sudden impatience in his tone made me open my eyes, to find him staring at me with a certain grimness.

"Oh, don't worry," I said. "There are sure to be some bookings left for last-minuters like me! If not, I'll just have to stand up on the deck, I suppose, or find a corner to curl up somewhere. I don't really mind, now, so long as I get there."

56

"I believe," Hamilton told me, "you have to book at the company's offices in the Via Layetana, in Barcelona. Still, if the *Ciudad de Barcelona* doesn't sail till midnight, there should be plenty of time to get it sorted out. I'll come along to the offices with you, and then we can have a meal."

"All right, thank you," I said. I wondered how well he knew the city, and Majorca, but I didn't ask. I thought he was fussing unnecessarily about the Majorca ferry, and pictured myself simply buying my ticket in Barcelona with time to spare, and then having dinner with him.

After lunch, we wandered down to the shops, and Hamilton bought a couple of picture postcards, and I fingered the hand-thrown pottery, and thought how good it was. I remembered the studio, back in the Mendip cottage, and suddenly experienced such a stab of longing for it that I had to shut my eyes.

When I opened them again, Ian Hamilton was looking at me strangely. A weird enough figure himself, with all that red hair, red beard, striped shirt and faded jeans, I couldn't understand why he should be staring at me.

"What's the matter, Ruth?" he asked quietly. "Are you feeling rotten again?"

"No," I said, "no—" and looked down at the piece of pottery in my hands. I realised, then, that I'd selected, subconsciously, I suppose, a white horse, with curling lips and tossing Spanish mane.

And as I grasped it, I saw Jenny again, in the Mendip studio courtyard, in that orphanage pinafore, her lovely hair in pigtails. And through all the chatter of the tourists, the roar of cars and coaches on the road beyond the frontier station, I heard that tense whisper again.

And when I want help, Ruth, I won't ask anybody but you.

"You look as if you've seen a ghost," said Ian, and grasped my arm tightly. "Do you fancy that pottery geegaw you're clutching so tightly?"

Looking down at it, I tried to match his mood. Gratefully, I knew he sensed something more than travel fatigue was upsetting me, and the attempt at diverting me was genuine.

"It's better than the stuff I used to turn

out, back home in Somerset. The glaze is nicer. But the horse I made looked less hostile—kinder, somehow."

"You're in Spain, now," said Ian Hamilton, and to me it sounded as if his tone had grown subtly harder, even threatening.

But before I could stop him, he'd called the fat Spanish seller forward, taken out some *pesetas*, and bought the white horse.

"Here," he said, grinning, and thrust it into my hands, "Keep it. As a little memento, let's say, of an interesting journey."

Clutching it, I found I was suddenly doing battle with an overwhelming sensation of desolation.

"Look," I said, "I'll see you in Majorca, surely? I mean, after our dinner tonight, we ought to meet, on the boat?"

He gave me another of those straight, hard glances, cast a look at the coach, and at Pepi prancing about amongst some of the passengers who were already beginning to climb aboard for the run down into Barcelona.

"Beautiful creatures, horses. Aren't white ones supposed to be symbolic of something—in folk lore and magic, that is?"

"In antiquity, in the English West Country, they carved them on all the chalk hills and downs. Something to do with the old gods, I think."

"They used to sacrifice the poor beast," Ian told me. "A sort of rite. In the ancient world, as you say. And especially, I think I've heard or read, in Scandinavia. They ate the flesh and buried the skull in the grave with the person who owned it. Or who might even just own a representation of it. And then the person, too, would be sacrificed. Oh, usually, it was for kings and important personages—"

Ian looked toward the coach. "Come on, we'd better go—"

We got aboard. Ian said he was tired, and went almost immediately to sleep, leaning back against the upholstered interior of the vehicle, and sleeping, indeed, like a relaxed child.

Was he really that relaxed, or was some of that a careful pose? Long hair, voluminous beards, are perfect disguises.

He was, I decided, a man who, by inclination, seldom betrayed his real feelings or personality. But, if one can catch a person in real sleep, this is often a sure pointer to character.

Something told me Hamilton didn't sleep, but merely dozed. Perhaps the expressed need for sleep might be to gain privacy from me for awhile.

What did it matter? I would never see him again once we got off the Palma boat, or perhaps, not even then. If he had a cabin, and I had to join the homogenous crowds on deck, we should probably disembark by separate gangways.

If he really wanted to find me again, he had the address of my casa in Majorca. I, on the other hand, had no idea where he would be staying. And that, too, I thought, could be deliberate.

4

HAMILTON grunted.
"Look out, here comes Laughing Boy!"

Pepi had begun his gyrating dance up the aisle. About midway, he stopped, and began to address us all through a small hand microphone, the lead of which dangled behind him to the driver.

"Ladies and gentlemen, we enter Barcelona in one hour. Those of you who are going on to other parts of Spain will find the railway station almost directly opposite our hotel, the Park. Again, those of you who have return tickets with Esmeraldo Agency, will meet there in one fortnight from tonight. For the rest of you, we shall not meet again, so I hope you have a very happy holiday in sunny Spain."

Here, the admirable Pepi dropped his voice to almost a conspiratorial whisper, and went on:

"Ladies and gentlemen, it is customary for to make a small collection, an honorarium, for the driver. I shall now pass around the envelope, if you would be so kind, if you feel you have been well-served, to put a little something inside—"

"And what about a little something for Pepi," murmured Ian Hamilton wickedly beside me. "I guess we're supposed to hand that out at Barcelona, with a sly smile and an adroit slide into the hand."

Pepi and his trailing microphone lead reached us. We were treated to the flashing smile. "I believe you both are going to Palma, Majorca, yes?"

Hamilton's nod was somewhat dour.

"And you have your passages booked?"

Now it was I who explained that Hamilton did; I didn't.

"Oh, it will be all right," reassured Pepi, plainly not caring at all, only anxious to be rid of his two most troublesome guests. We could hear the furtive clink of money as the other passengers slipped their *pesetas* in through the top of the somewhat battered brown envelope that was going the rounds of the coach. "There are always seat and cabin cancellations. The ferry, she goes from a little further down from the railway station where we stop. But the taxi drivers, they are very good, they will get you there in plenty of time after you have had a look around Barcelona."

Plenty of time—except that we stopped for petrol on the outskirts of some village, and, when the driver tried to drive off again, the coach refused to start. At first we thought little of this, but when, after five minutes, the engine still refused to turn over, we were escorted out of the coach and into the nearest cafe.

Here we sat, consuming coffees or mineral water, afraid to go for walks or do any exploring of the village because, as Pepi said, the driver, now bent over the engine with a youth from the garage, would coax it into life at any second.

In fact, the coach refused to start at all. After an hour's vain waiting, the driver telephoned his agency in Barcelona, and a relief coach was dispatched. By the time it got there, the Esmeraldo Agency's party, bored and irritated, had been taken to the nearest hotel, given the run of the garden, plied with the Spanish version of tea and sticky cakes, and charmed into waiting by Pepi, who ran between the hotel and the garage, his smile getting more and more fixed every second.

"This is going to ruin our dinner date," said Ian, as we drank yet one more cup of tea, brewed from tea bags. "Rotten luck, just on the last leg like this."

It was dark when the relief coach finally rolled into the garage courtyard, and Pepi came to hustle us along.

And, somehow, in the confusion, as we got aboard, the back seat where Ian and I had been sitting got filled up by some of the girls, and Pepi shouted irately that we were to take the first seats we came to, that it was essential we speed towards Barcelona and our various destinations, especially, he added, for those passengers bound for Palma, who must catch the midnight ferry.

I found myself sitting next to one of the more elderly passengers, an Englishman visiting his daughter who had some sort of boardinghouse on Minorca. But he'd booked for the Minorca ferry for the next day, intending to spend the night in Barcelona in any case, so he was comparatively unmoved by the turn of events.

The relief driver (our old one sat in

disgruntled silence beside one of the passengers) made good time, and soon the
outskirts of Barcelona were speeding past
us. I had glimpses of the ocean on my
right, and of old and new houses built
mostly in the European villa style on my
left as we sped along.

Then we began to pass factories and
electricity plants. The houses fell away,
and there were shops and emporiums,
most of them already putting up their
shutters.

By then it was half-past eleven, and it
was doubtful Ian Hamilton and I would
ever arrive in time to catch the Palma
ferry.

I had a glimpse of what looked like
trolley buses and a vast park, of big wide
avenues, tree-lined, and people strolling.
Then the vehicle pulled up outside a tall,
elegant-looking building with the words
PARK on the outside.

As we all spilled out on to the pavement
amid the tall buildings, on a street jammed
with cars, lorries, and coaches, Ian
Hamilton struggled to get us both to the
ferry.

"Got any luggage in the boot?" he called.

"No, just a small suitcase. It's here."

"Come on then, we might just make it. I'll get a taxi."

He grabbed my arm. Immediately from behind us there suddenly came a rush of people, some sort of outing or social gathering, with young men and women with flowers in their hair, and all singing some Spanish song. They effectively separated Ian Hamilton from me, like a torrent of water.

I had one glimpse of him, face turned in my direction, as a taxi drew up opposite him. The driver seized Hamilton's knapsack and other grips and threw them adroitly in to the cab.

"Come on, Ruth," yelled Ian, beckoning frantically, one foot on the taxi step, the door held open for me.

The driver turned, impatiently, yanked Ian into the cab with one brawny hand, slammed the door shut, and drove off, leaving me and the pigskin case forlornly on the pavement.

A deep melancholy akin to malaise, and not unmixed with panic, settled on me.

The thought of launching myself out into the teeming streets of this enormous Spanish city, with its frightening streams of traffic, its policemen directing the traffic with rifles on their hips, and the heat, pressing like some gargantuan blanket on the tops of the houses, suddenly appalled me.

"You want taxi, lady?"

With a stab of relief, I saw another cab draw up, wondered why he'd addressed me so positively in English, till I noticed the Esmeraldo Agency's coach was still parked a little further up the curb.

"Palma ferry?" I cried. "It sails at midnight."

He nodded. I scrambled in as he threw open the door. Off he drove following Hamilton's cab into the maelstrom of cars and coaches. We raced down a wide avenue, with ships again upon our left. I had a glimpse of an ocean liner, many yachts, and surely what looked like a ferry boat, as remembered from the illustration on Hamilton's *Compania Trasmediterranea* pamphlet. We turned left. I saw Customs buildings, and beyond them, surely, a glimpse of the ferry boat.

A siren sounded. We entered a compound, and the taxi driver braked, jumped out of his seat, and seemed to grasp me, suitcase and all, in one professional hug, as he rushed me to a glass-walled hall.

"Ah," he said, peering. "Lady, I am so sorry. You not make ferry tonight. Look!"

He pointed. I stared, blankly, at a sign beyond the glass which said, tersely, in large white capitals, *PALMA/BARCELONA— FERRY COMPLETO.*

He pointed again. The ferry, now between the Customs building and some other structure, was inexorably moving away from the quayside.

And there was no sign of Hamilton. As I looked at the lights of the ferry, now fast vanishing into the distance, I realised that Hamilton's cab, just beating the traffic melee ahead of me, had landed him at the quayside in time for him to get aboard.

"Lady, you want hotel stay night?" demanded my taxi driver.

I gazed at him uncertainly.

"I know very good place," he insisted.

Hot, tired, and oddly lonely now that the gregarious Hamilton had departed, I could only nod. Unless I wanted to spend the night on one of the hard wooden seats outside the Customs House, what alternative was there? I knew it was quite useless going back to the Park Hotel seeking Pepi's aid. He'd earlier informed one of the girls who'd neglected to book herself any accommodation in Barcelona that the Park was full up, and that he couldn't help her.

The taxi driver, small, dark, middle-aged, and eager, was simply out to get my *pesetas*. That I couldn't avoid, since I knew nothing about Barcelona and its hotels.

All I did know was that the rate of exchange was 132 *pesetas* to the English pound. Remembering the perilous state of my finances, I said, "Nothing too expensive, you understand?"

"Si, si, Senorita!" And he waved me back into the cab, and shot off, left of the quays, till we came to a tapering monument nearly two hundred feet high, with a man in a medieval mariner's uniform pointing over the city. Beyond lay a wide, tree-lined avenue with cafes and their clusters of outdoor tables.

70

Instinct told me the bronze statue must be that of Christopher Columbus. Light from a vehicle coming around the corner into the wide avenue showed me a name on a building, high up: Plaz Puerta De La Paz.

The driver set the cab at breakneck speed down the avenue. People sat at the cafe tables, drinking wine or coffee, some before plates of food, and there were more tables, with people, under the trees lining the middle of the road.

"Ramblas," called back the driver, pointing, with obvious national pride at the crowds. Many were obviously European tourists, but there were also Spanish citizens, the women recognisable by their intensely black hair and olive complexions, the men by their fierce, handsome faces. Hippies and teenagers, bearded and long-haired, a few barefoot, moved amidst the pavement throngs. Most shops were open, crowded with customers.

Presently the driver drew up with another screech of brakes, seized my case, and set off down an alleyway between buildings. At a breathless pace, fearful of losing him, I followed.

We arrived at some marble steps with a glass door and portico at their top. The driver urged me up them into a dimly-lighted hall. Here he flung down my suitcase (good thing poor Jenny got an expensive one, I thought ruefully), and started a lively harangue with an old man in a navy-blue uniform behind the counter.

I caught the phrases "Engleesh," and "Palma ferry completo," followed by more exchanges of excited, liquid Spanish. Giving a shrug that took both hands to the level of his eyebrows, the old man shook his head decisively, "No."

"Come," commanded my driver. He would have been quite at home in ancient Rome, cracking a lively whip over the columns of slaves. "We try again. Me, I know other places, Senorita. All much, much good, si!"

Two more stops, two more alleyways, steps, potted palms, and blankly staring, shrugging hall porters. By now, I'd stopped perspiring, and staggered along behind the driver, too spent to even call a halt and demand he take me to the Park, and the ministrations of Pepi, who, even at his most devilish, could surely do better than this!

By now, I owed the driver a certain sum beyond his due fare for service and gloomily I realised he would do his utmost to stretch my indebtedness to the limit!

The fourth alleyway. Now, a fat, moustachioed proprietor, outraged, waved his pudgy hands. *His* popular, much-in-demand establishment with a vacancy, at twenty minutes past midnight during the tourist season? He was insulted, his pride in the dust.

Pedro, the taxi driver, wiped his own brow. Wildly I wondered if I was destined to end up in a Spanish police court, an alien, found wandering the Barcelona streets, with no fixed abode. For I knew that visitors were not encouraged to demean Spanish etiquette and decorum. Could I go back, then, to the hard seats outside the ferry terminal? Or, if I tried that, would I get a policeman's hand on my shoulder, and some searching questions put?

Sighing, I realised I must, after all, direct Pedro to return me to the Park Hotel, where I should have to throw myself on Pepi's mercy. Perhaps, if he intervened for me, I could sleep on one of the hall chairs?

"Wait," hissed Pedro, "I think . . . Si, you come . . ."

Divining the exhausted rebellion simmering in me, he seized my arm, piloted me a few steps further down the same passage, up yet another flight of marble steps into surely the most dimly-lighted foyer of them all!

There sat a white-haired Spanish lady, with sharp features and cavernous black eyes, wearing the long black gown favoured by elderly Spanish women. She listened imperturbably to Pedro's babblings, now starting to verge on the hysterical, then turned the open hotel register towards me! In heavily-accented English, sharp with authority, she said:

"Passport then, Senorita! You have passport?"

"Ah," almost sobbed Pedro, "you see, Senorita? Do I not swear I get the Senorita a hotel!"

"Wait," I almost sobbed. "How—how much?"

Madame regarded me glacially.

"Fifteen hundred *pesetas* a night, which includes the breakfast and the shower, Senorita. These is Hotel Phoenix, in the Avenue des Ramblas. Now, your passport."

Since she seemed perfectly capable of snatching it from my handbag if I didn't immediately produce it, and since the sum she named was ridiculously low, I handed it over.

"You very comfortable here," beamed Pedro.

He named his fare. It seemed, I thought, reasonable. Forty *pesetas*, and he had done a lot of chasing about, on my behalf, so chancing it, and under the wholly sardonic eye of Madame, I added another ten.

As I handed it over, I saw from the gleam in his eye—and Madame's—that his harvest was quite satisfactory.

I was then conducted into a hall, through a succession of corridors with dangling bead curtains, and up several flights of narrow stairs. On a dismal landing Madame threw open a door.

More beaded curtains, immediately upon my left, cut off a minute chamber with a shower stall built into a corner and a wash basin set in the wall. I noticed a stench, but in Madame's august presence dared not even sniff.

The room beyond harboured a double bed which ate up almost all of the floor space. But, on the whole, the room was scantily furnished, with frail-looking wooden furniture and rush mats scattered about.

Like the chatelaine of some noble castello, Madame advanced proudly to the window, throwing open the wooden shutters, letting in the heat, noise, and revelry of the Ramblas.

Like London, Barcelona seemed to be one of those cosmopolitan cities which never slept. London, I thought, it seems so far away I could be on another planet! In fact, I felt like a citizen from nowhere on this world. I was stateless, rootless, and —almost—penniless.

"The Senorita breakfasts at what hour?"

I explained that I wished to catch the Palma ferry. "Si, si, the ferry, she sails at noon. If you have not a ticket, Senorita, you must queue in the morning. At the Compania Trasmediterranea offices in Via

Layetana. And get there early, Senorita, for they have the long queues . . ."

"Could I have breakfast at eight then?"

Graciously, she nodded.

I felt so grateful I had to say something friendly. "You speak very good English, Madame."

"I was a governess to an Earl, Senorita, in Sussex. Before I marry. Me, I did not like it. Him, nor his house, nor his family. Still less your grey damp country."

Fixing me with another patrician glance, she nodded, and left. Diving between the beaded curtains, I was assaulted by an odour so foul I nearly vomited. It rose from the shower drain, although that coming from the wash basin was not much more agreeable. Retiring precipitatedly from that room, I set out in search of the lavatory. It was in a small, boxlike room, and the odour there was even worse. Defying convention, I left the door slightly open, praying I wouldn't die of asphyxiation.

Back in my room, I inspected the bedclothes with morbid interest—grey sheets and blankets defied too close inspection in the dim light.

There were two oranges still in my suit-case. Peeling them, I carried the skins to the shower compartment. The only deodorant on hand, they at least did some-thing to mask the odour of the drain.

Then I snapped out the light. Taking a cigarette, I lay there in the strange little room, smoking, looking toward the window, and thinking.

I thought about Jenny, and my lips began to twitch. I heard myself giggle. Jenny, darling Jenny, would never have endured this dreadful little room for five minutes! My mind wrestled with a picture of Jenny and the Spanish proprietress engaged in a battle royal over the room. And Jenny would finally win the woman over to allot her the best room in the hotel, even if she had to turn someone else out to do it.

Without self-pity I knew that I would always be fobbed off with second-best because I looked the uncomplaining, meek kind. Well, I should have to learn to be more aggressive, firmer, not quite so polite and so subservient. Ralph, indeed, had taunted me once with the epithet, "servile," and perhaps, then I had been

because I'd thought I loved him. *Love*—
my mind rejected the word in disgust.

I wondered now what I should find to
do on Majorca when I'd finally lain my
wreath on Jenny's grave. Go and call on
Lars Sven? For some reason my mind
shrank from that idea. Still, if I wanted to
get a clear picture of her last days, he
would be able to supply it. Then perhaps
her ghost, or whatever that psychic wraith
was, would stop haunting me.

I would stay on the Island, I thought,
till my money was nearly gone. Then
I'd come back to England. Perhaps I
could emigrate to New Zealand, say, or
Australia, or America? But *not* Canada,
my mind directed quietly . . .

I wondered how Ian Hamilton was
faring aboard the ferry. He was probably
asleep by now, never giving me a second's
thought. And the schoolmistress, her
inhibited husband, the young men and
girls, the middle-aged man? All would
have settled down somewhere for the
night. The Spaniards would be in their
own homes.

Home, I thought wistfully, what a lovely
word it was! Hamilton and I were ships

that had passed in the night. It was unlikely we should ever meet again.

Suddenly, consumed by restlessness made feverish by the heat, I got up and went to the window. People still promenaded up and down the thronged thoroughfare that was the Ramblas, where many cafes and shops were still open. A group of youngsters with guitars began singing. Under a tree were a man and a woman. And they, for some reason, held my attention. They were both seated, he wearing a cool-looking grey suit, she in a flame-coloured, flowing evening gown, diamonds sparkling in her ears, her raven-black hair cascading to beautiful shoulders.

Then from out of the shadows behind them stepped another man, whose silhouette took on an odd, teasing familiarity. Ralph, I thought—and then, in self-contemptuous disgust, reminded myself I'd come all this way partly to forget Ralph.

But before I could see more of the couple and their companion, the group of guitar players moved directly in front of them. Still curious—perhaps because of the rare beauty of the woman's face and figure—I waited impatiently, indeed eagerly, for them to move away, so that I could again study this group.

But the guitar players didn't move for as long as I watched, and so I went to bed. There I dreamed of my friend Jenny Midnight.

Once again I saw her in the same orphanage pinafore, with her hair braided in those awful pigtails. In her right hand she carried one single red rose. And in the left, a big iron key. With her was a man whose back was toward me, but whose figure I instinctively knew to be that of Lars Sven. I trembled in my dream, for as I watched, breathless, I saw he was stealing up on Jenny, something bright flashing in his right hand. Everything around them was white, dazzling white, but, as in most dreams, this background was shifting and nebulous, and I couldn't see it clearly.

Then two other figures came on to the margins of the dream landscape. One wore a grey-coloured suit, the other a flame-hued evening dress. Irrationally I recognised these two as the figures under the tree in the Ramblas, and then my subconscious forgot even that, as Lars

Sven raised the glittering, bright instrument and held it, poised, over Jenny!

I tried to scream to warn her, but the dream suddenly vanished as someone dug sharp fingers into my arm. I awoke to find the proprietress standing over me.

"The Senorita has had a bad dream?" she inquired. "The travelling, the upset about the boat, perhaps made her ill? See, here is your breakfast. Drink some coffee, Senorita."

Still half-hypnotised by the remembrance of the nightmare, I stammered out my thanks and was glad when she left. The breakfast consisted of coffee, rolls, and honey. And the bill was there, too, enclosed with my passport.

In the shower, I noticed that Madame had piled my orange skins into a tidy heap and left them, like a reproof, neatly on the glass shelf above the basin as if to say, *she* could not be held responsible for an inefficient drainage system.

As we parted at the reception desk, my bill paid, our eyes met.

"*Buena sera*, Senorita!" she said, and handed me some *pesetas* in change. "You travel all this way, from England, alone?"

I nodded. Again the dark eyes swept over me, and she suddenly leaned forward to pat my hand benevolently.

"Never mind, my child," she said warmly. "Me, I read faces. There is trouble and grief enough in yours. And loneliness. Si, si, much of that. Sometimes, too, I read the futures. Take comfort! For you, at the end of it all, the sun is shining!"

But that frank piece of sentiment, after the night I'd passed and the weeks that lay behind me, shadowy with their memories of Jenny and Ralph, was, all of a sudden, too much.

Terrified that I was going to burst into tears in front of her, thus destroying my image as a reserved, ever-dignified Englishwoman, I picked up Jenny's pigskin case and fled.

5

THE *Santa Maria Del Pino* drew in to the Paseo del Muelle at Palma as darkness was falling the same evening. The eight-hour crossing had been calm, but the ferry was crammed with passengers, cargo, and cars. I'd seen nothing of the voyage, or the approach to the Island.

In Barcelona, I queued for thirty minutes, as Madame had prophesied. However, the fates relented enough to secure me a first-class cabin.

With my head dizzy from the sleepless night, I sank down on my bunk, closed my eyes, and knew no more till the cabin steward drew back the curtains to inform me we were approaching Palma.

I'd never allowed for arriving in the dark. Now, seeing the brilliantly-lighted city ahead of the ship, with a Gothic cathedral highlighted amidst the modern hotels and other buildings, I was over-whelmed by panic.

Beyond the ferry, yachts rode at anchor and at another quay I glimpsed still larger ships, ocean liners among them. Cars moved along the waterfront and a building, much like a Moorish fort, was bathed in the glow of floodlights.

The Palma waterfront at night was a magical sight, but our arrival was marred soon by the passengers crowding the spot where the stewards had indicated the gangway would go down.

I had no idea where the Casa Saint Paul was situated, but the girl at the Esmeraldo Agency had said they would send a car to fetch me.

So I waited, till the hundreds of luggage-burdened, knapsack-carrying travellers had, at last, all slowly filed off, and the great cranes were winching down bags of fruit, mail, and cargo.

All the cars had disembarked, too, having been driven off from the rear of the ferry. So there was nothing more for me to do but pick up my suitcase and walk, with a reluctance that was beginning to amount to dread, down the gangway.

People were getting into private cars, and others were hiring taxies. Greetings were called, and I saw people embracing. I took up a position a little away away from all the other travellers, looking, of course, for a car bearing the mark of the Casa Saint Paul.

Gradually, however, the crowds began to diminish, and soon there were no more people waiting for taxies. The taxi rank lay beyond the Customs building. Several times, thinking the car from Casa Saint Paul might be there, I had walked down the rank, but there was no sign of any vehicle bearing that name.

Some cars came, and turned around in the space below the taxi stand. People came from the Customs shed, got into them, and were driven off. The *Santa Maria Del Pino* seemed deserted. Her gangways were still down, but there was no sign of life about them. A cat came up from somewhere, and began to weave, purring, around my ankles.

A night wind blew off the water and I felt chilled. There was a waiting room next to the Customs shed. Fortunately, it was still open, so I went in and sat down.

Still there was no car. No one came inquiring for the guest for Casa Saint Paul.

And a taxi driver who had been waiting by his vehicle at the head of the rank, now put his head into the waiting room.

"You want taxi somewhere, Senorita?"

I hesitated, then shook my head. The Casa had promised to send someone, and it might be miles out of Palma. The hotel car, I reasoned, would be less expensive when it did come. Moreover, I would be certain I was being taken to the correct destination. I simply couldn't afford to go on handing out *pesetas* like confetti.

Getting really concerned now, I looked at my watch. The *Santa Maria Del Pino* had left Barcelona thirty minutes late, and then she'd stopped, unaccountably, halfway to Palma. All in all we had lost about ninety minutes, and now, as I stared at my watch, I saw that it was 10:45. They must have finished dinner at least an hour ago at Casa Saint Paul, even allowing for the late hour at which I'd heard—was it in one of Jenny's rare letters?—that they dined in Spain and her islands.

It was then that I looked harder across the space between the dock, where the *Santa Maria Del Pino* lay, and saw a small arcade of shops and coffee bars running parallel to the waiting room.

At the top of this corridor there was a brightly-lighted booth with a sign attached indicating that it was an Information Bureau. Outside of this, dressed in an immaculate white suit, and looking as I imagined a Spanish grandee would look, was a fine-featured gentleman with a splendid white beard.

From time to time, people approached, pulled slips of paper, or letters, or travel books, or maps from pockets or bags, and obviously asked him questions.

With some hesitation, as I was, by this time, in that state of nervous fatigue which breeds indecision—I went out.

On the glass door of the Bureau, stamped in gold, were the words: English Spoken, and other phrases indicating a variety of other foreign languages were also known. The Spanish grandee's magnificent brown eyes flashed as he strode towards me. Absurdly, I felt that he was likely to seize my hand, bend over it, and kiss it.

"The Senorita looks lost," he said very kindly in a fascinating Spanish accent.

How could he have known I spoke English?

Then I saw the label on my suitcase. But in my insular fashion, I decided it was probably because of something about my manner or my looks that made him guess.

"Senorita, how can I serve you?"

From my handbag's muddled depths I dragged up the colourful brochure of Casa Saint Paul, and explained my difficulty.

"Ah, si, si, I will telephone them for you, Senorita. There has obviously been some small mistake. The *Santa Maria Del Pino*, she has been docked more than an hour. The hotel car, it would not be that late. No doubt they have sent someone, but it has broken down—some small accident of that kind. Do not worry, Senorita!"

And he urged me inside the Information Bureau while he telephoned the hotel. Oh he knew of it, he assured me, a small, quiet place about twenty minutes ride from the centre of Palma.

He sat me down on a hard wooden chair and turned to a desk telephone. Soon I heard him pouring out a torrent of Spanish in which I caught, oddly, my name,

"Senorita Ruth Foundleeng . . ." I saw him reading it off the label on the pigskin suitcase.

Soon his noble countenance took on a puzzled look. He waved one of his white, ringed hands quite kindly at me, beckoning me forward.

"Senorita, I think it best you talk."

I seized the receiver. A young woman's voice, accented, sulky, and tired, said, "Casa Saint Paul. I am very sorry but we have no accommodations booked for Miss Ruth Foundleeng, from England. A mistake, Senorita . . ."

First *Miss*, now *Senorita*—I felt I'd begun to change nationalities already!

But anger took over from anxiety, as so often happens in intense fatigue. Fingers tightly gripping the receiver, I yelled into it, "Look, I definitely booked with your establishment. Through the Esmeraldo Coach Agency! Over ten days ago, in London."

In my fury, I'd added three days, but such niceties no longer seemed material.

"Wait, please . . ."

Silence, then a whispering in Spanish, then a deep, masculine voice took over, "'ullo, 'ullo, Casa Saint Paul! What you want, please? My reception lady already say . . ." The voice sounded angry, not at all conciliatory.

"What do I want! I've been kept hanging about here for almost an hour after your hotel promised to send a car for me. Now you're saying you haven't even got a room for me! And I'm stranded here, on Palma quayside, with no transport!"

"I say I am very sorry, Miss Foundleeng!"

Ugliness now, in the voice, with a hint of weariness beneath the boredom. He had heard too many complaints about over-bookings. There were too many tourists, all no doubt vociferous about things gone wrong.

"I say again I cannot accommodate you! It is eempossible!"

"But I know nobody on Majorca! I'm a complete stranger here! And at this time of night—The Esmeraldo Agency definitely assured me I was booked in with you!"

"Senorita, my hotel she is booked to the seam bursting!" exploded the voice wrathfully. "Me, I tell you, you ring this

Esmeraldo Agency, okay? Then you explain, si? There is no room for you here! Me, I know nothing about you! I am again sorry, but good-bye, Senorita!"

The line went dead.

Stunned, I laid down the telephone receiver. The Spanish grandee looked at me in apparent sympathetic inquiry. His large, dark-brown eyes also went mournfully to the clock above the counter. Twenty minutes to midnight. Soon he would, I suppose, shut up the Information Bureau and go home.

"This Tour operator," he said, tapping with one white forefinger on the lurid leaflet still grasped in my hand. "I ring him for you, yes? You have the number, I suppose, Senorita?"

Now, underneath the courtesy, a hint of Spanish contempt. This stupid little Englishwoman, coming all this way, most of the details about her journey incomplete. How he must despise her!

I found the information sheet of the Esmeraldo Agency, the one issued to clients giving them the telephone numbers and addresses of the various hotels used on the journey out from Victoria. The address and telephone number of Esmeraldo's representative in Palma was also there. In Barcelona, of course, it had been the ubiquitous Pepi and, presumably, the proprietor of the Park Hotel.

The Spanish grandee almost snatched the leaflet from me now, rang the representative, established contact, and handed the receiver to me once more.

"This is Miss Ruth Foundling, a passenger on one of the Esmeraldo Agency's coaches out from England. I booked a room, in London, through Esmeraldo, at Casa Saint Paul. On Marjorca. In Palma. Through your tour company. But no car was sent to fetch me off the boat, which docked two hours ago. And the proprietor of the Casa Saint Paul claims he knows nothing about it. Can you help me, please?"

"Please—one moment—I look at the papers. You wait. I look . . ."

Heavy breathing at the other end of the telephone. Then, a frenzied rustling of papers.

"Senorita, I am sorry. There is no Senorita Ruth Foundling booked through Esmeraldo Agency. Not only not for Casa

Saint Paul, but none of the hotels on Palma have your reservation. I regret, but you are mistaken . . ."

"The mistake is on your company's part, not mine," I said icily.

"Senorita," said the voice gently, but with that ever-present hint of steel, "you have the receipt for the booking, si?"

"Why no," I said. "The girl on the phone took it verbally! But she assured me it would be all right—"

"I am very sorry, Senorita!" It was beginning to sound like a record. "There is no booking. I suggest . . ."

Then, a great spluttering and crackling and the line went dead.

"Hullo, hullo!" I said desperately, and jiggled the telephone button. All that happened, was that a multitude of voices, all jabbering in Spanish, assaulted my right ear.

Out of the corner of my eye I could see the Spanish grandee locking up drawers and cupboards, and getting more aristocratic by the second. Clearly, I couldn't spend the night in his Information Bureau, his attitude said. And what more could he do? I thought, wildly, of the British

94

Consul and the Spanish police. Then the name of Lars Sven and Castello Minerva flashed into my mind. Oh no, I thought, I can't, not at this time of night, and in these circumstances—unbidden and unannounced!

But the Spanish grandee was now carefully shrugging himself into a long white silk coat.

"Senor," I said, and took a desperate breath, "you have been most kind. And I am truly grateful . . ."

I got hotter and hotter, as handbag on the counter, I began to hunt through it for the letter from Lars Sven. Surely it was there! I distinctly remembered putting it into my handbag when I left the Somerset cottage, not with any idea of calling on Lars Sven, but just thinking to myself that I might go and look at the place where Jenny had spent the last few weeks of her life.

But now—if I'd lost it I would have no letter as evidence and neither the servants nor the housekeeper would take pity on me for the night.

"Senorita?" said the silken-steel voice of

the Spanish grandee. "Senorita, I too, am very sorry . . ."

"Wait!" Almost sick with relief, I finally pulled out the letter with trembling fingers, and thrust it at him. "There is one last favour. This telephone number—if you would be so kind—please ring it for me."

A woman on her own has all the dice loaded against her in this sort of situation. And especially, or so I began to think, in this beautiful but antique land, where masculine privilege still held undisputed sway.

He bent over the letter, frowning, as if now suspicious as well as tired of this idiotic Englishwoman and her unbooked hotels and dubious travel agencies.

Suddenly, he shot me a very speculative look from those magnificent brown eyes.

"Senor Sven? You know him?"

Could I be truly said to know him? I bent my head, in the suggestion of a nod, keeping silent, suggesting an intimacy totally false—but necessary to my circumstances, for I was getting desperate.

The Spanish grandee dialed a number. Then, as we waited, I saw Jenny again, in that awful orphanage pinafore, hair in braids, staring in through the window glass, eyes dark with horror! Fatigue, I thought, and looked away.

"Castello Minerva?" said the liquid Spanish voice. "Is Senor Sven available? Si, I speak in English. For there is a young Englishwoman here. Si, a Miss Ruth Foundleeng. Please tell your master she wishes to speak with him most urgently."

He turned and gave me the receiver again. I waited, heart thudding against my ribs. Outside, somewhere on Palma's waterfront, a ship sounded her siren. Music drifted in from a cafe. The slap of the water was hypnotically soft against the wooden quaysides. And I was tired, so tired.

Then, a deep, level voice, very cultured, very musical, with a trace of an accent which I presumed must be Norwegian said, "Miss Foundling? Jenny Midnight's friend? But, I am delighted . . ."

6

CASTELLO MINERVA stood poised on the top of a rise, looking down on the southwest coast of the island, some twenty miles west of the beautiful and ancient city of Palma. Around the castello, within the pine belt, lay three or four acres of cultivated land. The terraces, overflowing with roses, carnations, and flowering shrubs, stretched southwards of the house. On the west a capacious kitchen garden supplied all the vegetables and fruits needed for the household.

The way to the cove lay beyond the southern terraces. A flight of somewhat worn stone steps, hewn out of the solid rock, and down which one had to carefully clamber, led to the pebbly beach. There was an iron balustrade to the right of the stairs, but on stormy or misty days, it must have been quite a nerve-racking experience negotiating those steps.

The castello had a turretted tower on the

eastern side. In the centre, an arch led to the courtyard at the rear, where there were old stables, now used as a garage.

Built around the end of the sixteenth century for some Spanish nobleman from Barcelona as a holiday residence, it had, for me, the frowning attraction of all the castles looming out of fairy tales and legends.

The tower apartment, as it was called, had large, lofty rooms decorated in Moorish style. Lars housed and photographed his collections there, and it was there he also held his fashion shows.

The servants lived in a suite of rooms above the arched portico; Lars and his guests staying in the east wing. Comparatively modern, the latter was cunningly built in the same old, yellow stone, locally quarried, of which the central and tower portion of the castello were built. It was hard to tell where old and new began.

After the Spanish nobleman died, the castello passed to his descendants, the last being killed in a duel at the end of the nineteenth century. The owner before Lars Sven, a wealthy American, had added the east wing, and then went home to lay his own bones in his native Arizona soil.

Lars bought the place some time in the late fifties. He was inclined, or so I'd vaguely gathered, to move between the castello and his Oslo flat.

One statue of the Greek goddess after whom the castello was named stood on the central terrace. There had been Greek and Roman occupation of the Island, and, according to local lore, a temple where the healing arts were practised had, at one time, stood on the castello's site.

Listening now to the song of the sea, the lullaby of the pines, I thought that, in antiquity, the castello might well have been such a healing shrine. But now— well, no doubt it was my own mood which made me ascribe to it aspects less than therapeutic.

Eight bedrooms, each with a separate bathroom, lay on the second and third floors of the east wing above the white dining room, salon, small library, and modern kitchen. My own bedroom, which overlooked part of the tower, the gardens, pine woods, and sea, was exquisitely done in rose and green.

From the inner courtyard, a drive wound around to the back of the castello, terminating in enormous iron gates which were flanked on either side by two more gargantuan statues of the goddess Minerva. This was the main entrance to the castello. All of Lars' guests, and all deliveries came that way. Other entrances were the steps from the private beach, or through breaks in the pine forest beyond the perimeter of high fencing which marked off Sven's land from the rest of the hill.

On the third morning of my arrival at the castello, I sat in a luxurious lounge on the verandah of my bedroom. The verandah had a gay striped tarpaulin awning which shaded it from the sun, and striped matting on the stone floor.

I could just see the small motor cruiser nosing out into the mist. The *Belle Isle* was painted a distinctive blue and silver. At her bow a small blue silk pennant, bearing the entwined initials *LS* fluttered in the morning breeze.

Just visible at the wheel was the tall, bearded figure of Lars Sven, his powerful body clad in white silk shirt and slacks.

Beside him was his Majorcan chauffeur, butler and general handyman, Felipe, a small, dark man, very quick and alert in all his movements, but inscrutable and enigmatic in his mood.

Felipe was courteous and attentive to me, as I sensed he would be to any of the guests who came to the castello, but I always felt vaguely uneasy when his eyes, almost as dark as his master's, were turned in my direction. Absurdly, I felt he knew that I came, in a sense, under a false front.

As the motorboat halted on the edge of the mist, Lars Sven turned, his binoculars catching the light. He had them focused upon the castello, and suddenly I found my colour rising, for he'd raised his left hand in a laconic salute, obviously having got me in full focus.

Felipe and he had gone fishing that morning. Lars had told me they were going the previous night at dinner. The dining room at the castello was a magnificent place, high and long, with polished wooden floors, walls lined with white silk, and a huge marble fireplace. Around the walls were hung portraits of the Spanish nobleman and his descendants, some of them clad in heavy armour. Their ladies, wrapped in lace mantillas, grasped elaborate fans.

The salon was more comfortable, smaller, capable of evoking an intimate atmosphere, with a grand piano at the eastern end, and a smaller dining table.

The household guests usually took breakfast and tea in the salon, where the French doors opened on to the central terrace, before which Juanita usually set the table.

But I was remembering the night the *Santa Maria Del Pino* docked at Palma, and how, after my panic-stricken call to Castello Minerva, Lars Sven himself came hurrying down to the quayside in an enormous dark-blue Mercedes Benz.

"But I am enchanted that you do telephone," he'd exclaimed, when I tried to explain how I'd been let down over my booking at the Casa Saint Paul. "I should have been most hurt, most angry, in fact, if you had not let me know you were on the Island! Did I not write inviting you to come?"

"Yes," I acknowledged, confused, as he drove the powerful car at what I considered a dangerously high speed along the waterfront, then up and up, past the cathedral and the old city walls, and a grim-looking palace which, he informed me, was called Almudaina.

"Built by Moorish kings," he said. "The Moorish influence is strong on the island. Later, members of the Mallorcan Royal House lived there. But you will see. There is so much to see here, I hope you will be my guest for a long time."

Soon we were on a great street called Via Roma where there were trees in tubs. Via Roma reminded me of Barcelona's Ramblas; there were hundreds of people strolling, going into restaurants and night clubs, even at this late hour.

After that all I knew was that we'd left Palma behind us and were heading roughly northwest. The brilliant lights of Palma's streets all fell behind us, and we ran through country where, on either side, I glimpsed a vast plain with mountains rising up beyond.

It seemed to me that there were trees everywhere, their serried ranks visible under the moon that peeped in and out of the cloud cover. I saw a windmill, its arms turning, and an old, white-washed farm-house, set in behind more trees. Then the mountains upon our right appeared closer.

"What mountains are those?" I asked, but Lars Sven grinned.

"You will love Majorca," he said as if I'd never spoken. "It is so old, just like Norway."

Then he laughed and drove on like a fiend, along roads that got narrower and more precipitous until at last we came out of a sort of canyon to find the sea heaving upon our left like a quilt of liquid gold under the moon. Glimmering through the pine forest, clearly visible upon the summit of a hill, lay the Castello Minerva.

After that, mine was a confused medley of impressions. I was greeted by Felipe, who took my bags, and then handed me over to the care of plump Signorina Juanita, with her great bun of shining black hair, and her flashing smile.

She took me off to my bedroom, unpacked my suitcase, and ran a bath for me. Finally, too exhausted to even sort out my impressions of Castello Minerva and particularly Lars Sven, I fell between sheets smelling of lavender and drifted off into blessed, dreamless sleep.

I didn't dream of Jenny, nor of Ralph, nor of anybody to do with my old life. And, when I woke in the morning, a slim, pretty maid in a black dress and frilled white apron came in with coffee and rolls, and a folded English edition of *The Times*.

"I am Maria," she informed me, revealing a flash of sunburned legs as she set down the tray. "Senor Sven, he hopes you have had a good night, Senorita! Perhaps, when you have rested, he say, you will join him on the terrace?"

There was just a hint of sullenness under the smiling courtesy. As I looked at her, I wondered if she had brought breakfast to Jenny like this, and impulsively, as she crossed the room to the door, I said, "Did Senor Sven tell you I knew Jenny Midnight? That she was a very dear friend of mine?"

Maria halted, head half-turned back towards me. Her dark eyes were cool, without regret, or even pity.

"Si." The rather curt monosyllable was non-revealing. "The beautiful young

English model. So very sad. But Senor Sven, he did everything that was possible."

Then, with a last glance at my face, and as if courtesy, at least, demanded it, she said, "Of course I am very sorry, Senorita, about your poor friend." Then, still lingering, morbidly curious, she asked, "And you come here to visit her grave, is that it? You want to see where she is buried?"

"Yes. You see, Maria, my friend Jenny is a long way from her homeland now."

"But a long way for you to come, Senorita. And so sad a pilgrimage. But after you have been, you have a little holiday on our island, yes?"

"Yes," I said. "Yes, perhaps I will, Maria."

An hour later, bathed and dressed in one of Jenny's sun dresses, a lovely thing of green silk, I sat on the terrace, and heard Lars Sven saying much the same thing.

"But, Ruth," he had swept into the use of my Christian name as a matter of course, "you must not think of going back to England till the late autumn at least!

Unless, of course, there is something you must do there after you have been to Jenny's grave?"

"No," I said, "there is nothing there for me. I am very free."

He was wearing shorts and a silk shirt, and in the sunlight his dark beard was like a shield around the lower part of his face, a mask, a disguise.

His lips were well-shaped, and rather thin. Did they denote sensitivity or cruelty? Tenderness or sadism? His nose was aquiline, with wide, flaring nostrils, and his eyes were black. I'd never seen such black eyes before, and I found his at once fascinating and enigmatic.

I realised we'd never talked of Jenny, and he went on, as if to make it easy for me, "You are very attractive, little Ruth, but in a way different from my exquisite Jenny. You know, her death was like a knife in the heart to me. She was such a wonderful inspiration! So vital! So—so compellingly alive! When she put on a dress—even if it had been botched up by some hack—you know it acquired style, chic, elegance, all at once!"

That was true. Even in our orphanage

days, Jenny could drape a sheet around her, and make it look like something straight out of a top fashion house.

"About her death, Lars. Was she in much pain?"

Lars shook his head. Half-resentfully I thought, he's not a doctor, how can he be so sure? It was possible he was trying to spare my feelings, I supposed.

"No. Or perhaps just for a little while. I was not here, you understand. We'd spent the morning together, in the tower, going over our ideas for the autumn fashion show. A long way off yet, we joked, but better to be well prepared. Jenny bubbled with enthusiasm. She would wear this dress, or that, I would get more models from the mainland . . ."

His speech was full of idioms I found strange in a Norwegian, till I remembered how widely travelled he was. Abruptly, he set down his coffee cup, looked almost morosely away from me. The blue sea sparkled beyond the pines. I could smell the fragrance of the trees and the tang of sea air. So old a scent, I thought.

A magical place, this island. It seemed colourful, peaceful, gay. But underneath, as with Castello Minerva itself, what stories lay untold?

"I went out. I felt jaded. Felipe took me out in the boat. The Gertaes were down at El Pino. Jenny collapsed. Someone— Juanita I think—telephoned the doctor. He came at once and took Jenny to his clinic and operated immediately. It was too late. Dr. Max said she must have been hiding the pain . . ." Sven's voice grew gentler. "Ruth, my dear, everything possible was done—"

We stopped talking about her then; it was too painful for us both.

"You must, as Jenny's special friend, stay here for as long as you wish," he said.

Immediate refusal was on my lips, dictated by the way I'd practically forced this friend of Jenny's to extend hospitality to me. Nor was I certain I really liked Lars Sven. Oh, I found him unusual and deeply fascinating, and although I'd spoken against him in Ralph's company, now I thought that was probably more to provoke Ralph than out of any genuine dislike for Sven.

Well, all that was finished now! The time had come for me to find a new maturity, to stand on my own feet. That was one thing about Jenny: there'd been a tremendous toughness about her.

Sven set down his coffee cup—we'd been talking on the terrace later that afternoon—and came to stand beside me. He put one darkly-tanned hand lightly on my wrist. I started slightly, for the magnetic strength in that hand seemed to burn into me like an electric current.

Was that what had appealed to Jenny, this tremendous magnetism? The difference in their ages no longer seemed so important, although I had an idea that more than twenty years separated them. Jenny had never told me his exact age, but he must, I thought, certainly be in his early forties.

"When I called for Jenny, at your charming Somerset cottage," he said gently, "you were living with a young artist, Ralph. He was a painter, I believe."

I looked steadfastly over the pool to the pine forest and the sea, and a small yacht which was beating before the breeze.

"Ralph and I have parted company for good. He's gone to Canada."

"Poor little Ruth!" he said, after a

pause. "That sensitive little heart of yours has been subjected to some hard knocks, lately! Now, let us make a pact. It is easy to tell you are still upset over Jenny's death. I, too, am mourning Jenny. Though you are not like her physically, you remind me of her in so many ways."

His proximity made me nervous. Although I found him fascinating, there was something about him which did put me slightly on my guard.

"Do I? How?"

"You are both so very independent—fiercely so! You see I talk of her as if she were still alive! Isn't that a tribute to her vitality? But this independence, it makes it very hard to do either of you a favour! And you are both enclosed in a shell—a beautiful shell which cuts off the woman within from the outside world! You—like she used to—seem to me to be a woman entirely on your own."

Well, that wasn't true of me—or at least it hadn't been till very recently. It was true enough of Jenny. Yet, how strange Lars Sven should plumb any independence in me, after what I'd just been analysing in myself.

Had Jenny told him about those orphanage years? I knew she'd never made any secret of it to Courtney Grafton. He had been very fond of her, and I don't think he troubled at all about her background; and she certainly didn't know much about his.

What had she really felt about Sven? She'd confessed to me her hope of marriage, shyly, and happily, but not in words suggesting she was deeply in love with the Norwegian. None of her letters home said much about him either. But then, Jenny was a very poor correspondent.

As he stood there, large and dominating and, in his way, magnificent, something prompted me to test him.

"Perhaps it was because of the way we were brought up," I said.

His eyebrows rose, and the black eyes became guarded.

In some obscure desire to shock him, or give vent to my own rankling feeling of inferiority, which his lovely home, of course, did nothing to mitigate, I said, "Yes. In a state orphanage. Both of us. From the time we were tiny babies. Didn't

Jenny ever say? Or that that was how we got our names—Jenny Midnight and Ruth Foundling!"

And then, in a flash, I remembered that old newspaper cutting in Jenny's suitcase. Presumably, she'd never spoken of that Christmas visit to the orphanage to Lars Sven. Perhaps she feared he would think it, somehow, damaging to her career? A sentimental gesture that betrayed too much about her humble origins? *If* they were humble, that was! For all that anybody could tell, Jenny might have been the daughter of a princess!

She could be secretive with people she knew well, yet open as the day with strangers—the newspaper reporter, for example, to whom she'd confided that she might come back to the area one day and try and find her parents.

Well, the revelation couldn't harm her now. And if Lars Sven was really shocked, then that showed what sort of man he was! I reminded myself they'd been on the verge of announcing their engagement. Or had they? Jenny certainly thought so, but she could well have been mistaken.

Lars just didn't have the air of a man who was heartbroken.

He stood between me and the sun. It was hard to tell from his look whether he'd always known, or whether he was hiding the slight shock that this news must have been to him if he'd just heard it for the first time.

"Charming names," he murmured. "Ruth, Jenny's dead. I'm desolated, as I told you." He hesitated, and then went on, "We hadn't known each other very long. And I was a little uncertain of her true feelings towards me. But—well, I thought these few weeks on the island, together, here at the castello, would help us both to make up our minds!"

I held my breath. Was he going to tell me he'd wanted to marry Jenny, had actually asked her during those hours when they were closed in the tower, ostensibly planning the fashion show? His hesitation vanished. He seemed to make up his mind.

"But that's all over now, Ruth. And life has to go on. For all of us. She was never the girl to want anybody to mourn for her . . ."

And that means you, I thought.

"And now, you came out of the night, as if destiny had sent you to replace her, as if it were meant to be." Had destiny meant that Jenny should die, in this place, beautiful though it was, so far from home?

He'd given nothing away. Impossible to tell whether Jenny had told him about the orphanage or not. Impossible to say whether he'd really meant to ask her to be his wife. Or was just—amusing himself. Still, Jenny wasn't me, and could, in that sense, certainly take good care of herself.

Still, I thought, I shouldn't like to step on this man's pride! Perhaps, too, he was just sparing my feelings about the orphanage?

"I'm not a model," I said. "I don't have any of Jenny's gifts—"

Feeling my stupid colour rise, I caught the flash of his smile—amused, just a little patronising perhaps, but, it seemed, very kindly, even beginning to betray a definite concern.

"No matter. You have gifts enough of your own, Ruth. And it is those I want to use."

Astonished and uncertain, I must have

given him an inquiring glance, for he went on, "Jenny was always praising your practical mind, Ruth. 'Ruth is so logical,' she would say. 'She works everything out ahead, a step at a time. She isn't slapdash and impatient, like me.'"

I accepted this accolade from beyond the grave. Brilliant, accomplished, beautiful Jenny Midnight had never needed to cultivate my painstaking logic or anxious care for the future.

Yet, I thought, it might be true I had the better intelligence. Destiny is supposed to offer some compensation for every yearned-for, but denied, gift. I'd always craved beauty, and above all, poise and self-confidence. Instead, I had brains—no personal credit to me, just a biological accident.

And, in the same way, Jenny's gift from destiny had been that flame-like beauty.

"I badly need a secretary, Ruth. When I left Oslo this spring for Majorca, my secretary resigned. These weeks, I've managed without one. Now, it's imperative I engage someone."

He casually mentioned a sum per month that would have kept me, back in England, for at least twelve! Financially, the offer was enormously tempting. But it came from a man who was virtually a stranger.

Yet what did I have left in England?

Well, I thought, is there any real reason why I shouldn't accept his offer? I came to the island to lay a wreath on Jenny's grave, obsessed with some foolish idea her ghost was urging me to make a pilgrimage to this place where she'd died. I'd always supposed ghosts came to warn their percipients either of some trouble in store for them or because there had been something strange, unusual, or evil about their own deaths and were not able to rest till their trouble was put right.

Taking that last grim thought out, and exploring it for what it was worth, it seemed, frankly, absurd. Jenny's collapse had been witnessed by the two women at Castello Minerva. The doctor and nurse at El Pino Nursing Home had treated her and her death had been certified by the former.

As well as that there was the letter from the British Consul, and her perfectly proper interment in the cemetery, attended by Lars Sven and the members of the household apparently, for he'd told me that he, Juanita and Marie had all been driven to the graveside by Felipe.

How could there be anything wrong there? Had something happened before she died? Something on the island, which she'd kept secret from Lars? Her own letters though, contained not the slightest hint that anything at all had been amiss. They were almost lyrical with delight at her relationship with Lars.

If there was anything here causing me the slightest misgiving it was the instinct I had, growing stronger day by day—in fact, almost hour by hour—that Lars Sven wasn't as upset about her death as I should have expected from a man supposed to be deeply in love with her.

Could he be hiding his hurt? If the wound had gone deep enough, that could be so. But it was unlikely, surely, that Jenny, beautiful though she had been, was, when they met, the only woman in his life.

There was the difference in their ages. He must be at least fifteen years her senior, and probably even older. And, looking at his face, hearing the way he spoke to a woman, even the castello servants, I could tell he was very experienced, sexually and emotionally. This being so, I could hardly expect him to mourn Jenny forever.

Then again, there had been something ambiguous in Jenny's own attitude towards him when she spoke of him to me, briefly though it'd been! And I wondered if she'd been mistaken in his feelings for her, that she found this out when she got to the castello, but that he would never acknowledge so intimate a thing to me.

Yet Jenny continued to haunt me like a ghost unlaid. It was becoming difficult to separate imagination from whatever psychic reality there was in her comings and goings. At night, when I lay in my bed in that luxurious, unfamiliar room, I'd seem to hear, amid the song of the pines and the sea, that quiet, tense whisper, "And when I want help, I won't ask anybody but you, Ruth."

Or I'd imagine I saw her on a corner of the east wing's stairway in that orphanage pinafore, hair in braids, staring at me, wordlessly, but with an infinite appeal in those midnight blue eyes—just as in those other flashes.

What did she want? Or did she really want anything? I'd heard, or read, somewhere, that hallucinations of such a kind often came after some emotional shock.

While she was alive, we'd both known, and often laughed over, those telepathic flashes, and thought little about them, one way or the other.

It was possible I'd invented both her wraith and the idea that she, as a discarnate presence, wanted help, simply fitting that remembered little speech of hers into my mind as a comfort and protection against grief. I wanted her to still need me and so those voices and visions could be pure invention, which I'd subconsciously created.

I'd already asked Marie which room she'd occupied during her tragically short stay at the castello, wondering if, out of sentiment, they'd put me into it. Deeply though I'd loved her, I'd no particular desire to sleep in the same room and, in identical circumstances, I could imagine Jenny herself shuddering, widening those dark blue eyes, protesting, "Oh, no, Lars darling! Positively too, too creepy!"

Maria, answering in that courteously sullen way, told me that Miss Midnight's room was at the end of the corridor above mine.

"Next to the master bedroom occupied by Senor Sven," added Marie, with a meaningful look at me, an obvious hint that Lars and Jenny had been sleeping together. Jenny had never said so to me. Yet, knowing Jenny, it was not difficult to accept that they probably had. For Jenny viewed most sexual relationships with cynical realism. And I'd thought, in any case, that her own feeling for Lars had, somehow, transcended the sexual.

Yesterday afternoon I'd gone up to Jenny's room. Lars Sven had driven off into Palma, and I'd carefully watched Juanita waddling up the stairs of the central block to her siesta. Felipe and Marie gossiped in the rear courtyard.

There was no reason why I shouldn't explore the castello, I told myself, for Lars Sven himself had urged me to have a good look around, after he showed me over it perfunctorily the first full day I was there.

Even the tower apartment wasn't locked, although it was tacitly understood no one went over there except when Lars was working on his collection. He visited it frequently—but invariably alone—his studio being on the ground floor.

One reached the upper corridors by a broad wooden staircase built at the side of the east wing. Halfway up this curved stair a huge picture window let into the wall gave a view of the beach and the top of the pine forest.

It was very quiet. The corridor seemed wrapped in an almost deathly hush. I reached the top of the staircase, and saw the hallway stretching out before me, the polished olive wood gleaming in the sunlight.

I suppose this momentarily dazzled me. I halted at a half-open door, and realised, instantly, that this must be Sven's bedroom. It was exquisitely furnished, with a robe of Lars' I recognised draped over the foot of a modern four-poster bed hung with rich green silk curtains.

There was, from these windows, a view of the courtyard. Marie and Felipe seemed to have vanished. There were fine carpets on the floor, and beautiful curtains. This was obviously the room of a sybarite, a man who loved luxury.

I turned away. Marie had said the room at the top of the corridor. I turned the handle, experiencing a sudden, and unexpected, flood of tenderness. This was where Jenny had slept, dreamed her dreams about marriage. And something of her would surely linger here, something to which, now, I could bid farewell.

And I realised, then, that much of my own sorrow about Jenny's death was because this farewell had never been said, so swiftly, so unexpectedly had fate struck her down. I turned the handle again. It resisted my fingers. I tried again. The door was locked.

I looked back along the corridor. All the other doors were slightly ajar. As I stood there I suddenly saw Marie breasting the top of the staircase, a pile of clean linen over her arm.

Feeling like some child absurdly caught out in some misdemeanour, I just stood there. After all, she must be perfectly well aware of what I was doing, why I was there.

"Hullo, Marie. I just wanted to look at Miss Midnight's room. You said this was it . . ."

Silence from Marie. Was it hostile, or merely that she, too, felt awkward, and embarrassed?

"The room is locked," I went on.

"Yes." Again the monosyllable gave nothing away. "Si. On Senor Sven's orders."

And she had passed on, ostentatiously, I thought, flinging open the door beyond Lars' room, as if to show that none of the other rooms were locked.

I'd not known what to make of it, at the time. Probably there were one or two personal objects in there that had belonged to my friend that Lars proposed to hand over to me. And, till now, not being certain I was coming, he'd kept the chamber locked. So there was really no need at all for me to turn the castello into some sort of Bluebeard's castle.

I sighed, and got to my feet. Jenny wanted me to be happy, always. She had worked for that, in her own way, all through her life. But would she have wanted me to take the position now offered to me by the man she'd hoped to marry?

I reminded myself of my resolve to come to my own decisions, and I could almost hear her saying: "It's not what I want, it's what you want, Ruth darling!"

Whatever post I took in England, I would probably know no more about my new employer than I did about Lars Sven. Although, of course, it would be easier to check up on someone in my own country if I was at all doubtful.

As I changed, slowly, I remembered how he'd left the matter.

"I wouldn't think of your starting, anyway, till the period of your intended holiday is up, Ruth. But as I shall have to start sending advertisements out to the English and Norwegian newspapers soon, if you don't want the appointment, I would be very glad if you'd let me know. Let's put the deadline at Wednesday evening shall we? I'm having some friends in for dinner, and you shall tell me, yes or no, before then."

Today was Wednesday. Lars had gone off in the boat and wouldn't be back till late afternoon. He went out with Felipe in the *Belle Isle* nearly every afternoon, fishing, or just exploring the coast to the north, so he told me. I gathered that they often landed at one of the smaller, little-known bays beyond Formentor, where he enjoyed a lazy swim, or worked at his book—he was writing one on English fashion design—and his new secretary would be required, as part of her duties, to type the manuscript.

"I must introduce you, Ruth, to some of my secret places, up there," he'd said, smiling. "Jenny often came with me. She'd sunbathe, or read, while I sketched or wrote, and Felipe fished.

"You know, although she died so tragically, it was a very lucky day for me when Jenny wrote, right out of the blue, to say she'd seen some of my fashion displays and would love to model for me. Otherwise we might never have met! Oh, I'd heard of her, naturally; who in the fashion world hadn't heard of the lovely Jenny Midnight?—but I thought she was full up with modelling contracts for other designers—"

And then, there in the bedroom, I stopped, staring at my own reflection in the wardrobe mirror, remembering that letter, in his own writing, that I'd found in Jenny's suitcase . . . a letter, from him to her, suggesting they should meet!

Then, after a second, I thought: well, surely there's nothing particularly sinister in that! He's a man under tremendous pressures, and he's just forgotten that it wasn't Jenny, but he himself, who made that first approach. Probably after his own letter Jenny answered, said she would, indeed, love to model for him, and they met, and their relationship went on from there.

I gave myself a little shake, reached out for the dark green silk shirt and dark green jeans which I proposed to wear that day. Jenny's choice, and they fitted me perfectly.

For now the moment had come for me to do what I'd originally left England and come to this Island to do, to lay a wreath on Jenny's grave.

I was going that morning, and I hoped that, in the interval of time, I'd be able to make up my mind what I was going to tell Lars that night.

I'd already informed Maria and Juanita,

at breakfast, where I should be going, and that I'd not be back till after siesta.

I saw no sign of either of them, as I walked down the stairway of the east wing into the hall, and on to the salon and out through the French windows to the terrace, where I'd left my sunglasses on the table. I picked them up, and went around the side of the east wing and into the courtyard.

From there, I struck out down the winding drive which ran through the rough grass planted with a few olive and walnut trees, till I reached the massive iron gates. These were ajar, as they were usually left during the day, when Lars drove out.

Now the pine forest closed in again, cool and pleasant. I walked through it for about ten minutes to emerge at the top of a hill. Here, he had told me, I could catch the local bus into Palma. He'd given me the schedule, and I had only to wait about five minutes till one came along.

He had given me directions as to how to get to the cemetery, too, and had offered to take me there in the Mercedes.

But I'd thanked him, and said I wanted to go alone.

"I understand, Ruth. But remember, now, it is the old Cementario—you must ask for that, or they won't understand your English 'cemetery.' And it is at Genova, where the graves of the English are. Not the new one, the other side of Palma. Still, if you make sure the taxi driver knows you want the Genova Cementario, that is all you need to be sure about. The graves of the English you will find right at the top. They are bricked up in tiers."

There was, to me, something rather forlorn, even upsetting about that, but Lars spoke about it in an almost business-like fashion.

Before I had time to explore that thought any further, though, I saw a little green-and-cream omnibus bowling smartly along the road and, on its destination plate, the word *Palma*. So I hailed it, and paid out my *pesetas*, and found a seat at the back.

The vehicle was crowded, mostly with foreign holiday-makers, but there were one or two Majorcans, men and women with black scarfs around their thick, black hair, and lined faces wrinkled from the sun. These people were elderly. Most of the younger island population seemed to travel around in their own cars, and one saw quite a few bicycles and motor cars.

Lars' castello lay in a lush, if lonely, part of northwest Majorca. The nearest popular beach, so he'd told me, was Puerto Soller.

I had no wish to visit such places, but I was interested in the Royal Carthusian Monastery at Valldemosa, where George Sand and Chopin had stayed for some months. Lars had suggested he might take me there, and also to Manacor, where there was a pearl factory.

"Tourist stuff," he'd said, smiling, "but it might amuse you."

The bus rattled along, and we passed now through what seemed to be typical Majorcan scenery. There was a backdrop of distant green mountains, and in between vast plains sown with olive, walnut, and almond trees.

"Wait till the spring, Senorita," Juanita had counselled me, beaming, hands upraised, "and then see our almond trees in blossom. Ah, it is so beautiful a sight!"

In the spring . . . Should I still be here? Majorca was a beautiful island, even in the heat of summer, with glimpses of the sea never too far away. We passed white farm-houses, surrounded by plantations of almond trees.

Grape vines were set out in the fields, along with melon and tomato plants. Men and women worked away amongst them, and I also saw donkey carts, the patient beasts between the shafts, and I smiled at the sight of the little straw hats which some wore over their great ears to shade them from the sun.

The roads were dusty, though, their surfaces bumpy. Lovely villas, their tops just visible between more pine and almond groves, marked the residences of the wealthy.

We came into Palma by the way Lars had driven out on the night of my arrival. Immediately, I recognised the Via Roma. Here some sort of small market was taking place, with fruit and vegetable stalls, and clothing booths, and a lot of fascinating pottery and leather work on display.

The streets were already packed with holiday-makers, Majorcans on their way to work, recognisable by the fine light suits and rather formal dresses they wore. The police, their pistols noticeable in their holsters, controlled the street traffic.

From Via Roma the 'bus went on through a maze of streets I didn't recognise. Then I spotted the Cathedral, and began to get my bearings.

I got out on the waterfront, by the Paseo Maritimo. There were some flower shops in the ranks of buildings behind it, and there I purchased a dozen lovely red roses, still in tight bud.

Next I looked around for a taxi, and luckily found one cruising amidst the pack of private cars, motor bicycles, 'buses, and lorries which thronged the streets of Palma.

"Senorita?" queried the driver, drawing up.

"Do—do you speak English?"

"Si. A little. So, what you want, Senorita?"

"Cementario Genova," I told him. "There and back. And I shall want you to wait a while, say fifteen minutes or so."

He stared at my red roses. Then, as his glance came back to my face, I noticed the dark, Spanish brown eyes soften.

"Okay, I take you Senorita. One hundred and thirty pesetas, si, including the wait?"

That seemed reasonable, so I climbed in, and he shot off through a maze of narrow streets beyond the Paseo Maritimo, overlooked by huge, towering concrete blocks, some modern hotels, some flat complexes, with shops on the street level, and almost every one having a cafe or a sort of bar, outside of which people sat, drinking, eating ice cream or fruit, reading newspapers on poles, or just smoking and watching the passing throngs.

Lovely, I thought wistfully, to sit relaxed like that, with a companion, with no problems to shadow past or future, only a sunlighted world on which to gaze. And, for the first time in days, I suddenly found myself thinking of Ian Hamilton, wondering how he'd got on when he disembarked from the night ferry, and where he was now, what he was doing.

7

NOW the sea was upon our left, blue and very calm in the heat-haze. There were a few yachts, further out, and what looked like one of the ferries, bound, I supposed, either for Minorca or Ibiza since the twice-daily ferry between Palma and Barcelona sailed—as by now I knew!—at noon and midnight.

We passed through more narrow streets filled with holiday-makers, shops, piles of leather goods, pottery, wines and spirits, cigars and cigarettes. At one point we went right by a studio with the artist's canvases on display, and I thought, wincing, of Ralph.

Still, I was getting better, for it was the first time I'd consciously thought of him in twenty-four hours, although he persisted in staying in the back of my mind.

And, as the taxi wove in and out through the narrow streets, and the perfume of the roses, in their wrapping on

135

the seat beside me, drifted up, haunting and evocative as Jenny's real ghost, I began to feel aware of a sensation almost of escape.

But not from Ralph, nor Jenny, but from Castello Minerva, that luxurious, lovely home, beautifully equipped and furnished, in its pine woods and terraces, like a jewel in its setting.

Jenny could, I thought, have belonged there as the wife of Lars Sven for, although her own beginnings, like mine, stayed sheathed in mystery, it had always seemed to me she was born to such a life, and would have worn the diadem of chatelaine to Castello Minerva as one taking up something she had been born and bred to.

But I didn't belong there. I felt uneasy, surrounded by all those trappings of wealth. I knew I should never like to live there permanently, and certainly not as its mistress—although I had no illusions that Lars Sven was ever likely to fall in love with me, or ask me to accept that status.

I could, I supposed, remain as a servant —if only for a month or two. That seemed, after all, a harmless diversion.

The taxi came to the end of a narrow

street, and started to climb inland, under a bridge, and at the top of a steep street, which opened up after about half a mile, I saw country on either hand, the houses, hotels, and shops left behind us.

Looking through the rear window, I could see, on my left, another quayside, with more ships anchored there, and, immediately in the foreground, a small beach with sun umbrellas and people stretched on what looked like rather grey sand.

Then, the taxi swerved left, and we were on a twisting, curving road, where the vegetation grew high above the bordering ditches, and where I again got sight of the mountains between the plains, and the olive and almond trees, and the small white farmsteads.

And suddenly I couldn't look at it anymore, this exquisite, alien landscape, for I was back in the little flat Jenny had shared with me during our first years with Courtney Grafton, and she was saying, smiling, "Funerals depress me, Ruth, and all that goes with them. I don't think I've got any last wishes but, if I go first, then you can put red roses on my grave . . ."

Well, here I was, and I had the roses, and maybe, after this, I could exorcise her dear ghost, and begin to think about my own future again.

And as that idea entered my head, I remembered how Lars Sven had looked when he spoke of Jenny, and of the belief I had, that most of the love had been all on her side, and in that moment, I decided not to accept his offer.

"I'll go home to England," I told myself, as the taxi slowed down, caught behind a single green 'bus making for a small village ahead which, I presumed, was Genova. "I don't belong at Castello Minerva, and I can't see myself really making a success as Lars Sven's secretary. Indeed, I'm not really sure, in my heart, that I like him, kind and attentive though he has been. Yes, I'll go home in a few weeks, and if I can't find something useful to do there, I'll go to New Zealand . . ."

I'd always cherished a dream to visit that land of mountains, glaciers, and hot springs, and at least, it was a long way from Canada.

Again, the taxi swung left, and we entered an even narrower lane, between fields sown thickly with melons and grapes. There were no trees, and the sun beat down brazenly, so that I felt it through the thick top of the taxi.

Far on the horizon I glimpsed the dark shape of yet another castello, black and grim and cruel, somehow, against the bright Majorcan sun. An antique world, this one, in which, it seemed to me, I caught the drift of old magic, both good and evil.

Then, in a few minutes I saw, ahead on the right-hand side of the road, a sight that suddenly made my heart lurch. Tombstones, hundreds of them, lining a green hillside, almost like ranks of people, standing there, waiting for eternity.

Iron gates, ajar, came into view around the last bend of the road. There was no lodge, as there often is at such places, only the serried ranks of stones, rising to the top of the valley.

The taxi driver grunted, turned and said, "Cementario Genova, Senorita."

Holding on very carefully to my precious roses, with my bag swinging from its strap across my wrist, I climbed out and immediately felt the heat of the sun, almost like a blow between the eyes.

"You—you will be sure to wait, won't you?"

His stock English phrases served him well enough, and he seemed sympathetic. But I didn't want to be abandoned here. I wanted reassurance.

"Is okay, Senorita, I wait," he said, and smiled suddenly in an almost fatherly fashion so that I wondered: is he married, does he have daughters, and does he think, perhaps, that I am like them?

Satisfied that he would wait, I turned towards the cemetery. But then I saw him get out of the vehicle and approach me. He put a hand under my arm, and walked me toward the iron gates.

"The graves of the English, Senorita," he murmured, "they are up the steps. Go through this main place, as far as you can go, then take the steps upon the right. Not the ones in the ground, you understand, but in the rock."

He swung open the right-hand gate, looked at me and my roses again, and said, with real concern, "As we Majorcans say, Senorita, nearer to heaven—"

Warmed by this gallant attempt at comfort, I smiled, raised a hand in salute, walked through the iron gates into the full fury of the noonday sun.

The graves of the Majorcans lay all around me, marble slabs, columns, angels, urns, some inscribed with the names of the dead, others with little valedictory verses. No different, really, to tombstones in England, except that many had little photographs of the deceased, placed on the stones and protected by little circles of glass.

The eerie quiet that seems to hold all such places, even in the heart of great cities, held this one also. Somewhere an insect buzzed. The distant hum of traffic, on the road to the left, was reassuring. So was the sight of the taxi, as I nervously half-turned, the driver back in his seat now, bent over what appeared to be the daily newspaper.

Unaccountably, my nervousness increased. For some reason, it took an effort of will to push one foot in front of the other.

"Don't be idiotic," I told myself, almost violently, "the dead can't hurt you."

141

I wound around the path, skirting the graves of the main *cementario*. The flight of stone steps led up to a sort of wall, almost twelve feet high, and railed off by an iron bar.

Lars and the taxi driver had prepared me for what I should see. Otherwise, I'm sure, the actual sight would have shocked me.

"They bury them in tiers, Ruth, one above the other, with the names just printed on the front. They aren't in separate plots. The part of the *cementario* given over to foreigners is quite small."

I'd seen the same tiered burials before in Italy. Only then it had all been so much more impersonal, when I gazed, unconcerned if sympathetic, at the graves of strangers. Now, Jenny was one of those walled-up figures. The red roses in my hand began to quiver, my heart started to thud, and there was a queasiness in the pit of my stomach. The heat, I thought.

I'd reached the top of the steps, and found myself in a sort of stone corridor with names printed in layers, as it were, of five. At the end of this corridor a

142

bulkhead of stone was made by more layered coffins.

Suddenly, I saw her name, right at the top of the last section on the right just where the stone corridor ended.

I had to halt, step out of the sunlight into the shadow made by the left-hand bulwark.

Jenny Midnight
Born: 29 September 1949
Died: 2 August 1972

This bald announcement, and no more. I didn't quite know what I'd expected, except that I'd imagined, if I'd been in Lars Sven's shoes, I'd have added something about keeping her memory green, using the phrase "In Loving Memory."

But there was nothing, nothing about love at all, in fact, just her name, and her birth and death dates. So cold, so unfeeling!

He's a man, I reminded myself, and a Norwegian. I've always heard they are not a sentimental race. But she believed he was in love with her, my heart protested. And, once more I reminded myself, Jenny was wrong about that. That is not his fault, only her mistake.

I looked at the stone, all the same, in sad loneliness. Where was I to place my valedictory roses? There was no niche, no place at all on the smooth face of that poignant layer of tombs. At the foot, I supposed, only I'd brought no vase, no urn, and nothing was provided.

Heartbroken, I decided I must just leave them at the foot of the rock, when, to my left, in the shadows, something moved!

Emotionally off guard, distressed, battling with the flood of memories that had been released at the sight of Jenny's name on the stone, I cried out swaying.

Then someone stepped forward, put very wiry, strong arms about me. I clung, blindly, trustingly to him.

"Ruth, it's all right! I've got you."

Through eyes blinded with tears, harsh sunlight, and dizziness, I had one startled glimpse of a tall man with close-cropped red hair, clean-shaven cheeks, and strong chin. A stranger, yet not a stranger.

He led me away, back to the steps, sat me down on the topmost one, my head against his shoulder, while the *cementario*, with its hundreds of stones, and below that, the taxi, the patient driver still hunched over his newspaper, waved about before my vision.

"Now, just take it easy, girl," said Ian Hamilton. "Though I don't know what you expect, climbing about in this place in the heat of the noonday sun. Mad dogs and English women, eh?"

The scent of his jacket against which his firm hand had pulled my swimming head was immensely comforting. Amid the tainted, sepulchral miasma of that alien graveyard, it was as refreshing as English summer rain—and as welcoming. Why, I must be homesick, I thought, incredulously. How extraordinary! And how delighted I am to find him here!

For a few minutes, all I wanted to do was lie there, getting my breath back, waiting for my heart to stop pounding, and my mind to clear.

"Better?" said Hamilton, after a few seconds.

"Oh, my roses!" I cried, remembering, and looking around for them in distress. "The roses I brought for Jenny—"

"Stop worrying," commanded Hamilton. "I've got 'em here, quite safe, beside me."

He'd cut his hair, close to his skull, like a helmet. It showed some remarkably good bone construction. He was clean-shaven, too, and the lines of his cheek and jaw were also good. He looked altogether younger, more respectable, but somehow also more formidable. The troubadour of the coach was gone. I found, somehow, that I missed him. I'd felt then on an equal footing. Now, there was something just a little daunting about Ian Hamilton.

"I thought," I said, withdrawing myself from his hold, and feeling, amongst all the other sensations that assaulted me, remarkably foolish, as well as dishevelled and gauche, "that you were on a walking tour of the island."

It flashed over me, rather absurdly, but in a way I couldn't quite dismiss, that he'd, somehow, been spying on me and had followed me here. What a strange place this was for us to meet!

He helped me to my feet, began to brush off the minute particles of yellow dust and stone that clung to my clothes from the steps.

"Why—why did you come here, to the *cementario*?" I demanded, when he stayed silent.

He stared down at me, then put the roses into my hand. "I might have come," he said, "to lay a wreath on Jenny Midnight's grave. Like you—"

When the taxi dropped me at Castello Minerva that night, my head was aching, my senses still in a whirl. I paid the man off, thanked him, and managed to slip in, and up the staircase of the east wing to my room, without attracting the attention of Maria or Juanita.

Lars' car wasn't in the double garage, and, considerably shaken, still, by the events of the afternoon, I took a bath, put on a wrap, and locked the door.

Then, taking cigarettes and lighter, I went out on to the balcony. The *Belle Isle* was back at her moorings, and I could see Felipe moving about on her decks. Evidently, Lars was still on the island, somewhere, in the Mercedes, and I wouldn't see him till dinner, which, in Castello Minerva, would probably be any time between nine and ten o'clock. He tended to appear some time then, and demand a meal of Juanita, if he wasn't entertaining guests. Otherwise, he set the hour formally.

Thankful for the time to myself, I sat down and stared out at the shimmering sea. It wouldn't be dark for another hour, but the sun was dipping towards the west, and it was perceptibly cooler.

As I looked down on the deserted cove below the terraces and the pine woods, I heard, in my imagination, the voice of Ian Hamilton, "Going to work for Lars Sven? As his secretary? Is that such a good idea, Ruth? Why can't you get a job back in England?"

We'd stood at Jenny's grave, with my lovely roses placed upright in a cranny at the bottom of the stepped catafalque.

Ian had asked me when I was going home, explaining how he'd just managed to catch the ferry I'd missed, but that, next morning, when he got to Palma, he telephoned Casa Saint Paul and enquired for me.

"And they'd never heard of me, of course," I said, bitterly, savouring that abandoned moment on the quayside all over again.

So I explained, and told him that I was now a guest of Lars Sven, where my friend Jenny had been staying when she died, and how kind and considerate he'd been.

By this time Ian had said there was a little cafe in the village, and he got the taxi driver to take us there.

It was only a modest place, with a few iron tables set out in a stone courtyard, and some steps leading to the shop where they sold wine and mineral water and simple refreshments.

Ian had asked the taxi driver to wait, and, amicably, he'd gone inside with his newspaper and was talking to the Spanish proprietor, an old man with waxed moustache.

"Have you tried sangria?" asked Ian, and when I said no, introduced me to the light, red wine of the country which had lemon peel and lumps of ice floating in it. I found it very refreshing and palatable.

The village had a few curio shops, and hikers in mountain boots frequently toiled up to it. There was a trickle of cars but, on the whole, the village was very quiet.

149

"I got worried about you Ruth, when I realised you'd have to spend the night in Barcelona all on your own."

"Oh, it was rather funny, really—quite a little adventure, in its way," I assured him, and told him about the taxi driver, and the aristocratic Madame in the hotel, the shower with its smell, and the crowds in the Ramblas, and my arrival, next night, on the Palma quay, and the Spanish grandee at the Information Bureau.

"I thought about going to the boat to meet you," said Ian. "But I wasn't quite sure whether you might not think that an interference. I mean, you'd said somebody was meeting you from your hotel. And, when the Casa Saint Paul said they had nothing booked for you, I just thought I'd misheard the name."

I drank more sangria.

"Then I found I wanted to see you again. And since you'd told me you were going to visit Jenny's grave, I thought, well, when I'm walking that way, I'll go in and see if there's any sign of Ruth. I mean, I wasn't sure of finding you there when I went to-day, but I'm staying at a small pensione, up near Castle Bellver, and

150

so I've done most of my walking, so far, around this area of Genova where the old *cementario* is . . ."

It was then, after I'd filled in all the missing bits and pieces about what had happened to me since we parted in Barcelona, that I told Ian Lars had asked me to stay on and work for him.

"And are you going to? Is it definitely decided?" he asked.

"I like you better clean-shaven," I said inconsequentially. "It shows up your skull and facial bones. You've got nice bones." And added, for no reason, "Ralph told me about that—about bones and things, I mean . . ."

"Ralph?" Ian's tone was oddly gentle.

"The man I was engaged to," I lied, "back in England. We—I broke it off. We —we weren't suited."

"I'm sorry," said Ian, still in the same, gentle voice. Then he grinned, drained the sangria in his glass, and poured out still more for both of us from the glass jug on the table. "I can understand your thinking of staying. Normally, too, it would be your own business who you stay and work for here."

Normally? What did that mean? After Ralph I wasn't inclined to enter into any relationship with a man that wasn't strictly platonic, or, as with Lars, businesslike. But I wouldn't have been normal myself if I didn't guess Ian was attracted to me. And I had no desire to wound him, as I'd been wounded.

"Oh, look, I'm sorry, Ian. It's just, I suppose, that I'm a bit unsettled and uncertain . . ."

"Tell me," invited Hamilton. The story of my life, I thought, cynically? Well, although that would have been a relief, there wasn't much left to tell. He knew most of it already, in bare outline, if not the details.

I reminded myself that I hardly knew him. His appearance at the *cementario* had been a shock and that was taking its time wearing off. He'd explained it plausibly enough. A little too plausibly, perhaps?

I lighted a cigarette and surveyed him through the smoke.

"Look, that story about going to the *cementario*, in hopes of meeting me—"

"Found it a bit thin, did you?" he said. "Well, that's fair."

He continued to study me, though, in that harsh, bright sunlight, as if making up his mind. Then he nodded, took a letter from his wallet, dropped it on to the table between us.

The envelope, addressed to Mr. Ian Hamilton at some address in North London, was in Jenny's handwriting! The shock of that hit me like cold water. Instantly, Ian's hand covered mine, closed steadfastly about my fingers.

"Please," he said quietly, "don't worry! Before you read your friend's letter, I'd like to explain. There's nothing supernatural about it. I was going to tell you, on that damned coach, but somehow it didn't quite seem the time and place. I could tell you were upset, wanting your own company, for a bit."

I had to grin, at that, remembering the serried ranks of starers, the schoolmistress and her acid comments, Pepi's sculptured curls and total personal indifference, the chattering youngsters.

"I thought I'd wait till we met in Majorca, as I intended we should meet."

Feeling my colour rising, I looked across

153

the dusty road to the blue and distant mountains.

"Jenny and I met in London. At a mutual friend's house. We were attracted."

He frowned, looking immediately like the angry young man who had come late to the coach at Victoria.

"I knew, at the time, she was working for Lars Sven." His tone was hard, so were his eyes.

"And you didn't like him?"

"No," he answered bluntly. "Suave, smooth, polished—and dangerous."

"Dangerous!" I was prepared to admit Lars Sven could impress anyone, particularly another man, as having the first three qualities but the last one? And yet, I thought, perhaps there was that quality in him.

"Ruth, open the letter," commanded Ian quietly.

The cafe was empty except for us and the taxi driver and the proprietor, whom I could just glimpse, through the open doorway, heads bent over their game.

It was Jenny's writing on the envelope, all right, and now, as I opened it, on the

154

letter—the capitals were big and heavy, and each word, too, was large and heavily-inked.

Dear Ian,
I'm enclosing a copy of the Esmeraldo Coach Agency brochure. You said you might come out to the island. A girl I met on the plane said she had tried Esmeraldo in the spring and that it was very good, considering the price.

Two young men, in shorts and shirts, strode into the cafe, sat down beyond the doorway, and called for drinks. Under cover of their arrival, Ian bent forward.

"That explains, I think, Ruth, even to the most Doubting Thomas, how we both happened to be on the same coach. Neither coincidence nor conniving destiny are to blame. Just cause and effect."

And, I thought, this is a hint that he wasn't following me for some purpose of his own.

"Jenny told us both about that Esmeraldo tour. And, as we both happened to be her friends, were anxious to see the place where she was laid to rest . . ."

155

"Yes," I said slowly. "Yes, I see." It sounded perfectly reasonable, up to a point. "So when I spoke to you about Jenny on the coach, you already knew I was a friend of hers?"

"She spoke of you, certainly. Not often, as people don't tend to chatter inconsequentially about folk who mean much to them . . .

"She told me, 'Ruth and I now live our separate lives, but there's nobody who is closer, or who means so much to me.' Ruth, won't you finish the letter?"

Brushing the tears from my eyes, I took it up and went on reading:

I've been feeling very fit, Ian, since I got here. The marvellous weather and sunshine help, of course, not that I'm ever really ill, and Castello Minerva is an exquisite place. You know, I've never even been in hospital, except for that sudden attack of appendicitis when I was seven years old, and the matron took some of the orphanage kids away on holiday. They rushed me to hospital in Weymouth and I was operated on at once. Ever since then I've been perfectly fit. The surgeon, I remember, said I was lucky not to get peritonitis.

I dropped the letter on to the table. Ian's fingers closed around it.

Suddenly, I felt very, very cold. And then, from back in the past, memory pushed open a door. I wondered how, when the news came about Jenny's death I could ever have forgotten. They divided us into two sections that month at the orphanage, for a camp at Weymouth. Jenny and I were, I remembered, inconsolable because we were separated. Not till I got back did I hear about that near-fatal appendicitis.

I did recollect now Jenny showing me the abdominal scar, a scar which, through the years, faded like my childhood memory of the incident. If I'd actually been with her at the time, I would have remembered. Childhood experiences, especially those known only second-hand, get subconsciously buried, till something triggers them to mind. And, of course, when news of her death did come, there'd been that revolting preoccupation with Ralph.

Looking across the table at Ian, I whispered, "Can you have appendicitis twice?"

"Certainly not. You might have an exploratory operation, if there was any pain around the original operation site, but that's not appendicitis."

"The doctor's letter? The British Consul's letter? Lars Sven's letter?" I whispered.

"The Consul wouldn't view the body. He'd take the word of the doctor issuing the certificate. Here, read the rest of the letter . . . *quietly*, if you please!" Ian jerked his head back in the direction of the two youths.

But there is a doctor within close call if I should fall ill. His name is Dr. Max Gertae, of El Pineo Nursing home. His wife, Elsa, I have also met. We are already good friends and both are frequent guests at the Castello Minerva . . .

There the page, not Jenny's letter, stopped. Looking at Ian enquiringly, I saw he seemed just a little out of countenance.

"Ruth, I've got the last page. Jenny's

158

final letter to me. But I'm not proposing to show it to you. She could be pretty extravagant in some of the phrases she used. We'd known each other pretty intimately, you see. And in London, we were both—lonely."

Well, that was no great revelation. If Jenny had been promiscuous, it was only because early years had starved her of normal affection—just as they had made me inhibited, as Ralph had never hesitated to tell me.

"No, Ruth, I never loved her. Or she me. What we shared was transient. But we weren't using each other, either. She was very generous, and mature and she taught me a lot. We parted, in London, knowing that what we had together had burnt itself out, and was over forever. But we were still very good friends. I'd have done anything for her . . ."

Yes, that was the way Jenny made you feel—not under any debt, but grateful for the experience she gave you. And gave was the word, I thought, tears suddenly blinding me again, which was why she was so singularly loved.

"No strings and no holds," said Ian,

guessing my thoughts. "A great girl, Jenny. So, you see, I wouldn't want to think anybody had hurt her.

"Ruth, I came to Majorca to find out what I could about the way Jenny died. I agree the death certificate could just be genuine. She may have died of complications from that old appendectomy, but, in that case, why didn't they say so, as most competent surgeons would?"

"Do they know at Castello Minerva about you, that you are a friend of Jenny's?"

"She could have mentioned it in passing. But if so, Lars Sven never wrote to tell me she'd died. I suppose she had a diary and address book on her."

I told him it had been returned to me with most of her effects when she died. How could I remember whether his own name had been in it?

Ian frowned. "All right, she probably never mentioned me. But look here!"

He produced a cutting from *The Daily Telegraph* of August, 1972. It was headed, FAMOUS LONDON MODEL DIES IN MAJORCA.

Jenny Midnight, whose lovely face and

160

figure will be familiar to thousands of newspaper and magazine readers, died in El Pino Nursing Home in Majorca yesterday after an operation for acute appendicitis.

It was understood that the operation for the removal of the appendix was quite successful, but that Miss Midnight later suffered complications after surgery, to which she eventually succumbed.

Miss Midnight, who had been a guest of the international fashion designer Lars Sven at his Castello Minerva, a few miles outside Palma, will be buried on Majorca. Miss Midnight had no family.

Again I'd stared at Ian Hamilton, finding, now, a look in his brown eyes which completely baffled me. I remembered he'd once studied medicine, and wondered if that accounted for his probing diagnostic intentness.

And I wondered, of course, what his profession or business might be, after he'd abandoned medicine, even while my mind struggled with the implications of his story about Jenny.

"It's possible I'm wrong," admitted Ian. "But well, like you, I had a bit of a holiday due, and I thought I'd come out here and take a general look around."

Was he, then, a private detective? Or was there some deeper story behind all this, and had he only cultivated Jenny's companionship, used her, to find out what he could about Lars Sven and Castello Minerva?

But what reasons could he have? His own highly personal ones? He'd helped me lay the flowers on Jenny's grave, but left none of his own.

"Look," I challenged. "There could be a perfectly rational explanation about Jenny and that story about the appendicitis. The scar was well-hidden. I remember now, even when she wore a bikini, you couldn't see it. It faded fast. They often do after surgery in childhood."

"I know," he said, nodding.

"Well then, what? And what's your business with Lars Sven?"

But he by-passed that one. His manner had changed. Gone, totally, now, was the buffoon, aggressive and self-assertive, who'd come late to the coach to exchange

162

duel verbally with Pepi and the school-master. That Ian had utterly vanished now along with his beard and long hair. I knew the man in his place—quieter, more mature, on his guard—no better, for instance, than I knew Lars Sven.

Beating down my fear, I realised that my only intimate experience of any man had been gained with Ralph. And, of him, I'd known not the slightest fear. Only, at the end, a contempt.

Realising I was afraid both of Lars Sven and this new Ian Hamilton added some-thing to my concept of both. And, remem-bering how I'd seen the orphanage Jenny, in pinafore and pigtails, at the Mendip cottage, and again on the road to Majorca, and here, on the Island itself, I went cold again.

"You're saying there's something wrong about her death? Something faked?" I'd asked him.

"I don't know. But I do know this. You take out an appendix. The patient recovers. Nowadays peritonitis is rare. And with antibiotics, rarer still. But peritonitis would happen within hours of the original operation, certainly not four-teen years later."

I'd fallen silent, sick and wondering, till at last I said, "We could go to the British Consul, demand an autopsy, an exhumation?"

Even as I said the words they sounded so horribly unreal as to be laughable. Grotesque. Surely it couldn't be Jenny—lovely Jenny—we were talking of? For now, what Hamilton was hinting at was ugly, sinister, but, of course, could be explanation enough for those glimpses of Jenny. The ghost who came to warn . . .

A lizard ran from the nearby wall, flopped on to the table, ran across and dropped, again, to the shingle of the court-yard. An exquisite blue thing, it was the same colour as Jenny's eyes.

"Not yet—not on the evidence we've got."

Silence. The youths at the table above got up, paid their bill inside the cafe, and departed.

"I've been thinking," said Ian, almost conversationally. "If you did take that post, Ruth, there's a great deal you might find out."

To take any sort of job under false pretences was repugnant to me. Hamilton, as he himself had just admitted, could be all wrong in all his surmises. Lars Sven had been very kind to me—as Jenny had said he had been to her.

In the end, I left Ian, telling him I'd think about what I was going to do on my way back to Castello Minerva.

"I don't like the idea of acting the spy," I said.

"You could be in danger yourself," said Hamilton, curtly. And, like one suddenly annoyed, he called for the bill, paid it, found the taxi driver, and soon had the latter seated in his vehicle, directing him to drive it to Castello Minerva. Then, grim-faced, he handed me in.

"But Ian," I called, "I must see you again! We need to talk!"

"I'll telephone," he said quietly. "For the moment, say and do nothing."

The taxi driver swept on, down the narrow, twisting road to Palma.

Now I looked down at the delicate glass ash tray I had brought out from my bedroom behind me, piled high with all the cigarettes I'd smoked, reliving that extraordinary episode in the little cafe beyond the *cementario*.

Out at sea, the *Belle Isle* bobbed at anchor. The water flowed like silk around the rocky promontory and the guardian pine escarpment and the sun, setting now over the water, made a pathway of gold towards Barcelona and the mainland.

The view was breathtakingly beautiful, the air scented with the flowers and the pines, but the castello seemed a place of ugly and frightening surprises.

8

IT was already Wednesday night, and Lars Sven would be waiting for his answer. As I dressed, and thought back on the talk with Ian, a profound disquiet, mounting, minute by minute to fear, grew in my mind and refused to be banished.

The burning sunlight was now mellowing, setting behind Puerto Soller, turning the island, the mountains, the plains, and the trees, to pinky-gold. Paradise. But now, for me, paradise tainted. One minute I wished Ian Hamilton hadn't told me of his dark and nebulous suspicions. Then I was reminding myself that I'd come to Majorca just because I felt Jenny herself had, somehow, summoned me, though I didn't know why, and wasn't yet convinced her shadowy appearances, and her small, clear voice, were not hallucinations.

If, too, common sense suggested that what Ian had hinted must be absurd,

Jenny's life had been a strange one. She'd moved in a rarefied world, darting here and there to parade herself in her gowns, keeping company with all sorts of men.

And what might she not have found out, for instance, in those feverish wanderings around the world? Perhaps her real enemies were not Lars Sven, or Dr. Max Gertae as Ian thought, but someone else?

How far, though, was I justified in trusting this Lars Sven, about whom I really knew less than nothing, only what Jenny herself had told me? Sophisticated, suave, very much a man of the world, he could very easily, I believed, have fooled her.

As for Hamilton, it was true he had that letter in Jenny's handwriting, which seemed to indicate she'd also trusted him. Or, at least, that he was a friend, for those few casual medical details she'd put in might have been simply because Jenny knew he'd been a medical student, and the fact that Dr. Max Gertae was Lars' guest at the castello would, presumably, interest Hamilton, like those facts about her early appendectomy.

Jenny's death certificate, according to

Hamilton, could have been faked. By Lars, by Dr. Gertae, or possibly, his wife. If this was the truth—and I was far from accepting that it even might be—then what had Jenny done? Or, possibly, found out? Was there some sinister secret here at the castello upon which she'd stumbled?

I jumped slightly, almost as if I'd been speaking these sinister thoughts aloud, and could now be heard by the man whose car I now heard in the courtyard outside. There was the noise of a car door being slammed, and Lars' voice, followed by that of Felipe. He was back!

It was then that I made up my mind what answer I should give to him. And I would tell him that night, when opportunity served, either during or after dinner.

Dressing with some care, so that Lars' sharp and strange black eyes should find no clue to the deep disturbance in my mind from my appearance, I chose a pleated green silk dress, softly flared to the ankles, matching sandals, and an imitation jade necklace.

All these were Jenny's things, part of the wardrobe in the pigskin case. I wondered whether Lars Sven had given them to her, and if he would recognise them, for I knew he passed on to Jenny dresses and other items from his various collections, when the publicity conferences were over.

Not for the first time I began to wonder about the collection housed in the tower apartment. I supposed Lars would have to get a new model to work the show, or would he simply abandon the idea now that Jenny was gone? Yet designing and selling to the big fashion houses was his livelihood.

Marie knocked, calling out immediately to identify herself. She came in, looking very handsome in her black silk dress, frilled apron, and high-heeled shoes.

"Senor Sven brings guests," she told me. "He telephone this afternoon to tell Juanita and Felipe to prepare dinner for four in the big dining room. He asked me to let you know, and to ask you to go down as soon as possible."

Guests! A hint, obviously, to wear something formal. Well, that was all right. Taking a last critical look at myself in the mirror, I went down the stairs, knocked perfunctorily at the salon door, and entered.

Beside the open French doors Lars Sven stood with his guests. He wore full evening dress, a clove carnation glowing in his right lapel. His dark hair and beard were sharply-outlined in the light of the enormous crystal chandelier. Strangely, for all that he was Norwegian, I thought he seemed quite at home in that ancient place where the mark of its first Spanish noblemen owners still seemed stamped upon everything about it.

Beside him stood a man I judged to be in his late thirties, but he could have been older, for he was thin and wiry. He had a small, elongated skull, brown hair worn long, and rather a clever face, lean and somehow vaguely questing, the high cheekbones glistening under very pale skin. He also was in evening dress. About him there clung such an aura of the professional man that I was sure this was Dr. Max Gertae.

I also disliked him heartily on sight.

The woman with him radiated vitality, just as did Lars Sven, whereas the doctor radiated a kind of cruel strength deliberately held in leash. Elsa Gertae's raven-dark hair was styled straight and long. It brushed her magnificent shoulders, and set off her perfectly formed, sharp features. Then, as Sven hurried towards me, I caught the flash of her lovely green eyes as she, too, turned in my direction.

I suddenly knew where I'd seen these two before!

They had been at the Hotel Phoenix, in Barcelona, when I looked out on the Ramblas. There they had sat with the pop group just about to shut me from their sight.

Had, then, the third figure, the man who hovered on the edge of that picture, been Lars Sven? When he brought me to the castello in the Mercedes he told me, quite casually, that he had been in Barcelona the night before, and that he'd wished he'd known I was there.

Well, there was no particular mystery about it. If it had been him, obviously he'd joined his friends the Gertaes for some little celebration. And then had gone back to the island next day, so that I was able to telephone him at the castello when I found myself stranded on the Palma quayside.

The words almost were on my tongue, "Why, how strange, our meeting like this, because I'm sure I saw you in Barcelona, the night I was there!"

But I never said them. Instead, I smiled, shook hands, murmured polite and meaningless words of greeting, as, from Lars' introductions, I found out that these were indeed, Dr. Max Gertae and Elsa, his wife.

Coming, as I did, almost straight from Ian Hamilton and his story, I felt they must, all three, be reading every suspicious thought in my mind!

Dr. Gertae, however, only bowed and smiled. But his eyes, a sort of slate grey, bored into me, confirming that first impression which I felt I would have made without benefit of Ian's insinuations. Here was a man whom I not only instinctively mistrusted, but who I also found revolting for some unexplainable reason.

"Charmed!" he had murmured automatically at our introduction. Elsa Gertae's smile, like her husband's, never reached her eyes. Dr. Gertae took my hand and bowed low over it, an obvious gallantry which I only found annoying.

Was his charm too deliberate or was it the fact that I was on my guard, deliberately looking for something false? We chatted perfunctorily over drinks and cigarettes. I was told that they ran the El Pineo between them, in the summer, but that it was closed for most of the winter, and that they took only a few patients because of the very small nursing staff.

"How do you like Majorca?" she asked me, in a fascinating, throaty voice. "Very beautiful, is it not? But too hot for you, perhaps, coming from cold grey England?"

"The sun shines there too," I said drily, "but perhaps not all that often in the part I come from."

We fenced with each other, sizing one another up. From something in her eyes I could tell she wasn't much impressed with my looks. I found her beauty fascinating, yet slightly repulsive.

"You have been sunbathing today, perhaps?"

A direct frontal assault, as it were, might be a good idea here.

"No. I've been over to the cementario, the old one, by Genova."

She stiffened, or was that, too, my imagination?

"I went to take some flowers to my friend, Jenny Midnight's, grave."

If I'd expected to shock them into guilt or remorse or fear I was sadly disappointed. Lars nodded without comment; he'd known where I was going, anyway. Dr. Gertae murmured something politely sympathetic, which sounded like "Poor young girl!" and Elsa said, "Yes. Lars tells us how attached you were. It was indeed very sad. But I don't expect you want to talk any more about it just now? We were all, of course, very upset."

"I understand that it was in the El Pineo Nursing Home that Jenny actually died?"

Normally, women like Elsa Gertae tended to inhibit me, with their poise, sophistication, conscious appeal, and beauty. Yet, the haunting thought that they might, all three of them, really have done something awful to Jenny robbed me of my customary reserve. Still, I hadn't meant to say it quite like that, as if in deliberate challenge. Or perhaps it hadn't

175

sounded so, and was I just remembering what Ian had hinted?

"I did everything humanly possible," said Dr. Gertae, "but she'd left it too late."

"I thought the antibiotics were useful with conditions like peritonitis?"

If I was quoting Hamilton, they weren't to know it. Dr. Gertae frowned, then went on, soothingly, as if to a relative of the deceased whose lacerated feelings must be considered, "Antibiotics are useful, certainly, if one can get them into the patient in time to prevent the spread of the infection. Unfortunately, in Miss Midnight's case this wasn't possible."

"She hated having to confess that she felt even the least little bit unwell," Lars Sven said, thoughtfully. "Ruth, my dear, our two very good friends here really did all they could."

There seemed, I fancied, to be a slight edge to his tone, under the gentleness and superficial courtesy. In his profession, no doubt, the latter was often a necessary defence. Yet I felt I was being warned that my questions were becoming too direct, too searching.

"Of course," I said quickly. A withdrawal was not only tactful, but expedient. I had my own careful defences to man.

"Lars," said Elsa, pitching her cigarette through the open French windows, "your gardens are charming, if the island stays short of rain. You could try growing vines on those terraces, yes?"

The accent, so far as I could place it, suggested she was European by birth, possibly Austrian. Dr. Gertae's, on the other hand, puzzled me. There was a nasal intonation to the a's that could have indicated Australia as his birthplace. But his English was carefully polished, and any accent was difficult to place.

"Oh, Felipe has enough to do," Lars said, idly.

"You also. What with your book, and the designing and soon your new collection to present, you must be very busy. A splendid idea to have Jenny model for you in the tower apartment. What will you do now, Lars?"

He stared rather sombrely out at the sea now silvered by a young moon.

"I don't know, Elsa. Jenny was to have modelled the bulk of the collection with the help of some professional models from Barcelona, probably. The gowns are already here. They came from the Parisian dressmaker in the early summer. I haven't had much heart to do anything about them since Jenny went . . ."

Jenny went, I noted. Why not *Jenny died*? Still, that might be just his way of putting it, in the same way that other people referred to death as "passing away" or "passing on."

Lars said, "You've a lovely figure, Elsa, not unlike Jenny's. I thought of it the other day, whether you might consider modelling the autumn collection?"

Elsa stared, surprised, and Lars went on, "So long as Max agrees, of course."

"Did you hear that, Max?" she called back. "Lars would like me to do some modelling for him! What do you say?"

The doctor didn't answer immediately, and I thought the two of them exchanged a baffled look, as if something about the offer puzzled them.

"If it's going to help Lars out of a difficulty, by all means," Dr. Gertae said politely. "But I don't want you turning into a full-time professional model!"

"Oh, it would only be for one afternoon," Lars assured him. After that, the talk on that subject lapsed, but it seemed to me that the two Gertaes were uneasy, almost as if they suspected Lars of making the suggestion for some deeper, hidden motive.

And, I thought, he could get a model easily enough with his reputation. Jenny thought it was a great feather in her cap when he made her his chief model.

Strolling casually to stand between the French doors, I looked out on the terraces and the sea. "Just exactly where is the El Pineo Nursing Home situated? Is it possible to see it from here?"

Lars shot me a rather speculative look, and the doctor turned that stone face upon me. Although on the surface no emotion was allowed to show, something in his face, I fancied, seemed to stir.

It was Elsa who told me, coolly, without undue curiosity marking that lovely voice, "Of course. Look, I'll show you."

We stepped into the garden. Lars didn't follow, but Dr. Gertae was at our elbow in seconds, as the woman pointed to a white villa, some half mile to the west, the flat top of which was just discernible through pine trees.

No other building was anywhere near it. Below more pine woods, as with Castello Minerva, fell to the Mediterranean, and behind lay open country.

"There is a road," said Dr. Gertae, "but you can't see it from here. We need isolation, you understand, peace and quiet for our patients."

Yes, I thought, at night El Pineo would be very isolated.

We went in. In a few moments, Felipe entered to announce dinner. Felipe's glance found his master's immediately. When it came next to me and lingered, I felt it was faintly but unmistakably hostile.

Lars escorted Elsa into the white dining room; the doctor smilingly offered me his arm. Such formality irked me. That elegant room, with its silk-covered walls, glass chandelier, long olive-wood table, loaded with crystal and silver and flowers from the castello's gardens, seating the quartet we made with ease, was oppressive.

I felt physically and spiritually dwarfed as if all the aristocratic Spanish owners of the castello, looking down at me from the ornately-framed oil paintings, contemptuously dubbed me an intruder, a little peasant, with no real name or background.

Then, glancing down at the table's end which lay in shadow, I saw Jenny again! She was so faint, I caught only the shine of her braids, golden in the gloom, and the top of her figure and face. But she stared straight up at Lars Sven, midnight blue eyes blazing!

Catching an involuntary breath, I thought, surely he must see her . . . surely, they must all see her! But they went on talking, sipping their wine, nodding, smiling, Elsa using her histrionic gestures as she'd done that night on the Ramblas.

I nerved myself to look once more. The chair at the very end of the long table was vacant. Lars Sven's eyes suddenly met mine, as if he'd sensed that psychic shock in me. Well, he'd invited me to the castello, certainly, but I could scarcely say he'd lured me here, whatever he might have done to Jenny.

On the other hand, one could interpret the detached coolness of his letter as a clue he'd never wanted me to come, had confidently expected I never would! But now I was here, and perhaps must be kept—as his secretary, if necessary. That I might myself be in any kind of danger had never occurred to me till then.

Juanita was an accomplished cook. Course followed course, and with each, wines of excellent vintage. Lars, I noticed, drank freely; Dr. Gertae moderately; and the lovely Elsa, not at all. Her figure, I guessed sardonically, watching her send away the fattening *gazpacho* with its pressed bread, tomato puree and olive oil. She toyed with the *empanadilla*, a meat-filled pastry. This was followed by *escudella*, the main course, a stew with chicken and potatoes floating in it. For dessert, there was a dish of *buñuelos de limon*, a kind of lemon cruller.

"You will need to know the names and natures of our Majorcan dishes if you are to stay on here, my dear Ruth!"

"Stay here?" murmured Elsa, raising her eyebrows as Felipe came in with a great silver platter of peaches, grapes and plums. She, of course, had waved away the *buñuelos* with a shudder of distaste.

But Lars was looking at me, smiling. And I looked around again at the three of them, decked out in their ultra-smart clothes, and wondered what was really going on in their minds, and what secret there might be here that had concerned Jenny—and might, indeed, have sent her to her death.

After dinner, Elsa played and sang for us in the salon. She had a strong, rather powerful mezzo-soprano voice. A voice suited, I thought critically, to the woman herself.

Lars listened, waving a hand in time to the music. He still held his wine glass, I noted, and seemed able to drink as if liquor were water. His speech was quite unslurred, his strange, near-black eyes quite clear, and his manner unfuddled.

Later, Dr. Gertae and his wife went down the central terrace towards the swimming pool, and I was left alone with Lars.

Somehow, I found myself out on the central terrace too, with his hand under my elbow, and then he was guiding me around the side of Castello Minerva, so that we stood in a little dell, shut in by trees.

To the east I could see the Bay of Majorca, and all the lights along the paseo maritimo, where the taxi driver had taken me that morning. Further off lay a golden haze that must be where the Cathedral and the Almudaina Arch and all the other historic sites were.

"What a beautiful night!" I whispered involuntarily, catching the drift of all the exotic scents of the castello gardens. "It's so very lovely."

"There is sadness in your voice again," said the man beside me. We'd halted beneath the shelter of an ancient yew. Beside it, his figure, moon-limned, was very strong—and very attractive.

"You are thinking of dearest Jenny."

"Yes," I admitted.

"It's inevitable—for a little while. But you must not mourn her too long. You are yourself too young. And she—would not want it."

No, I thought, nor would she want to be hurried out of life before her time! It seemed to me that both Lars and Elsa were urging me to forget Jenny, and in a way that seemed unnatural.

For to me it was equally unseemly, and unnatural, that they couldn't mourn at all.

"Ruth?" I tensed; I knew from his tone what was coming.

"Yes, Lars."

"Have you decided?"

In the moonlight he bent towards me, the clove scent of the carnation in his buttonhole almost overpowering, his dark eyes fixed intently, almost hypnotically, upon me.

"Why yes, Lars," I told him, and stepped back a pace. "I have. I mean, I've thought it over well, as you asked me to . . ."

"And—Jenny?"

I cried out at that, so startled and shocked was I. In another second, I could have bitten my tongue, for I realised he'd just made a verbal slip, and he would be the more puzzled at my reaction.

He stepped forward instantly, and grasped me by both arms, his fingers and thumbs digging cruelly into my flesh. But I could tell he didn't mean to hurt me.

"Hush, foolish little Ruth! I didn't mean to frighten you! I'm so sorry, my dear. But we had just been talking of her, and you are her friend. It was just the association of thoughts."

Or had her name been in his subconscious and, in the nervous desire to know my own decision, had he been taken off-guard, and cried it out?

Looking up into the dark, handsome face bent above me, in apparent chagrin and self-reproach, I saw, indeed, nothing there that betokened guilt or fear. Only, I thought, vexation for this faux pas.

"I understand, Lars. Please, don't let it bother you." But with a thrill of self-contempt, I realised I was joining him in this artful game of camouflage.

Why in the world couldn't I put my cards on the table? Tell him about the letter from Jenny that Ian Hamilton held, ask him to explain? Or call Dr. Gertae here, and get him to explain?

"You are so sweet," Lars murmured. Just for a moment, his hand hovered over my hair, and then was withdrawn. And gone, too, was my impulse for honesty.

I knew I never could ask him; all that was left was either to stay, and try and find out if Ian's suspicions were rooted in anything positive, or change my mind, even at this eleventh hour, and run from Castello Minerva and everything to do with it.

That latter impulse, for a black, whirling second, was very strong indeed. After all, the castello hadn't brought poor Jenny much luck. It might be just as much a place of bad omen for me . . .

But I found it was too late, that I'd hesitated and procrastinated too long, for Lars was standing straight before me, blocking my path, plainly not intending to move till I'd told him what he wanted to know.

"Well, Ruth?" he said again, smiling.

I took a deep breath, set a smile on my own lips, and hoped he couldn't tell how forced and unreal it was, reflecting nothing of the turmoil in my heart and mind.

"I'll accept your offer, Lars. For a few months, at any rate. Shall we say, a provisional period till Christmas, till we see if we suit each other?"

There was then a gleam in the dark eyes that I couldn't at all identify. Disappointment, frustration, or—anger?

"Half a loaf, eh?" he said at last. "Well, if you want it that way, Ruth. Myself, I see no need for any provisional period."

"But you may find me hopelessly incompetent," I told him. "I feel you should be free to withdraw, that we should both feel free to withdraw."

"A way of escape, eh?" said Lars, and laughed. Mocking laughter, with a harsh, ugly edge to it. "So be it, Ruth. You're engaged as my temporary secretary then, till Christmas! And I'm absolutely delighted, my dear!"

His hand came out, took my right one, pressed a kiss to it.

"You mustn't mind, Ruth my dear. We're both, I fancy, two very lonely people. But I shan't take advantage of your youth. Or your particularly vulnerable position. You're quite safe with me."

Under the circumstances, I couldn't help feeling that that was an odd statement, but before I could say or do anything else, he released my hand, put his own under my right elbow again, and was saying, in a brisk, business-like voice, "And now, we must go and tell Max and Elsa. They will be enchanted. You will see a lot of them from now on, especially if Elsa can be persuaded to do some modelling for me."

I couldn't help wondering if they would be as charmed and delighted as Lars supposed.

Lars was as good as his word, not bothering me or approaching me on any aspect of his work till the last two weeks of my holiday were finished.

In those two weeks, we went out and about together quite a lot. The Gertaes never came to the castello again, and I saw nothing more of Ian Hamilton, although, tempting fate, I went once more to the Genova cementario. My visit to Jenny's grave completed, the dead red roses removed and a fresh bunch placed there, I went back to the small cafe where we'd talked.

Knowing the way that time from a map of the area, I was able to dismiss the first taxi driver at the road to the cementario, and pick up another in the village to return to the castello.

When there was no sign of Ian, no hint that he'd been again to Jenny's grave, and no word, or telephone message or letter, left for me at the castello, I was inclined to dismiss the whole affair as the product, on his part, of an overactive imagination, and on mine, as grief and strain.

So Lars and I motored about Majorca, and he took me to see the pearl and shoe factories at Manacor, and, laughing, bought me a rope of pearls as a memento.

Sometimes Felipe accompanied us, and then I wasn't so contented for, although the man was perfectly polite and courteous, I felt that underneath, he resented my presence.

One day we went to Valldemosa, climbing up the rocky road between the mountains, with the monastery perched on its hill, and below, the fields spread out and enclosed within crumbling stone walls. Here there were olive trees which looked incredibly ancient, and Felipe assured me that they were hundreds of years old.

We wandered through the Carthusian Monastery where George Sand stayed with Chopin in the winter of 1838. I thought it very pathetic, seeing the very rooms where this young, tortured genius had agonised over his music, whilst George Sand tyrannised his mind.

The view from the terraces was magnificent, with oranges and lemons growing in the small gardens, and a breathless view down the valley.

"You are fortunate to see it as it is now," Lars told me when we emerged from the Chopin suite, with its photographs and letters and piano of the musician, to walk in the cool of the Carthusian cloisters. "In the season, one cannot move for the tourists, with their cameras, and their guide books, and their gaucherie!"

My ire rose at that, although I had the sense to conceal it, for I was learning that Lars wasn't the type of man to tolerate much verbal opposition. It was better to keep one's opinions to one's self, and reserve judgment.

Oh, he was a fascinating and utterly considerate friend and employer, but there was too much about him that stayed hidden, that I couldn't probe or understand.

"I wonder if they knew any real happiness," I said, as we sipped wine at one of the inns below the Monastery.

"Who?" Lars asked.

"Chopin and George Sand. They must

have had something in common, at least to begin with."

"I dislike dominant women," said Sven distastefully. "He, of course, was a genius. All his real love was given to his music. I think it was too much trouble for him to stand up against her."

He said this with such a look of burning intensity in his dark eyes that I felt uncomfortable. Lars, too, was an artist. He had that single-minded attitude toward his work which also suggested that it was the only thing that mattered in his life.

"She believed in free love," Lars went on. "And lived with Alfred de Musset, the poet, in Venice, after she left her husband. She was a remarkable creature, I grant you, but not one I should ever want to cultivate."

"I should have thought you'd have admired her courage and enterprise," I said lightly enough. I didn't really care about George Sand at all; I was just interested in probing Lars' mood.

He shrugged. He looked tired that afternoon, as if he'd not slept well, with dark circles under his eyes, and his skin pallid.

"Oh, I can do that, my dear, without admiring her as a woman."

He seemed restless, unwilling to linger. Soon we were in the Mercedes again, Felipe driving us skilfully and smoothly along the rather winding, rough roads of the north-western corner of the Island. Here I caught enchanting glimpses of the Mediterranean, blue against the red and green of the pines and firs, and a panorama of rocky headlands putting me in mind of Cornwall's north coast, if without that mystical, fey quality of the latter. And there weren't so many windmills in Cornwall.

Although I enjoyed the trip, I wasn't altogether at my ease, and it was a relief when we finally drove back to the castello.

After dinner that night, at which Lars again seemed somewhat preoccupied, he asked me, rather formally, to excuse him. He was going into the tower apartment to work on the autumn collection, having now decided there was little point in not holding it.

Photographers and representatives from European and American newspapers and fashion magazines would be coming. He didn't propose to offer them any more hospitality than would be necessary for the day on which the show would be held.

"They'll be going on to other shows or exhibitions," he explained. "But there will be a great deal of preliminary paper work. Juanita and Maria will see to the domestic hospitality—drinks, lunch, some sort of afternoon tea. After that, they'll be gone again. But I shall rely on you to get out the invitations, arrange for the printing of the catalogue, programmes and so on."

"It sounds exciting," I said.

I went off early to bed with a book. The sound of the sea and the pines was usually soporific and soothing. That night they seemed to infect me with something of Lars Sven's restlessness.

I pictured him poring over his drawing board, adding this or that touch to a sketch or design.

The rooms in the tower apartment were small, though the ceilings were lofty. Those upstairs, which were unused except for an office on the second floor, were furnished in the Majorcan style with olive-wood furniture.

Lars' studio was on the ground floor.

Stacks of sketches leaned against the walls as well as paintings he'd either done or was working on for stage productions. He told me he was keeping the used ones to illustrate his proposed book on design.

He had also shown me the racks of beautiful clothes that had already arrived from the Parisian fashion house—apparently more were expected. They were day dresses and evening gowns Lars had designed modelled on Majorcan peasant fashions.

Still restless, I got up, put on a robe, opened the windows, and stepped out on to the verandah.

Here the heady perfume of pines and sea was much keener. The wavelets broke on the private beach more audibly. Lights from solitary boats glowed out on the bosom of the Mediterranean, and I could see the diffused glow from the mass of ships anchored at the docks in the Bay of Palma.

A jet climbed, its green and red lights lost amongst the stars. I caught my breath. The moon was out, and the scene had a magic that momentarily arrested the senses.

The beauty of the night and the loveliness of the landscape only intensified my curious sense of yearning for some vital quality missing in my life. I knew what it was: a sense of belonging. I was frustrated and lonely.

Sadness engulfed me, till I remembered Ralph, and bitterness swallowed up the sadness. Love was overrated. I could do without it if I used enough self-discipline.

And if the desire to find out what had happened to Jenny was becoming an obsession, as common sense and logic warned, at least it was better than dreaming foolish dreams about love, marriage, and children. All of these I'd cherished when I first met Ralph. Oh, he'd promised marriage, or I'd never have agreed to our liaison in the first place. And, having met Lars Sven, I was wondering now how much he'd promised Jenny, and perhaps disappointed her in?

My mood of depression and melancholy deepened; to my horror I found I was on the verge of tears!

Blinking them angrily away, I suddenly noticed that the one solitary light burning in the tower apartment had been extinguished. I waited, for some reason, to see my employer emerge, watch him walk across the intervening space to the door of the eastern wing, enter and go up to his room.

Five minutes went by. There was no sign of the tall, strong figure in evening dress. The door remained fast. A nightbird swooped low over the tower battlements and suddenly I was shivering in my thin, nylon nightgown and filmy robe.

Why on earth was I lingering there, staring, waiting for Lars Sven to emerge? If he did come out, though, it was imposs- ible for him to see me, for I was well back on the balcony, within the shadows cast by the overhanging eaves of the castello.

Still, I moved even further back, my gown clutched fast about me, as a wandering breeze stirred the hem and played coolly around my ankles. Ten minutes. The light was out and still he hadn't emerged. He must have slipped by unnoticed, I thought, in the split second when a cloud covered the moon and put the tower apartment in darkness.

There was no rear doorway to the tower apartment. Built and shaped like a military tower, with the battlemented roof, it seemed to have been designed as a model of what such towers were like when they were defended against siege.

But so far as I knew, the castello in the pines had not been the scene of any bloody battles, not even in the days when the Moors invaded the island.

"He's gone back to his room," my mind informed me coldly. "And you'd better do the same, not stand shivering here, like some moonstruck schoolgirl, imagining all sorts of idiotic things!"

But could he have got accidentally locked in the tower by Felipe, who went the rounds each night? I looked at my watch. Only eleven o'clock! Felipe never locked up till midnight, or later. This I knew because Lars had informed me that if I ever wanted to stay out late, I must let Felipe know.

"And he will wait up for you," said Lars, rather forbiddingly. "I do not like people to come late to the castello. It would be better, if you do wish to go on an evening excursion, that I escort you."

At the time this had seemed presumptuous, but I'd just nodded and said nothing, for the simple reason that I'd no intention of attending late cinemas or night clubs in Palma, with or without his chaperonage. I'd come to Majorca to rid myself of a ghost, and of an obsession.

The moon came out again. Yes, the iron door was firmly closed.

I was turning into my room when I caught the flutter of movement beyond the swimming pool where the rough steps led down to the private beach.

The movement quickly resolved itself into the figure of Lars Sven, still in evening dress, walking quickly up the ornamental path between the terraces.

That's strange, I thought; he's coming from the beach. Evidently, I decided, he must have gone, unnoticed, down the side of the eastern terraces under the rose pergolas and taken one of the paths through the pine woods to the beach.

A long way around, surely, when he might have walked straight down the central terrace, along the side of the swimming pool and so to the stone steps?

Still, it was a lovely night. No doubt, after working so hard on his designs he felt the need for air and exercise.

As he neared the castello he stopped, raised his head, and looked directly up at the facade of the east wing, and I could have sworn, particularly at the room which I now occupied!

Standing there behind the curtained French door, shivering, I felt, absurdly and totally irrationally, that those dark eyes had pierced behind the glass to pick out my own figure, and examine it, sardonically.

The moonlight was full on him now, on his hair, his beard, the strong, powerful features, even the carnation in his button-hole. So strong now was the illusion that he could see me that the space between us seemed to fall away, so that I could smell the clove aroma of the carnation, glimpse the well-cut mouth and the smile that seldom, if ever, reached the eyes.

The next day I took my bikini, and a book and towel down to the pool. It was too hot to go walking, or even to clamber down the steps to the private cove.

The pool water was warm, and for a while I swam around and sunbathed on the side. Once or twice I turned around to survey the castello. By now, Juanita would have gone to her customary siesta. Presumably Lars—and Marie—were still in the tower apartment. I found my mind playing with the picture of Lars, rising from his drawing board, with Marie, handsome and expectant, before him, tray in hand.

Oh well, I thought, if that's what they both want, and wondered if Jenny had been troubled by that thought.

As to that, and Ian Hamilton's suspicions, there could be nothing in them. I'd been at the castello over a month now, and no place could have been more peaceful. Lars was temperamental, certainly, given to moods, and I still thought there was something on his mind. But that applied to a great many men who had achieved the kind of success Lars Sven had. It was, I supposed, the price of ambition.

"Ruth!"

From the depths of the pine forest opposite, someone had called my name. Startled, I dropped my book, and stared into the massed foliage. Nothing.

Irritated, I again picked up my book. It

had been my fancy, or just the wind, rustling through the pine forest, or even the sea, breaking down there on the private cove.

"Ruth!"

There was no mistake. Someone was calling me. The voice was muffled, hard to identify. A shiver went over me, for, of course, the weird notion came to me that it was Jenny, somewhere there in the pine forest. Jenny, or that waif who was her ghost, calling me!

"Ruth! Ruth Foundling!"

No, not Jenny, she would never call my second name like that. Remembering that eyes might be upon me from the house, I walked, as firmly and as steadfastly as I could, round the edge of the pool, and a few yards into the forest.

I went another few yards into the forest, looking around at the serried ranks of trees. My heart was pounding, and I found perspiration trickling down my temples.

Then, from a group of pines, a hand shot out, closed around my wrist, and yanked me forward; I stood face to face with Ian Hamilton.

"Ian!" I said, angry now that the worst

of my fears were proved groundless. "What a stupid trick!"

"I'm sorry. I didn't mean to frighten you. But I had to see you. And I wasn't going to walk up to the front door and bang on it. Lars Sven, for all I knew, might have come in person to answer it."

"Well, from all I've been able to discover, it wouldn't have mattered if he had. He's not the Bluebeard you've been trying hard to make him out."

"Isn't he, Ruth? I watched that chap Felipe safely away in the boat, and then I came up through the wood, hoping to get a glimpse of you."

Had he, then, been spying on me? How could he tell I'd not driven, or walked, out by the main entrance gates?

"Well, you have, for what it's worth," I retorted, still angry. This clandestine hole-in-the-corner way of meeting now seemed to me ridiculous and unnecessary.

"Look, I've no intention of saying what I've come to say in earshot of the castello," said Ian, equally grim.

"I'm not sure I want to talk to you anywhere." I was remembering the three silent weeks that had passed since our last extraordinary meeting, weeks in which there'd not been the slightest signal from him.

"You left me right up in the air," I went on. "It was very unkind, to say the least, filling my mind with all sorts of dark and horrible suspicions! Sven has been very kind, and Dr. Gertae and his wife have been here as his guests. I think you're mad, even entertaining the ideas you have!"

"Did you ask the doctor about Jenny already having an appendectomy?"

"No," I admitted. The truth was that I'd allowed the days to slip by, never really facing that question. I'd thought about it, at intervals, then buried it again. Jenny could have had some obscure, but dangerous, internal condition which Dr. Gertae mistook for appendicitis, I decided.

It was also true that I hadn't really wanted to believe what Ian had suggested, so I'd spent the time shutting my mind to it.

But now here was Ian again, aggressive and demanding, destroying the illusions I'd wrapped around myself. If part of me, the weak and yielding part, hated him for it, another part of me admired his tenacity, clamoured with curiosity to know what else he might have discovered.

"I've a boat, hidden in the rocks just beyond the point," said Ian. "Will you come, Ruth?"

No harm in that, at any rate. We reached the boat by the simple process of plunging down through the wood, out on to the sand, across it, over a line of rocks, and then into the stern from the small, sea-washed platform with its handy iron stanchion, put there, I guessed, by some seaman years ago.

"Hired her, from Palma," said Ian of the boat, as he started the motor. "Do you suppose anybody can spot us from the castello?"

"It doesn't matter if they do," I said with spirit. "After all, I'm perfectly at liberty to go out for a trip with an old friend if I so choose."

"Thank you for the accolade," said Ian, his lips quirking. It seemed unlikely that we could be seen at that point, for the rock overhung the sea. Ian carefully kept the small motorboat under the overhang till we were round the nearest western point, far away from the castello.

"We'll get around to the south side of the island, Ruth, back to Palma, I think. I've got to take her back anyway, and we'll find a sheltered cove there."

The coast was beautiful, but Ian, finding a bay of sand just westwards, he said, of Andraitz, put in there, tied up the boat, and we set out.

We walked over scrunchy shells to a line of whiter sand. Ian spread his coat under the shelter of a rock, and we sat down.

"Cigarette?" he asked, and as I nodded, took one for me and lighted it.

"Why have you stayed away so long?" I asked abruptly. "You could have telephoned—made some excuse—if you didn't want Lars to know who it was. Besides, Juanita, his housekeeper, or the maid, Marie, usually answer the phone."

Ian looked at me gravely, his eyes narrowed against the sun. I'd have expected him to have been more deeply suntanned after those days on the island. But he looked thinner, too, and tense; not at all like a person who'd been on a relaxed walking holiday.

"As a matter of fact, I haven't been in Majorca much since the last time we met," he told me.

"Where have you been?"

"In England—making certain enquiries."

When I didn't answer, he took a wallet from his trousers pocket, opened it, and extracted a sheet of paper. It was a greyish colour, the printing on it very black and smeared looking. I realised, as he gravely handed it over, that it was one of those things you get from copying machines.

For some reason I was reluctant to look at it. Then I realised this was because I feared to read it, was frightened of what Ian had found out.

"I've been doing some sleuthing," Ian said, "in old newspapers—those that go back to the month and the year that your friend Jenny was abandoned on that orphanage doorstep."

"Like me," I said, reading it. It appeared to be the fourth page of a London daily newspaper for April, 1950. There wasn't much national news. There were pictures of a girl getting married, just entering her taxi. Some actress going to

Caxton Hall. A column concerned a man who'd fiddled with his income tax. Another was about some London politician's views on the chance of war in Korea.

Aware of Ian beside me, studying me intently, watching, as I realised, for my reaction, I scanned the page diligently. There was a photograph, at the top of a column, of a man's face—a young, clean-shaven face, with close-cropped hair.

I passed it, at first glance, never recognising it, till, suddenly, I was caught by the eyes. Even in the newspaper, they were deep set and looked very dark, black.

And their expression was exactly the same as that I'd recently seen at breakfast time at Castello Minerva.

"Lars Sven!" I said. "Only a much younger Lars! Thinner in the face—"

"Read on, Ruth," said Ian.

I did. And was immediately transported from that pleasant, sunlit beach on Majorca to a court at the Old Bailey in London where one Judge Baker was summing up a case evidently known as "The Rosalie Saunders Murder."

"Murder!" I gasped. "Ian, was Lars . . . ?"

Ian plucked the paper from my nerveless grasp. He began to read.

At the trial this afternoon of Gordon Ayrton, designer and artist, on a charge of murdering Rosalie Saunders, a prostitute, living at Burton Mansions, Chelsea, Lord Justice Baker directed the jury they might only bring in a verdict of guilty against the accused if they were satisfied, beyond the shadow of a doubt, that his was the hand that killed her.

Most of the evidence was highly circumstantial, the Lord Justice pointed out, a fact that they must bear in mind in their deliberations. They must also dismiss from consideration the fact that the dead woman was a prostitute. Her moral code was not under judgment in that court.

The deceased was found stabbed to death on the morning of February 10, 1950. Witnesses have testified they saw Gordon Ayrton, a frequent caller at the flat, slipping in and out of the house twice on the night of the murder.

Gordon Ayrton has pleaded not guilty. The prosecution admits his fingerprints were not on the Indian paper knife that killed Miss Saunders, but they were found elsewhere in the room on many objects. However, Ayrton has a solid alibi. A young woman with whom Ayrton lives has testified he was with her the night of the murder, a fact which Sir Edward Bates, gifted counsel for the defence, has made the most of during the closing stages of Ayrton's trial.

There will be a full report on the outcome of the trial in our later editions.

Ian took another photostat from his wallet. Puzzled momentarily, I stared at photographs of racehorses, but Hamilton's hand travelled down to the bottom of the sheet. Under the racing results printed there I read,

Gordon Ayrton found not guilty of the murder of Rosalie Saunders. Verdict was given as murder by person or persons unknown.

"But, if that *is* him, he's changed his name!" I said. "And grown a beard, and long hair! And made a distinguished career for himself."

"Quite so," said Ian, and twitched the second paper away, brought up the first sheet, and handed it to me.

"Notice anything else?"

For a little while, still wrestling with the discovery that Lars Sven wasn't Norwegian at all, and that, twenty years before, he'd apparently been lucky not to have been hanged for the murder of a London prostitute, I saw nothing, only that darkly-handsome face and the strange, near-black eyes that had always, I thought, had a weirdly-haunted quality.

"At the foot of the first column, Ruth," said Ian very curtly. "There's her picture, and a small paragraph."

It was the photograph of a baby, a round-faced smiling infant, about six months old, in woollen coat and a bonnet with strings tied, bow-fashion, under the dimpled chin. There was a short paragraph below it.

BABY LEFT ON ORPHANAGE STEPS

211

This charming stranger was placed on the steps of the Greystoke Orphanage at around midnight on April 28, 1950. There was no clue to her identity. A nurse at the orphanage smilingly told our reporter they planned to call the baby Jenny Midnight, unless, of course, her real identity can be established.

"My God, Ian! He, Lars—or Gordon Ayrton—must have kept this old report and when Jenny started, or said she would start, her own investigations, feared she'd find out about him."

A sea bird swooped low, cried hauntingly, and flew away over the sun-dappled sea. And I looked into Ian's steadfast brown eyes, and felt, suddenly, as cold as death in that burning sun.

9

"I BEGAN to suspect when you told me about finding that newspaper cutting in Jenny's suitcase. The one where she's photographed taking the toys to the kids in the orphanage. She must have told Lars she thought about starting an investigation into her past."

"At the time, I'm sure, it must have been just one of her romanticisings, Ian. You see, she said the same thing to me, many times. The idea was that we should both try and find out who our parents were, where we'd come from. I wasn't keen on it. And I think, too, Jenny was half-afraid to actually do it. I mean, we might have found out more than we ever wanted to know. Actually, she was rather inclined to let sleeping dogs lie."

"Very likely," Ian nodded sympathetically. "For her, the idea, told to some admiring young reporter, with a picture of her holding the teddy bears and dolls and so on, was pathetic and nostalgic. Good publicity. And she probably reckoned it wouldn't do the orphanage any harm. Rich people, not knowing where to leave their money, can be directed to a deserving cause."

One of the exploring goats ventured nearer to the cliff edge. We heard the musical tinkling of its bell.

"If Lars Sven, though, didn't know she was just romanticising—" I ventured.

Ian inhaled deeply from his cigarette. His attitude toward me was subtly changing. On the coach, I'd been the immature and, at times, slightly tiresome child to be looked after. Here I was gradually being accepted as partner and confidante.

"I've still got the white horse you bought me," I said with total irrelevance. "It's on the chest in my bedroom at the castello."

"Keeping you in mind of me?" he said, and suddenly grinned. "And just like a woman, to go off on a tangent like that!"

"Sorry," I said defensively, and Ian leaned forward, seized my chin, and kissed me swiftly on the mouth.

"Ruth, isn't that just the point, about

Lars Sven and Jenny? I mean, how far could he be sure she was just romanticising? He's changed his name in an attempt to leave the past behind him. I found out that after he was acquitted of the Rosalie Saunders murder, he went to Norway. He has relatives there. And he took their family name."

I stared at Ian. "How do you know all this?"

"A fair question. And one I knew you'd get round to asking sooner or later. Apart from being Jenny's friend, and wanting to know what happened to her, I write about crime in my spare time. So it was easy enough for me to explore the sources from the London end."

"You mean the newspapers, the record of the trial and so on?"

Ian nodded. "Yes. But I wanted to trace Gordon Ayrton's history after he left London, so I used a detective agency."

A part-time crime writer! That and the fact that he'd had Lars Sven investigated somehow made me uneasy.

As if reading my thoughts, Ian grinned and said, "My darling girl, consider yourself lucky. I made a search amongst the

London papers for news of your connection to Jenny, but there was nothing."

"But we were always together," I pointed out, slightly annoyed that my life was such an open book to him.

"I know. She told me. It was almost as if you'd been twins, at least in spirit. But they gave you no publicity! By then either that reporter was interested in other activities, or maybe—and this is more likely—more important news crowded you out. Jenny got all the publicity then, and later!"

"Jenny would have been the last person to gossip!" I said fiercely. "Surely even Lars Sven must have known that."

Ian appeared to consider this gravely.

"That's a point. But once she'd begun such investigations, there was always the possibility other people might get interested—too interested."

Ian paused. "Ruth, don't misunderstand me. You're very loyal to Jenny. Perhaps too loyal."

"What do you mean?" I said indignantly.

"Well, you did only see one side of her —the best side. Because you were the only person in her world for whom she entertained an utterly selfless and sincere affection, you weren't in the way of any of her plans or ambitions. She could be pretty ruthless when she chose."

Another hot denial was on my tongue till a stab of uneasiness checked it. There was truth in that.

"Surely you're not suggesting she would have been blackmailing him? Why, that's a horrible insinuation!"

Ian stared at me again, half-irritably, half-sympathetically, then suddenly leaned forward, tilted my face up to his, and kissed me full on the lips.

"Ruth, don't you trust me?" he said quietly when he'd released me.

"How can I know who I can trust?" I snapped.

"Well then, do you trust Lars Sven and this chap, Dr. Max Gertae, and his wife?"

On the boat, I'd told him about the situation at the castello. And now, at the direct question, my eyes fell.

"No—not altogether," I had to admit. "There's something on his mind. And he does have queer moods. But he's brilliantly gifted, that could be the reason."

Ian nodded, and I went on:

"Anyway, if he was acquitted, why should he bother about that twenty-year-old trial? I can see what you're suggesting, and I admit it does seem feasible. He either read that newspaper report or she told him. And because it's rather a horrible coincidence that a London newspaper carries the report of his trial and her arrival at the orphanage on the same page with his photograph, he fears—or feared—Jenny would find out. But what if she did? He had been acquitted!"

"Agreed, Ruth. But can't you see the effect on his career if it were established that he was tried for a particularly sordid murder, under his real name, and that he isn't even Norwegian at all? His career means everything to him."

"But surely there would have been other people at the trial who knew him and are still alive, Ian? What about them?"

"Twenty years is a long time. The way he was living, in London, he probably had only friends like himself, students eking out a living. When he went to Norway and began to climb the ladder to success, they were deliberately put out of his life."

"This girl, the one he was living with, who gave him his alibi, what about her?"

Ian told me he'd spent most of the time in London studying the reports of the Rosalie Saunders murder. The girl who alibied Gordon Ayrton was another art student.

"Well, what happened to her?"

"She was found drowned in the Thames the night after Gordon Ayrton disappeared from his London lodgings. The police could prove nothing, and it could have been suicide. Publicity, after the trial and during it, malicious gossip—who knows?"

"Are you suggesting he killed her?"

"I'm not suggesting anything, Ruth. I'm just giving you the facts as I've got them."

"You're altogether too cagey for my liking," I said bluntly. "I admit that photograph looks like the man I now know as Lars Sven. But he could have a double. How can you be sure that Gordon Ayrton later did become Lars Sven?"

"The detective agency is a reliable one. They showed me photostat copies of photographs of him soon after his arrival in Norway. It was young Gordon Ayrton to the life. They also found out that he legally changed his name in that country, from Gordon Ayrton to the one he now uses. He worked with an Oslo dress designer for many years, and became well-established in Norway before broadening his career. I've got proof, but as I say, and we both agree, changing his name is not a criminal offence."

"No," I said.

"I told you all this to put you on your guard, Ruth, that's all."

"But I'm not in any danger!"

"Not yet. But you could be. If, for instance, he finds out you came to the castello to discover the truth, the real truth, about the way Jenny died!"

"All we know, so far, is that Jenny was buried under a faked death certificate."

All we know, I repeated silently and remembered Jenny again in her orphanage garb; her eyes staring, staring, in blind and mute appeal! God, am I really going mad? I thought, and covered my eyes.

"I only wanted to warn you. Ruth, I think you should abandon your original idea of staying on at the castello, and go back to England. I know I said before it was a good idea, but now I'm not so sure."

"What about you?"

"Well, I can move about without the surveillance to which you may be subjected. You're probably being watched right now."

I shivered, remembering those nights when I felt certain I heard footsteps in the corridor outside my room.

"I'll keep an eye on Lars Sven. See what breaks," Ian said.

"What about the Gertaes? Do you suppose they know about Lars Sven really being Gordon Ayrton?"

"Probably. Remember, Gertae signed that death certificate."

"Well, I'm not going home. Even accepting that Lars Sven is not what he claims, that doesn't make him guilty of murdering Rosalie Saunders or my friend Jenny."

"*Our* friend Jenny," said Ian quietly. "You're very obstinate, in your own quiet little way, aren't you?"

"Well, it's only fair—till I'm sure Lars Sven is the cheat and imposter you say he is."

"Except that I personally don't think he deals in fairness. Go back to that house

221

and in my opinion, you step straight back into danger."

"You're exaggerating."

"Isn't it enough for you that three women with whom this man has associated have died under violent circumstances! Do you want to be the fourth?"

The proprietary note in Ian's voice suddenly reminded me so maddeningly of Ralph at his most hectoring, that I sprang to my feet, hands clenched, cheeks burning.

"I think it's a case of giving a dog a bad name! Oh, I admit I gave you to understand I wasn't happy about the way Jenny died. But that doesn't make Lars Sven, or even the Gertaes, into murderers!"

"Well, follow your own instincts, then," Ian said very curtly. "This feeling you have that Jenny comes to you, keeps trying to tell you something! What do you imagine she wants to tell you?"

"I don't know," I admitted. "I wish I did. Every time I see her, hear her, it makes me feel so dreadful, Ian!"

Ian came nearer, took me by the shoulders, looked long and deeply into my eyes.

"Do you want to drive yourself into a psychiatric hospital, Ruth?" he said softly. "All that—thinking you see her, the voice . . ."

"But I *do* see her! I *do* hear her!"

"Have you told Sven or the Gertaes about this?" he asked.

"No, of course not! How could I trust them after what you told me?"

"Well, that's all right then! Only, we don't want them suspecting what we're up to till we know more."

Ian released his grip on my shoulders, took my hands and held them tightly. The child Ruth is back again, I thought despairingly. He doesn't believe me when I tell him about seeing and hearing Jenny. In that sense, I'm just as much alone with him as with Lars Sven or the Gertaes!

"It's all this anxiety about her," he reiterated gently. "And that's justified by the facts, which I do believe. Ruth," he went on, his voice subtly altering, "when Jenny was with you in Somerset, did she say much about Lars Sven, and her relationship with him?"

"No. Not really. She did hope to marry him. She mentioned that in her letters."

"Nothing else?"

I was puzzled. Something in Ian's attitude began to alienate me, ever since he'd inferred I was getting hysterical, or mentally disturbed, over the wraith of Jenny. I knew she wasn't a wraith, that if she was dead, or alive, my subconscious clothed her in that orphanage form because that was how she'd printed herself on memory, when she told me that, if she ever wanted help, she'd ask nobody but me. Ian's total failure to understand, or even to try to understand, angered me.

"What else would there be, Ian? Unless you mean the dress show, Lars' autumn collection, that she was to model for him?"

He shook his head. "No. I just wondered, you see, if she had found out anything about him or his past as Gordon Ayrton, if she let anything slip. I mean, she could have done it inadvertently, not wanting to let you know she'd found out she'd made a mistake about him. Because, at first, or so I gathered from you, Jenny was in love with him."

"I don't know," I admitted again, miserably at sea now. "And I can't really remember. I had other things to preoccupy me—more's the pity, Ian! But she seemed delighted, thrilled is really the word, at the prospect of marriage to Lars. As to whether she loved him—well, I don't think Jenny loved any man in that sense."

Breaking off, I struggled for words, wondering how to explain to Ian. Then, thinking it no disloyalty to Jenny, hoping it might help him, I told him about Courtney Grafton and the early years.

"I know about that. She told me," he assured me. "God knows I never blamed her. But that's not what I meant, Ruth. I wondered if she said anything about Lars and his background; if she was worried about her fitting into it. I mean, if she didn't know he was really a sort of imposter, it could have bothered her, I suppose."

"Do you mean was she ashamed of her orphanage upbringing?" I said indignantly. "No, of course she wasn't! Any more than I am! We regretted it, yes. Naturally if we could have talked of our families, our homes and backgrounds, or even better yet, experienced family relationships of our own, it would have given us both a greater sense of emotional security. As it was—" I broke off. "Her compensation for that was to get all she could from life. But except sexually—and even there she was careful, as you know —she chose from experienced partners. Nobody got hurt by Jenny's ambitions. She was much too honest to let that happen."

"Yes, she was blazingly honest, wasn't she?" said Ian.

"Look," I said, feeling suddenly, utterly exhausted, "I'm going back to the castello. I'll have to go soon, in any case."

"And you're fed up with me and my insinuations, isn't that it? You're half-inclined to believe me, but at the same time, you don't really trust me."

"Well," I said coolly, "if it comes to that, I don't know any more about you than I do about Lars Sven, or the Gertaes, do I?"

And I turned, scrambling up the little path from the beach.

"Wait, Ruth!" Ian called angrily, but I rushed on, fully expecting him to pursue me, catch me up, stop me. I got to the road, which wound dustily and narrowly between almond and olive trees above the meadow where two white goats stared out at me, curiously, as I stumbled past. At the top of the road a signpost listed Palma, among other names, and the distances to each in kilometers.

I hesitated, then looked back to the beach. Ian Hamilton, in jeans and green shirt, was clambering from the rocks to the boat, not turning a glance in my direction.

Hot, tired and disturbed, I was standing there, wondering what chance there might be of getting a taxi by telephoning one from the nearest farmhouse, when a 'bus came trundling along. It halted by the signpost and let several Majorcans, in black dress and white straw hats, into the road.

Racing madly after it, I made sure it had Palma on the destination board, and thankfully climbed into it. Fortunately, I had a few *pesetas* in the little bag I'd brought with me, and that was enough to take me into the city.

From there, in a mood of bitter defiance, I telephoned the castello, got Lars, and revealed my plight to him. Of course I didn't mention Ian Hamilton. I only said that I'd got lost.

"So, you are stranded again, are you?" he said in a light, amused voice which told me, I confess to my relief, that his dark and curious mood of last evening was gone. "And I am to come to your rescue again, is that it? Well, I have been working hard all morning, but it has been worth it. I evolved several superb designs for the new autumn collection."

What about Marie, I thought, and wondered, ruefully, and in a flash of personal insight, whether I could possibly be jealous of the dark-eyed handsome Spanish maid?

I also wondered, uneasily, whether Lars could possibly have seen me leaving the castello in Ian Hamilton's company in what could have been construed as a sly and clandestine fashion. If so, his voice gave not the slightest indication of it.

"Well, now that my morning's work is successfully completed, I shall come and pick you up and take you for another drive around the island."

Another drive around the island was the last thing I wanted to do. Yet to reveal this to my employer, or even to show any sense of tension or disturbance, would be a mistake.

I waited in Palma, in a cafe near the Ramblas whose name I'd noticed and given to Lars Sven. There I drank two cups of black coffee, and tried to expunge from my mind everything that Ian had told me. And found, on this cooler, saner reflection—without that note in Ian's voice to bedevil me with its memories of Ralph —that I couldn't.

I turned from lighting a cigarette to see Lars Sven driving along the cobblestoned way towards me. He was immaculate in a white suit, a red carnation in his buttonhole. Then—catching my breath—I saw Jenny the child again, wraith-like, wide-eyed, at the next table!

That afternoon, or what was left of it, Lars took me to Inca, where there were a lot of old stone houses faced with pink tiles, and where I saw a mule harnessed to a pole threshing the grain. We dined at an old inn, and afterwards there was Spanish dancing and singing to a guitar.

"Perhaps you would like to see a bull-fight some time," said Lars, as we drove back to the castello under the stars.

"Oh, no," I said, shuddering violently, "I couldn't stand anything so barbaric."

It had been a magical evening, in wonderful contrast to that horror-haunted morning on the beach. Only when Lars laughed, long and low, did my uneasiness suddenly return.

My uneasiness increased when, driving back by the road by Castle Bellver, Sven told me how it was built for Jaime II in the fourteenth century.

"It's now a museum," said Lars, halting to stare at the huge yellow building. The sombre, brooding look was back on his face. "Under the Moorish kings it was used as a prison. One of your countrymen, dearest Ruth, was here. The Inquisition tortured him. He was of the Protestant faith."

"Oh, poor man!" I murmured.

"He was also a galley slave on a Moorish ship and then shipwrecked here on Majorca. He got away, was captured again, and brought back. They put him to the torture again, and flogged him brutally."

There was a curious note in the voice

of the man beside me—almost, I thought, shuddering inwardly, of sly pleasure!

"He was like all the English," said Lars, and it was very hard to remember then—so well did he play his part—that he was English himself. "Obstinate and proud. His name, as I recall, was Richard Hasleton. He escaped in the end to North Africa, and then the Moors got him once more. But he finally got home to England."

"He deserved to," I said quietly, and wished he'd not told me Richard Hasleton's story, or sounded so sadistic as he spoke of the torturing and the flogging.

Lars asked me to come to the salon to have some wine and talk for a while. But I needed to escape to the privacy of my own room and think, and so I made the always-acceptable excuse of a sudden headache. He came with me to the foot of the staircase, kissed my hand, and bade me pleasant dreams.

Pleasant dreams! I knew I'd never sleep, except in snatches. I'd brought some sleeping tablets with me, but when I went to my case, the tablets were missing.

Startled, for I was sure there'd been a

half-bottle full when I last went to the case, I looked carefully around.

The room seemed to be as I'd left it, except for the disturbance I'd caused by moving about, taking a shower, undressing. But I'd done most of that in the bathroom, and I'd not disturbed the contents of the wardrobe or any of the drawers.

My clothes, in fact, still hung on hangers in the bathroom, for I intended to launder them in the morning. Grimly, I began a reconnaissance.

Whoever had stolen the pills was something of an expert in breaking and entering. Now that I looked closely, it was easy to tell some hand had been through the wardrobe and the drawers and Jenny's pigskin case at the bottom of the wardrobe.

There were telltale clues. An untidy packer, I tended to heap all my underwear into the drawers, seizing a piece as I wanted it, or pushing it in hastily after I'd laundered it. Now, although skirts, pants, and stockings, were apparently lying in the same clean but careless confusion, there was an order to that confusion I never would have imposed!

In the wardrobe, dresses, coats and shoes were tidily assembled, because of the rails and shelves. Even so, I was certain one particular pair of evening shoes had been put back on the wrong shelf.

Nothing had been taken except for the sleeping pills! Why that?

Deeply disturbed, I went at last to bed. I thought it likely enough Marie was the person who had been through my possessions, though I couldn't fathom why she would steal the drug.

And, I thought grimly, if she tries taking those tablets without the medical prescription to their dosage, she'll either feel very ill, or even kill herself. I had better drop a salutary word or two in the morning, and watch her reactions.

Lars? It was possible he'd taken it, although he'd been with me for most of the day. Elsa? Dr. Gertae? I'd no means of knowing yet.

If Ian Hamilton was right, then Lars Sven was not only a man going under an alias, though we'd both agreed this was no crime, but also one who might have killed

Rosalie Saunders was his lover, and he hers. That much was clear from the newspaper photostat. But had he killed her? And that other unfortunate woman who gave him freedom through her alibi? And Jenny?

Suddenly I was shivering, recollecting the glint in his eyes, the note in his voice, as he spoke of gallant Richard Hasleton and his sufferings. And his mention of bullfighting, like one who approved and condoned that barbaric practice, frightened me.

Even so, many men could be capable of such reactions who were neither murderers nor criminals. A great majority of men, in fact, seemed to like such bloody "sports."

The doubts, chaotic and unnerving, returned. How did I know, beyond that one piece of evidence, that Lars Sven was Gordon Ayrton? True, from that newspaper photograph, the likeness was staggering. There was also the extraordinary coincidence that Jenny's photograph as a baby had appeared on the same day as that story detailing Gordon Ayrton's trial.

And there was the haunting way Jenny's

wraith kept coming between me and Lars, as if to warn me.

There was the fact that Jenny had been operated on for appendicitis when she was seven. And that Dr. Gertae, Elsa, and Lars all said she'd had an operation for appendicitis at Pineo.

I fell asleep, at last, but only to dream that Ian Hamilton was following me through the Genova cementario, a bunch of red carnations in his hand, while I ran away from him, shouting in the dream: "No, keep away—keep away!" I awoke, the sheets twisted and knotted about me, the counterpane on the floor, and the bright Majorcan sunlight streaming in through the window.

When I started working for Lars, he installed me in one of the empty rooms over in the tower apartment. He justified this with the explanation that it was quieter, away from possible callers and other distractions.

It was an eerily fascinating place, cool because of the thickness of the walls, and oddly silent, when one was once inside it. It had a stone staircase, winding up on the left, from which each of the three stories opened off to a landing and a corridor leading to the various suites of rooms.

An iron door at the top, where the steps terminated, gave access to the battlemented roof. But the door was bolted and barred, kept shut by Lars' express orders.

Apparently, when he first came to the castello, he'd had the tower surveyed. Because of crumbling masonry, and possible falls of portions of the ramparts, the roof was considered unsafe, although the main tower was all right.

No one slept there now. I could see that there might be danger during storms, of bigger portions of the masonry hurtling down.

In any event, the only callers we had continued to be Dr. Max Gertae and Elsa. Lars seemed to have few friends in Majorca.

I had little to do. Lars had a typewriter and a filing cabinet put into the office. There was also a telephone. Felipe brought what post there was each morning, after Lars had extracted his own private letters and papers.

The mail I did attend to was mostly

about Lars' work. There were many invitations to fashion shows. He seemed to accept only those for Europe or America. Everything for London, I noticed, was refused. He would scribble Yes or No on the margins of the letters or cards, and leave me to answer these invitations.

As I examined the files and correspondence about his fashion shows, the sets and costumes he'd done for plays and films, I also noticed he'd done nothing in London for more than a decade. He'd designed some sets for ballets in Edinburgh, Paris and Rome, but he consistently kept away from the English capital. Ian Hamilton, of course, would find that very significant.

As to the new book on design on which he was supposed to be working, there was no sign of the manuscript. When I sought him out in his studio on the ground floor wanting an answer to some query, I would find him immersed in a drawing, but he seldom wrote.

I evolved a filing system, arranged and catalogued the quite sizeable library on design which he kept in the room next to the office. But after lunch, brought by

Juanita on a tray, there was really nothing left for me to do.

As time went on, I grew bored. I was left alone some days when Lars was out in the boat with Felipe from morning till night. It was at such times that ugly conjecture knocked at the doors of my mind.

It had occurred to me, of course, that if something sinister was going on at Castello Minerva, if Lars Sven was a cheat and imposter, engaged in some dark design which had engulfed my friend Jenny, the servants might be discreetly pumped with the idea of getting some information out of them.

When Marie brought my morning coffee, I had two questions to ask of her. One concerned the missing sleeping pill bottle. And, as I put the question, I studied Marie over the rim of the cup. Had she seen a small brown bottle with a white cap containing some white tablets? Not a feature of the girl's sullenly handsome face altered, yet it seemed to me that the question touched her, beyond the ordinary curiosity a maid might feel in such circumstances.

The shake of her dark head seemed rather too emphatic. So I went on to ask about Jenny, and her habits.

"I know she loved walking, Marie. So I suppose she would have found some favourite haunts around here. I'd like to visit them. Do you know where she particularly liked to go?"

"Oh, she did not leave the castello grounds much, Senorita Foundling." Her tone was too eager; again the impression came that she was deceiving me. "Mostly she would sunbathe down by the pool. Oh yes, hours and hours she would spend there. Or, maybe, down on the private beach."

You're lying, Marie, I told myself, with a feeling of disgust. For Jenny seldom sunbathed. Her skin was so delicate and fine that she kept out of direct sunlight even in England, where it was usually diffused by cloud or mist. And, as for lying prone for hours upon a beach, that would have been anathema to vital, energetic Jenny.

So Marie, too, was covering up something, lying on somebody else's account. She was probably easy enough to bribe.

239

For all her attractiveness, she seemed, I felt, singularly stupid.

"What about the motorboat? Did she go out much in that?"

Marie shrugged. "Me, I don't know, Senorita. I have my own work to do, you understand. Besides, Senorita Midnight, she was not here all that long."

Marie was growing suspicious. She turned at the door tray in hand, to survey me haughtily, yet with that undercurrent of uneasiness.

"Look, why you not forget about her death, eh? I say it is not good for you, all this brooding upon Senorita Midnight. Perhaps it best for you to go back where you come from if to stay is to make you unhappy about her."

Impertinence, or another veiled warning?

"That's my affair, Marie."

She shrugged, and with a resentful flash of her dark eyes, was gone.

A small catastrophe that could also be construed as another kind of warning overtook me later that same morning. Returning to my room from the tower apartment for cigarettes, I saw the small white pottery horse, bought for me by Ian Hamilton at the Spanish frontier station, lying in four or five pieces. And it was not on the floor, but carefully placed on my bed, on top of the vividly embroidered Spanish counterpane, where, underneath, lay the pillow, and where, in sleep, my head must rest.

A cold finger, then, touched the nape of my neck. Quickly I stepped close and gathered up the broken pieces. And, as I held them in my fingers, suddenly, from out of the recent past, I heard Ian's voice, "Beautiful creatures, horses. Aren't white ones supposed to be symbolic of something—in folk lore and magic, that is?"

And my own voice, answered, "In antiquity, in the English west country, they carved them on all the chalk hills and downs. Something to do with the old gods, I think."

"They used to sacrifice the poor beast," Ian had said. "It was a sort of rite in the ancient world, as you say. And especially, I think I've heard or read, in Scandinavia. They ate the flesh and buried the skull in the grave with the person who owned it. Or who might even just own a representation of it. That person, too, would be sacrificed. Oh, usually, it was for kings and important personages."

The sun, pouring through the glass doors of the verandah, was fiercely hot, but I was shivering. Lars Sven was a cultured person, who would probably know all about the folk lore of antiquity, especially that of Scandinavia!

And I was remembering something else. Lars Sven and I had talked of horses a few days ago, especially of the famous Spanish horses used in the bullfights. I'd denounced this practice for the barbarity which, in my opinion, it was, and Lars Sven had answered, very curtly, "Life, not only the bullfight, is, in many respects, a barbarity. The bullfight only reflects one aspect of it. Why try to hide from the truth? That does not make it any better."

Because, then, there was something in him, aroused and passionate, which I didn't wish to further encounter, I'd hurried on, not exactly changing the subject, but diverting it to less controversial channels.

"I made a horse," I'd confessed, smiling. "A small white pottery horse,

242

back in Somerset. It was sold to a London studio."

Pride held me back from admitting the sale had been financially necessary, and that part of my fare to the island had come from its sale.

I went on, "In compensation a friend I met on the coach bought me another."

And not mentioning Ian Hamilton's name, I told Lars about the gift of the second pottery horse, and what Ian said about sacrificial horses and owners, in ancient Scandinavia. And Lars nodded, admitting he'd heard of the legend, that it was part of Viking mythology.

I couldn't help wondering if Lars, entering my room while I was at breakfast, had deliberately smashed the horse, laying the broken pieces out to frighten me off?

On the other hand, if Marie had embarked, for reasons of her own, or at the dictates of someone else, upon a policy of terrifying me, she could have overheard Lars and me talking, and broken the horse and laid out the pieces herself. Although I judged her unintelligent, she had resource and cunning.

Sickened, I laid the pieces on the

243

bureau. Whoever had done it, it was a cowardly and sadistic trick.

When Juanita came waddling in at lunch time with a dish of *empanadillas* and a plate of peaches, I repeated some of Marie's conversation about Jenny. And added, as if upset, the bit about Marie advising me to go home.

"Ah, you take no notice, Senorita Foundling," protested Juanita. "She is spoilt, that one, and gives herself airs and graces, as if she owned the entire castello!"

Juanita pursed her generous lips, leaned forward, and patted me reassuringly on the shoulder.

"Senor Sven, he would be most angry if he knew Marie speak so to a guest."

"Oh, please don't tell him," I interposed hastily. "Her English is not all that good, and it is possible she couldn't say what she meant. I would not like to make any trouble for her."

Juanita nodded. "Si, you would never make trouble for anyone, that I see well enough. But Marie . . ."

She shook her head balefully, and I said quickly, "Well, she's guiltless in one thing, Juanita. I don't suppose you know

244

anything about a little white horse in my room that got broken early this morning?"

When Marie brought the mid-morning coffee, I had asked her about the horse. But she disclaimed all responsibility, as she had over the bottle of pills.

Juanita couldn't help either, and said, "Marie is a troublemaker in many ways, Senorita. But she is not clumsy. And if you had the windows open, there was the strong wind this morning."

But that, I said to myself, would not break an ornament so neatly into four or five pieces, then waft them up to lie neatly upon the top of the counterpane!

I didn't want Juanita to think I was deliberately blaming Marie, and agreed that it was probably the wind.

She looked relieved.

"They make the little pottery horses all over Majorca," she went on, "so you can buy another easily, Senorita Foundling. Unless, perhaps, that one, it had the— what you say in English—the value of the heart."

"*Sentimental* value, Juanita," I returned, smiling, but I wasn't thinking of Ian Hamilton and his gift, or even of Lars

Sven or Marie, who, each for their own reasons, might have tried to terrify me by breaking it. I was thinking rather of the cottage in Somerset and myself crossing the courtyard, that other pottery horse in hand. Jenny had appeared out of the air then, staring across the space between us.

"Senorita Foundling!" exclaimed Juanita, and her deep voice was heavy with concern. "What is wrong?"

Shaking off the memory, I laughed and assured her it was nothing. Juanita was very plump, in her mid-fifties, but must, in her youth, have been as handsome as Marie, with the same clear-cut features, firm lips, and lustrous dark eyes. She was the widow of the man who had been caretaker at the castello during the time when it was empty before Lars Sven purchased it. Drawing her into talk about that, I learned little.

"Most of the place, it was shut up. A few visitors come, perhaps thinking to buy. It was most melancholy. Then, my poor man die. I am here alone. I think of all the poor peoples who die in this old part."

She came closer and I could smell garlic faintly on her breath.

"The very first owner of the castello, he was a tyrant, Senorita! A beast, a most cruel man! He owned the forest. Much of that land is now sold. Any poor peasant who anger him, he put away in the dungeons. And nobody ever sees him again! Girls, too, they say, that this Duke Manuel took, then had no more use for. Their poor families, they dared not speak of it—"

"The dungeons?" I said, and never recognized my own tone, it was so sharp. The room seemed to have gone suddenly dark, till I realised shock had dimmed my vision.

It cleared. Juanita leaned even closer, pressing me, involuntarily, against the desk back, the tray with the *empanadillas* and fruit laid down. In her large, still beautiful dark eyes, I glimpsed a slim girl in a sheath of green linen, with straight hair. She was a plain Jane creature, whose mirror image never revealed the terror clawing at her mind.

"Did you not know?" Like many plump, middle-aged women, Juanita had a keen histrionic bent. "Under this tower a stair leads to them. They are large rooms with iron rings set into the walls. These held the shackles for the poor prisoners starved or tortured to death. Si! Murdered, Senorita! Then thrown into the sea . . ."

Local history, I tried to reassure myself, probably much exaggerated.

"A Duke you said, Juanita?"

"Si. Duke Manuel. His other name I not know. But it is in all the history books about the island."

"I never heard about the dungeons, Juanita."

"Senor Sven, he would not wish to make you nervous. And the dungeons, now, they are all closed up."

"But you know the entrance to them, I suppose?"

Juanita stared at me speculatively, as if she was wondering just how much she might trust me. Then she smiled and nodded, with a mixture of eagerness and guilt in her manner.

"The Senorita, she is curious? You want I should show you them?"

We were almost like the women in the

folk tale, anxious, yet frightened, wanting, yet not wanting, to go and look at Bluebeard's chamber.

"I've always been interested in old buildings, and their histories, Juanita." I went on casually, "Juanita, I don't think you need tell Senor Sven you've shown me. Or Marie. Or even let anyone know we've talked like this. We don't want them thinking we've been gossiping, or poking and prying into things that aren't our business."

Then, I found it as hard to analyse the look in Juanita's dark eyes as I did those of her master. What did they reflect, I wondered, as for a moment longer they rested upon me, seemingly charged with some hidden, mysterious message! Almost as if Juanita, too, suspected why I'd come to the castello, had pierced my heart's secrets!

But all she said was, "Oh, si, si! Senor Sven, he is off with Felipe in the boat. And Marie is down in Palma, for the coiffeur."

Then, momentarily, there was another expression in her eyes. Astonished, I knew it for a tenderness, a romantic quality that could only have so shone from the eyes of one of our sex.

"Marie, she is very vain, that one. And Senor Sven, he is not really taken in, but he teases her."

Well, that was no affair of mine, I tried to assure myself. Marie might be vain, but she was undeniably attractive. Remembering Ralph, who had boasted that nearly all men had the same instincts for a pretty woman, I wondered what Jenny might have endured. I wouldn't ask Juanita, not that I thought the woman would gossip, but I owed Jenny certain loyalties.

"You come then, Senorita?"

Juanita wobbled and wavered about before me on the winding stairway. Through the open doorway below, the terraces and their bright flowers, the green pine woods, the blue sea, were framed between the antique stones.

Many an English castle had stones stained with innocent blood. Medieval cruelties such as those practised by Duke Manuel, or by the Moors against tragic Richard Hasleton, in Castle Bellver, could be matched by those as savage in my homeland. So there was surely no need for

250

me to try and fit any of Ian Hamilton's tale into Juanita's revelations?

We passed Lars' studio, moved towards the end of the ground floor passage, and the outer wall. It was dark in that corner, and windowless. The old face of the stone, timeworn, seemed, at first, to have no break. Then, peering, wondering what we should both say if Sven, Felipe, or even Marie suddenly walked through the open tower door, following Juanita's plump and pointing finger, I saw the suit of Moorish armour standing where the wall bulged slightly outwards.

Naturally, I'd observed the armour many times, but that corner was dimly-lighted.

Now, behind the standing armour I saw, with an involuntary catch of the breath, the outline of an old wooden nail-studded door, having an arched top, and an iron handle hanging under the keyhole.

"You see, Senorita?" whispered Juanita dramatically.

Indeed I saw! And wished I didn't, and pressed both hands to my heart to stop it from pounding. As for my mind, and what was going on there, I wished I could stop that, too.

"But it has not been opened," Juanita went on. "Senor Sven he say to me when he come, 'Leave it alone, Juanita.' I have never been down there. I am too frightened. I not know if Senor Sven even keep the old key . . ."

So from that, if there was a key, evidently Juanita didn't hold it. Her eyesight wasn't good. The space behind the warrior was dark. Without exciting even her slowly-roused suspicions, bending to examine the keyhole, and the space around the antique iron ring, would, in any case, not be easy even with my good, young sight. Unless, I thought, I came down alone at night, when the rest of the household slept?

We had become very absorbed, standing there in that dark little corner with the luminous figure of the warrior guarding the door to the dungeons. We never heard anyone approaching.

"Good morning, Ruth—Juanita! Are you interested particularly in medieval Spanish armour?"

Juanita spun around, with surprising

agility for one of her bulk, in her shock catching the lance of the warrior so that it rattled eerily in its hold at the figure's feet.

I turned more slowly, fear, as always, inhibiting me. And Lars stood there, in white shirt and dark trousers, black eyes enormous in the dim corridor, mouth, above the beard, uncompromisingly grim.

Plainly, from the expression on his face, he thought we had been snooping. Juanita's attitude conveying both fear and servitude in the cringing way she stood there, darting furtive glances from Lars to me, killed my immediate sensations of shock. And contempt began to flower, not for Juanita, who was elderly and already, no doubt, feeling guilt-ridden for having disobeyed an express command of her master's, but for Lars Sven, who, by his very presence, could put two women into such a state of cowering panic.

"You look angry," I said evenly, and stepped forward, putting myself between him and Juanita. I had no real worry that he would do anything to her. My action was instinctive, in protection of someone who had got herself into trouble through serving me.

He drew himself up, forcing a smile to his mouth, smoothing his hair back with a jerky, nervous hand.

"Of course not, Ruth," he said. And now, he was so far back in command of himself, self-possessed, urbane, and controlled, that I began to wonder whether that brief glimpse of another Lars Sven, accusing and condemnatory, hadn't been my imagination.

The whole atmosphere of the Castello Minerva bred in me a destructive self-mistrust. And, coming on top of Ralph's handling, did nothing to restore my always precarious self-confidence.

But I could always act for others, when fear kept me trembling for myself. Juanita was really frightened, and there was still Jenny, who might, herself, have faced that slit-eyed, grim-mouthed stranger who was the Lars Sven of only a few moments ago.

"I hope you don't really imagine Juanita and I were being too inquisitive. But you did tell me, yourself, I was free to wander about the castello . . ."

"The castello, yes, the modern part," he said, his manner light and easy now, although there was still something lurking, right at the back of the dark eyes, which discomfited me. "But the tower has dangerous aspects. I have already said no one is to go up on the battlements. I have the way to the roof barred. And the dungeons are equally dangerous."

His glance came back, darkly, to Juanita. Although he maintained a pretence of not being angry with me, more and more I was certain this was only a deception. I was certain he was quite furious.

"Juanita, I think you should return to your duties in the kitchen," he said evenly, his manner so divorced from the half-teasing, genial, smiling way in which he usually addressed the woman of whom I'd thought he was quite fond, that I felt immediately chilled. Juanita scuffled away.

In silence, Lars then escorted me back up the spiral staircase to the office.

"Your lunch is cold," he said, in the same politely forbidding fashion. "And you are shivering, too."

I gazed at him, baffled. The expression in his dark eyes was quite enigmatic, that ironic, mocking courtesy a shield behind which he successfully concealed all his real thoughts and plans.

"Poor Juanita!" I said, ruefully. "It really wasn't her fault, Lars. She was just talking about the castello and Count Manuel—"

His eyebrows drew into a fearsome frown at that, and I hurried on, "—and the prisoners in the dungeons. I asked her to show me where they were kept, that's all."

"She is far too fond of boring visitors and guests with her tales about the castello's history," Lars snapped.

I wondered what had brought him and Felipe back so soon from their fishing trip. But his manner was so forbidding, I didn't like to ask, my initial flare of rebellion dying away.

"Look, Lars, I'm very sorry," I said, and suddenly found I meant it. "Of course I won't go down to the dungeons, or on the roof. I know I can't unlock or force the door leading to the battlements, but I won't even wander about the tower, if you don't want me to."

As we stood there, something involuntarily fused between us, something like a spark of electricity, flowing from him to me, so that as he took a step towards me, I found I was drawn, in the same manner, towards him.

His hand came out and stroked my cheek, a hesitant, exploring gesture that almost seemed to show, in him, a deep-seated, unexpressed loneliness.

Our eyes met. Perhaps mine couldn't altogether disguise my innermost conflict, confusion, and uncertainty, my almost total ambivalence, so far as this man was concerned.

"I'm sorry, too, Ruth," he murmured, and turned a little away, letting his hand fall jerkily, abruptly, leaving me to wonder whether the gesture was something I'd totally misinterpreted.

"I'd no intention of alarming you or Juanita. She's a superb cook, a most faithful servant. But she does build things up in her mind. She has read too many of these old European folk tales. And now, here she is, in an antique castello, complete with a tower with crumbling battlements and dungeons. Can you wonder her imagination ran away with her intelligence?"

Like yours, that dark look now seemed to say.

"Tonight, I'll smile on her, praise her cooking, restore myself to her favour."

What a strange man he is, I thought, as he smiled and went away. But he was back, very quickly, bringing hot coffee and biscuits on a tray. Refraining from asking how Juanita had received him, only relieved at his looking so much less forbidding, I was glad of the refreshment.

Later Lars talked about the autumn fashion show.

"We will have it here in the tower apartment, Ruth. Elsa has managed to persuade Max to let her model the gowns Jenny was to have shown . . ."

Jenny. Wherever one turned, or looked, Jenny was there, as much woven into the life of the castello as she had ever been.

"Some Spanish models will fly over from Barcelona, to show the other clothes. I have based some on Majorcan costume. We can have a quick rehearsal on the morning of the show. It is not a big affair, although important, so we should be able to get through the rehearsal and show in one day.

He fixed a date in mid-September. There were letters to write to magazines and fashion houses, but, as he explained, the backbone of the work had been done when Jenny came. When all the telephoning was finished, letters typed and stamped, Lars looked up from his desk.

"Ruth, my dear, forgive me, but is anything worrying you?"

The direct question, so unexpected, sent a wash of colour up my neck and cheeks. I felt it glowing and burning under my skin. Lars saw it; his mouth twisted. Again, I felt, he thinks I'm a child! Like Ralph, and even Ian.

Ian. My mind was battling against the sinister ideas he had implanted there. Such was the personal fascination exerted by Lars that now, in his gentleness, his near-tenderness, I found it hard to give them credence.

"Ruth?" said Lars, even more gently, more persistently. Could he possibly, I wondered, be using some quality of hypnosis?

My eyes fell on the pile of letters, already stacked, waiting to be taken to the hall table where Felipe would deliver them

259

to the post box on the high road above the pine wood.

"The letters," I gabbled, and seized them and almost ran to the door. "I'll go over to the east wing with them now, then they'll be ready when Felipe comes."

Periodically, Felipe would go and examine the hall table, to see what mail, incoming or outgoing, might be there. Marie usually took in the packages for the castello, with letters and anything else that came from the tradesmen, with Felipe, when necessary, helping her unload.

"No, Ruth! Please wait!" Lars said curtly. "I must talk to you!"

But by then, I was running almost desperately down the circular stairway, letters grasped tightly in my hand, and absurdly fearful of even glancing behind me, lest my employer be in pursuit.

Only when I stood, breathless, in the sombre passageway before the still-open circular door, did I dare to glance upwards. But there was no sign of Lars, only the worn stone steps dappled by late afternoon sunlight striking them through the ancient doorway. And to the right, before the worn wooden door to the dungeons, the armoured figure glimmered, guarding the way below.

That evening, when I went to my room, the missing pill bottle stood on the bedside table.

Seizing it, I rang the bell angrily, with fingers trembling, and when Marie came, showed her the bottle. So far as I could tell, for I'd never actually counted the tablets, knowing only there was about half a bottle's supply there, none had been taken.

They looked the same, tiny white things, each labelled with the brand name.

"But Senorita Foundleeng!" wailed Marie, when I stormily taxed her with replacing the bottle and never telling me, "I swear by the Holy Virgin, I not know anything about your sleeping tablets!"

Plainly, I was going to get no confession out of her. Short of hauling her to the nearest police station, and demanding the bottle be checked for fingerprints, I could see no redress.

"You have your bottle back," Marie said, calming down. "Juanita, perhaps, found it. Ask her, not accuse me, who am innocent!"

But Juanita, lumbering up the stairs in response to Marie's loud protestations, assured me, equally firmly but less hysterically, that she had never before seen the bottle.

We were all three staring at each other, mute and hostile, even Juanita regarding me, I thought, with furtive suspicion, when there was a step I recognised beyond the half-open door.

"Is something wrong, Juanita?" Lars Sven called. "I just came in from the garden and was on my way to my room when I heard what sounded like a disturbance from Senorita Foundling's room."

With the most perfunctory of knocks, he stepped in. It was Juanita who explained. He took in her somewhat garbled account, though, with leaping comprehension, and striding forward, seemed about to lay hands on the bottle.

His white shirt was open at the neck. Under the bronzed skin I saw the large bones hard and firm against the skin. A powerful man, Lars Sven; more than a match for a woman.

"You say it was last in your suitcase, Senorita Foundling?" he demanded, almost as if I was defending myself in court, and he prosecuting attorney!

"Yes, it was. I'm positive," I said. But my voice faltered. His dark eyes raked me, and I saw them narrow, go more slit-like still.

Then Marie, like one seizing an awaited opportunity, cut in. "Senorita Found-leeng, she is not well. It is the heat to which she is not used. And no doubt her grief about the other Senorita has affected her. No doubt she put the bottle there, then forgot about it."

There was a smell of burning suddenly wafting up the stairs. Juanita stifled a scream, turned, and waddled swiftly away, muttering darkly as she went.

"Marie, please, have the goodness to leave us!" commanded Lars. And Marie, with a toss of the head in my direction, went.

"Ruth, I do not like these accusations against my staff. It is very disturbing to me."

It was my turn to toss my head.

"It is very disturbing to me to find something I'm positive I left in a suitcase missing for some time, and then placed clandestinely beside my bed when I am absent. To make me look, of course, either a fool or a liar!"

"No one, least of all Marie, Juanita, or myself, has said you are either."

"Words," I said, as coolly as I could contrive it, "are not always necessary, Lars."

"You are sure you feel quite well? It is true that for some people, especially those from England, the climate can be very trying."

"I've yet to hear that attacks of Spanish grippe, which I believe is the medical term for it, affect the brain and imagination," I said caustically. "I'd like to be sure I understand you, Lars. Do you think I'm going mad?"

He laughed, but I fancied there was uneasiness in that laughter, and his immediate assurances that of course he hadn't meant any such thing, that I was obviously upset, were just too pat.

"That bottle," he went on, "if you care to hand it over to me, Ruth, I could set your mind at rest perhaps, by getting the contents analysed, and the container checked for fingerprints. I mean, the whole idea that anyone in the castello should even want to harm you is—"

"I made no accusations," I said quietly, "about people wanting to harm me. I simply said the bottle was missing and has now been put back in another place from where I left it."

He bit his lip, like one who has made a palpable slip. But how odd, I thought, he should make the very suggestion with which my own mind had already toyed!

But now I had a better idea, especially in view of his last words. I should take the bottle and its contents to Ian, to ask if he could get the pills analysed—they could have been changed for some other tablet, the same name falsely and cunningly imprinted on them! And the container could be checked for fingerprints.

For how could I tell—if I let Lars Sven have them—what he would do with what might turn out to be damning evidence of some attack upon me?

"But perhaps it is preposterous," I took him up quietly. "That's what you were going to say, weren't you, Lars? So thank you, but I won't put you to that trouble. I mean, it would be foolish, under the circumstances, wouldn't it and make you look foolish as well?"

"There would have been no trouble, just so your mind was reassured. I understand you are still emotionally disturbed about Jenny." Lars hesitated, then asked, "Ruth, they are sleeping tablets? You take them for insomnia?"

"Yes."

The dark eyes grew darker still, and Lars took two or three steps in my direction. He seemed, I was then pleased to observe, both baffled and angry.

"Ruth, listen—"

"I was just dressing for dinner," I said, as if in weary protest. "And you haven't much time left, Lars. I'm sorry you came up here on a wild-goose chase."

"And I'm sorry if you were worried," he said, and gave one of his odd little bows and was gone.

A wild-goose chase, I thought, as I completed my dressing, the bottle safely shut up in my handbag, where it would stay till I had an opportunity to tell the story to Ian and enlist his aid.

I'd been in the tower apartment all afternoon, after leaving the letters on the hall table. Lars had disappeared soon afterwards, saying he needed to get some exercise. Juanita and Marie had been in the castello, too. Could the Gertaes be responsible for the mysterious theft and return of my tablets? They were always either in the east wing or the grounds. I sighed as the hot needles of the shower hit my skin. Anybody could have sneaked in to put that bottle where it was, for I'd not locked the door. In the future, I'd do so, but I was nearly certain all my suspects had their own keys, or could get one, from Marie or Juanita.

What would happen if, disdaining all suspicions, I took one or two of those tablets tonight after going to bed? Should I awaken in the morning to laugh at my terrors, as I'd pretended, just now, to laugh when Lars Sven was here? Or would I never awaken at all, and perish, like Jenny, in a foreign land?

10

"IAN! We—we can't! It—it would be against the law!"

We stood, the Englishman and myself, on the shores of the same lonely cove where we had met before. The weather had changed to a persistent drizzle, though Juanita assured me we had only temporarily lost the sunshine. Ian had sent me the most noncommittal of letters, simply suggesting we meet at this spot, indicating it by inference in case the letter should be intercepted.

And, although he put only initials to his letter, nevertheless its receipt made me uneasy, and when I'd digested its contents, I burnt it.

Lars was working in the tower apartment studio when I left the castello. I was in such a state of confusion and uncertainty, I didn't know if I wanted to see Ian again, wondering if it wouldn't be better for me to continue such investigations as I could alone—or even go on with them at all. Now that I had come, Ian had made a suggestion that caused my blood to run cold.

The rain had cleared a little, but the skies were overcast, the sea sullen. A swell rocked Ian's hired boat, tied up off the small promontory, discreetly hidden by the rocky overhang.

Apparently the Englishman was still temporarily domiciled at the same pensione, and now had the boat on indefinite loan.

I'd caught a 'bus on the road above the castello, and come down from the place where the Palma signpost stood. The paths, though, were wet, and the trees dripping.

Now, there were no cheerful brown and white goats with tinkling bells, only these weeping skies, matching Hamilton's determined dourness, and my own sense of growing conflict and indecision.

When I'd first come to the island, I'd had my purpose plainly before me, clear as a quest. I tried to fight off the reason for my inertia, but couldn't pinpoint it.

To give this journey, at least, some shape and form, I'd told Ian I'd come because I'd wanted to ask him about the small mystery of the missing pill bottle, and its restoration to the wrong place on the bedside table.

Ian, as I could tell, was not much impressed by the incident. Resentfully, I felt he believed I'd simply mislaid the bottle. And, as he knew no one on the island to whom he could take it for analysis, he said it would have to wait till he returned to England again.

I sensed his mind was geared to something he plainly considered far more urgent, for he pocketed the small phial impatiently. And then, to my horrified astonishment, spoke the words which had torn that shocked protest from my lips.

What Ian wanted from me had so taken away my breath that I could scarcely speak.

"Why not?" he said, his tone ugly as Lars' could be when I challenged him. "If he's the criminal we think . . ."

"The criminal you think, Ian! I'm by no means sure of it!"

The smile which now curved around Ian's own usually pleasant mouth was by no means reassuring.

"Another one?" he mocked. "Falling for the charms of the suave, sophisticated, successful, apparently-native-born Norwegian, known to the world as Lars Sven? But to you and me—and for all we know to Jenny—as Gordon Ayrton, escaping, by the skin of his teeth, from the gallows?"

"Hush, Ian," I pleaded in a nervous whisper, and glanced around, although the beach was deserted and only a few sea birds hung, apparently suspended, in the stormy air above the shut-in little place.

"Well, if you won't come with me, I'll have to go alone, that's all."

I shuddered, and drew the collar of my scarlet mackintosh closer about my neck. For what Ian had just proposed was not only macabre and dangerous but, to me, sacrilege.

"Look," I went on, in the same near-violent whisper, "if you really think Lars did something to Jenny why don't you take your suspicions to the Majorcan police? Let them arrange for this disinterment."

"No," said Ian obstinately. "I've reasons . . ."

Ian had told me he thought we should

go to the Genova cementario, at midnight, this very midnight, armed with suitable tools which, he assured me, would do what he required of them—break open the grave of Jenny Midnight!

"You said, to see if it was really her body—not a substitute," I said, feeling sick, angry, and, somehow, horribly tired. "If that's really what you think, then I still say you ought to go to the police and state your suspicions."

"And if I am wrong about him having planted somebody else there," Ian told me grimly, "I'll get myself hauled up before the Majorcan court and probably shoved inside some Spanish jail!"

"Then go to the castello and confront Sven himself! Or go to El Pineo and demand to see Dr. Gertae and ask him to explain about Jenny's death certificate."

But even as I suggested these perilous alternatives, I could see that, unless Sven and Dr. Gertae were completely innocent, Ian Hamilton would be putting himself, and possibly me, in pawn to them.

"Look," said Ian, "I can understand your scruples and I respect you for them. I only want to make sure . . ."

"And if you are wrong? If Jenny is there?"

"Then I shall want," said Ian Hamilton very coldly and clearly, "to examine that poor girl's remains. Don't forget I was a medical student. All I want you to do is stand well away from it all. You needn't look, only keep an eye out for possible interruptions. There really shouldn't be any at that time of night."

"But," I said desperately, "how shall I get out of the castello? Supposing Lars sees me and—and follows?"

"We've got to risk something," Ian said quietly. "Put pillows in your bed, and your nightgown over them. I take it it's very unusual for anybody to go into your room at night?"

His look was very straight and I could feel my colour rising, but I stood my ground, and just nodded. Ian smiled, an odd, almost tender smile, and touched my shoulder, as if in a kind of apology.

"Poor little Ruth," he said softly, "you are having a rotten time of it, aren't you? And today the sun isn't even shining for you. Never mind, when all this is over, I'll make it up to you."

"Why are you so—so desperately interested?" I asked again. "I mean, so personally interested, not calling in the police or anything?"

"We've been into all that," he said curtly, "and I told you. Jenny and I had some good times together. If anything's been done to her by that rotter, Lars Sven, I want to know why and how. Now are you coming, or not? If you won't come, I'll go alone. You can meet me here tomorrow and I'll let you know how I got on."

It occurred to me then that Ian looked like some medieval pirate himself, standing there in the sand, the rain running from his hair and mackintosh, his brown eyes fiercely resolute.

And I had a sudden, nightmarish vision of myself, lying sleepless in my castello bedroom, while, in my mind, I went with Ian, along the road leading from the village to the cementario, towards the grave where Jenny was buried.

Ian's expression changed. I saw him give a grim little nod, as if satisfied.

"The last 'bus leaves the road above the castello at 11 o'clock," he told me. "I checked. It's always practically empty. It'll put you down about a mile from the village where we had the wine that day. You'll have to walk, I'm afraid, we daren't risk a private car or taxi. I shall make my own way to the cementario gates. I'll be there at a few minutes before midnight. I'll not wait if you don't come."

After that, we said little, parting almost without words, me to hurry back to get the 'bus by the signpost, Ian to clamber back into his hired boat and return, over that sullen sea, to Palma.

But to face Lars and Juanita and Marie that night, downstairs in the formal salon, was something that turned my stomach over. So I sent down word by Marie, when she came in to turn down the beds, as she always did about six o'clock in the evening, that I had a severe headache and would stay in my room that night.

To lend credulity to this excuse, I lay under the covers, in my dressing gown, a cloth soaked in eau de cologne over my temples. The lights were all out too, except a subdued one, by the bed, and as Marie came nearer, I tensed.

"Poor little Senorita," she said in a

strange voice, and, between my eyelids, I could just see her there, in her fine silk black dress and white apron. "I am so sorry."

"Thank you," I said, wishing she'd go, and take my excuse to Lars, before he came enquiring after me, perhaps to penetrate my state of extreme tension, and wonder what might be causing it. "I—I sat too long over my book this afternoon. The light was bad, down on the beach where I took shelter from the weather . . ."

Silence from Marie. Then, "I saw you —you and Mister Hamilton!"

I don't suppose it was ever more difficult for me to hide my feelings than it was at that moment. I blessed the cologne-saturated cloth that covered my face, and tightened my mouth and chin muscles so that they should not betray my sense of shock—almost, indeed, of outrage. Marie, then, knew Ian Hamilton! But how?

I kept silent, deliberately provoking her into continuing.

"Oh si, it may surprise you, Senorita Foundleeng, but Senor Hamilton is not unknown to me."

She came closer, leaned over, her perfume becoming sickeningly strong.

"He has been on this island before. I do not know what he has told you, but me, I saw him with your friend Senorita Midnight, the one who die!"

"You're mistaken, Marie," I said quietly. "Though I really don't know what business it is of yours in any case. I do know Mr. Hamilton slightly. He is an Englishman. We met on my journey here. There is nothing clandestine about it."

"I am not mistaken when I say he and Senorita Midnight meet. I see them many times. You asked me about her, the other day, where she go, and what she do. I thought then, perhaps I will tell her about the Englishman. But I did not till today, when I saw you with him. So, I thought, that is strange. I will tell the other Englishwoman."

"They probably met accidentally and went on meeting so, as people of the same nationality tend to do, when on holiday."

"Perhaps," she said.

"Please, will you leave me?" I said. "My head is very bad. I must have quiet."

"Of course. I am sorry. And I will

inform Senor Sven you will not be at dinner.''

The soft, soft closing of the door set my nerves on edge more violently than if Marie had banged it. I got up, crossed to it, locked it, and stood with my back against it. My heart pounded like a sledgehammer.

Why had Ian not told me he'd come to Majorca to see Jenny? I was positive he'd never said anything to this effect, that he'd given the definite impression that he never saw Jenny after she left London! If he was lying why?

I was arranging the pillows in bed, dressed for my macabre expedition in dark jeans and anorak, when I heard, unmistakably, the firm, deliberate sound of Lars Sven's footsteps on the wooden floor of the corridor. My heart began to pound wildly, and I felt the sweat break out on my temples. He knocked, then called, peremptorily, "Ruth? Marie tells me you are not at all well. Is there anything I can do?''

Pressing one clenched hand against my traitorous heart, I willed my voice to steadiness—after all, I was supposed to be indisposed!—and called back weakly,

"No, thank you, Lars! It's just a head-ache! It'll go away if I lie here quietly."

"But I am worried about you! Let me telephone El Pineo and get Max to come up and prescribe something."

No thank you indeed! I thought grimly. That charming physician was the last person I wanted that night.

"Please, Lars," I called back, less strongly than before, "I don't want to be disturbed by anyone."

Silence, then he said, ruefully, "Which includes me, I take it? Are you still vexed with me for what happened in the tower apartment the last time we met?"

After that unfortunate and embarrassing incident, Lars had kept away from me; deliberately, I believed. He sent the post over by Marie or Felipe, with the usual scrawled instructions in the margins of the letters. When I asked Juanita, when she waddled in with the lunch, where he was, she said he'd gone off with Felipe in the boat, and would probably be away a couple of days.

A couple of days! That seemed a long time to me.

"Sometimes Senor Sven and Felipe,

they go to Tangiers or North Africa,"
Juanita volunteered, setting down the
cheese rolls and fruit which was all I'd
asked for. "Especially lately they are away
a lot."

"Are you still in disgrace, Juanita?
About showing me the dungeons?" I'd
asked.

"No, no, Senorita! Senor Sven, he
seldom stay angry for long—" She paused,
selected, as was her habit, one of the
choicest grapes, and popped it into her
mouth. "I think," she went on, deliberately watching me and smiling, "I think
Senor Sven, he is getting very fond of you.
So, with you, he not stay angry for long,
either."

Now, as I heard that rueful note in Lars'
voice, I began to shiver, remembering
what lay ahead of me, and trying, not
altogether successfully, to kill the attraction for Lars which was, day by day,
building in me. Suspecting what I did
suspect, under Ian's tutelage, and remembering how Lars had looked when he
found Juanita and me at the door to the
dungeons, the evidence of the newspaper
reports, and the strange anomaly of

280

Jenny's death from "appendicitis," I felt certain Lars hugged some dark and guilty secret to himself.

How could I even begin to harbour feelings of attraction for such a man who, at best, was a deceiver and probably a criminal, and, at worst, a killer! No, it was just that I was inexperienced, and lonely, and, I think, that Ian's continuing assurance irritated me.

Thinking, now, that silence was the most diplomatic way out of my present dilemma, I stood perfectly still and waited. Every instinct assured me that he was still there. If he didn't go soon I would be too late to sneak downstairs through the pine woods behind the castello to get that last 'bus that was to take me on my clandestine and macabre errand.

"Goodnight then, my little Ruth!" Lars called quietly. "Sleep well. Tomorrow, if you are not better, I shall insist on calling Max."

I let out my breath in a frantic sigh of relief, as, at last, the firm and determined footfalls gradually died away upon the polished olive-wood of the corridor.

Five minutes, I reckoned, feverishly, to

see him safely in the salon, with dinner before him. Juanita, Marie and Felipe would be in the kitchen. When the first course was served, that would be my moment.

Catching up a torch and a dark scarf, casting one last look at the bed, I slipped outside. Would it be best to lock the door? Or would that seem suspicious? Juanita and Marie both had master keys, so that if they wanted to get in, or Lars ordered them to unlock the door, my ruse would be discovered. Still, if I did lock it, any impulse the servants, or Lars, might have to just step in before bed and see how I was, would be defeated. They would assume I was quite indisposed if I felt it necessary to lock them out. I slipped off my shoes and hurried.

As Ian had said, certain things must be risked. Seconds later, the bedroom door locked, the key in my pocket, I stole down the stairway of the east wing. Just as I'd got to the top to halt, shivering slightly in the shadows, I had the good fortune to see Felipe cross the hall on his way back to the kitchens. From the open door I heard the unmistakable voices of Juanita and Marie.

Gliding like a phantom down the stairs, I halted at the foot, then ran lightly across the hall to the door. There was a slight wind, which covered the creak of it as I turned the handle, then I was out on the central terrace.

My hands didn't shake as I stopped to pull on my shoes, and then I was hurrying around the east wing of Castello Minerva to the courtyard and then up the main drive to the entrance gates.

Mercifully, there was no moon. Although, by then, I was certain none of those in the castello could possibly have spotted me, my shoulders and back felt naked, as I kept in the shelter of the trees. Then the statues of Minerva, set on either side the iron gates, glimmered blessedly through the Majorcan night. I slipped the gate bolt and let myself thankfully out into the road.

As I hurried down it, my confused mind seemed to have room for only two ideas: one, that if Ian Hamilton was bringing me out on this nefarious errand because he'd got hold of some facts which he'd misconstrued, then my most sensible course of action, under the circumstances, would be to confess to Lars everything he'd told me as soon as possible. The second idea was that I'd seen Jenny again the previous day when I walked in the rain back from the pine woods. She was still in that orphanage pinafore but now she, and all her clothing, were streaming wet, and her pigtails hung down lankly over her childish breasts. She stood on the edge of the pine forest, pointing towards Castello Minerva looking at me with terror in her huge blue eyes! I knew I owed her something. And I remembered her words:

"And when I want help, Ruth darling, I'll never ask anybody but you."

It was that which took me, of course, up through the pine woods and to the road, to wait for the 'bus, half-hoping it wouldn't come, not even daring to think what was waiting for me at the end of the journey!

Half an hour later, I hurried along the lane leading to the cementario. Ahead, in the great plain, I glimpsed lights glowing here and there amid the trees. Although there was no moon, the night was very clear, and hundreds of stars were winking and twinkling above my head.

Because I knew that if I once stopped, I should turn tail and hurry back the way I'd come, in the end I positively ran the last steps to the gates of the cementario, and almost into Ian Hamilton's arms.

"Good girl!" breathed Ian quietly. "I'd begun to wonder if you were going to let me down."

"Listen," I whispered fiercely, "I think you're crazy! And I'm crazier still. I swear, if you find her in that coffin, I'm going straight back to the castello."

"Ruth . . ."

"And you're coming with me. And we'll confront Lars Sven with that letter from Jenny to you and we're going to get an explanation. And if it doesn't make sense, then we're going down to Palma, and tell the whole story to the Majorcan police."

"Wait," growled Ian. "I can understand your feelings—"

"Thank you," I hissed, sarcastically. "But there's something else."

Perhaps it was the note in my voice, or something in my look. I've always been told I'd never make an actress. *All your*

285

feelings are on the bloody surface, Ralph used to growl in disgust.

Ian went strangely still, almost wary. "Well? What is it, Ruth?"

I repeated Marie's allegations. It was dark in the cementario. I could only see the blurred, glimmering outline of his face, having to judge his reactions from his body movements. Now, he stepped back a pace or two.

"And you believed her?" His voice was light, almost ironic, yet it was quite hard to plumb his innermost feelings. But I fancied, under all that irony, that Ian was hurt.

"Come on, Ruth," he went on more harshly and impatiently, "did you believe her? I want to know, please!"

"Well," I said doggedly, "you didn't say anything, didn't explain—not properly—about how it was between Jenny and you. And Jenny was never one for elaborating either. Or not on that particular topic. And I suppose it is really none of my business, if you and she—"

"Continued on here where we left off in London?" No mistaking, now, the irony in his voice. There was also a hint of compassion in his tone which, for some reason, both touched and angered me. "Well we didn't, Ruth, my dear. Cross my heart and hope to die!"

"In that case, why are you so very concerned about what happened to her?"

"Why are you?"

"I was her friend," I began again, hotly, and he cut in, quietly and steadfastly.

"And so was I, to tell it to you again, Ruth. And, though we were no more than friends at our last meeting, I did have high hopes we might have gotten together again if she'd lived."

Feeling deeply contrite, but not ashamed, for I felt, under the circumstances, the explanation was due me, I said, "Okay. And I'm very sorry if you're hurt because I doubted you. But I had to ask."

"It was a bloody lie of Marie's and Sven's," growled Ian. "Either he set her to watch you . . . she followed you to the Andraix cove, or she accidentally spotted us on the beach and told him."

"But, in that case, how would she know your name?"

Ian's grin flashed in the dark and I felt awkward again.

"Miss Detective Foundling, with the probing, persistent mind," he jeered. But there was soft, understanding amusement in the voice in the dark. "Lars Sven had ways and means of finding out. He could have found out from the chap I hired the boat from. Marie particularly would have had the opportunity since she's Majorcan anyway and could ask around at the boat stations. I've kept away from the castello, deliberately, but if they *are* suspicious they could have seen us together, made inquiries, and found out who I was."

Suddenly Ian stepped forward. "This is hardly the time, or the place, I know, but—"

I don't know why I found his kiss so strangely dissatisfying. It had been just the same with Ralph. I never felt really aroused or responsive. But then there was, as Ian intimated, the hideous incongruity of making love amidst the slumbering dead.

"Now," said Ian, "come on, and watch your step. If either of us comes a cropper

over one of these paths or tombstones . . ."

He left me to finish that thought. It
would have been very awkward, as he said,
if either of us fell and got injured, and the
other had to drag the one who was hors de
combat back to the road.

"What on earth could we say," I
muttered, half to myself, "if we had to get
help?"

"Come on," sighed Ian again. "Just
watch your step is all."

It was splendid for him, who had
brought sensible low-heeled shoes, leather-
soled and yet light on the ground.

In my panic-stricken, irresolute state,
I'd settled for sandals. The heels were low,
but I wore no stockings, and the straps
let in pieces of grit and earth and other
fragments whose nature I didn't much care
to speculate upon.

The stones gave off an eerie nocturnal
glitter, like banners in the gloom. My
imagination got to work on what lay
beneath the earth here—the coffins, the
shrouds, the mouldering flesh and bones.
As we got to the steps below the English

burial place, something flew out and, involuntarily, I half-screamed.

"Quiet, you little idiot," commanded Ian, turning. "It was a night bird—an owl or maybe a bat—It won't hurt you."

From down the road, we heard the soughing of wind in the street, and near at hand again, the screeching of a donkey.

"Come on. And for Pete's sake don't do that again," commanded Ian.

As we climbed the steps, I could see the terraced graves glimmering ahead. We reached them, and Ian hefted the crowbar he'd brought along.

"Just sit or stand by the steps," he said tensely, "and keep guard."

I don't know how long it was that I sat there, staring ahead at the standing stones of the dead. It was quite dark, but by now my eyes were getting used to the gloom, and I could just make out the stones.

Behind me, I shut my mind and ears to the sound of what Ian was doing. Only occasionally I heard a dull thudding, as of a bar striking stone. Because I couldn't bear to contemplate what, presently, we might see, I turned my eyes from the graveyard, and kept them on the few lights twinkling, like rubies, out in the soft darkness of the Majorcan plain.

I couldn't imagine how Ian could possibly steel himself to what he was doing—even out of love for Jenny—till I remembered how he'd once been a medical student. I suppose that did make a difference.

Ian had explained that he must have my help when, the concrete knocked away from the sides and top of Jenny's tomb, he lifted out the coffin in order to examine its contents. That particular moment I dreaded, and I had to keep reiterating to myself one taut, loving little phrase, "And when I want help, Ruth darling, I won't ask anybody but you." Only memory of that endearing, trusting phrase anchored me there, when every nerve screamed to bolt back through the cementario along the road we'd come.

"All right, Ruth? Coast clear?"

"Yes, I—I think so."

Scrambling up to where he stood, my heart thudded as I saw the top stone gaping and knew what would soon be required of me.

To control the worst of my terrors, I

291

said, "Ian? If there has been something clandestine, what about the local undertakers?"

"Lars imported a man, and an assistant, from Barcelona, presumably to avoid local professional jealousy, and gossip."

Well, that answer made macabre sense. Money can cover up a lot of crime, even in these days, if criminals have enough contacts. And nerve, I thought grimly, as Ian, rasping up deep, shaken breaths from the bottom of his diaphragm, took the top of the coffin, and motioned me to ease out the end.

A last service for Jenny, I thought, and that made it more bearable.

Another few moments, and we'd managed to lower the small coffin upon the rocky ground.

"It—it's about the right size, Ian."

Then we saw the brass plate with the words, JENNY MIDNIGHT and the rest of the pathetic inscription, and I sobbed. "Shut up," hissed Ian. "We've work to do."

Even when Ian took a screwdriver from his pocket and bent over the lid, my mind didn't flinch, nor did I want to shrink away. Curiosity, concern, love, all played their part. All I wanted—needed, now—was to know what lay within.

"Stand by, Ruth," said Ian. For just a split second, nerved up to the sight of whatever might be there, my eyes refused to focus, as if part of my brain had turned traitor and wouldn't obey my will.

Then, in the light of the torch, I saw that the coffin cover was propped against a neighbouring stone. I heaved a sharp little sigh and lowered my eyes.

Beside me, Ian Hamilton was swearing.

The coffin was full of books, heavy, thick-covered volumes that were piled neatly in the centre.

"Books," said Ian, in a shaken but deeply-satisfied voice, and put out a hand and began to turn them over. "Old volumes of the Medical Directory . . . in English. No names inside the covers, naturally, there wouldn't be."

Now that I knew I should not be forced to look upon Jenny's corpse, or indeed, upon any corpse, my resolution abruptly deserted me. My knees began to shake, and my stomach to heave.

"All right, Ruth, darling," said Ian swiftly. "You've been splendid. Look, you get out of here and back down to the gates. Do you think you can manage to wait there and keep guard for me?"

"But what are you going to do?" I asked.

"Put this little lot back where it came from," said Ian. "And cover up the traces of the night's work. Now that I know what's here, I don't need to do anything about it till I'm ready."

Glad to escape from the macabre little platform, I stumbled down the steps to the cementario gates. There, sickness engulfed me, and I fled a few yards down the road to a little clump of bushes.

After that, I felt better. I went back to the gates, and stood there, waiting for Ian, most of the time keeping my eyes on those comforting little flickers of light out on the Majorcan plain, those steadfast evidences that life went on, that people moved about, pursued an ordinary existence, beyond this tomb of the dead.

Which, though, did not enclose the remains of Jenny!

In those torturous moments of waiting —it added up to an hour in all, I learned later—I'd have sold my soul for a cigarette. I had no torch, so I couldn't even check the time by my watch, and each minute dragged by like a century.

Dreading that some late passerby might come along the road and see me loitering there, I decided to go back down to the shelter of the bushes. From there, I could keep a watch on the gates, and keep myself hidden. And there, too, I risked lighting a cigarette.

Inhaling the fragrant smoke, I dared to think again about the grave that was supposed to have been Jenny Midnight's, and which certainly bore her name upon the coffin lid. It seemed certain that, whatever had been done to Jenny herself, Lars Sven and Dr. Max Gertae and his wife must certainly be concerned in it. How could they not be, seeing she'd been taken from Castello Minerva to the El Pineo Nursing home, and that Lars, or so he told me, had been to see her corpse!

And Dr. Gertae's name was certainly entered on the death certificate, and under the column which gave the cause of death, was written "Peritonitis." The document lay, now, at my bank in England, with my few personal papers, in a safe deposit box, because I'd had nowhere else to put it.

The presence of the medical books in the coffin suggested that the Gertaes had arranged the faked burial. With, of course, the connivance of my employer.

But why? That was the question that tortured me! And where was Jenny now? Could she possibly be alive, kept prisoner somewhere? Naturally, my mind went to the dungeons, but that seemed utterly fantastic, till I remembered how deathly pale Lars Sven had turned, when he found us there.

I jumped, as I heard footsteps on the road. Moving from my hiding place, pitching away my cigarette, I hurried thankfully towards Ian, whose figure and face I could just make out, coming in my direction.

"Ruth? Wondered where the devil you were, till I caught the scent of your cigarette. You all right?"

"More or less," I said.

"Come on," he muttered, grabbed my arm, and hurried me along the road to the village. We passed the inn and the houses. A light burned in the upper storeys of one of the latter, and we crawled by with extreme caution. A dog barked, and Ian's grip on my arm tightened spasmodically, but then the creature stopped, as breathlessly we got to the top of the road.

Here Ian turned me into a little lane where, two hundred yards along, there was a small car parked inside a field with broken-down gateposts. Peering, I saw it led to an abandoned and ruined farmhouse.

We got in and Ian produced a flask of brandy and made me swallow some. Then we had a cigarette, and he turned to me.

"Look, Ruth, there's clearly only one thing to do now. And that's to go back to England and lay this story before the English police. You're quite right. I ought to have done so in the first place."

That took some of the weight of what we'd done off my mind. But I was also worried. Now that we'd become, in a sense, lawbreakers ourselves, I wondered how our actions would be received. Our tale was bizarre in the extreme.

"Sven came on you, Ruth, outside those dungeons, with Juanita. My guess is he now suspects you came to Majorca not just to put a wreath on Jenny's grave. You didn't, by the way, tell him about your—ah—visions and voices, did you?"

"I couldn't. He's too formidable. But Ian, if he's Gordon Ayrton, what about that Norwegian accent? It sounds very authentic."

Ian grunted contemptuously. "Easy enough to assume convincingly, to a man who's spent his life amongst actors and actresses, designing for the theatre. But you told me you came because you felt something had happened here to Jenny."

"Yes, something evil."

"I think, willy-nilly, you've conveyed that idea to him in your manner, and possibly to the Gertaes, as well. You also asked questions, and were seen trying to get in to her locked bedroom."

"Well, it was natural enough that I should want to know what happened to her. Ian, you sound almost as if you're blaming me. I thought you decided it was a good idea that I should stay on, ostensibly as Sven's secretary, to find out what I could."

Ian nodded. He looked gravely across at me, as if debating just how much he should say. And I could see that, though he didn't want to frighten me, he also thought it was getting more dangerous day by day, for me to remain at Castello Minerva.

"I didn't think they'd consider you as another victim. But now I'm worried. I think Jenny found out something to do with Lars Sven's past."

"Ian, I thought you said you had reasons why you couldn't go to the police?"

He nodded. "I did go to them before I left England." His tone was suddenly angry and bitter. "I've a friend, a detective-inspector at New Scotland Yard. I told him my general suspicions."

"I see," I said, understanding that he'd been rebuffed, his spirit bruised by the hard edge of officialdom. "I decided to come out here alone and find out for myself what had happened to Jenny," he added.

"And met me, a sort of ally, on route."

Ian hugged me around the shoulders. "And a brave, good, and resourceful little ally, too! But now I think I'll have to go back to England, lay these new facts before New Scotland Yard."

Suddenly, I yearned to go with him, to fly away forever from this place that had become a tainted paradise, and particularly from the strange figure who dominated Castello Minerva.

"Ian, if only I could come with you!"

He gazed at me searchingly, and seemed about to agree.

"But if we do both go," I said, "they'll suspect we've gone together. That'll just alert them. They'll leave, all three of them, to go on to commit some fresh devilry somewhere else."

Watching the struggle in Ian's face, I felt immensely sorry for him.

Then he said, reluctantly, "I don't like leaving you, Ruth."

"What alternative is there? Unless . . ."

"Unless what?"

I wondered why he'd never suggested my next alternative himself.

"Why don't we go to the island police and tell them what we suspect? And particularly what we found out tonight? I mean, surely that's reason enough for having Castello Minerva and El Pineo

Nursing Home at least entered and searched? There's been a faked burial and possibly a faked death!"

But Ian shook his head.

"They move more slowly in these places when it's the question of an alien's word against a person whose been well-established here for some time. Oh, I'm sure they'd go and interview Lars Sven and Dr. Gertae, but probably not both at once. And if one tipped the other off . . ."

I could see the sense in that.

"They wouldn't move before morning," said Ian. "And if I'm lucky with my aircraft, I ought to be in London before dawn and at New Scotland Yard soon after that."

"Suppose they still won't listen to you," I said.

"I've got Jenny's letter to me, haven't I? And those photostat newspaper copies? And I could hardly invent a yarn as macabre as what we found up at the cementario tonight!"

"All right, you go then," I said. "But Ian, please get back just as soon as you can with the police. I feel just a bit scared."

"And who could blame you," said Ian grimly, and pulled me to him and kissed me hard on the lips. "But I believe you're safe till I get back. I don't like it though, Ruth, not one little bit!"

He drove me back to the road above the pine woods and the castello, which was as far as he dared take me. Then, as he let me out of the car, he pulled me back for one last kiss.

"If they do suspect," he said fiercely, "and try anything on you, tell them what we found out tonight and say I'm on my way to England to return with the English police. It's our trump card, and we don't want to use it, but if it's to save your life . . ."

He kissed me again, and then thrust me down on the road to the castello.

Seconds later, I heard the sound of his car engine going along the road towards Palma, and the airport.

I approached the castello in a mood in which fear and anger jostled for dominance. Naturally, now, there was fear for myself, and there was anger, cold and terrible, for Jenny. Till now I'd not wanted to credit any of Ian Hamilton's story. But now I knew, from the ghastly evidence of that empty coffin, that something terrible had indeed overtaken Jenny. But how could I help her, if she was really dead? Ian had said she must be dead.

Stealthily unlatching the iron gates of the castello entrance drive, hugging the shadow as I crept down it towards the east wing, the question that now seared my mind was: is she dead? Or a prisoner, perhaps, in this place?

I recalled those long trips Sven took with his man, Felipe in the *Belle Isle*. Juanita said he sometimes went as far as the North African coast, or the farther Mediterranean. Maybe Jenny was being kept there. And perhaps I was wrong in all my conjectures, and Ian Hamilton, too!

The castello loomed before me. Flitting around the side of the east wing, I got to the French doors on the terrace. Before I left, I knew this would be my one likely mode of entry. The door to the tower apartment was always firmly locked at midnight.

The terrace doors had bolts at top and bottom. Felipe, whose duty it was to go around locking up, or Lars, who would sometimes do it for him, never neglected to shoot these bolts.

But on the left-hand door there was a hinged window, halfway up, that had been inserted at some time presumably to let more air into the salon when the double French doors had to be closed in bad weather.

This window had an outside iron ring that, properly manoeuvered, might be pulled out to open the vent. By standing on one of the garden chairs, I was fairly certain I could lower myself, feet first, onto the soft low chair under the window.

Now, as I played my torch light over the left-hand door, I spotlighted the loop. Leaning up, I'd actually grasped it, when, through the glass of the doorways, something white glimmered—a figure with long, flowing hair and huge, staring eyes —a woman's figure.

My fingers closed convulsively around the torch and I snapped out the light. Could this be Jenny come again, I thought wildly?

Behind the glass the figure wavered, seemed to grow taller, less nebulous. Backing into the darkness and cover of the garden, the rim of an iron chair bored into my legs. Terrified of sending it over with a crash and alerting everyone in the castello to my clandestine activities in the garden, I froze, immobilised with fright and shock.

I thrust my right fist into my mouth to deaden the scream welling up from my throat, as the hard rim of the chair's seat pressed painfully into the base of my spine. Terror-stricken, I crouched, watching and waiting.

Then, the figure moved towards me. I saw it stoop. The right-hand door opened. In the eerie darkness, the phantom floated out over the threshold and approached me.

"Ruth!"

My terrors died, stillborn. For the cool, clear accented voice was unmistakably of this world! "Senorita Foundling! What are you doing out here at this time of night?"

Elsa Gertae! The realisation that this was a living, breathing woman, and no wandering, pitiful ghost, destroyed the last of my terrors, but alerted me at once to the need to be cautious. Did my laugh sound as false to her as it did to me, ringing hollowly in my ears?

"I—I might ask you the same question!"

Attack, they say, is the best form of defence. But if I'd hoped to disconcert her, I was disappointed. Her gown was a swirling white nylon negligee.

"But that is very simple. Lars brought Max and me back from Palma on the *Belle Isle* for drinks. I think the poor man wanted company. He said you were indisposed. Then, he suggested we stay the night. Me, I could not sleep. I remembered, then, that there was a book I'd left down here . . ."

It seemed reasonable. She had the slightly disturbed air of the insomniac, her cheeks pale and her manner tense, even wary. But I couldn't help wondering if she'd spotted me from upstairs, coming in so stealthily from the drive.

"It's true, I did feel unwell earlier," I said, and walked deliberately forward into the light so she could see my jeans and anorak. Inwardly I shrank as those beautiful emerald eyes surveyed me, taking in everything about me. I felt that I must stink of the graveyard, and that my sense of outrage and guilt must be written plainly on my face.

And then I remembered the evidence of that empty grave, and my guilt died. I met that cool glance as openly as I dared. She was very beautiful in all that white drapery, her lovely hair about her face, eyes blazing magnificently under the light of the chandeliers. Lady Macbeth, I thought, and shuddered.

"But I felt quite recovered when I awakened around midnight, after a little sleep, so I let myself out by the front door and went for a walk."

"At midnight? All alone?"

It was one way of hinting she didn't believe me, but by then I was almost beyond caring what she thought or didn't think.

In the broader sense, though, I had to be careful not to antagonise her. Ian must be given time to get to London and return with the English police.

"I suppose it was rather foolish."

The inane laughter I forced out of my throat sounded to me quite as false as Elsa Gertae herself, but I found the role of deliberate deceiver very hard to play.

The lovely emerald eyes flickered over me. They held speculation and, I fancied, an ironic amusement.

Picking up the paperback book lying on the back of the chair, she said, "It is your own business, after all. But how did you expect to get in again? Felipe or Lars lock up at midnight."

"Oh, the French doors are sometimes left closed but not fastened," I said lightly.

She flicked off the lights, motioned me to precede her. In silence, save for the swish-swish of her long skirt, we walked up the darkened stairway.

On the landing I expected her to continue up to her own room on the corridor above, but she stopped and smiled at me. "Wait, you have not been well. I'll see you to your room. Lars would insist!"

One hand under my elbow, she propelled me there. The key to my room was still in my pocket. I caught, then, the malicious, amused glitter in her smile.

"Goodnight, Elsa," I said firmly, unlocking the door and, remembering the dummy figure within the bedclothes, edged in through the half-opened door and shut it on her.

Moving toward the bed, my heart still thumping from my uncomfortable time with Elsa, I didn't turn on the main lights, but felt for the bedside switch, and pushed it. At the same time that I saw the sheets flat and tidy under the plumped-up frilly pillows, the counterpane neatly folded at the bed's foot, I smelt the heavy, exotic perfume of a clove carnation!

"Good evening, Ruth. Or is it good morning?"

On the other side of the bed stood Lars Sven, wearing immaculate evening dress, the inevitable clove carnation in his buttonhole. His face was quite enigmatic, except for those dark eyes which glowed like coals.

"Where have you been?" he snapped curtly, and came around the bed to seize me by the right forearm and stand over me like the tyrant Ian had called him. Tyrant and murderer, I thought, remembering that pathetic, empty coffin.

Trying to collect my shocked wits I stammered out the tale I'd told to Elsa, remembering that it was important they should both be told the same lies. Deceit and intrigue, I thought bitterly; I'd certainly learned how to deal in these since I came to Majorca to lay a wreath on my friend Jenny's grave! A sense of betrayal and sickness welled up inside me, threatening to choke me.

Lars Sven, watching me narrowly as I faltered out my story, took a firmer grip on my arm, and with his other hand, seized my chin, turning my face up to meet his gaze. I tried to escape the burning scrutiny of those extraordinary eyes. Something told me that, if I looked directly into them, I should be lost forever.

"Don't lie to me, if you please, Ruth," said Lars Sven, evenly, coldly, and with menacing detachment. I began to shiver. Terror was making me almost dizzy, while the macabre rendezvous I'd just kept with Ian Hamilton did nothing to improve my nerve. Still, I must try and hide from him, at all costs, the fact that I was afraid.

"I'm not in the habit of lying—to you or anybody else," I said defiantly. "And I'm not a prisoner here, am I? Just because I felt suddenly better and decided to go out for a walk, hoping to slip back in and not disturb anybody . . ."

"And I've told you that's an excuse that won't stand up," he snapped. "You've been out with the Englishman, Ian Hamilton, haven't you? I say again, don't lie to me! Marie saw you, and told me."

That, of course, infuriated me! "Did you set her to spy on me?"

He shrugged. "As a matter of fact, my dear Ruth, no. Marie told me she saw you on the shore, beyond Andraix, together. She saw your friend Jenny there with him, too."

"*My* friend Jenny," I said, and heard my own voice falling away to the faintest of whispers. "I—I thought she was your friend, too, Lars!"

Again the shrug, again the careful avoidance of my glance.

"I didn't want to hurt you. But if you must know, I was bitterly disappointed in Jenny. We saw her with this Englishman many times before she died. Oh, it was nothing to me, if she found she was mistaken in her feelings for me."

Nothing to him! How proud he was! Or perhaps he was telling the truth at last,

311

thinking it no longer mattered what he divulged?

"I had thought differently," Lars went on, in the same bitter tone. But for remembrance of that empty coffin within the tomb in the cementario, I might have softened my heart at the sound of pain in that low, intense voice. Playacting, I told myself, designed to cover up whatever it is that they are in league to hide here. Lars, and the Gertaes, and the darkly-handsome Marie, were all in league together.

"She told me," I said quietly, "that she loved you dearly."

"She had a strange way, then, of showing it. Slipping out—just as you slipped out tonight—saying she was going out for air, that the night was hot, she couldn't sleep. Or going out alone, during the siesta time. And later, I found, from Marie and others, she was meeting this Englishman, Ian Hamilton."

"Well, she was never engaged to you," I pointed out. "She had a right to meet whomever she chose."

"In secret, after midnight, during the times when she told me she was asleep in her room? You are as bad as she was! It is as if you were in league together."

I took a step towards him, looked directly into his dark eyes and, at what I saw there, felt the world threaten to turn topsy-turvy again.

"How could I be in league with her?" I asked softly. "She's dead, isn't she? You told me that you, and the Gertaes, and the servants, all went to her funeral. Or is that a lie on your own account? Yes, Lars, you accuse me of deceitfulness and prevarication, but what else can you call what you've been doing to me since I first set foot in Castello Minerva?"

I saw the mistake I'd made the second I'd finished. Against all of Ian's express warnings I'd confronted Lars! But, somehow, in the face of what he'd said about Jenny, the words came tumbling out and I couldn't stop them.

For answer, if you could call it an answer, he bit his lips in that arrogant way he had when he choked back something either pride or anger wouldn't suffer him to say.

In the eerie silence that then hung over us, like a pall, I heard the soughing of the wind in the pines, and down on the shore, the lullaby of the sea.

"Or perhaps," I said deliberately, "you're not talking of the living Jenny? After all, you couldn't be, could you, if she's dead? Perhaps you mean I'm in league with her ghost?"

He gave a strangled sort of grunt, wheeled, and stalked out without another word.

Disturbed, I found the idea of bed utterly repugnant. I waited till I was sure Lars had returned to his room, and that all the guests in the castello were now also in theirs.

Then I quietly switched out the lights, left the bedroom, and stole down the stairs. Risking again the cold wrath of my employer, I unbolted the French doors to the salon (these were easiest to shift without the betraying creak of the hinges the front door would have given), and stole out into the garden.

The stark silhouette of the tower apartment, on my left, had now the fatal lure of all forbidden things. Although even I was not crazy enough to attempt to enter it at that hour, I flitted through the terraces, and reached its western side.

In any case, Felipe would have long since made all fast within the tower apartment, as he did everywhere else in Castello Minerva. Felipe, I brooded, another mysterious, enigmatic figure! Plainly fanatically devoted to Lars, he seemed to look upon everyone else, not excepting the Gertaes, with a hostile eye, despite his terrible courtesy, which, at times, could be as freezing as his master's.

Standing perfectly still, I looked up. No lights glowed, now, in Lars Sven's studio, nor in any of the windows facing west towards the cliffs and sea. The tower itself was just a vague outline in the dark, and suddenly, I was angry with myself for the idiot I was, mooning senselessly here in the dark garden, with the tower door locked fast against me, and everybody else asleep . . .

As I half-turned, on this thought, Jenny's voice breathed, "Ruth, be careful! Look out!"

From somewhere above, there was a rush of air, and a large object came hurtling down towards the very spot where I stood! With a stifled scream, I instinctively jumped sideways, my fingers scrabbling frantically at the wall of the tower, though I had no hope this would, in any magical fashion, give me protection!

The object smashed to the ground. Shuddering, I stared. It was a large piece of masonry from the battlements! In the dark, I saw the lump glimmering up at me with almost personal malevolence.

After a few horrible seconds spent screwing up my nerve, since what I really wanted to do was rush back to my bedroom and shut myself up in there, I stepped back, and looked up at the battlements. But there was only the jagged line of the ancient blocks of stone, weather-worn and immobile, glimmering faintly against the clouds above.

And I knew that if anyone was up there, someone who had hurled down that crumbling piece of masonry in a deliberate attempt either to kill or maim me, he or she would stay put within the tower till I moved away!

Shuddering, I recalled how Lars had looked and spoken, and realised he would just have had time, after leaving me, to hurry from the east wing to the tower apartment.

Was he up there now, concealed behind those ancient battlements, staring down at me as I lingered there, so incautiously, perhaps inviting another subtle attempt at assassination?

Turning at this thought, I ran around the tower, across the dark garden, and through the French doors into the salon. Stopping only long enough to fasten the doors behind me, I fled up to my room.

There I waited, moving stealthily between door and verandah, waiting, watching, to see if my employer crossed to the east wing, to come up the stairs, past my corridor, to his bedroom above. I maintained my vigil till dawn, but there was no sign of him. Nor, indeed, of anyone. If anyone had been on top of the tower, then he must be there still.

11

BREAKFAST, a few hours later, was a nightmarish experience. Lars Sven and I had, in fact, met an hour before it.

Watching my opportunity that morning, I waited till I saw Felipe go across to unlock the tower apartment, as he customarily did before breakfast. Then, under the guise of taking an innocent morning stroll, the minute Felipe disappeared under the archway in the direction of the stables, I ran to the iron-studded door, slipped within, and up the circular stairway towards the roof.

The stairway ended at a small stone landing where there was yet another iron-studded door. There was no key in this door, only bolts at top and bottom. With some difficulty I drew them, noticing that they seemed to have been moved fairly recently; for, although they were not oiled or greased, there was no dust or cobwebs upon them or the door itself.

Then, with a little gasp, I stepped out upon the flat roof. Momentarily I forgot I'd come up to find, if I could, any trace of the person who might have tried to murder me only a few short hours before. The view was breathtaking, with the calm, limpid waters of the Mediterranean lying around the island as far as the eye could see. The mountains lay veiled in blue mist to the north. Between the crumbling oblongs of the battlements, I could see them towering to a blue and hazy sky. The great Majorcan plain, dotted with trees, lay between them, with windmills and farmhouses and little outcrops of villas marking the hamlets. Immediately before me lay Palma. Its huge skyscraper hotels and apartment buildings were dazzlingly white, and the ancient Cathedral and Almuidaina Palace glowed softly golden against the backdrop of smaller mountains, and the vivid green of the palms.

Out in the bay, one huge liner moved gracefully. Several small yachts, with coloured sails, lay to the west of her. The combination of colour—sea, sky, and land—perhaps coming after my all but sleepless night, combined to dazzle me, and I put a hand to my eyes.

When I took it away again, Lars Sven stood before me in navy-blue jeans and crisp white shirt, the breeze just moving his hair.

Shock, at first, held me, and I had actually begun to stammer a few words of apology, in that I'd violated his express orders by coming to the battlements, when I remembered what had happened the night before, and my mind hardened.

"What are you doing up here, Ruth?" From his tone I deduced nothing, but instinct assured me he was angry.

"I'm sorry," I said crisply. "I know you told me nobody is allowed up here."

"Well?"

"Last night, after—after you left me, I felt more restless than ever. I came out again. To walk in the garden."

"Don't you ever sleep?"

"The heat is very intense. It seemed cooler in the garden near the tower, so I walked that way . . ."

He was now regarding me with the utmost intensity. And, appalled, I realised that my limbs had begun to shake.

Turning from him, I clutched at the battlements, and saw that, from the top of the nearest one, a large portion had either been deliberately chipped away, or had indeed crumbled and fallen.

From the look of the stone, it was impossible to be certain which was the case, for the stone was very porous and weatherworn. Even if it had been carefully prised off by some instrument, there would have been no sign.

"You're trembling, Ruth!" Lars was now behind me. In a moment I felt his arm around my waist. Deliberately, I disengaged myself, and walked a few paces away.

"Perhaps I was foolish but I stepped under the tower," I went on, "and a portion of the battlements fell—" I laughed, but the laugh was as shaky as I was. "Would you believe it, I only just stepped out of the way in time?"

Silence, in which I tried to summon up enough nerve to turn and confront him. Before I could do so, I heard his voice.

"You little fool! Didn't I tell you the battlements were unsafe? You might have been killed!"

He seized me, swung me around, and I was so close I could look directly into those dark, enigmatic eyes. He was very tense, and also very pale. Was he in a temper that it had been so near a miss, or did he feel genuine concern? He was doing an excellent job of feigning surprise, but it was also hard to separate this from his equally genuine anger. Ah, I thought, if only I knew the cause, the source, of that anger! But I didn't. All I knew was that, in his arms, something stirred in me that had to be ruthlessly subdued.

"Yes," I said evenly. "Yes, that's what I thought, when I heard the stone come rushing down!"

His fingers dug deeper into my forearms, and suddenly, I was afraid of what he might do. I disengaged myself rapidly, strode to the edge of the battlements and, with relief, saw Juanita waddling down to her kitchen garden.

"Juanita!" I called very loudly. "Juanita—"

She looked up, puzzled, saw me and Lars, and obviously concluding all was well, went on towards the garden for some herb or other. I was safe, I thought, for with Juanita as witness, he was hardly likely to try anything else.

"Look," I said, "if you come here, you can see where the portion of battlement fell away."

He looked at the broken battlement intently, then his face seemed to clear. His large, capable hands picked at the porous-looking stone, crumbling some of the yellow fragments between his fingers.

"Yes. I see what happened. Recent rain loosened the stone. It must have been about ready to fall when you so foolishly walked around the tower last night. Well, I hope that will teach you a lesson. When I put this area out of bounds, I did so for an excellent reason."

He turned again. Now his manner and voice both softened.

"But I am sorry, Ruth, if you were frightened, as indeed, you must have been. I will have the roof inspected again, see if some repair work is not possible. Now, shall we go down?"

"What about the others?" I said as, the door bolted again, we descended the circular stairway.

On the ground floor, as we paused

opposite his studio, his dark eyes raked me again.

"Well? What about them?"

"I mean, shall I tell them about the stone falling?"

"Why not? They should be warned, in case it happens again, surely? As I told you, I will have the roof inspected again. I am sure the rest of the tower apartment is safe enough, but keep away from the area immediately surrounding the tower. And remember, please, no more walks—before or after midnight."

We were at the iron-studded door. He opened it, and waited for me to go through.

"I'll tell them at breakfast," I answered, "and let Juanita and Marie know. After all, it could be equally as dangerous for them."

But Lars forestalled me, making the announcement himself when Juanita, Marie and Felipe were also in the room.

"I thought you looked pale, Senorita Foundling," observed the doctor, as Juanita gave a half-scream. Marie, like Felipe, betrayed no reaction at all and Elsa halted in the act of sipping coffee and stared, not at me, but at Lars. The brilliant eyes were wide open. In them I read only speculation. She must have told the doctor, and possibly Lars, too, how she'd come upon me practically trying to break into the salon last night.

"A nasty experience, Senorita Foundling," Elsa murmured, and selected dry toast from the rack with exquisitely-manicured fingers. She wore some sort of morning-wrap, all lace and nylon, rather too generously open above her breasts. Felipe's glance was on her, as was Lars'. Felipe looked thoughtful; Lars, wryly appreciative.

"I hope you really were not hurt?" The doctor said, the dead eyes meeting mine across the table.

"No," I said shortly. "But it could happen again. That's why I asked Senor Sven to tell you all."

There then fell one of those bursts of talk which often descends upon a group after the revelation of some crisis or ordeal which had befallen one of their members.

But what I was thinking, of course, was, if someone did conceal himself up in the tower, slipping up, somehow, without being seen when Felipe opened the door, was he present at this table, so glibly, and perhaps so hypocritically, expressing his concern?

It was now more than ten hours since Ian Hamilton had gone, and there was no word from him. No doubt, in London, at New Scotland Yard, there would be delays while he gave his evidence, perhaps while they insisted on checking his facts, even going to the orphanage and finding out all they could about Jenny and me.

After breakfast, Lars and Felipe went off in the motor-boat. The Gertaes took towels and wraps and a picnic hamper, saying they would spend the day on the private beach.

Consumed with anxiety, I decided, while waiting for word from Ian, to see if I could somehow get into Jenny's old room.

Juanita, as I knew, had the keys to all the rooms on a big steel ring which she kept in a drawer of the bureau in her room. She gave them to Marie on the days the rooms were cleaned, and to the women who came on Saturdays to help.

Juanita had taken me to her rooms,

above the inner gateway, several times, to show me this or that personal treasure, which was how I had learned about the keys.

But I was well aware that the bedrooms on the floor where Jenny had slept, where Lars and the Gertaes had their own bedrooms, had been cleaned yesterday: I'd seen Juanita and Marie up there, heard them calling to each other in Spanish.

Now I heard Juanita and Marie still in the kitchen, and hurried to the gateway, and up the stairs to Juanita's room. I found the keys, and hurried back. I'd have to trust to luck to return them.

But Juanita wasn't likely to need them till the next day, the cleaning now being done. The guests, and Lars, had their own keys.

It was only Jenny's room I was interested in. Juanita had the kitchen keys on her person, and with luck, I'd be able to slip this set back just before dinner. Juanita, too, was always mislaying things. If she did go to the bureau and find them gone, I could easily plant them somewhere for her to find.

Jenny's room was dominated by an

olive-wood bed with an ornate, luxurious bedhead and richly embroidered Spanish coverlet. Luxurious white pile carpet covered the floor, complemented by matching velvet curtains. A wardrobe stood empty against one wall, save for a layer of tissue paper on the bottom.

But, of Jenny Midnight, there was no trace at all! Every vestige of her, apparently, was gone.

The chamber was intensely quiet, charged, to my imaginative senses, with that air of waiting so noticeable in the rooms of the dead.

"Jenny?" I was whispering, though nobody could have heard me in that silent, empty corridor outside. "Jenny, darling Jenny."

I waited longingly—willing her to come. But I got no glimpse, then, of that small, ethereal figure in orphanage pinafore and golden pigtails.

I walked to the window, staring out with tear-filled eyes on the fairy-tale like beauty of the gardens, the pine woods fringing that incredibly blue, blue sea where everything quivered in the intense heat.

But it wasn't any use. Here, I realised,

was only an alien landscape, a stranger's bedroom, and the vital, joyous personality which had inhabited it for so short a space of time was gone. Then, why wouldn't the other Jenny come now, here in the quiet, she who had haunted me with her brief, tantalising appearances since that first one in the courtyard of the Mendip cottage?

I walked forlornly to the door. A shaft of sunlight fell with peculiar brightness on the small, olive-wood chest that sat, like an ottoman, close to the door.

"Ruth," said Jenny's voice, somewhere inside my mind, "Ruth, darling, look in the chest!"

That chest was the only piece of furniture I'd not examined. My subconscious was telling me to look. Logic and reason informed me, coolly, that that was the source of the voice, not Jenny, talking from beyond the grave.

Dropping on one knee, I put a hand on the smooth lid, and tentatively tugged. It was locked fast. Remembering Juanita's keys, I feverishly took the ring from my pocket, and tried one after the other. At first, I thought none would fit, till I came to the last but one, a slender, iron-cast thing that slid so easily into the lock I knew it must be the one.

The fragrance of myrtle and rosemary rose to my nostrils as I pushed back the lid. I saw three or four neat piles of woven Spanish blankets, with some towels next to them in a smaller heap, very colourful and gay, with bright designs stamped on them.

See, jeered logic and reason, just household linen! What did you expect? Then my right hand, slowly turning those scented, orderly piles, halted at one piece on the very bottom of the last pile. Pushed into the darkest corner on the left was a gaudy crimson bathrobe, almost the same colour as Juanita's sturdy household towels. This was why I'd nearly passed it over in my first, preliminary sorting.

I had given this particular bathrobe to Jenny when she left for Majorca! Ralph jeered at the colour, but Jenny loved it.

Now I drew it out, and examined it. Inside the right-hand pocket lay something small and light. I drew it out and almost laughed aloud in tender, reminiscent memory. But then I remembered where I was, and who, at any moment, might come along this corridor, to listen and betray me —as they'd betrayed Jenny.

In my hand was a small green velvet mascot in the shape of a Cheshire cat. It had large green velvet eyes and a huge black smirk sewn on its face.

A visitor to the orphanage had given him to Jenny one Christmas. I'd thought the present foolish. "Whoever heard of a green cat, Jenny darling!" I'd laughed. But Jenny adored him, took him everywhere, and when last we met, at the Mendip cottage, she admitted, grinning, that she still had him. Sometimes, when she was lonely, she put him on her pillow when she went to bed.

When, after her death, I went through her things, I remembered the green Cheshire cat, and concluded that the foolish, valueless souvenir (which was what he would be to any eyes but hers), had been thrown away.

Downstairs, a door banged. I heard voices. Thrusting the keepsake into my bag, I got to my feet, after carefully replacing the towels as I'd found them and locked the box.

A few minutes later, I walked down the

stairs of the east wing. From the kitchens came the smell of garlic and bread, and the sound of dishes clattering. Then reassuringly, the sound of Juanita, lazily scolding Marie.

It was ludicrously easy for me to slip back the key.

I imagined Jenny coming back from a walk, or a quick dip in the pool, going into her room to pick up the cat and pat him on the head, or pinch one ear, as I'd often seen her do in our orphanage days.

Would Jenny hide something in him? Jenny, perhaps desperately frightened, might leave a message for me, who would know the significance of her mascot, when other, enemy hands, would not.

Juanita could have plucked up the robe and thrust it into the chest with the towels by accident. And Jenny could have been killed soon afterwards, so that she never had the chance to ask Juanita about the robe or the cat.

I crossed the courtyard to the tower apartment, now determined to go one step further and explore the dungeons below.

Later I would examine the green Cheshire cat more closely. My plan hung on finding the dungeon key. Lars Sven might have it on his person, but I thought it unlikely. Surely he wouldn't want to risk losing so sinisterly precious an object.

Slipping across the courtyard, I stared down at the terraces. There was no sign of the Gertaes, so they must still be on the beach.

Lars' studio door was locked, but I'd already made the discovery that the key to the small office I used also opened his studio. Nobody else, so far as I was aware, knew this, but I'd found out one day when I wanted a sketch in Lars' workroom and, finding the door locked, in some temper thrust the office key into the lock.

Afterwards, I saw he assumed he'd given me the sketch, and I did not disillusion him.

Now I opened drawers, cupboards, boxes. Lars had a quick, very appraising eye. He would surely notice any sign that a search had been made unless I was sure to put back every brush and sheet of paper exactly as I'd found it.

I went meticulously through packing cases crammed with theatrical masks, costumes, and lengths of silk and velvet.

There were at least a dozen of these boxes, and I plunged my hands deep, my fingers feeling for the key. If these seemed unlikely hiding places, Lars Sven, if it came to that, was just the man to choose them.

Every second, of course, I dreaded to hear Juanita's light footfall on the outside flagstones, and some motherly query about afternoon tea. Or, infinitely worse, Marie's sharper, more staccato footfall, her voice, subtly challenging, mocking, like Elsa's. "Senorita Foundling, are you looking for something lost?" For I should have to open the door to whoever it was, and peering beyond my shoulder, they would see.

Well, I am, I told myself violently, savagely, fearfully. I'm looking for the key to the dungeons, but more than that, I'm looking for the key to the mystery about my friend Jenny Midnight!

And I'm going to find out, if I have to stay here forever, if Ian Hamilton, who's supposed to be my ally, never comes, and if Lars Sven should return and find me here, hands deep in his possessions, hunting, searching, for the key to the place where he's expressly forbidden me to go!

There was no sign of the key. Perhaps it was in his bedroom, then, or maybe in the small library, over in the east wing? But he used the latter scarcely at all, I'd noticed, working almost always in the studio. The bedroom, on the other hand, was a possibility. Why hadn't I thought of looking there first, when I was up in Jenny's room?

I stared around, angry and defeated. Lars' desk was placed under the wall. Above it, high, long windows cut deeply into the old stone, looking out on a corner of the tossing pine woods and the intensely blue Mediterranean sky.

The desk was never locked. The top held his sketching board, pens, pencils, little pots of paint and brushes, knife, and erasers. I'd seen him wander between desk and larger canvases, propped on the easels which were ranged around the walls, in the untidily tidy manner of the true artist, who, in the midst of appalling clutter, always knows where to lay his hands on the very object he needs.

The drawers, each side, yielded nothing,

and I knew their contents by sight already. Dozens of sketches, many half-completed, old invitations to fashion shows, the backs used for making notes, odd scribblings about ship and plane schedules, a name here and there that was presumably that of some model or, perhaps, a woman known even more intimately.

As I stood back, baffled, the telephone rang. Scarcely daring to breathe, as if the person ringing could actually see me at my underhanded work, I thought, let it ring! But then Juanita or Marie would answer. And, if it was some query about Lars, or, maybe, the proposed fashion show, they would come hunting for me. Marie, certainly, would later report to Lars how she had found me snooping.

I plucked off the receiver, mentally cursing the caller.

"Castello Minerva here. Senor Sven's secretary."

Most of his callers would answer in English. But I all but jumped out of my skin when a low voice, a man's, but which, disguised though it was I recognised, said, "Ah, good morning Senorita Foundling! This is the American Express Bank in

Palma. I am very sorry, but those cheques, they will not be ready until tomorrow. There has been some little delay in the transfer of funds from Barcelona."

Ian's voice, except to me who caught those faint, clipped, betraying Scots vowels, was like that of any other English-speaking teller in an international bank. Even as my heart sank at the implication of his words, I understood his intention—the need to keep secret our arrangements.

"Thank you," I said formally. The telephone was one of several extensions. Any curious listeners—in the salon, my own office, Lars' bedroom, or, significantly, the kitchens—might hear what we discussed.

"I will let you know, Senorita, when the funds have been transferred."

"Thank you," I said again.

There was a click at the other end of the line. Ian Hamilton was gone. So, he hadn't got off the island even! The gist of his message was that he was at the airport trying to get a flight and that he would be with me as soon as he could.

Perturbed and uneasy, I wondered just how long, now, I should have to hold the fort. Would Ian ring again, or was he simply waiting for the first available plane he could get off the island? On the other hand, though, it could be a question of days before he got in touch again.

Unnerved at this unlooked-for turn of events, I abandoned, at least temporarily, the idea of searching the dungeons. A more sensible, certainly safer, plan, would be to take the 'bus down into Palma, mingle there with the sightseers and Majorcans, and come back late to the castello.

My foot struck something under the carpet. I felt a projection, an unevenness. Over the old stone bricks the covering was a heavy crimson carpet that ran right up to the thick walls. Quickly I bent down, flicked back a corner to expose a small area of bricks, time-weathered, and apparently undisturbed, but for the laying of the contemporary carpet, for centuries.

Kneeling down, I saw that one of the bricks was set slightly lower than its neighbours. Moving my right hand cautiously over the surface, I found a nick on one edge. My finger in this nick, I gradually levered up the brick.

In the space under it, I saw a heavy iron

key, with an ornate carving on the handle —a Moorish design. Five minutes later, with the figure of the armed knight protecting me from anybody who might come suddenly into the tower apartment through the shut, but not locked, central circular door, I inserted the key into the wooden door leading to the dungeons.

As I turned the key, I irrationally found myself half-hoping, half-dreading that the door would not yield. But it did, moving easily upon its hinges—too easily, surely, for a door that, so Lars Sven had said, hadn't been opened for centuries.

I'd brought a torch with me. A stone passage yawned blackly beyond. In the focussed beam of my torch, I saw that the walls and floor were free of dust and debris.

After a second's hesitation, I secured the door, pocketing the key for safety. Better to be entombed, temporarily, within the dungeons, than risk having Marie, or Lars, or the doctor and his charming wife, in secret pursuit. Then, in the eerie light, my mind conjured up the vision of an agitated Juanita wedging herself along the very narrow passage. Why, she'd surely get herself stuck, poor soul! I thought. And had, sternly, to check the giggle that threatened, for it was semi-hysterical.

A hundred yards further on, the passage suddenly ended. In the light of the torch —I prayed fervently that the battery wouldn't suddenly give out!—I saw I stood in a large, circular chamber from which three smaller chambers had been hollowed out.

Shuddering, I remembered those invaders, the Moors, and imagined the moans and groans of the hostages and captives they might have incarcerated here, for there were iron rings fastened to the walls of all four chambers.

Still, there were no piles of bones, no signs that anyone had perished here. Testing the floor with my toe, I found this, too, was solid rock.

So whoever had been confined here, they must, as corpses, have been disposed of elsewhere, for that rock was too hard to make a grave! I found myself contemplating a second passage, one leading outwards to the sea. That way some of the prisoners could, no doubt, have found a way of escape. And there also would be a place where contraband could be landed.

I stepped further into the circular chamber, but saw no sign of any seawards-leading passage. The light glinted on those rusted, circular rings. My mind on that other outlet, I lost all sense of caution and moved quickly, almost feverishly forward. My right foot slipped, and grabbing for some support, any support, in horrible panic that I should do myself some serious injury and lie here, perhaps for days, perhaps to die, my hand closed around the nearest of the iron rings.

Half-lying, half-crouching against the wall, I heard, next, a strange metallic grating, and, to my astonishment, shock, and a certain cold, clawing apprehension, felt the ring in my hand moving outwards with a portion of the old stone wall into which it was set!

Recovering my balance, I stood perfectly still, unwilling to look within the cavity, for fear of what I should find there. Again, Jenny entered my thoughts. Jenny, my friend Jenny, as Lars had so oddly described her, now dead these past three months! Oh no, I thought, in utter revulsion, no, not this, not for lovely, beautiful, Jenny, not down here, in this pressing dark, and clammy cold, in this hideous dungeon where unnameable tortures have been inflicted on other innocent, despairing souls! Please, dear God, don't let me find her—Let there be anything, anything else, even the mummified, ossified remains of one of Duke Manuel's victims, but not my lovely friend Jenny Midight!

"I thought," said a voice coldly and contemptuously inside my brain, "that you were determined to stay at the castello till you found out what happened to her? And, if she is here, surely it's no worse for you to look at what may have been done to her, than for Jenny herself to have endured it. Don't be such a coward, Ruth!"

Holding the light with hands that, on that thought, were as firm as the rock upon which I stood, I looked into the cavity.

And saw, with sickening relief deepening to profound curiosity, that the space was not large enough to entomb anything bigger than an infant.

There was an iron box, about eight

inches long by five inches wide by five inches deep. It was of weathered metal of the kind used to store deeds or old documents. Extracting it without difficulty, I laid it on the ground and crouched beside it.

The box was fastened with a hasp and iron loop, but it was not locked. The loop was big and heavy, and resisted my fingers, which were clumsy with cold and the mingled sensations of fear, curiosity, and excitement which gripped me.

At last I prised up the lid. Inside, I saw a bundle of letters tied around with blue ribbon. With them there was a faded photograph of a young woman. It was too dark to make out her features clearly, for the torchlight merely distorted them, but she had been, I thought, very beautiful.

Then I hesitated, looking down at the pathetic bundle of letters in my hand. I almost thrust them back, unread, when my mind hardened, and I silenced the voice of conscience, remembering my friend Jenny.

Setting down the torch so that its beam directed a fair light, and sending one nervous glance back along the passage, I opened the letter on the top of the pile. The script was very faded in what seemed to be brownish ink. The handwriting was large and very feminine.

They were all signed simply, Rosalie. Rosalie Saunders, of course, for whose murder Gordon Ayrton had been tried by the courts of England, and released!

All of the letters began "My darling Gordon," and were written in tenderly endearing terms, warm and so loving I felt the sudden prick of tears behind my eyes.

And, although they were signed Rosalie, what went before the actual name was equally loving, being "Your devoted," or "Your fond," or "Your precious."

So she had loved him, I thought in pity, and he'd rewarded her by killing her, then running away, sheltering behind another woman's alibi. Like the criminal who can't keep away from the scene of the crime, he'd kept these evidences of her devotion.

Picking up the box again, I stared down, half hypnotised. Any peril I myself might be in was completely forgotten. For, glowing like a submerged pearl in the corner of it, I saw a six inch length of fair, silky hair that was exactly the shade and texture of Jenny's.

Snatching up the photograph again, I looked at it. That woman was very dark in her beauty, as I was sure I'd remembered the newspaper reports of the trial describing her.

"No!" I said again, "no." But this time, without any hope of denial, my whispered words went into silence.

Ten minutes later, I furtively pushed open the door of the dungeons to see the black metal of the armed knight before me. I listened tensely. All seemed quiet within the tower apartment.

I managed to get into Lars' studio, slip back the key, and then hurry back to my own office, where I was, in fact, supposed to have been all this time, working.

For camouflage, I spread account books and papers all around the desk. Then, I took out my cigarettes, lighted one, and sat there, smoking, and thinking, heedless of the time, or how the afternoon was wearing on.

The criminal returned to the scene of his crime or to some object associated with it which he was compelled, by some ghastly malaise, some twisted psycho-logical quirk, to handle.

He'd probably destroyed all of Jenny's letters. All that remained as evidence of his crime, serving his psychological perversion, were Rosalie Saunders' letters and photograph, and a lock of my friend Jenny's hair!

Was she down there then, not under that rock, but tucked away somewhere, in some niche or cranny, where he expected nobody would ever come upon her?

Why hadn't I stayed, examined in greater detail the circular chamber and all those smaller ones, tried, with more persistence, to find out if there was some other passageway leading to the sea?

Coldly my reasoning mind informed me Lars could have taken Jenny's body out that way, and thrown it overboard from the *Belle Isle* many miles out to sea. Was that why he and Felipe went out so often, searching to make sure she had not floated up from the depths of the ocean again?

It was then I heard that little whisper again, so gentle, yet so compelling, only, since I'd been on the island, strangely sounding so very very faint and far away.

Almost indeed, like the ghost of a ghost voice.

"And when I want help, Ruth darling, I won't ask anybody but you!"

Whatever it cost me, I must return to Sven's room, raise the brick, get the key, and go back down there.

"Senorita Ruth!" My heart lurched so violently I half-started from my chair. Seated at my desk, staring out at the sea and a shore I never saw with my physical vision, I'd temporarily forgotten where I was.

Juanita, moving with that ease and gentleness common to all the plump, had climbed the circular stairs with afternoon tea on a tray, and a dish of Spanish-style crullers, to beam at me like some benevolent witch.

Rising hastily, I seized the tray, and began hurriedly to thank her. But Juanita had some news of her own, which caused her, no doubt fortunately, not to pay all that much attention to me.

"Senor Sven and Felipe, they come back from the fishing trip," she said, and sighed gustily. "Si, they return early. So now, I get on with my dinner preparations, certain there will be people there to enjoy my cooking. Myself, I thought they would be away all night, or come back late."

I remembered the Gertaes, who would be remaining for dinner now that Sven had returned, and probably lingering on at the castello for a few days, Elsa having to confer with him anyway, about the autumn fashion show, and what she was to model of the dresses already in the tower apartment.

So, no chance now of making a second trip to the dungeons! Indeed, I could count myself lucky that I'd emerged when I did. Another few minutes and Juanita would have caught me. Another five or ten, and Lars would himself have come upon me. For he would have been sure to have come to the tower apartment to see what I was doing.

"Senorita Ruth!" Juanita peered short-sightedly at me, her large, languorous eyes heavy with concern. "You are deathly pale! And your eyes, they are so big! You look as if you are about to have a sickness. Is there something wrong?"

That wouldn't do! If she suspected

something amiss, Lars would pinpoint the source of my distress.

Shaking my head, forcing a smile to lips that felt stiff as cardboard, I assured her it was just the heat.

"Juanita, is Senor Sven actually in the castello?"

"No," said Juanita. "I see his boat from the terrace, coming in to the private beach. Dr. Gertae and Madame Elsa were on the shore waving."

Reprieve, if only for a few minutes! Juanita lingered, expecting me to drink the tea, or eat at least one of her buns. Not to make her suspicious—she was not malicious, just a great gossip—I forced myself to drink a cup of the tea, and bite into one of the sweet, sticky crullers.

That cold, reasoning part of my mind which seemed to have become detached from the rest of it informed me Lars had still to tie up the boat, greet his guests, come over the beach, up the steps, and over the terrace. That was long enough for me to play the insipid English secretary to Juanita, and then make my escape before those dark, shrewd eyes of his could take in my state!

Juanita chattered about her planned dinner menu. Because I thought she would be some sort of bastion between myself and my employer, if I did encounter him on the way, I rose and went back to the east wing with her on the excuse I needed something from my room.

Marie moved, now, between kitchens and salon. I caught the flash of her dark eyes. From far down the terrace came the low, musical intonations of Elsa's voice, and the steadfast, entirely level one of Lars Sven.

In my room at last, I shut and locked the door, and stood against it, heart racing, fighting the heat, the heavy brooding atmosphere now enveloping the castello, pressing down upon my over-wrought senses so that I felt I wanted to turn and run out of the place, escape from it forever.

It took all my strength to beat down this impulse for the self-protecting thing it was, and I called to mind, deliberately then, Jenny's wraith-like figure, evoked again, that small, whispering voice. *No, Ruth, you're not going.* I was able to say then, You're staying here, no matter what it costs, even your life itself; but you're going to find out what happened to Jenny Midnight!

Somehow or other I must get back into those dungeons with a stronger torch, and plan it so that I should really be undisturbed!

Now, if I tried to get to the airport, to tell Ian what I'd discovered, there was a possibility I'd still miss him. For all I knew, Lars or the Gertaes, all of whom now seemed to me to be growing suspicious, would follow me.

There was also this: to the island authorities, they were persons of prestige and substance. I was just an unknown English-woman, with, moreover, not a soul in England to vouch for me. The orphanage matron was dead. All the other staff I'd known had long since retired.

If I did go to the Majorcan authorities alone, without Ian to back me up, and tell them about the empty coffin in the Cementario Genova, they would probably be so incensed at what, rightly, they would call desecration of a tomb, they'd put me in jail!

Then they would, of course, go and see

Lars or the doctor. But the latter, by then, would suspect I'd found out something and, carefully covering his tracks, would then move off the island.

Or else they'd somehow get hold of me, and treat me the same as they'd treated poor dear Jenny! No, there was still only one thing for it—to wait for the return of Ian, and his Detective-Inspector friend from New Scotland Yard and meantime, find out all that I could.

Keep your nerve, girl, I told myself. *They can't be sure that you do know anything yet, whatever they may suspect!*

I moved away from the door to look warily out on the gardens, empty, drenched in sunlight, oddly menacing, though, in their fairy tale-like loveliness. Like the poisoned apple the old witch in the story offered to the beautiful princess, they were a lure disguising horror and wickedness beneath their tempting sur-face.

I thrust my hand into my pocket, wanting a cigarette. My fingers touched something soft, almost cuddly, like a toy. Jenny's green Cheshire cat!

Drawing it out, I stared at it, lovingly

and with tender regret for the person it called to mind. And thought again, could it be possible Jenny laid it away in that bath-robe pocket not accidentally, but with some message tucked inside it? Fearing herself threatened, her very life in danger, hoping someone might come to the island seeking her (not knowing, then, she was to die), did she leave the Cheshire cat in that robe, expecting anyone else who found it to pass it by, whereas a friend would take it up, finger it, and find what she had left?

There was a pair of scissors on top the olive-wood dressing table. Feverishly seizing them, I began to unpick the seams that some benevolently-minded person had sewn up, more than twenty years ago, to make a present for an unknown child in a London orphanage.

Snip—snip—snip—a hurried, backward glance at the door. Despite the fact it was locked, Juanita had her master key and so did Lars. I put the point of the small gilt scissors into the back seam, and cut on through the tiny, neat stitches. A few minutes later, I stared at the dismembered and disemboweled Cheshire cat.

One tail piece, two body pieces, one under-body, and four legs, all carefully laid out with the kapok stuffing they used to use before foam came in. There, too, were the whiskers of twisted black thread, and the two pads of black velvet with green embroidery and lashes for the eyes.

Nothing. There was no note, no key, no signal of any kind from Jenny. Had she abandoned the idea of leaving something in the cat? Got interrupted, perhaps, and thrust the mascot down in the robe pocket till she could resume? Or had somebody, after all, divined her ruse? Taken out what she'd left there, and then killed her?

And I remembered grimly how Elsa had told me, with pride, that she was a very good needlewoman, and made many of her own clothes.

Sweeping up the mutilated creature, I looked around for another hiding place. Going through into the bathroom, I snatched up my cosmetic case which was very large and had several capacious inner compartments. One had a small inner purse of waterproof plastic, like the case itself. Thrusting the pieces of velvet inside it and zipping it closed, I then went over to the large black marble cabinet set in the wall above the hand basin.

This had a medical compartment, containing tins of ointment, pots of anti-mosquito paste, little phials of eye lotion, and a large, unopened package of cotton wool.

The cotton wool was sealed at both ends in thick blue paper. With a nail file from my bag, I slit open these ends, unrolled the wool, laid my plastic bag at the end, and rolled up the wool again, then looked at the flapped ends.

They'd been lightly stuck down with some adhesive and if the package was not to betray me, if my room was searched, must be re-sealed. For a moment I felt baffled, till I remembered there was a small tube of adhesive in my writing case, part of the studio equipment from the Mendip cottage which I'd pushed in just in case it came in useful on my travels.

The glue was sticky with the heat, and oozing from its tube, but I finally managed to get enough on to the ends of the blue paper to reseal it so that it looked as if it had never been opened since leaving the factory.

Then, critically, I felt the package. I supposed for anyone deliberately and methodically searching, there was a telltale heaviness and thickness about the roll. But to the eye it was impossible to know it held anything but the cotton wool. I should have to be satisfied with that for the time being.

Possibly I was all wrong about the cat, and Jenny had simply shoved it into that bathrobe pocket and forgotten it. Only, I thought, as I hurriedly showered, changed into a pale blue silk dress and matching costume jewellery, she had, as I knew, been very attached to it.

Then I prepared to go down, remembering Lars had parted from me in cold, hard anger, and that I must be wary, careful, not to arouse that curious, slumbering hostility again. Nor the more impersonal, detached, but, therefore perhaps more dangerous, enmity of the Gertaes.

Jenny had believed in prayer, that there was some dimension into which we all went, as human souls, at death. Such faith was, for me, much more difficult, but as I went down the stairway of the east wing, ears tensely alert to the murmur of voices beyond the dining room door, I found I was praying, seeking to draw down to myself some of her own bright and shining courage, that superb disdain of all personal danger.

Despising my cowardice, and remembering her, strength and steadfastness, of a kind, did come.

Deliberately, I'd got down a second or two late, so that, under cover of the general entry into the dining room, I could go in without too much attention focussed upon me.

Elsa and Max were already seated. Lars was just lowering himself into his chair. All were in evening dress tonight. Lars wore the inevitable clove carnation in his buttonhole. The men sprang automatically to their feet. Elsa, in a purple evening sheath whose decolletage was so very deep that few women would have dared to chance it, bowed her head. That lovely countenance was animated, charming, even friendly. But her eyes were guarded and uneasy, and I sensed a tension in her.

"Sorry! I'm a little late," I murmured. Felipe, standing behind Lars at the sideboard, turned and pulled out my chair. I caught the Majorcan's slightly wooden stare, and thought, He's devoted to Lars; he'd do anything Lars asked of him.

"I—I stupidly fell asleep on the balcony. It is such a very hot evening. Do excuse me, everyone."

"But of course. It is very understandable, Senorita Foundling. We ourselves have only just been seated."

But the doctor looked across the table at me critically, and I saw those light blue eyes, with their curious, empty deadness, narrow. Was he trying to find, perhaps, some legitimate reason for my excuses of yesterday? To allay his own suspicions, and those of his wife? Had the three of them been talking about me, comparing notes as to what I'd said, how I'd behaved, pumping Juanita, perhaps, who would tell them I was in the tower apartment for a large part of the afternoon, finding out I'd looked strange, and distressed?

Lars crumbled bread; already, his wine glass was half empty. He looked sideways at me, across Elsa. In that inscrutable glance I read nothing. He did, I thought, look extremely tense and tired under all that control. Still, it was scarcely to be wondered at if, at times, Lars Sven, too, wore a haunted air.

"Felipe, fill Senorita Ruth's glass, if you please," he said peremptorily, catching my glance, as if, aware of every dark suspicion searing my mind, he was determined to be the solicitous host. "I don't think she is quite recovered from that curious indisposition. Perhaps we should get you to have a look at her, eh, Max?"

Juanita, coming in with a huge silver tureen of *gazpacho*, smilingly ladled a generous portion into my soup bowl. Ignoring the deliberate irony and definite condescension in Lars' tone, I stared at him across the blaze of candles which, in their ornate silver holders, always graced the castello dining table despite the great crystal chandelier blazing above our heads.

"Forgive me, Senor Sven," I said coolly, "but I cannot congratulate you, either, on your own looks this evening."

Elsa, languidly spooning up *gazpacho*, didn't flick an eyelash. Max stared inquiringly, as if wondering just what had prompted my remark.

"Are you, perhaps, also feeling the

heat?" I went on, warning myself, nevertheless, that I wanted to soothe him, at least for this evening. "I've never seen you so pale. Perhaps you're troubled about the coming autumn show?"

"You are very perceptive," he said drily, and without any apparent anger or disturbance of manner at all. "It is very hot, certainly. As for the autumn collections, I have no worries. The gowns are all assembled in the tower apartment. The show should go smoothly when the buyers and newspaper people come."

Well, I conceded, that needs nerve, to go on with such a project, knowing what is in your past, and what lies below the very tower apartment where you propose to hold your show! Still, you are a man of tremendous nerve—dark, passionate nerve —that won't be gainsayed.

"We all feel the heat, no?" murmured Elsa languidly. "There is thunder in the air. When the storm breaks, we shall have some relief."

Nevertheless, she and Lars immediately plunged into animated discussion about the autumn fashion show, the date for which, I remembered, was only a few days away. Despite my own lead, Lars didn't include me in their talk, and I couldn't decide whether this was a deliberate snub, or if he thought I was not concerned with the actual modelling of the collection, and therefore could be excluded.

And, listening to the two of them discussing the cut and colour of this gown or that, deciding what she should wear, what should be allotted to the fashion models who would be flown in from Barcelona, both of them couldn't have sounded more normal.

I made a pretence at eating the excellent dishes. The main one was a superb *graisonera*, a Majorcan delicacy of eggs and meat, with small artichokes, beans and peas—only the sauce was over-seasoned, heavy with oil and garlic. As I drew the crystal water jug towards me, the doctor, with an admonitory, smiling wag of his finger, filled, instead, my half-empty wine glass from the jug in front of him.

Juanita placed the jug, full of the local red wine, on the table each mealtime. Felipe would come around with the more select wines, at Lars' command.

"I do not recommend the island water

for you, Senorita. Oh, it is quite good, but English systems do better with our wine."

Too thirsty to argue, I smiled automatically and drained the glass. He filled it again, but then the *graisonera* was served.

After it, we had an elaborate whipped cream and spun sugar confection of peaches, and more wine. Felipe brought in coffee, Lars decreeing we should not have it on the terrace that night.

Dr. Gertae again turned to me, cigarette case open.

"We are better here; it is too steamy-hot outside. And the mosquitoes are very active."

I thought of the anti-mosquito paste in the bathroom, upstairs, and of the cotton wool packet and what was in it. Shaking my head at the proferred cigarette, I took a firmer grip on the wineglass, and wondered if more of the local wine might, perhaps, steady me.

It had crept on gradually, that strange, disassociated feeling. I couldn't keep the room or its occupants in proper focus. Elsa and Lars began to shift about, then merge weirdly into each other, like shapes in one of those distorting mirrors one sees at fairs.

Max's voice faded, the dining room whirled, and I saw Jenny again! In orphanage pinafore, hair in those familiar pigtails, blue eyes blazing, she stood just beside Lars and Felipe, and was amazingly, weirdly clear although all the rest of the huge room spun and gyrated around me!

There was from somewhere, then, a crack like a pistol shot followed by a sharp pain in the palm and fingers of my right hand. Stupified and dazed, I looked down. The glass was snapped in two, and blood trickled down on to the white napkin beside it.

"Ruth!" Lars' voice, harsh and very clear, cut through every nightmarish picture and sound, wiping Jenny's wraith from behind him. "What is it? What's the matter, I say? Are you ill?"

I tried to get on my feet, heard a crash behind me and realised I'd sent the dining room chair over on to the floor.

"Please," I croaked, as Elsa, Lars, and the doctor all wavered about in front of me like pieces of a jigsaw puzzle thrown haphazardly into the air. "Please, I think I'm going . . ."

Nausea gripped me, and an agonising pain in my abdomen. Remembering Jenny, terror was added to my physical distress. And the sickness gathered strength, as I picked out, amidst all the other surrounding odours of food, wine, flowers, the night fragrance of the pines, the scent of a clove carnation.

"Ruth!" Lars Sven's voice was frighteningly, threateningly close. I felt him near then, but couldn't pick him out from that whirling background. "Don't move. It's all right; I've got you."

But blind panic engulfed me as I felt his arm close around my waist and knew, instinctively, that the other two were closing in on me. Putting out both hands, I tried to fight them off. There was a moaning sound, a half-sob, and bewildered and ashamed, I realised it was coming from my throat. I pitched forward, temporarily breaking free from Lars' hold, then he caught me again. In bitterness of spirit, I went into darkness.

When I opened my eyes again, it seemed not much lighter. But I saw I was in my room, with Marie coming towards me, tray in hand.

I'd been undressed, and lay in one of the luxurious night dresses, of black nylon and lace, that had also been Jenny's. I caught my breath, remembering how I'd seen her, so clear-cut, behind Lars, and then buried the thought, lest Marie should mark the disturbance in me.

Her figure grew bigger. For one bizarre, disoriented second, I wondered if I'd died, and if Marie and I, she having also met her end, drifted in that borderland of human souls known as limbo, the dimension between heaven and hell.

For the chamber was filled with dull grey mist through which her still-pert, advancing form seemed to float. Then, as I half-rose, turning towards the window, I saw that this weird effect came from outside, that a sea-mist whirled sluggishly outside the windows.

"Good morning, Senorita Foundling!" Marie set down the tray of black coffee and toast. "I hope you are better?"

My head felt as if little men with hammers were beating maliciously all over my skull. My limbs were weighted, but that horrible nausea was gone. Had I, then, been doped? Or drugged? I remembered the doctor's apparent solicitousness, when he warned me not to drink the local water, as he plied me, instead, with wine!

Marie's eyes and manner were as veiled as the morning. She'd left the bedroom door halfway open. A hand tapped smartly upon it. Without waiting for my invitation to enter—was it Lars?—in came Dr. Gertae, in crimson silk shirt, dark blue trousers, and rope-soled shoes. His tread was always quiet. That morning it was catlike. A very suitable way to approach an invalid, I thought, sardonically, watching him through my half closed lids.

Marie made no move to go; immediately, I understood why. They were both trying to be as conventional as possible.

Dr. Gertae bent over me, took my pulse, then my temperature, while primly, almost coyly, hands folded under her apron, Marie waited. Perhaps, I thought, she had been told to wait, not out of false etiquette, but for some other reason?

"You will be quite recovered by tomorrow," the doctor said, straightening up. My experience of the ritual used by medical men wasn't all that extensive, yet there seemed nothing clumsy or unpractised about his. Well, there wouldn't be, I thought, otherwise how could he run El Pineo, or that practice he was supposed to have over on the mainland, at Barcelona?

"I will have some remedy for an upset digestion sent up from my nursing home, Senorita! And it would be best to remain here, in your room, for the rest of the day, and keep to a light diet. I will advise Juanita of the best food for you."

"Thank you, Dr. Gertae," I said. Marie came primly forward, straightened the bedclothes, playing her own role of nurse to a nicety. Then, I forgot even him, forgot to wonder whether he, or Lars, or Madame Elsa, had slipped some drug into my wine or food that previous night, as there came the melancholy hooting of ships' sirens.

The doctor walked to the door, Marie following. He turned, one hand on the handle, his slim, taut figure, clean-shaven face, and well-kept hair giving him a look of youth—all but for those eyes, with their empty wariness.

"Hear the fog signals, Senorita? It came

down at midnight. The planes at the airport are all grounded. There won't be any in-coming boats and planes until the fog lifts."

The dead eyes flickered over me again. Although I was always on guard now, the doctor was beginning more and more to make my flesh creep.

"I fear we are at least temporarily cut off from the rest of the world."

Deliberately, I made my face a mask, concealing from him the desolation I felt at that news. For it meant, of course, that Ian too, was grounded, that he wouldn't get off the island now for at least another twelve hours, and possibly longer, if the fog didn't lift.

Then I thought, well, twelve hours isn't going to make all that much difference. From what I've heard, nobody ever goes up to the cementario. All I've got to do is continue to play the stupid Englishwoman.

"Well, that won't trouble me, Dr. Gertae," I said, demurely, keeping my eyes down, "as, under doctor's orders, I shall be keeping to my room for most of today at least."

"But how sensible!" His voice was

lighter than Lars', but I felt there was greater potential menace behind it. This man could be fanatical, utterly ruthless, I judged, when the cards were stacked against him.

"And how fortunate, Senorita, you made no plans to travel today! Good day, then. Rest well."

Snatching up a wrap as he closed the door, I ran to the window. My heart sank at sight of the fog, pressing, thick as a blanket right up against the glass, so that I couldn't see even the verandah's outline.

I drank black coffee, crunched at toast, and wondered. If some drug, opiate or tranquilizer had been dropped into my dinner wine, had the intention been to kill me, put me to sleep just for the rest of the night, or warn me off so that I should flee from the castello and the island, too frightened to breathe a word of my suspicions and experiences?

My system, of course, had reacted violently. I thought it likely enough that this reaction of almost instant rejection started before they'd expected it. And they probably counted on my being in bed, or at least in my room, before oblivion overtook me.

Or had that *graisonera* been too rich for my English palate? The torridly-hot evening, following on that hazardous, nerve-racking expedition through the dungeons, had also played its part.

My head still ached; critical reasoning was difficult. So many possible explanations added to my confusion.

Another even more nasty one now presented itself. An incompetent Dr. Gertae might have over-estimated the amount of the drug, supposing it was he who dropped it into my wine. On the other hand, if he was acting on behalf of Lars Sven, the doctor, by mistake, might not have given me enough. Shuddering, I reflected that I was thus alive, as it were, only by accident.

12

THREE days later, the forecourt of Castello Minerva was packed with cars that had come over on the ferries from Barcelona. Lars Sven was holding the autumn fashion show as planned.

The fog had persisted for two whole days and nights, only completely lifting that morning. But no word at all, not even a coded phone message or innocent postcard, had come from Ian Hamilton.

He must be lying low somewhere on Majorca, unless, by some lucky chance, he got off by one of the smaller fishing ships which, so Juanita had heard from Felipe, sailed for Marseilles on the first night, cursing the sea-fog but braving it.

Congestion at Palma Airport was severe, with hundreds of delayed passengers trying to get off Majorca. Apparently, too, a few flights had left Minorca on the second night, where the fog wasn't so thick.

The morning after my attack, I struggled down to breakfast. The Gertaes, to my surprise, were still at the castello, and greeted me with apparent warmth. The elixir from the doctor's dispensary had been delivered to my room. Tasting it warily, it seemed to he nothing more deadly than a chalk and bismuth mixture, but after consideration, I poured it down the sink drain.

My cotton-wool parcel, which I'd examined carefully, had plainly not been tampered with.

Lars didn't appear. When, later, I went to the tower apartment office, he came up, dictated some letters very formally, asked me curtly if I was better, then shut himself up in his studio again. I did not disturb him.

Next day he threw himself, with Elsa, into the final plans for the fashion show. The room where the dresses were kept was unlocked, and he and Elsa flitted up and down stairs, gowns draped over their shoulders, calling to me for tape measure and pins, or pencils and pens.

Later I helped him bring up the huge vases of flowers and trays of potted plants ordered in from Palma, or cut by Felipe and Marie and Juanita from the castello gardens. But with the latter three there, he was rigidly correct to all of us.

We met alone on the terrace while Elsa went to her room to change for lunch. The exquisite Elsa, even when there wasn't a fashion show being organised, changed her costume about six times a day. One was never quite sure what she would appear in next.

I sat there, absorbing sun and pine and sea-scented air, eyes on the line of the lazy blue sea beyond the pine forest, tracing the smudge of smoke from a liner, wondering if she was bound for England, or east-wards, through the Mediterranean, envy-ing her happy passengers, enjoying this old world without fighting any of the shadows which lay over my part of it, when I heard Lars behind me.

"Ruth!"

I rose, turned, saw him in white silk shirt, brown velvet trousers, beard and hair glowing in the bright, clear air.

I stayed mutinously silent. Let him speak, I thought, speak, and somehow betray himself.

"Ruth, please, look at me!"

As, reluctantly, I met his gaze, it was to find him faintly smiling, as if he guessed my thoughts and was ready to annihilate them. His eyes were narrowed, against the sun, so that I felt the real Lars was hidden somewhere at the back of those dark eyes. But then, there was no real Lars. Lars Sven, I reminded myself, was an imposter, a man hiding a criminal past under a false identity.

Perhaps this contempt showed in my face, schooling myself though I was, to control it. For his expression imperceptibly changed; the mouth grew less firm, there was an indecisiveness, a blurring, about the whole.

"You wanted to say something?"

"Yes. About your friend Jenny. And Mr. Hamilton, the Englishman. I am very sorry I spoke as I did."

"My friend, Jenny!" I repeated, slowly. "Look, I don't understand why you keep talking of her like that. I thought, at least till very recently, that she was . . . well, close enough to you to be more than just a friend."

He moved away from me slightly, to

374

stand within the shade of a cactus, an enormous thing with pointed leaves and giant, purple-tinted flowers, shifting his position either to escape that blazing sun or me.

"So did I," he answered sombrely, surprising me by this lack of prevarication, this apparent sincerity and honesty. "But I have no selfish desire to blacken your memory of her. I know how very much you loved her."

He turned again, half-smiling. I had to beat down, then, the sudden flowering attraction I felt towards him, a yearning, almost, to step nearer to him, to tell him all that I'd learned, to ask him, vehemently and hopefully, to deny it.

For he said, in that dangerously sympathetic fashion, "And to be loved by little Ruth, that is indeed something to warm the heart and strengthen the mind."

"We were parentless orphans," I reminded him, and saw his face change again, grow wary and tight. The newspaper report, I decided, and Jenny, saying she should search for her parents and her past. Compassion, and that other, darker attraction, died. I suppose few women would not have found him compelling. He was handsome, eminently successful, and the very knowledge that he possessed a hidden past, gave him an added lure. But it was the wrong kind of lure, and I was an indulgent fool ever to allow myself to warm towards him, to begin in my mind to make allowances and excuses for him. For I was beginning to wonder if he might even be what he represented himself to be, and no fake at all.

That was what part of me yearned to believe, and, in mounting self-disgust and horror, I knew why!

He stepped nearer, put his hands on my shoulders and kept them there. I suspected, the second I tried to move away, he would tighten his grip—to indicate the mastery he could exert over me, if he so chose.

So I just stayed still under his hands, unyielding, and tense. And I heard him give a little sigh under his breath, as if he realised he couldn't conquer me.

"Ruth," he said very quietly, in an odd tone that I couldn't decide was baffled anger or even thwarted desire. "Ruth, my

376

dear girl, I wish you'd go home. Back to England. Where you belong."

Even though this was so much an echo of my own thoughts as to be almost telepathic, as if he'd been reading my subconscious mind, and divined my true feelings, I was still astonished.

"But it's scarcely a month since you asked me to stay on here, and be your secretary!"

"Yes," he said curtly. Dropping his hands, he took out a cigarette, lighted it, and stared out over the blue sea. "I know. And I thought it would work out. But it hasn't."

"I'm perfectly satisfied," I lied. "Of course, if I haven't given you satisfaction . . ."

This was absurd. Any girl straight from a secretarial college could have given him satisfaction, for all the work she had to do! What could he possibly mean?

"It's Jenny, isn't it?" I accused, when he didn't answer. "Somehow, in my coming, I've reminded you of her— perhaps too much for your peace of mind!"

His face darkened. He pitched the

cigarette onto the nearest flower bed, and turned to me.

"What do you mean?" he asked curtly. "My peace of mind?"

"You said she'd not been loyal," I reminded him, realising I'd gone too far, that I must soothe his suspicions. "You made those unpleasant innuendoes about her and Ian Hamilton, and you were angry when I defended her."

"If I hurt your sense of loyalty again, I apologise, Ruth. But only for the wound to your feelings. Jenny was promiscuous —all her friends knew it. Most of them, including you, I see, thought none the worse of her for it."

"That's not quite true, Lars," I returned, with considerable dignity. "She was a girl who yearned to be loved, really loved and wanted. She pursued love, because she, and I, had so little of it as kids. But I never approved of the way she —flitted—like a butterfly from affair to affair. At the beginning, I told her so. But it was useless. The early years in the orphanage hurt her, left a wound, and Jenny tried to heal it by reaching out, with both hands, for all she could get. I didn't think any the worse of her. She was my friend, and so I would never have condemned. Anyway, we'd been through too much together—crying ourselves to sleep in each other's arms in the orphanage many a time . . ."

I stopped, lips trembling, horrified at these revelations which had come tumbling out. But he—he was still staring, apparently unmoved, at the sea, and after a moment, in control of myself again, I went on, "Anyway, you are a man of the world. You must have known."

"No," he said and turned, his tone quietly savage. "I knew all that, Ruth. Yes. As you say, I am a man of the world. But between Jenny and me, there was an understanding. Or so, you see, I foolishly thought. As my intended wife, that sort of amorality was to have ended. We talked, and it was mutually agreed. But she didn't play fair, as I discovered. It was that Englishman."

Well, if that had been true, I felt sorry for him. But I didn't believe it. Ian had told me it was a bloody lie.

"You said nothing about this when I

first came to the castello, Lars. Why these sudden revelations now?"

"I see you don't believe me. But it is the truth that I couldn't bear to hurt you. She was dead. And, I thought, why drag it all up again, to besmirch her image for this lonely, so dear friend."

"You're very considerate," I said bitterly. "But no, I don't believe you—"

"And that's why I want you to go home. I have sensed your growing antagonism towards me these past few days. I fear we can no longer live, or work, in amity. And Castello Minerva, with its dreams of her, is bad for you. You keep brooding about her, imagining you see her here. It is becoming a malaise in you."

Bewildered, I suddenly wondered if that, indeed, was the real truth, and all the rest of it a dream, evolved from sick fancies and imaginings.

"Go home?" I faltered. "You mean now, at once?"

"No. That would be inconvenient and distressing for us both. I have grown fond of you, little Ruth. I am sorry it has to end like this. But I am thinking only of

380

your ultimate happiness when I suggest it."

"Suggest?" I threw back. For, of course, he was master of Castello Minerva. I knew a command when I heard one!

"Perhaps you would consent to stay till the end of the month? That would give us both time to make our necessary arrangements."

So that I could apply for my tickets, book myself in, in advance, at some English boardinghouse, let it be known, by Ian Hamilton and others on the island who might enquire, that I'd made genuine plans to leave?

So that, if anything sinister should befall me on the journey it could be arranged to look like an accident?

Ah, how cunning, how fiendishly subtle and clever! Why should I feel so hurt, so personally rejected, when he could think up such a plan?

"Very well, Lars. If you wish to dispense with my services, as you so obviously do, I'll make arrangements to leave at the end of the month."

Relief, and something I couldn't define, flitted over his face.

"But," I went on, "I shall probably not leave the island. I think I'll stay on to find other employment. You see, as you really must know from what I've been foolish enough to tell you, there's nothing for me to go home to."

"Foolish enough," he said very sharply disregarding the pathos and the self-pity in my words. "What did you mean by that? Foolish enough?"

I'd meant something entirely different to the interpretation I now gave him, but it seemed wiser not to provoke him too far.

"I fear I've bored you," I said gently. "Babbling of my life in the orphanage, my loneliness, Jenny's loneliness. How could you want to hear all that? I'm sorry."

Back in the tower apartment office, typing away at some quite unimportant list, just in case he decided to pursue me there, I wondered had I made another mistake by hinting I should stay on the island? If I'd gone away, they might have just let me vanish, forgotten, the English nuisance, the poker and pryer who had finally taken herself off. But, on the island, freelancing, having to be watched, I must be a perpetual threat.

I telephoned Juanita, saying I didn't want lunch. I was busy, I said to her protests, with last minute details for the fashion show.

As I typed my ridiculous list, one eye on the door, I wondered about Ian, frightened that they had found out about our visit to the cementario, perhaps even got Felipe or Marie, unknown to us, to follow us there. And now had Ian hidden away somewhere, trying to make him talk, tell what he knew.

Ought I to go to the Majorcan police? Or to the British Consul? What if I hurried out and down to the English Club in Palma, to put in a call to New Scotland Yard? I'd never have enough money for a coin box, or enough time. And what if I had? Could I say, "Come at once to Castello Minerva. I believe my friend Jenny Midnight was murdered here. And an Englishman is masquerading under an assumed identity. He, and two friends, Doctor and Madame Gertae, are dangerous criminals."

They would demand evidence, proof.

"Please! Go at once to Cementario Genova and open the coffin of Jenny

Midnight. The coffin that's *supposed* to be Jenny Midnight's . . ."

Even to me, it sounded bizarre, unbelievable. I'd go on waiting, just a little longer. After all, the fog had really only cleared completely that morning.

The fashion show went on. There were even moments when I forgot the peril I was in, forgot to worry about Ian, or even to remember Jenny consciously, although she was always there, at the back of my mind, an elusive presence.

For there was magic in Lars' command of his creative world, in the atmosphere and gaiety and sophistication of the fashion show! He created a kind of other-worldly oblivion, bringing, oddly, a touch of the real domain of fairyland, of make-believe into the old castello, giving it a romantic enchantment. Almost as if, I thought wistfully, it had come into its own, for just these few happy, busy hours.

"Madame Elsa wears an evening robe of ivory jersey, designed by me, the material coming from the Paris fashion house of Gita, having a gold thread interwoven—"

And I came back to the immediate present, to the sight of Elsa, hair piled high, real pearls encircling her throat, Sven's gown clinging seductively to her superb form, poised halfway up the circular stairway. Cameras whirred, pens and pencils flew. Sven looked, furtively, at his watch.

I stood, then, on the second corridor. Lars, the correspondents and photographers were grouped below Elsa. He looked up. Our eyes met. Very curtly, he said, "Number twenty-five. The penultimate piece of the collection. Mark it off in the catalogue, if you will be so kind, Miss Foundling."

And attend to your duties, insinuated the tone!

So, he'd noticed my preoccupation, and was no doubt speculating on whether I really did intend to leave the castello, and the island.

As Elsa flowed through the open circular door of the tower apartment, to pose for other photographers in the grounds, the six other Majorcan girls descended.

This was Lars' pièce de résistance. There were murmurs of approval, and some clapping, as the Majorcans, all wearing evening or day dresses cunningly adapted from aspects of their national costume, paraded down.

"Zoe, wearing a night piece," Lars intoned professionally. "Pepita, in an afternoon ensemble. Marguerite, ready for the opera—"

He talked, the cameras whirled, the girls smilingly paraded and pirouetted, moving down the antique, shadowed setting of the circular stairway, out through the door, and into the sun-flooded gardens, following Elsa.

I ached for them to go, and at last it was over. The notebooks were closed, the cameras and programmes packed into the backs of cars, the coffee, sandwiches, and local delicacies Juanita and Marie had spent all morning preparing, consumed.

What orders Lars got, of course, would come not directly to him, but through the distinguished handful of fashion houses which he served.

Wearily, with aching legs and head, I went back to my office to tidy up the chaos and speculate on the brilliant paradox this man presented. His flair for design, colour, and texture, taking him to the top of his professional tree, bespoke an instinctive love of beauty, but his baser instincts and ambitions had been responsible for the death of three helpless women!

When, later, I went outside, the gardens were deserted. I suddenly remembered, fear gripping my heart, that Dr. Gertae had not been at the castello all that day. Elsa had driven herself up, early that morning, after dropping him at the El Pineo Nursing Home!

The previous night, at dinner, he'd made some ironic excuse about not being interested in fashion shows. At the time, I'd fancied the jest had a hollow ring.

The sun was glinting on the water. I thought, with real longing, of the private beach, and the cool waves lapping at it. Since, to enter the east wing again meant I must encounter Lars, whom at all costs I wished to avoid, I decided not to return for my bikini, but to go down to the beach and have at least an hour or two alone, before the ordeal of dinner with Lars and the Gertaes, and Marie slipping in and out with her eternal smirk, was forced upon me.

Marie was another mystery. What did

she really know? What could she know? Unless she was in the confidence of Lars and the Gertaes, she must be innocent.

There's something missing, I decided, eyeing the terraces warily and slipping around the side of the castello, just in case any hidden eyes had me under surveillance from the tower apartment or the remaining portion of the castello. I was sure that, at the heart of this mystery, there was still a fact which Ian and I hadn't yet uncovered. And it was that which Jenny found out, and why she met her death.

A path, covered by thick crimson rose bushes arranged like a tunnel, led to the swimming pool from that side of the castello. Bees hummed amongst the blossoms. The rich, heavy essence of them was all about me. The petals, like blood-red confetti, were bruised under my sandals. A drowsy loveliness held the castello gardens. Here something of the fairy tale-like atmosphere generated by the fashion show had spilled out, and held me captive.

Emerging from the arcade of roses, I saw the swimming pool almost under my feet. In any real fairy tale, I mused, there would be, of course, a lake, with the enchanted castle set in the centre of it.

The knight who was to rescue the princess would either swim or row across those waters, to knock upon the iron-studded door, sword in hand, and demand instant entrance. The password would be, "In the name of love."

Smiling, I relished my fantasy till, looking down, I saw blood-red petals floating forlornly on the pool's waters, and a twig of pine, and then a cone. Felipe dragged the pool with a net every few days.

Jenny had never been much of a swimmer. The ugly thought that followed on that violently destroyed the spell I'd been creating. But I thought, they'd never dare that, not in daylight, with the risk of some stranger coming up those beach steps, private though they were. And then there was Juanita, who would surely not remain silent at something like that.

The pine branches swayed and murmured, and in their soughings, melancholy yet languorous, I caught the echo of a remembered voice. But this voice was not Jenny's, nor Ian's, but that of Lars

Sven, and it was harsh and grim "Ruth, I
want you to go home! Ruth, you must go
home!"

And myself, answering, forlornly, "But
I have no home! I have no home!"

Small paths, mossy and overgrown,
lined with thorn and bracken, wound away
through the forest. There were acres of
untrod forest in there, dim, hidden clear-
ings, where any unmarked grave could
stay undiscovered—perhaps for months,
years, even decades or centuries.

Caught thus on the forest's edge, I
looked back. The castello was now black
against the afternoon sky. I pictured Lars
within, talking to the photographers or
correspondents who remained; Elsa, lying
on her bed, resting; the pretty Majorcan
girls chattering and laughing over their
successful debut.

And forward again, into the green,
mysterious, subtly-inviting shades of the
pine forest. Once inside it I, too, might
fight and scream, but those thickly-planted
trees, that crowding undergrowth, would
insulate all human sound.

I clambered down the steep stone steps

beyond it, to emerge on to the rough shingle of the beach.

Halfway along, between the steps and promontory, I found a little enclave of sand edged with grass. In this sanctuary I lay down, the pines just shading me from the sun, took out my cigarettes, and allowed my mind to drift into that deliberate reverie which is often conducive to the deepest subconscious revelation.

"Give a dog a bad name and hang him," I thought, remembering that this was the accusation I'd flung, so indignantly, at Ian Hamilton.

But, accepting that Lars Sven could not be tried, certainly under British law, for a crime of which, twenty years before, he'd been judged innocent, was there, conceivably, some other crime of which he was guilty and for which he'd never been brought to trial at all?

And I wasn't thinking of Jenny then, but of something done between the death of Rosalie Saunders and when Jenny had met him.

Obviously the Gertaes were implicated, insofar as a bogus death certificate had been issued, and there was the matter of the concealment either of Jenny's body or of Jenny herself. Was I then to assume that Jenny might still be alive somewhere? Kept prisoner, perhaps, either in the castello, or somewhere else—perhaps not even Majorca?

The motorboat trips which Lars Sven and Felipe took were described by my employer as fishing trips. True, Juanita, when they did come back, got plenty of fish of all kinds for our table, but with such a man, he would make sure to keep his feints in countenance, if only for my benefit.

Jenny might have stumbled on this secret, whatever it was. Marie, infatuated with her master, made out she'd seen Ian and Jenny together. So, was Marie Lars Sven's spy, or had the girl, in jealousy, invented the tale?

Juanita had hinted Lars made love to Marie. That wasn't all that significant, one way or the other.

That she would serve him, without asking too many awkward questions, I was fairly certain, but of the fact that she would actually break the law on his account, I was less sure. That sullenness, unpleasant though it could be, hinted at a strong will. If Lars went against her moral code, which in women of her class and race was deeply-rooted, I felt she would turn against him.

From the evidence of that iron box, I felt it was psychologically possible Lars Sven had loved only one woman, ever, and that one was the exquisite Rosalie, whom he'd killed in a fit of dark and jealous passion.

The sound of the waves, the soughing of the scented pines, made a lullaby. Pitching away my cigarette, I soon slept soundly as I'd not slept for days, ever since I came, in fact, to that luxurious bedroom now fast assuming the feel of a prison cell.

But when the first soundness of sleep was spent I dreamed I was in the pine forest, Lars Sven pursuing me. I dodged in terror from tree to tree, hair flying, dress front open, like a woman fighting off her seducer. Then I saw Ian Hamilton, waving a newspaper, on which was printed, not Jenny, or Rosalie's picture, but my own! And before me yawned an open grave with a coffin in it. I dared not approach it, for I knew my name would be on it.

Lars caught up with me, was pushing me towards the grave! But all the time he was smiling diabolically, and whispering, "Ruth—my little Ruth—I won't ever let you go. You won't get off this beautiful island, or away from me."

With that cry ringing in my ears I awoke, to find that the sun had disappeared. The Mediterranean was an uncharacteristic and decidedly stormy looking slate grey, and the breeze had risen to a wind, which moaned amongst the pines and sent pieces of debris rattling over the pebbles of the deserted beach.

Even as I scrambled, in some dismay, to my feet, not wanting to add to my troubles by getting drenched in a semi-tropical storm, rain suddenly came down in torrents, and, within seconds, my light linen dress and straw Majorcan sandals were soaked.

I eyed the stretch of beach between me and the steps. A quarter of a mile, at least! Behind lay the pine forest, but that, although offering shelter from the elements, was still, for me, eerily-haunted and forbidding, especially in light of that unpleasant dream.

Immediately westwards lay the rocky promontory at which Ian had, only a few days ago, tied up his boat.

Before stupidly drifting off to sleep, I'd noticed the mouth of a small cave close to the shore. Shelter enough, I decided, till the worst of the storm had spent itself. From my growing knowledge of the island, storms blew up, and out, usually in ten or fifteen minutes, and I could afterwards, if the sun came out, dry myself out.

Majorca was honeycombed with caves, I remembered, as I shuffled across, my sandals squelching over the shingle and pebble to the entrance. There was the *Cuevas del Drach*, or Caverns of the Dragon, holding a lake six hundred feet long, with stalactites growing in it, that was one of the wonders of the island. Then there were the caves of Arta, over by Puerto Cristo. Juanita had urged the merits of both upon me, and, in the early days of my coming to the castello, Lars had promised to take me to see them.

The small cave into which I awkwardly came, however, seemed to contain nothing miraculous or marvellous, being very dark, its surface strewn with boulders and smaller stones. No sooner had I got inside it, however, then there was a tremendous crack of thunder from above my head, and lightning zigzagged over the sea.

Instinctively, for I am afraid of thunder, I retreated further into the cave, once plunging almost up to my knees in a pool of icy-cold water, and giving a small, involuntary scream which sent weird echoes reverberating along the passage.

Deciding that since I was a voluntary prisoner till the storm passed, I might as well explore my cell, I clambered further on into the cave.

After ten minutes or so of this groping, the daylight behind me faded, and I was in the dark. Without lights or a torch, it was difficult to go on, and I was just turning back, when, ahead, light of a kind gleamed and lured me on again.

Rounding a sort of pillar, I emerged into a clearing open to the sky, with a sandy floor, but with rocks all around it. Evidently, through storm or accident, at some time in the past the ground above had fallen, letting in the daylight. Staring up westwards I had another glimpse of the pine woods, and far to the left, the steps to the castello's terraces. On the other hand the rocky coast below the castello and the pine woods fell away to the sea.

I caught a sharp breath. Immediately ahead was a great standing rock, but between it and the bulwark of land margining the shore, there was a space. Slipping behind this, I found myself face-to-face with an iron door upon which was stuck a notice: CASTELLO MINERVA. PRIVATE. KEEP OUT.

And I knew that this was another entrance to the castello dungeons, that it was kept private, indeed, since it stood, anyway, on a private beach. Stepping forward, I tried the rusty iron handle. The door was locked, and I didn't doubt, behind the lock, bolted and barred.

Then, as I stood shivering and excited before it, common sense told me that there was, very naturally, an outlet from the old part of the castello; in the days of the Moorish occupation, and in the time of Duke Manuel, this outlet from the dungeons was probably used for ordinary enough purposes. Indeed, anything could well have been landed right at the entrance, by a small boat coming up on the seaward side, or perhaps, hauled over the short bastion of rock. There was space enough, where I stood, for cargo to be thrust in from the sea or out again, I mused, into the waters of the Mediterranean!

Surveying the door again, and particularly the keyhole, I could detect no sign that it had been recently opened. Wind and weather, anyway, would beat upon it, through those fissures and cracks in the breached way before it. Like the door in the tower apartment, it was heavily studded with iron, and on the bottom, centuries of water dripping down from the rocks, had eroded the strip of heavy metal which buttressed it there.

Then I realised that either the large circular chamber, or one of the smaller dungeons, must have an exit, leading to the passage to the sea which ended at this door. And, in that innermost passage, what?

Another vicious crack of thunder sent me cowering against it, so that the iron studs pressed cruelly into my flesh. When imagination again suggested what might lie behind it, I shuddered away from contact with it, and carefully picked my way back down the passage to the entrance to the cave on the private beach.

Heedless, now, of the flailing rain, I stumbled across the scree and pebbles to the wooden steps, and gasping partly from shock and partly from effort and hurry, hauled myself to the top.

There, I halted, staring at the castello, eyes raking the terraces and the building. There was a light burning in the salon, where I guessed Lars was taking tea with, perhaps, some of those dilatory guests. Otherwise, there was no sign of movement or life.

Dodging along under the shelter of the pines, although not entering that hated wood, I made a breathless way back under the rose tunnel. I'd go to the tower apartment, I decided, and dry myself out there, keeping well away from the east wing, in case, in a clandestine attempt to climb the stairs to my room unheeded, I was seen by Lars or the Gertaes.

The door to the tower apartment was half ajar, and I slipped thankfully inside.

There was a spare pair of jeans, and an old working blouse which I kept in the office. I could change and go back to the east wing, and even stroll in on Lars for tea, thus keeping up the fiction that I'd not left the castello.

I had one foot on the circular stair when, to my horror, his studio door was thrust open, and there he stood, in the crumpled smock he often wore when he was working, a brush in his hand.

"Ruth!" he said quietly, and came towards me. "You're drenched to the skin, girl!"

Head high, I faced him, suddenly curious to know what he'd say, how he would react, if I told him where I'd been, and what I'd seen. That folly, at least, I didn't commit, and the half-lie came glibly enough to my tongue.

"Yes." Even the rueful little laugh I essayed came, I thought, with strange, equally cynical facility to my lips. "Your charming island is full of surprises, Lars! I thought it never rained here. I went for a stroll and got caught in the storm."

"For a stroll?" he said gently, but his dark eyebrows were elevated, and I did not like the mocking twist of his lips above the immaculate beard. Deliberately I avoided his eyes, dreading what I should see there.

"Yes," I returned, defiantly. "Along the road beyond the entrance gates."

His glance travelled, thoughtfully, but in the same mocking fashion, to my feet. Not making the mistake of following it, I was well aware of my sea-stained, rock-scratched sandals, and the mud on my naked calves and ankles.

"I see," he said, in the same diabolically gentle tone. "Why did you not go at once to your room to change?"

Anger and indignation stirred in me, but I subdued them.

"As you've already noticed, I'm in something of a mess," I returned coolly. "The road surface beyond the gates got churned up by the storm. Not wanting to spoil Juanita's lovely polished stairs I came here first to dry off and change into some other clothes I left here."

That he believed me I never credited for a second. All I was interested in was whether he would challenge me, assure me he knew I was bent on deceiving him, and that I'd been doing that for days.

But he only gave me another silent, inscrutable stare, and nodded. Then, just as I thought, with a surge of relief, he was turning away, he said, "Look Ruth, I—I wanted to find you, in any case. To thank you, for all the work you put into the fashion show. It was a great success, despite the number who couldn't come because of the fog."

The fog, I thought, yes, the island mist that had come down so inconveniently for myself and Ian Hamilton.

"I did very little," I told him. Obviously, he was just making the fashion show an excuse to keep me there, no doubt wishing to allay any more suspicions his recent attitude had aroused. If I was going, let me depart as innocent, and ignorant, as I arrived.

"Your designs were superb," I said, truthfully. "And your Parisian dressmaker magnificent."

"We have worked together for years," he answered.

Another mystery. All these men and women, professional colleagues, yet none of them knew this man was a fraud. Still, many brilliant artists used a professional name. As I'd told Ian several times, this didn't make Lars Sven a criminal.

"By the way, what happened to your idea for that book on design I was to type for you?"

Or had that been another trick to keep up his facade, and to keep me at the castello while he found out how much, or how little, Jenny might have told me?

"I've been too busy with the fashion show and—other things. But I haven't abandoned the idea. I'm sorry I shan't have the pleasure of your help in preparing the manuscript. I'd hoped you would have found it interesting—with your artistic flair."

He gives nothing away, I thought; that's how he's climbed to the top, stayed there, and kept his secrets hidden.

"Perhaps I may have the pleasure, though, of sending you a copy? For of course you'll leave us your address, on the island or wherever it may finally be, when you depart? We shouldn't like to lose touch with Jenny's friend forever."

He really must think I'm naive, I decided, and said, "Once I've left, I don't really think it's likely we shall meet again.

After all, we do live in two quite different worlds, don't we? And come from two entirely different levels of society."

He moved quickly at that, as if my words had touched some hidden nerve.

"But I'm sure I shall see your book, Lars, in one of the book shops or reviewed in the papers. After all, you're quite famous."

It was his imperturbability which maddened me and moved me to malice. For, after that small, recent start, he'd recovered at once, so that I couldn't be sure it hadn't been some natural movement.

"You really ought to write your autobiography, the story of your life."

The well-shaped lips turned up at the corners. There was the glimmer of a smile.

"But perhaps that would mean revealing all your secrets? And that might be distasteful?"

He frowned, as if over my choice of the last word. Cowardice or self-preservation had made me substitute it for the one in mind.

"Autobiographies make rather indifferent reading in my opinion, Ruth. Either the writers tell all, which is boring—one should surely leave something to the imagination—or they fall back on invention to give the work verisimilitude. And I don't care for cheating."

You hypocrite, I thought angrily, and I turned away, lest he should see how moved I was.

"Excuse me," I said formally, "I think I'd better, after all, return to my room and change properly."

I made to move past him towards the door of the tower apartment. But he caught me by the right arm, quite gently, but firmly enough so that I should feel his strength and purpose.

"Ruth, wait a moment, if you please."

And, just for a moment, my flesh shrank in terror. We were alone there, in the tower apartment, with only his allies, the Gertaes, and the servants, somewhere in the rest of the house. He was immensely powerful, tremendously strong. What was to stop him from putting his arms about my throat, choking the life out of me, then unlocking that wooden door behind the warrior in armour, and hurrying, with my corpse, down to the circular dungeon?

He would keep it there till he found the opportunity, as with Jenny, of disposing of it in the sea.

Now he stood very close, in his white working smock, in sharp relief against the dark stone of the tower's interior, fingers pressing gently yet inexorably into the flesh of my right arm.

And I caught myself thinking, is he going to attack me? Shall I scream for help? And if I do, will anyone come?

Or is this, too, prearranged, an evil contrived by the Gertaes and Marie?

"Ah, you're frightened, aren't you, little Ruth?"

His hand left my arm, very gently stroked my hair. By then, my breath was coming in long, shuddering spasms. I couldn't have answered him to save my life. I was like one hypnotised.

"Ruth," he said sharply, "don't look like that. There's nothing to harm you— not while I'm with you."

But, by then, I had my back hard against the stone wall, and with that bastion supporting me, drew freer breath again. Lars Sven dropped his hands, moved a few paces away.

"I'm sorry, Ruth. I should not have startled you like that. It's obvious to me that you find my presence distasteful. Please forgive me."

"It's all right. And I don't find you distasteful. I just can't explain . . ."

I could only gaze at him, baffled, angry with myself and, in that moment, the whole world.

"I can," he told me quietly. "I terrify you because of Jenny. That's it, isn't it?"

Impossible to tell him the truth about that! Plunging wildly into words, any words so long as they were not the traitorous ones my heart longed to speak, I cried out, "I should never have come here. It's too much, all the sadness, and the upset, about Jenny. I—I can't forget her here, you see!"

Again he stepped nearer, towering over me, his face etched in angry lines. "Why should you want to forget Jenny Midnight if you loved her as you say you did? Or did you just love some false picture of her? You didn't like what I said about Jenny and Ian Hamilton, did you?"

Wordlessly, I wrenched myself free, but

he put one arm between me and the wall, barring my passage.

"Come, tell me! This Englishman, this Ian Hamilton, how well do you know him, anyway? Any more really than you know me? Jenny knew both of us."

What did that mean? His tone was savagely cold.

"I mean," he went on deliberately, as if he'd picked up the frightened query in my mind, "that it's obvious, Ruth, from your manner and attitude, that you believe I've done something to your friend. Well, what about him, this Hamilton? He was with her on the island . . ."

"That's a damned lie!" I ground out. "I asked him. He said you or Marie made it up, that he hasn't seen Jenny since he last met her in London!"

"And you believed him?" Lars challenged. "Did Jenny ever mention him to you? Say he was a friend? As I was a friend?"

"No," I admitted. But I remembered that letter, and I straightened up, and said, "But I've good reason to trust him, and to believe what he tells me."

"I was Jenny's friend," Lars reminded me, "till Hamilton came along."

"Look, why go into all this again," I said wearily, "if this is what you kept me here, shivering and cold, to hear."

"No," said Lars. "Max and Elsa will be in the salon tonight. Elsa will be entertaining us with some songs. The atmosphere in the castello has been so disturbed of late. I thought if we had an hour or two of music, of—of conviviality, we might all be able to relax better. You will be going in a few weeks . . ."

"You told me you wanted me to go!" I reminded him.

"I think it best," he said curtly. "I really need an older woman, someone more mature. Oh, you've managed beautifully and I'm more than satisfied, but you are, at heart, an artist. You need yourself to be free, to express your individuality, to follow your own bent. I do not like to think of you, in fact, tied to an office and a routine."

I'd not felt clay or a wheel under my hands since I finished the white horse in the Mendip Cottage. Remembering it, marvelling, I felt that the Ruth of that time was an entirely different girl. Yes, that Ruth Foundling was a stranger.

"Come," he said, almost coaxing, "there is no reason, is there, why we should part in enmity? It hurts me, now, to watch the way you look at me, so scornful and yet so wary! Do I really terrify you that much?"

"Don't—don't be absurd, Lars!" I temporised, while wondering. Was this a harmless olive branch or another subtle trap? Still, an hour or two of listening to Elsa's admittedly lovely voice wouldn't harm me. I didn't see how they could hurt me any more, in the salon, than if I was locked up in my own room, or took refuge in the tower apartment.

Even if I got desperate and locked myself in the dungeons, they'd find me. My only hope lay in fighting to preserve an appearance of absolute normality. That was why I'd answered Lars as I did about my departure from the castello. It seemed to me normal to feel a certain chagrin which had produced the reaction I'd striven so hard to suggest.

Ian, I told myself desperately, Ian, please hurry up and return! As for Lars and his reproaches that I appeared terrified

410

of him, that, in one sense, was true enough, but if I played my role with sufficient finesse, I might induce him to believe this fear was that of some inexperienced girl, still recovering from a blighted love affair.

I recalled his taunt, that I believed he'd done something to Jenny. It was the first time he'd dared to put it into words, the dark suspicion that lay, like some malignant shadow, between us.

Had they noticed the absence of Ian Hamilton from his usual haunts? Perhaps Lars' probings had been made in an attempt to make me let something slip in anger or terror.

Still two hours—two desperate, dragging hours!—to the ordeal that was dinner.

Courage, I told myself, for, within that time, Ian himself could turn up with the English police and a search warrant for the examination of the castello.

"I have no wish to quarrel, Lars," I said quietly. The tragic thing for me was that part of my mind meant it! "And I should like to come to the salon concert this evening. Madame Elsa has a really lovely voice."

Well, that was the truth, in all this welter of lies, evasions, and half-truths. Perhaps thinking he saw yielding, even surrender, in me then, Lars put one hand around my waist, pulled me to him and kissed me, with great force and passion, full upon the lips.

Dear God, I thought, why should love prove so traitorous? I heard the sighing of the pines, the background murmur of the Mediterranean, felt my treacherous flesh wanting to surrender. With a gasp, I pulled myself free. Lars, without another word, let me go. There wasn't any need for me to say anything. That kiss had told me what, in myself, I dreaded to learn!

I dressed for dinner with the utmost care, choosing, after much deliberation, a plain black dress, a single rope of crystal beads and matching earrings. It chanced that the dress was the only one of my own I'd brought with me, but I felt freer in it, less chained to Lars Sven's subtle dominance.

Going down the stairs, and glancing again at my watch, I found I was early.

Entering the salon, I thought there was no one there. Then I heard, discreetly muted, the murmur of voices, with Elsa's coming through clearly at intervals.

I stood perfectly still. The dinner was laid in the dining room and Juanita and Marie talked to each other. They were unlikely to enter the salon for a little while, and probably not at all till dinner was past, since it was invariably Felipe who came in to announce this.

The french doors were half open. I realised Lars and the Gertaes must be somewhere on the central terrace or on the paths leading to the beach. Only one lamp was on by the right-hand window. Satisfied I couldn't be seen, I deliberately lingered there, my way of retreat—the door to the hall—clear behind me.

It was Dr. Gertae's voice, however, that I heard next. ". . . can't wait much longer. We've tried all the most likely and unlikely places . . . Marie's not been much use. I told Lars . . ."

I bit my lip in sheer frustration, yet I dared not go any nearer, for I had no idea just where they were, and if they came upon me eavesdropping, it would be not only embarrassing, but would shatter my carefully-played role of the gullible, stupid innocent.

Elsa's reply did nothing to reassure me either, on the latter point.

"She's very intelligent. I wonder if she's busy playing some little game of her own?"

". . . how much Jenny Midnight told her." Infuriatingly, it was the doctor's empty voice again.

". . . great friends," said Elsa, and now her voice, too, grew fainter. Then stronger again, as if she was walking to and fro. Peering through the half light, I caught only the shadowy glimmer of the trees and terraces, and the gleam of the sea beyond. "Perhaps she might not have, Max . . . protect her."

Well, that was clear enough, and pointed to some shrewd psychology on Elsa's part. Max Gertae again, sharper now, with a note of anger, and something else, in his voice.

"Wait. Which did you say her room was?"

"There. Max!"

"Yes, the damned light's gone out! She must have come down . . ."

Waiting for no more, I backed to the door and slipped into the hall, then across it and into the small, little-used library. The previous American owner had furnished it, left some of his books on art and Spanish history there, all in crimson velvet-bound volumes, lining the room from ceiling to floor. Lars Sven and the Gertaes never seemed to use it.

Obviously, the doctor and Elsa had been watching the light in my room. But I'd left it on when I went out, knowing Marie would soon be slipping up, as she usually did before helping Juanita with the dinner, to turn down the bed sheets, and lay out my night dress. No doubt the girl had gone up while I lingered in the salon.

A large, heavy green velvet curtain closed in the small library window. Breathlessly, heart thudding, I slipped behind it, and was just there when I smelt the heady perfume Elsa affected and got a whiff of the doctor's cigarette.

Mercifully the curtain was long enough to cover my feet. I stood well back against the window, so that the drape didn't bulge outwards.

Would they examine the window and the curtains? If so, what excuse could I make? There was a fairly wide window seat, but extending myself on its empty, cushioned length was awkward in the dark, and with the need to be silent.

My heart began to hammer again as Elsa's staccato footsteps neared the window.

But anger for Jenny was conquering every personal terror. For if I'd wanted confirmation they'd done something terrible to Jenny, surely I had it in those sinister, clandestine phrases.

Oh, if only Ian and the English police would come, I thought, or if Ian, at least, would telephone, send me some sign, some word!

"She's not in her room," Elsa said. "I caught Marie coming downstairs, and asked her. She saw the girl leaving it a few minutes ago."

"Then she must be in here!" the doctor said in an ugly voice. "By God, Elsa, if she—"

"Quiet," returned Elsa, and I pictured

her jerking her head towards the window, since the book-lined walls offered no possible hiding place.

Waiting tensely for the twitch of the curtain, the betraying flood of light from the crystal chandelier, I heard, instead, the small library door open, and a step, firm and strong, that I instantly recognised.

"My dear Max—Elsa!" came Lars Sven's voice in mild astonishment. "I didn't expect to find you two here! I thought we were to have a concert in the salon for Ruth."

"It's Ruth we're looking for," explained the doctor, his voice more controlled. "Marie said she came in here."

"Ruth? I saw her in the gardens a few moments ago."

Hardly able to credit my own ears, I then heard Elsa say, in obvious relief, "In the garden? She must have strolled out, then, without our seeing her, just as we came in."

"Evidently," returned Lars Sven coolly. "Elsa, what did you say to Marie?"

"Nothing, my dear Lars—don't worry! Only that we wanted to talk to her."

"The library is not the place for

talking." Lars sounded, I thought, irritated. "Come, shall we adjourn to the salon? I have some excellent sherry there, Max, which I'm sure you'll enjoy."

In a very few minutes, the small library, except for me, was empty. Creeping cautiously out, I straightened the window curtain, made sure I'd left nothing there, and turned to leave.

As I was opening the door, emerging in the same cautious manner, Felipe, in his chauffeur's uniform, came in. Instantly he saw me, frowned, then hurried forward and opened the door, very formally and correctly.

In the same manner Felipe escorted me to the salon and showed me in. Lars, Elsa, and the doctor were all gathered around the piano, Elsa with some sheets of music in her hand, the chandelier lights flashing on the diamond rings on her fingers, emphasising the midnight blue of the gown she'd chosen.

Across the length of the magnificent room, Lars—like the doctor in evening dress, with a clove carnation in his buttonhole—stared at me.

"Ah, there you are, Ruth. I hope you

enjoyed your pre-dinner stroll in the grounds. I told the doctor and Madame you would be remaining with us, after dinner, for some music."

So, he was persisting in that story. Had he imagined he glimpsed me in the castello gardens, mistaking me for Elsa, perhaps, as she hurried back into the salon? We were of the same height, and our gowns of similar hue.

"Yes," I said. "Thank you. I shall be pleased to remain."

Had he informed the Gertaes that I was, in fact, under notice to go? Uncertain of this, I felt a slight falseness in my own position, although, knowing what I did know, or what Ian and I suspected, this was no cause for shame. Perhaps it would be better if they didn't know, so that whatever they contemplated, they would be urged on to do it, and be caught in their guilt when Ian and the police came.

Lars could have seen me, too, hurrying into the small library, perhaps as he himself descended the east stairway from his own room. Or he could have gone along to my bedroom, and found it empty.

For such a big man, he moved about with uncanny softness at times.

"But we are desolated," Madame Elsa said, in her histrionic fashion. "Lars tells us you are leaving at the end of the month."

I flashed him a glance, but he was turning over the pages of her music, his face downcast. So, they knew!

"Yes," I said. "I find that I am not suited to the post which Mr. Sven was kind enough to offer me, after all."

"But we all thought how well you had accomplished your duties," put in the doctor smoothly. "You seem to me to be the perfect secretary type, if I may say so!"

He made it sound like an insult, as if all secretaries were meek and subservient, and fit only for obeying commands.

"You're very kind, Dr. Gertae. And Madame. But, as Mr. Sven himself says, an older woman is really needed here. One with more experience and, possibly, poise."

"But I did not even hint that, Ruth," Lars interrupted. "It is just, as I told you, that I myself think you should be concentrating on your own studies."

"Ah, yes, you make pots, do you not, on the wheel?" questioned Madame. "That is strange, because I should never have thought you were artistic! A quiet little mouse, like you."

It seemed to lie somewhere between a jeer and a compliment, but I said, coolly, "Perhaps, Madame Gertae, you would feel me to be more in character if I went about with lumps of clay in my hair? Or wearing dirty jeans and a sloppy blouse?"

Madame shrugged. Her look said, plainly enough, I do not care what a little peasant like you does . . . I cultivate you for only one reason.

"Ruth, we were just going through Madame's repertoire," interposed Lars. "Now, what is your preference? The classical, perhaps, or a ballad, something—"

"Sentimental and simple," cut in Madame, "in keeping with her character. So charming!"

No doubt it was foolish of me, but I'd been provoked and insulted.

"I'm sure you must all know by now," I retorted, "that my education was of the scantiest. In an orphanage, or certainly in the one which reared me, we got little opportunity to hear any music, save for the plainest and dullest of hymns."

"Ruth," began Lars with an embarrassed look for me, "I don't think . . ."

"You and your charming guests want to hear the story of my life?" I responded brightly. "I'm sorry. I'm sure you don't. Shocking bad taste on my part. Still, there is a thing I like, but I shouldn't think Madame Gertae would know it. There was a middle-aged old nurse, sentimental and old-fashioned, like me. She used to sing it to us, when Matron wasn't around . . ."

Again Lars' look came to me, charged now with that peculiar, searching expression which both baffled and intrigued me.

"Us?" he said.

"Yes. Jenny and me." I found that there was a lump in my throat. Because I felt so peculiarly vulnerable, and defenceless, I decided not to withdraw, as wisdom and prudence were now imploring me to do!

Madame, by now, was looking piqued; the doctor surveyed me with his curiously cold, scientific stare—as if I was some strange creature in a specimen jar.

"Perhaps you could sing it?" suggested Madame, in a tone wholly idle. "If I could hear it once I'm sure I could manage a suitable rendition. I pick up refrains very easily . . ."

Almost as if he could read my mind, Lars Sven put down the glass he was holding and stepped nearer.

"Yes, Ruth, let's hear it! I should like to know something of your taste in music."

"Jenny's taste too," I said steadfastly. "All right . . ." Was that my laugh, self-confident and almost brazen, without a trace of worry or fear? Well, I was fighting for her, not myself; it made all the difference.

I stepped away from them, the glare from the chandelier hypnotic and confusing, almost as mind-deadening as Lars' stare. I took refuge in the cover of the shadows. My hands shaking, I clasped them behind my back, dug my nails viciously into my palms, and took a deep breath.

My voice is thin, but I have always been told I render the notes true. As I heard that reedlike contralto though, wavering uncertainly out into the huge salon, it sounded like the voice of a complete stranger.

Some letters tied with blue,
A photograph or two,
I count them all
Among my souvenirs . . .

I broke off, unable to continue, and stood there thinking only of that box down in the cellar, and whatever else might be hideously bricked up there. I prayed those walls didn't hold the rotting flesh and bones of someone once infinitely dear to me!

From the others, silence—weighty and more clamorous, somehow, than if they'd all burst into talk at once . . . a silence that, to me, was loaded with guilt and screamed of secrets.

And I wanted to scream too, breaking it, crying out my suspicions, my discoveries, accusing them, breaking their nerve, winning from them some betraying gesture, some clue or hint as to what they had really done to my friend.

Then from across the hall came a faint clattering and the sound of Juanita's deep voice as she and Marie completed their dinner preparations.

I felt a faintness growing in me, a sickness, as the figures of the Gertaes seemed to grow smaller, fade away into the background.

But Lars stepped deliberately forward like, I thought, someone answering a challenge. His eyes had narrowed to slits and his face was contorted, the well-cut lips twisting downwards. Was it pain, anger, or perhaps only chagrin that Jenny's friend had so far betrayed her own humble beginnings, her lack of sophisticated taste, in warbling out, and so badly, the verse of that sentimental little song?

"I congratulate you, Miss Foundling. You are overly modest. In its way, that is quite an attractive little voice and I remember the song. One hears it now and again but, of course, it was popular very long ago."

Then his voice, so low only I could possibly have heard it, whispered, "What the devil do you mean by that, eh? What subtle little game do you think you're playing?"

And, looking up into those near-black

eyes, that dark and frowning countenance, I thought: was this how he spoke, how he looked when Jenny met her end?

"You must excuse me," I cried wildly, "but I—I don't feel well again. I think it was probably the song. It brought back—old memories."

I turned and fled up the stairs to my room. There, I locked the door and flung myself down on the bed, to give way to such a flood of tears that I sobbed myself into a torpor, and lay there as the sun set over the Mediterranean.

The tears were, of course, a necessary catharsis. Afterwards, I rose, showered, changed into my night attire and, taking a book and cigarettes, prepared grimly to spend yet another night of torment under the roof of Castello Minerva.

I heard Lars Sven come to my door and knock, towards midnight. When I didn't answer, he called, very softly but clearly, "Ruth? Ruth are you awake? I want to talk to you."

The safest answer, of course, was silence. Yet it took all my nerve to lie there when he knocked again and called in that obstinately persistent voice, "Ruth, do you hear? I must talk to you!"

Would he batter down the door? Was he alone, or did he have the Gertaes with him, all three of them waiting for me to unlock the door and be entirely at their mercy?

My silence continued, but I furtively rose and went to the verandah door. The moon was up now. The terraces, rose arbors, guardian pines and sea were etched silver and black. The magic scent of pine and sea drifted languorously through the air.

"Ruth! Ruth!" The steady beat of Lars' voice seemed to blend with the sea and pines, becoming one with it, a lure working on my heart and mind. As he called "Ruth, Ruth!" the loneliness, the frustrated yearning searing my heart, longed to respond, even though I knew what he was, and what he might be!

Had Jenny, I thought in horror, finally surrendered? Then, finding herself over-whelmed, killed herself? Had these strangers within the castello seeking, for reasons of their own, to hush up this pitiful self-killing, then arranged that monstrous charade of a funeral?

Yet why did I feel so persistently that some personal destiny directed my footsteps here; that although I'd rationalised my pilgrimage as allied to that old telepathic link with Jenny, I was to be the instrument for some other purpose now but dimly comprehended?

Then I heard Jenny's voice again, but it came, as I knew, from out of the past:

"There must be something, somewhere, into which we go. Otherwise our lives here would make no sort of sense . . ."

Lingering there, armouring myself against opening the door, I saw something white thrust under the door and then, Lars' voice, level and quite loud, as if in signal to any who might wish to hear, "Goodnight then, Ruth."

Switching on the light, and quickly pulling the curtains—in case anyone lurked in the shadows of the garden—I moved to the door, bent down, and retrieved the letter. Enclosed within a thick white envelope in Lars' bold, heavy script was the message laconic and, as usual, as enigmatic and ambiguous as the man himself.

> Ruth,
> I have asked you to leave the castello. After tonight, the sooner you go the better.
> Please make yourself available to see me, for the last time, in my studio at eight o'clock tomorrow evening.
> Lars Sven

The note was a command. If I didn't come, clearly, he would have me brought.

So I was right! He'd got the message of that song, knew I'd plumbed at least part of his secret, and was going to get rid of me by this feint of sending me away.

Nothing, of course, would induce me to keep that rendezvous. The thing was, should I run away now? But, if I did, how would Ian know where to find me? If I went to the airport, how could I be certain of finding him there? Or to the cementario? If he came in daylight, that would be all right, but to spend a night there was more than I could bear!

Because there was nothing else to do, I

went to bed. I even slept to wake, around dawn, to the sight of bright rays striking the french doors and the realisation that another day of suspense lay ahead of me.

13

A FALSE dawn—a betrayer—like everything else, it seemed, about Castello Minerva and its setting. Falling at daybreak into an exhausted, unrefreshing sleep, I wakened again to the sound of wind howling around the ancient walls dropping, now and again, to small, sobbing gusts.

Outside, pines and garden shrubs leaned forlornly inland, blown down by the wind. Whitecaps edged the Mediterranean wavelets. Small sticks and branches, torn down from the pines, floated in the swimming pool.

The ocean was so grey it might almost have been the Severn Sea. The pines and terraces, falling to the beach, seemed like the valley cut in the Mendip cliffs, where I'd shared the early summer, the idyll that turned sour, with Ralph.

Now it wasn't Ralph, but Lars who had turned on me so brutally and so openly, showing his hand at last. As I recalled the night before, I rose hastily, showered and dressed, and made my way downstairs to breakfast.

Lars and Felipe had gone out early, in the motorboat. As I'd dressed I'd noticed the small vessel bobbing about on the unkind seas, till, as usual, it vanished out of sight over the horizon. But I recollected, too, those powerful field glasses; they could easily keep the castello in sight.

Lars' attitude alarmed me, so much so that before actually going in to breakfast, I hurried over to the tower apartment. Going immediately to the studio, I found the door unlocked.

After that, it seemed pointless bothering to raise the carpet and the brick. But I did, and the yawning, empty cavity mocked me, like the look, last night, in the dark eyes of my employer.

Still, that didn't necessarily mean he'd taken the key because he was certain I'd been down into the dungeons. He might, for instance, suspect Juanita or, for all that I could tell, Marie.

I had sung the song, on impulse. Now, it was likely enough to prove a fatal one. It was as if I'd said through the words of the song, "Yes, I've fallen in love with you. That I can't help. But all the same, I know you're a fake, and a cheat, and I'm almost certain, a murderer. You're not worth loving. Unfortunately, one can't command love. But after this is over, I can put you out of my heart and memory. And I've still to do what I came here to do—find out what you did to Jenny."

I'd shocked him. Frightened him, too. But even so, he could still have decided I only knew about the iron box, the letter and the photograph, because Jenny told me. Because she'd gone down there and found out for herself.

It didn't follow he had any proof I'd ever been down into the dungeons myself. I wondered how Jenny, if she had found the box, discovered behind which one of the iron rings it lay. I, of course, had literally stumbled upon the secret.

Recalling that quiet, sinister whisper, "What did you mean by it, eh?" fear returned again. Lars Sven, had looked then as if he'd like to murder me on the spot.

Standing there beside his studio, with the armoured figure glimmering outside the dungeons' entrance, I found I was suddenly shivering uncontrollably.

And I realised that, after last night, I couldn't remain at the castello alone and under threat from so many forces, declared and undeclared. Ian might come, or telephone, today. Or, it might be another two or three days or longer before I heard from him.

Or never, I thought, and suddenly stopped shivering. What if I really was waiting and depending on Ian all in vain. Not, after all, because Lars Sven or the Gertaes had done anything to him, but because he'd lost his own nerve, and quietly gone back to England to selfishly leave me to face the music?

Then logic and common sense asserted themselves, and I realised that Ian, from his past behaviour, would never be capable of such a craven-hearted act. No, if he left me to cope alone, it would be because he, too, had been dealt with—just like Jenny.

But if by tonight, say after dinner at the latest, I'd not heard, then it was clear I must act alone.

I decided that after dinner would be the best time to make my escape, when we moved from the dining room to the salon. I wouldn't wait beyond then for I knew that my nerve must crack if I dared to accept the grim challenge of the rendezvous with Lars. It was a challenge he knew I should find hard to resist.

I reminded myself of those smaller mysteries, the missing pill bottle, the piece of crumbling masonry flung from the battlements, my collapse at the dining table. Yet to go immediately to the airport, or down to the docks, would be an almost fatal mistake. Safer to loiter in Palma, slipping from one cafe to another; then, in the small hours, take a taxi to the airport. I realised, when I gave it more thought, that my chance of getting a berth aboard a ship was minimal, even if it was nearing the end of the summer tourist season.

Back in the east wing, Juanita said "La Tramontana," the storm wind from Africa, was blowing, but that it would last only another twenty-four hours. Then, she had said, "Senorita Ruth, the world, it will be all sunshine again!"

She had told me this at breakfast. The Gertaes weren't down yet. Hearing them coming, I followed Juanita over the hall into her kitchen, carrying an empty dish as if going after rolls, butter, or jam.

"Why you leave here, eh?" she astonished me by saying as she ladled jam into the held-out dish. So she had been told.

"You not like it here, Senorita? Something is wrong, si? We not treat you right?"

We stood in the large, modern kitchen, with its walls of Moorish tiles, and its big windows looking out on her capacious herb and vegetable gardens. And I couldn't help wondering what she would say if she knew I would be gone from the castello that very night.

Juanita, though, looked hurt. Perhaps she imagined I was leaving because of her cooking or her housekeeping. Both were impeccable, yet, as I recollected the green velvet Cheshire cat, I absurdly felt my colour rising.

Absurdly, since it was evident that whatever evil things went on beneath the surface at Castello Minerva, Juanita knew nothing of them.

She separated egg yolks into an aluminium dish and added olive oil in her preparation of mayonnaise. I wondered that so unimportant a detail should register in my mind at such a time.

Over-plump, self-indulgent, and lazy, Juanita was also kind, and she had integrity. Should I warn her? What could I say? Either she'd laugh at me, or go straight to Lars Sven. As it turned out, Juanita wasn't so naively simple. Only, perhaps, infinitely wiser than Jenny, Ian, or I.

Like any conscientious cook, she went on with her delicate blending of oil and egg, as if her recipe was the most important thing in the world. But, lowering her voice, she said, "Senorita, something goes on here, yes? Something you sense, something that is—not nice!"

Oil and egg emulsified. The plump hand rotated the mass steadfastly.

Startled, I cast a glance back at the door. Juanita said, still in the same quiet but careful voice, "Those two, they are still at breakfast. The wooden floor is a telltale. Do not worry, I shall be warned if anyone comes."

Her words had momentarily robbed me of speech. In any case, despite her reassurance, I was horribly conscious of my enemies, breakfasting so coolly across the hall.

"The other English girl, Jenny, the beautiful one . . ."

But Juanita halted, stared at the mayonnaise, flashed me a very understanding smile, then said gently, "You are beautiful, too, Senorita Foundling, but it is a different sort of beauty." She resumed her beating, and went on, "Something happened to her. That is why you come, to find out, yes?"

"Juanita! How did you know something happened to Jenny?"

"I don't know how to make anyone believe it, Senorita. But the little senorita Jenny, she was so very frightened!"

"Nothing frightened Jenny!" I said stoutly, but I felt it wasn't true, not here in the Castello Minerva.

Juanita's dark eyes narrowed. "Oh, she never say she feel fear, you understand. Only I watch her, when she is alone, walking in the gardens. Or in the salon, before the others come at night for the drinking. And I tell you, there was much fear in those so beautiful eyes!"

Juanita's hand went rhythmically on and on.

"You too, Senorita, are frightened. You come, I think, to find out what happened to your friend. From the moment you come I sense this. Also your fear. And when you say her name, 'Jenny,' there is the great heartbreak in your voice, Senorita!"

Juanita had the peasant's near-uncanny ability to probe to the heart of a matter in seconds. But what did she know aside from what she instinctively suspected? My tears fell on the table top.

"Senorita, dry the eyes! If someone comes . . ."

Frowning, she moved to a tall wooden cupboard, took packets from it. Flour, fat, other ingredients I'd no real eyes to see. Accepting the cue though I began to relieve her of these packets as she handed them out, although I suspected they were entirely superfluous to her present culinary needs.

"So kind of you, Senorita Foundling! Juanita, she grows old and fat . . ." She dropped her voice to a whisper. "She went down to the dungeons alone several times.

And me, I often see her come out from the tower apartment at the dead of night. Si, and Senor Sven, too. But never together."

I dumped a giant jar of black olives upon the table, fingers convulsively sliding down the glass.

"The olives I need for my *pollo*. And afterwards, the fresh fruit." Again, the whisper, "I do not sleep well. Often I get up to refresh myself with a look at the pines and the sea, or the big ships sailing to places where Juanita never goes. Often I tell myself it is no affair to me what Senorita Midnight does. Only, till Senor Sven comes, nobody used that tower. And they do not ever go into the dungeons. But I am, what you say, only curious. I think perhaps they are planning something for their fashion show till, Senorita, your friend Jenny dies!"

She grimaced, nodded, waddled to the kitchen door, opened it. From across the hall we could hear voices murmuring. Juanita, returning, seized a huge knife, took a chicken from the refrigerator, and began to joint it deftly, with a certain viciousness.

"The day she die," Juanita whispered, "there comes a telephone call from El Pineo Nursing Home. And she say, 'Oh very well, Max, I'll come now.' She go, walking down that very road outside, so beautiful, so graceful. Me, I never see her alive again. They say she collapse at El Pineo. There is an operation. She does not recover. Dr. Gertae, when I ask, say they do not bring her body back here. She is—what you say—disfigured after the illness."

And the Gertaes and Lars Sven had all told me Jenny collapsed at the castello!

"I overhear them tell you she is taken ill here. I think that is a lie, that something is wrong."

"The police . . . Why didn't you go?" I breathed.

"Senor Sven, he has been so kind. But those Gertaes I never liked. And the police, how they take one old woman's babblings, eh? You lose your little bottle with the medicines. The stone falls on you from the tower. Yet nothing is wrong Juanita can prove!"

You and me both, Juanita, I said to myself.

"I debate if I should tell the priest. Only I think he say, Is it your business? But I watch you. I see you suspect, as Juanita, she also suspect . . ."

Suddenly Juanita all but shoved me off balance with a massive thrust in my ribs. Seizing from behind her an enormous kettle simmering on the great stove top, she poured boiling water into an empty basin just as the door opened. Elsa, coffeepot in hand, entered the kitchen.

She wore a smart green pants suit and a scarf of green chiffon loosely bound about her dark hair. By then, Juanita and I were enveloped in clouds of steam.

"Now this part, it is very important, Senorita Foundling. You put the chicken joints, so, into the hot water. Then the skin, it can later be—what you say—"

"Peeled," said Elsa, and smiled brilliantly. "Juanita, are you telling Senorita Foundling one of your recipes?"

"Si, si!" answered Juanita, stirring busily at her mayonnaise again.

"Splendid, Juanita. So useful for when she sets up housekeeping on her own. Now, if I could please just have a little of that hot water for some coffee?"

Smiling with apparent goodwill, Juanita brought water from another simmering kettle. Through the second cloud of steam, our eyes met.

I should have told you, anyway, soon, Juanita's eyes warned. *But now I know you are going, I have told you all I know. And, if you want me, I am here.*

I remembered there was a fashion magazine in the salon out of which Lars, before we quarrelled, had asked me to photostat an article on designing. I went to get it.

"We shall be leaving ourselves after tea today," Elsa said. Idly, she asked if I'd like more coffee. Imitating. her own apparent casualness, I hoped, I accepted another cup.

"We must return to El Pineo. We close it down, you understand, during the winter months when my husband takes over his practice in Barcelona."

"Yes, our pleasant holiday interlude is over," the doctor added. I had found the magazine, and I picked it up. "But we shall not lose sight of you altogether, Senorita, since you will be remaining on the island. We shall come over to visit

Lars from time to time. And hope we may have the pleasure of calling upon you, wherever you may have settled."

Not if I can help it, I thought, and said, "I think that very unlikely."

I'd rolled up the magazine, and held it convulsively clutched in my right hand. In the heat I felt my fingers adhering to the shiny surface, caught the faint odour of print.

The doctor in his white suit, and Madame, in her svelt outfit, were slightly to my right. Beyond, the terrace, the garden, and the sea were all obscured by rain.

"As I told Senor Sven, in the future, my way and his will lie far apart."

Elsa, her coffee finished, took a compact from her bag, and began to inspect her makeup.

"What will you do all alone, and so far from home?" she asked. An echo, almost, of Lars' words, and with as little genuine concern behind them.

"Oh, I'm used to caring for myself. I'll find something to do."

"Still, I wonder you should actually choose to stay on the island, with its poignant memories of your charming friend!"

Dr. Gertae's voice was as dead as his eyes. Smooth, ever-courteous, bland as cream, he had the deadliness of the iceberg, which keeps its fang hidden in the depths of the ocean.

"It was for Jenny's sake I came," I said steadfastly, like one repeating a protective litany. "But I'm not haunted by any morbid memories of her."

And that was true, too, even remembering the wraith in pinafore and pigtails.

"Haunted? A strange word to use, Ruth," said Elsa. Her eyes had narrowed, and her mouth was hard-set.

"Is it?" I said quietly. "But they say the dead can, and do, return, sometimes."

But Elsa just gave one of her aggravating shrugs, and Dr. Gertae shook his head, almost as if he doubted my sanity.

For the rest of the morning, I stayed in the tower apartment, peering out through the rain to see if I could catch any glimpse of the motorboat returning, or even, miraculously, of Ian, though common sense said he'd not return that way.

I telephoned the kitchens saying I

wanted no lunch. I couldn't contemplate the mockery of it now, with the Gertaes. Besides, I felt it was dangerous. Juanita waddled over herself with ice-cold *gazpacho* and some fruit. Before we could exchange any further confidences, the telephone rang. Juanita, nodding, finger to lip, discreetly withdrew. Presumably she just thought this must be some client of Lars'.

"Castello Minerva, Senor Sven's secretary."

"Ah, good afternoon, Senorita Foundling. This is the American Express Bank in Palma."

Ian Hamilton! I found I was clutching dizzily at the desk as the office spun crazily around me.

Shaken and sick, but filled with relief, I heard him go on, "Your travellers' cheques are ready, Senorita. However, the bank closes in thirty minutes. Can you come to the office today to sign for them?"

Was he back with the English detectives and a search warrant to examine the castello? Or hadn't he even gotten off the island? The questions seethed through my mind, but they were questions I dared not

446

ask, and Ian wouldn't dare to answer. Not here, and now.

A fevered glance at my watch. In exactly ten minutes a 'bus would trundle down on the road above the pines. Ian must have realised, too; it was my best chance of getting to his rendezvous.

"Thank you." With some difficulty I made my voice crisp, brisk, business-like. "Please expect me in fifteen minutes. If anything delays me, I'll come tomorrow at nine."

"Very good, Senorita Foundling. At either hour, then, we expect you. But preferably, this afternoon."

As Ian hung up, I wondered if I dared risk returning to the east wing for stronger shoes and my burberry? Crossing to the tower that morning, I'd worn light shoes and my plastic raincoat, but now the weather was turning nastier.

By great good fortune, my passport and all the money I should need was in my bag. I'd placed it there only last night, knowing I might need to move in a hurry.

Abandoning all idea of entering the east wing, I slipped down the circular staircase, around the tower's circumference, and down to the road.

My spine crawled, so strong was the sensation that eyes were upon me as I moved swiftly toward the iron gates.

Once past them, I dove to the cover of the pines lining the road, hearing their melancholy soughing breaking over my head.

The sense of surveillance, of someone watching me, that had assaulted me ever since I first set foot over the castello's threshold, now grew immeasurably stronger. Mingling with the soughing of the pines, the background beat of the sea, I fancied I could hear furtive footsteps pursuing me. I halted, gasping, and dared to look back. But I saw only the castello, lashed by rain, and the tower grimly outlined in the unusual gloom of the Majorcan afternoon. And, in that light, it seemed to hold only malevolence.

But ahead lay the turn in the road which ran straight on to the main highway. Once around that bend, I should be only ten minutes away from the safety of the Palma road.

The low cloud ceiling, the encroaching

pines, the knowledge that no building lay between the road and me, increased my fear, my sensation of being held in some green prison.

Then terror took on a positive form for suddenly, on my left, I saw movement. From the tree cover, two figures darted out, one cutting me off in front, the other running in from behind.

Swerving blindly, I ran sideways into the other section of the pine forest. I had some crazy notion of losing myself in it, crashing through to the Palma road, to the 'bus, and to Ian Hamilton, my saviour.

But the shorter of the figures, muffled in a dun coloured mackintosh, rushed forward and seized me around the waist and neck. Something damp and sickly-smelling was pressed over my mouth.

Fighting to get free, I had a last minute impression of a car hidden halfway down a track opposite the woods. Then everything went black about me.

14

WHEN I opened my eyes again, I lay on a small white bed. There was the smell of beeswax, disinfectant, and drugs. And Dr. Gertae loomed over me, setting down on a bedside table an aluminium vessel covered by a white napkin. The stone eyes raked me. The bland mouth smiled.

"No need for alarm, Miss Foundling. You are in a private suite of El Pineo. We told you a few lies at lunch. The nursing home closed for the winter a week ago. We sent the patients home, knowing we should need to offer you our hospitality, as it were."

Ian, I thought, dredging his name, its blessed associations of rescue and safety, up from the depths of half-drugged consciousness. Hold on till Ian gets here!

And then I remembered how I'd given that other, alternative meeting time, that if I didn't turn up this afternoon, Ian would simply assume I'd believed it safer to come in the morning! The morning . . .

"Thinking of your supposed ally, the Englishman, Ian Hamilton, are you?" sneered the doctor. He closed one reptilian-cold hand around my wrist. I snatched my hand away.

"Come now, you aren't going to be obstinate, are you?" Elsa sat on a white-painted hospital chair. She still wore the green pants suit. Jewels of rain glittered on her dark hair; her mackintosh was flung hurriedly beside the bed.

"We're going to give you some necessary treatment," Dr. Gertae went on. "Unless you care to tell us voluntarily where they are?"

Then I thought perhaps I am mad, and this is the absolute hell of non-reality, the nihilistic no-man's-land where nothing can have any meaning? Perhaps I've been in that nightmare state ever since I crossed the courtyard, back in the Mendip cottage, and saw Jenny staring at me in her orphanage pinafore?

"Come, stop masquerading as the naive innocent, Ruth!" commanded Elsa coldly. "A splendid performance. We let you go on with it, expecting to find out without having to do you any physical harm. But that nonsense must stop now! Where are they?"

The doctor snatched the napkin off the aluminium dish. Light from the ceiling globe flashed on a syringe charged with pale yellow liquid.

"Pentathol, Miss Foundling, the so-called truth drug. Now, let's get you out of this mackintosh."

Elsa got up, moved towards me. I thrust myself back against the bed head, holding on to it with both hands.

"I'm a British subject! If you force me to submit to that injection against my will the police in England—"

"They'll never find you," said the doctor, and dragged off my mackintosh with Elsa's help. Struggling seemed a waste of valuable energy. Determined, though, not to be injected, I knew I must wait till the very last second, when the needle was all but ready to prick the vein.

"This room," said Elsa, "is sound-proofed—for very disturbed patients, you understand. Nobody outside would hear you if you shrieked your attractive little head off. There's nobody here save Max and me and, as you know the nursing home is as isolated as the castello."

"Miss Foundling," the doctor threatened, "the mind—any mind!—is a bastion which can be breached by suitable drugs. These cut out individual will, making struggle useless. But I'd prefer you tell us voluntarily. In that case, no doubt, we could come to some sort of bargain."

"Bargain? With the pair of you? Anyway, I don't know what you're talking about!"

"Oh, come now, my dear." Elsa sounded weary, as well as angry. "We know that Jenny Midnight told you about the Ellerman Emeralds and that she came to Castello Minerva expressly to find them!"

Of all the things I'd expected to hear, this was the most ridiculous!

"The Ellerman Emeralds," went on Dr. Gertae, "are two huge individual gems, part of the collection of a White Russian duke murdered during the Revolution."

"And worth," Elsa said lightly, "half a million sterling!"

"Henry Ellerman, wealthy London

merchant banker, bought them when they were smuggled out of Russia. Thereafter, though the gems retained his name, they had many owners. They've a reputation for being cursed, bringing ill luck and bad fortune to all who own them."

Elsa's tone as she interrupted her husband was light, but it held an undercurrent of conviction. "Superstitious rubbish! The last owner gave them to one Rosalie Saunders . . ."

Inevitably, I caught my breath. Elsa and the doctor exchanged glances.

"I see you've heard of the lady. Somehow we thought you had. Now, just who gave them to Rosalie, nobody is quite sure. Nobody in our little world, that is. You see, they changed hands at a London jewel auction. The buyer was anonymous. Anonymous, that is, to jewel handlers and criminals, as the world calls people like myself and Elsa!"

I struggled with a weird sensation of déjà vu as if I had received confirmation of information until now only subconsciously known. Of the Ellerman Emeralds I'd never heard. I sighed, remembering the kind of woman Rosalie Saunders had been.

"The police never knew Rosalie had them. Only certain people in the criminal underworld would have known."

"How do *you* know?" I cried. "And where's your accomplice, Lars Sven? Or did he tell you? And what about darling little Marie?"

The doctor's smile grew narrower, stretching his facial muscles like those of some ghastly puppet's. But Elsa looked over her shoulder. Instantly, Gertae moved a fraction closer.

"Marie? She did a little necessary spying for us, yes. But she knows nothing about the emeralds. Oh, she took that pill bottle from your suitcase. We got her to search your room for clues. Then we instructed her to put it back on the table. Nothing had been done to it. And the drug I slipped into your wine that night in the dining room was really quite harmless, if unpleasant in its effect."

I strained further back from him as my eye caught the metallic glint of needle and syringe.

"And I'm afraid little Marie was the naughty girl who pushed that piece of stone over the battlements. She had strict instructions not to let it fall too near."

I gasped, horrified.

Elsa went on, "I had a duplicate key to the tower made. I let her in, when we saw you go out again after our little meeting in the salon. Marie had already seen you with Ian Hamilton."

"You—you just wait till he finds out about this!"

The doctor's smile was very peculiar indeed. Elsa's laugh held triumph.

"You murderers!"

"Marie," said Elsa, "is strong and active. Her eyesight is good, and she knows the terrain around the tower like the back of her hand. You were never in any real danger."

"Then why?"

"You were so obstinate!" said Gertae. "We knew why you'd come, and that Jenny must have told you. We expected you would cooperate once Jenny was gone. When we realised you'd come to hunt on your own, we tried to frighten you off, hoping you'd give up and go home like a nice, well-behaved young English lady."

So it had been Marie, not Lars, in at least two of the attacks, and the doctor in the other!

"Marie is very vain," Elsa said, reflectively. "She is also poor. She watched your movements, reported on them to us."

"Want to hear the rest of it, do you?" taunted the doctor. "Well, if it makes you realise the hopelessness of your position. Rosalie Saunders' maid had a husband, then awaiting trial for some petty crime. He was, I fear, a common sneak thief. But he found out Rosalie had the Ellermans. After Rosalie's death, the maid searched the flat. Not finding them, she realised Gordon Ayrton, known to you as Lars Sven, must have taken them. Afraid to do anything further herself, it wasn't till twenty years later, on her own death bed, that she told her only son. And he, Miss Foundling, was a man already enjoying the easy living that comes from an intelligent pursuit of crime."

But I was thinking, appalled, of the emeralds and Jenny's love of beauty and luxury. Jenny—warm, tender-hearted, joyous Jenny Midnight—a thief? Conniving and consorting with creatures like these? It was as if Jenny, too, had betrayed me.

And for a moment, I didn't much care whether Ian Hamilton came or not.

"I was one of Rosalie's many lovers," said Gertae. "Her favourite, apart from young Gordon. But I never knew she had the emeralds till the maid gave me the word. She was going out that night, and the coast was clear. She was positive they were somewhere in the flat, but she'd searched the place herself and never found them. I told her I'd sell them, give her a share. Afterwards I learned that while we talked outside the house, young Gordon Ayrton arrived. But when I slipped in, he'd gone."

"Max," warned Elsa, "get that stuff into her!"

But I saw the truth in her eyes.

"Why it was you who killed Rosalie Saunders!"

"Yes, Miss Foundling. She was obstinate. I told her I knew she had the Ellerman Emeralds, that I wanted them. She laughed, and told me to go to hell, that they were where I'd never find them. Not believing her, I killed her. I searched her person and turned the bloody flat inside out. I wore gloves and took every precaution, but then I heard someone coming. Fortunately I got away unchallenged. When I heard the police had arrested Gordon Ayrton, I suspected he had the gems. But I dared not go after them then. I started a new life in Australia, qualified out there as a doctor. For a while I prospered, and even forgot about the gems."

Oh, how I wish you had, my heart cried. How I wish you had never come back to involve us all in this hideous nightmare.

"Then I lost everything playing the stock market. I risked returning to England. My mind was on the Ellermans again. I traced Ayrton to Norway, then Europe. He had taken the name Lars Sven. Oh, medicine interests me, Miss Foundling, and I am fully qualified. My Barcelona practice is quite bona fide, but there's no real fortune to be made out of the profession. Besides Rosalie Saunders had been a demanding mistress. I felt she owed me those baubles."

My heart almost stopped, then began to

race. Outside in the corridor I heard the sound of feet—a tread I knew. Not till it was too late did the significance of those undisguised footsteps burst upon my reeling mind!

A man in a dark blue mackintosh of traditional English cut and style stood there. Rain glistened on his red hair and strong, clean-shaven chin.

"Hullo, Ruthie dear."

"No! Not you!" He kicked the white painted door shut. His big, familiar right hand held a small gun, which gleamed malevolently bluish-black in the light from the ceiling.

And Ian Hamilton smiled gently, terribly, at me!

I struggled to sit up, but Max's snake-cold hands thrust me back.

"After I signed the death certificate," Gertae went on, "Elsa found the faint appendicitis scar on your friend's body. Elsa used to be a nurse, you know, a fact I found most useful when I met her after I returned from Australia."

Beside myself, I cried out in anguish and horror, "What did Jenny die of? And what have you done with her body?"

"I'd already telephoned the British Consul with the story she'd died of appendicitis. I fear we really did panic a little then. Supposing—though there was no real risk of it—someone came from England, asking to bring the body back there for burial; someone who knew her medical history? In view of what was at stake, we couldn't risk that, so we enlisted the services of an undertaker from the mainland. Roderique is—or was—an old, valued friend. He coffined the so-called corpse and arranged the burial service beautifully. Then, suitably rewarded, he flew off to take a long vacation in Mexico."

"Jenny?" I croaked. "Jenny."

"Somewhere at the bottom of the beautiful Mediterranean, weighted down with lead," Ian said in a new, cold voice. And coming forward, he slapped my face with his free hand. All this time Ian had been a trap to deceive me into telling where the Ellerman Emeralds were! I had believed their confederate was my ally!

"Max filled her up with pentathol, but the obstinate bitch still wouldn't talk. Max finally gave her a massive injection that finished her off!"

461

"Oh, Jenny, Jenny!" I wept bitterly.

"Save your pity. You'll need it for yourself. We took her out in Lars' boat one night when he was away in Barcelona, and dumped dear Jenny Midnight down into the deep blue sea."

"You—you're lying!" I muttered. "You filthy Judas! As if Jenny would ever stoop to conspire with criminals like you!"

"Tch! Such loyalty!" jeered Ian, and slapped the other side of my face so that my senses rocked, and all three of them wavered about in front of me like paper figures. "Silly, trusting, naive little fool! All right then, read this!"

With dread, and through mists of pain and terror, I recognised the writing on the letter he dragged from his pocket. It was the other half of the letter from Jenny he'd shown me in the Genova cafe.

My eyes leaped over the phrases about her keeping well, about there being a doctor in the house if she needed him, and then about the appendicitis on the orphanage outing.

"She hadn't known the Gertaes intimately when she wrote that," Ian said softly. "And I didn't show the doctor or

Elsa the letter till after she was dead. But by then, Elsa had spotted that telltale scar. We decided to use the letter as a lure to fox you. Read on, trusting little Ruthie."

From this you'll gather I'm in, Ian darling! I've yet to make myself properly known to the Gertaes. It's vital Lars doesn't suspect you told me who they were, and why they're here, so I'll need to choose my opportunity to whisper that I'm here to contact them.

I'm looking for the loot, and so far, no luck. I'm sure LS doesn't suspect anything. If I can get the key to the dungeons I should soon know where it is.

I don't want to put any more in writing.

Love,
Jenny

So, I thought dully, it was true. Jenny had become a thief, hunting for the emeralds to share with these thugs and criminals.

"The law will get you for this," I threatened. "You must have forced poor Jenny into it."

"The law got me a year ago in England," confessed Gertae. "For doing illegal abortions in the nursing home Elsa and I were then running. So now you understand why we eventually came here."

"To many awkward inquiries," said Elsa, "and all of them a little too near home."

Yes, I could see that. Then they were on the trail of the gems. Jenny must have found them and then been callously put out of the way!

The rest of it poured out of Ian Hamilton in a sick, malevolent stream. Ian encountered the Gertaes in Norway. Primed by revenge for his dead mother, Rosalie's maid, he trailed Lars, believing that he had killed Rosalie. Soon instinct informed him that the Gertaes were on the same hunt, although he was ignorant of the fact at the time that Max Gertae had ever been Rosalie Saunder's lover.

These twists and quirks of fate, did they mean anything, save that we were all helpless victims of blind destiny?

The doctor had never changed his name. He was plain Max Gertae then, an Englishman of Austrian parentage, a petty criminal. But he believed the English police would never catch up with him in the Rosalie Saunders affair, since only Ian Hamilton's mother knew he had been in the house that night.

"So," I said, "all that on the coach, the meeting up with me here, Ian—" I thought of something particularly vicious. "The white horse! You got Marie to break it, to put it on my pillow, remembering our talk at the frontier station. You said that in Scandinavia, the horse was often a symbol for the sacrifice of the owner!"

"Yes, Ruthie dear, my telephone call, the visit to the cementario, all were designed to throw dust in your beautiful, innocent eyes. Jenny gave you the emeralds after she found them here. Or you acquired them, accidentally or innocently, after her death. She double-crossed us!"

"Marie telephoned to let us know when Lars and Jenny were out," said Elsa. "We searched the castello, at intervals, from tower to dungeons. Marie saw Jenny coming from the dungeons one night carrying something very carefully in her hand. But when we searched, we found nothing. So from that we suspected, Jenny found the Ellermans and wasn't going to tell us."

"You see," Ian said, "we knew either Lars or Jenny still had the gems because they've never been passed to a fence. With our contacts, we're sure. Now, little Ruth, will you talk? Or do we get Max, here, to make you?"

"Jenny didn't talk," I said defiantly.

Dr. Gertae's voice was very ugly. "No, she passed out under the drug, in fact. It was easier, then, to finish the job. But you'll talk. I'll be more careful this time!"

The needle was about to prick my flesh. All I could think of was my friend Jenny had betrayed me! Then, incredibly, Gertae's hand began to shake! Elsa turned, staring at the door. Ian Hamilton levelled his gun at the slowly-turning handle.

Slowly, very slowly, an infinitesimal degree at a time, it revolved and the door began to open. Hamilton swore obscenely, and the doctor dropped the syringe. From Elsa, a shuddering breath, dredged up, as it seemed, from the depths of her being.

"No," I whispered, looking at the now fully-opened door, at what was framed in the entry. "No, dear God! Jenny, Jenny! Go—go away!"

But she didn't go back to those shadowy realms of the dead where she now properly belonged. Nor did she, this time, even fade. And she certainly didn't smile, or greet me with that loving tenderness in her dark-blue eyes.

Her figure was wraith-like enough, wrapped loosely in a white coat. Over her shoulders her bright hair hung unplaited. Her face was as if carved from marble. Shuddering, I thought, if I dare to touch it, now, it will surely have death's chill!

Her eyes opened, suddenly, to their widest. They were blazingly, furiously alive!

"No!" shrieked Elsa, as I'd done, but on a full horrified cry, lips open, figure convulsed, arms outstretched, to ward off Jenny. But Jenny came inexorably on, like an avenging fury. "No! Keep away, damn you!"

"Jenny—Jenny Midnight!" croaked Ian Hamilton, and his gun went clattering to the floor. "You—you're at the bottom of the Mediterranean!"

The doctor stared, kept on staring, but

he trembled convulsively from head to foot, that glacial calm of his smashed at last.

Jenny, smiling, glided towards my bed. Then, behind her, I saw other figures, human forms that would surely never have played custodian to any ghost. A group of uniformed men that I recognised as Majorcan police stood there. Beyond them were another two or three plainclothesmen, and a slender, dark man with a very professional air.

And there, at the very back of the group, was Lars Sven, staring towards Jenny. His dark eyes soon found mine, and our gaze locked.

"Don't be frightened, Ruth, darling!"

Surely that was Jenny's voice, as in life, low and vibrant, so warm and alive! She took me in her arms, just as she'd done to comfort and reassure me in the old orphanage days. The uniformed men seized the Gertaes and Ian Hamilton. "You've done a perfectly splendid job. Didn't I tell you, when we were kids, that if I ever wanted help, I'd ask nobody but you?"

15

THE segments of velvet that had been the green Cheshire cat were layed out on the coffee table in the salon of the Castello Minerva.

The English detectives whom Jenny had brought with her had opened up the two large velvet eyes, finding in them the Ellerman Emeralds, so cunningly cushioned in the material that my exploring hand had failed to find them.

"I'm sorry, Lars," Jenny said, her arm around my shoulders, "I suppose my early years made me greedy. When Ian sought me out in London, and told me he had reason to believe you had two valuable emeralds concealed somewhere in the castello I was tempted to find them."

"So you went down into the dungeons, poked around till you found that iron ring and the box," said Lars grimly.

There was a silence. Jenny nodded, and the dark-haired man behind her leaned forward, and pressed her shoulder. She

469

half-turned, gave him one of her loveliest smiles. As his dark grey eyes returned it, I read Jenny's future.

"And the emeralds. Yes, Lars. I read the letters, and knew at once that Rosalie Saunders was your sister! She was, wasn't she?"

Lars nodded, biting his lip. I recollected the woman's photograph, those telltale phrases, "To my own darling," "My precious Lars." How could I ever have been so blind?

Reason, logic, and common sense, I remembered remorsefully, and felt the tears start. Jenny's hand tightened on my shoulder.

"Rosalie was my older sister, yes. We kept our relationship secret because of the way she lived. About that, now, I say nothing. Only that, whatever the world may think, she was always good to me."

Daring, then, to reach out and touch his hand, my heart fluttered as his fingers closed hard around mine.

"I adored her. Felt terribly, perhaps wrongly, protective towards her, even when I knew she had stolen the emeralds. The man was a most distinguished name,

470

high in public office, and much esteemed. He promised to marry her, make a lady out of her. Then laughed in her face. She stole the emeralds in retaliation. Then, she realised she was being secretly watched and that her maid's husband was a petty criminal. The night before her death—I never knew until now that that devil, Max Gertae, killed her, of course, or I'd have done the same to him, long ago! Rosalie gave me the emeralds."

Lars sighed, his dark eyes brilliant with pain. The pressure of his fingers grew strong again. "She repented the theft, and was terrified someone would steal the emeralds from her before she had a chance to return them. She was actually about to tell me the name of the owner when she heard the maid outside. 'Come back,' she whispered, 'tomorrow night. I'll tell you then. But take the gems. I don't trust that girl. You can return them to the owner . . .' But next night, when I did go back, I spotted the maid talking to someone in the garden. Suspecting some sort of trap, I slipped away, coward that I was. Then, fearful for her, back I went.

By then it was too late. She'd been murdered by that devil."

"We have his confession on record, sir," said the Detective-Sergeant."

"That girl—the one who alibied for me —lied," Lars went on. "I left the emeralds with her. She drowned herself, terrified of discovery, because she was going to have a child, and she thought, poor kid, they'd put her in prison as some sort of accessory. It was my child."

"Oh!" I said pitifully.

"I determined, as I promised Rosalie, to return the gems . . ." Lars' grimace was ironic. "But I didn't know to whom! So I just kept them."

"You could have sent them to the police anonymously, sir!"

"I was a fool. After a childhood spent in poverty, I was embittered. Rosalie was good to me. I adored her. But my childhood and adolescence, all the same, were sheer hell. I had no background, no real identity. No one I could get close to. I never knew who my father was."

Now his look focussed on Jenny with a searing pain. "Then I met you, Jenny. I'd read that story in the newspapers about

472

your orphanage upbringing. Oh, I denied it to Ruth. I thought how perfect Jenny and I were. We were brilliantly successful in our careers, but socially we were two outcasts."

Lars stopped, shaking his head, and Jenny said, "Darling Lars, I know. And when I read those letters, I just couldn't go through with the idea of stealing the gems. And then, that lock of her hair you'd so carefully laid away with them."

"Rosalie's hair!" I gasped. "But I thought—"

"You thought it was Jenny's, that I'd murdered her, leaving that—*souvenir*—" Lars' expression was like a knife in my heart, "to gloat over, Ruth."

Twisting the knife still further, I nodded, in guilt.

"But it was marked," Jenny said, astonished. "A little twist of paper wrapped around it, saying 'Rosalie's hair.' Darling Ruth, you must have missed it down there, in the cold and the dark. You were frightened . . ."

"No," said Lars, "I knew Ruth had been down there. I found the twist of paper on the floor below the iron ring."

Reason, logic, and common sense, I told myself again, and a grown young woman, surrendering to hysteria, too frightened to search for that truth she boasted she'd come to the island to uncover.

"Jenny," said Lars, "I saw you coming from the dungeons one night after midnight. I realised you'd found out where the key was, and taken it. When I went down the next day, the Ellerman emeralds, also in the tin box, were gone. But I couldn't believe you were just a common thief. So I said nothing, waiting, sure you'd come and tell me why you'd taken them."

"Oh, Lars!" said Jenny, and her eyes were full of tears.

"I even had some weird idea you might have found out who the real owner was, that there might also be some relationship between the owner and you."

And he told us that deliberately he then left the key where it was. He already suspected the Gertaes, possibly Ian Hamilton, as well, had searched the dungeons, never finding the box behind its iron ring. Then I came along.

"In the shadow of Jenny, as it were,"

said Lars, in that cold, curt tone which I now realised was a cloak for his most passionate feelings. "I wanted, desperately, to trust you. You could have been my one ally. But you obviously mistrusted me. I felt, then, that all your loyalty, all your love, was for Jenny Midnight. And I was that much older, and Jenny and I——" He shrugged. It was painfully obvious how well he'd read any thoughts.

"But Jenny," I cried, remembering, "the iron ring? Obviously the Gertaes and Hamilton never found out the box was behind it. And I only stumbled on it by accident."

"How strange," said Lars sombrely. "How very strange."

"Yes, as if Ruth was led to it," said Jenny solemnly. "Lars, darling, it was no such inspiration with me. You talk in your sleep, I'm afraid. And I heard you talking, one night when we were together, about the circular chamber, and the iron ring, and murmuring Rosalie's name.

"But I swear I was going to come to you, Lars, to warn you about the Gertaes and Ian Hamilton, tell you they'd asked me to split with them, four ways. Then, from the coldness of your manner, I suspected you'd found out something. I— I lost my courage, even wondered if you'd go to the police. Marie was also watching me, and Hamilton and the Gertaes threatened that, if I exposed them, they'd kill me. Then I got a message from El Pineo. Max said you had had an unfortunate accident, and I'd better come and bring the emeralds. Somehow, they'd found out I was double-crossing them."

"Marie," I explained. "She's been spying for the Gertaes all the time. And she also saw you coming from the dungeons."

Jenny nodded. "At El Pineo they injected me with pentathol. The night before, suspecting they were closing the net, I sewed the two emeralds up in the eyes of the Cheshire cat, then stowed it away in the chest. I was desperate. It was all I could think of. Juanita suspected something, I knew. I hoped and prayed she'd find them if I was prevented from confessing to Lars. I got over the threshold of the private suite at El Pineo, then they seized me and I was injected. But I don't remember anything else till I found myself being hauled aboard a Greek steamer somewhere off Ibiza!"

A dark young man with the air of quiet authority stepped forward. Jenny's hand left my shoulder, as, smiling, he pulled her gently to her feet.

"We don't quite know what happened to the weights the Gertaes and Hamilton put around her feet. But both calves and insteps were badly cut as if her legs, mercifully, had hit some projection. Mercifully because this projection, a piece of iron or something from a wreckage probably, cut the ropes holding the weights and released her, still unconscious, to the surface."

More bits of the puzzle fell into place. The Greek steamer took Jenny to Athens. The dark young man, Dr. James Norman, was temporarily working there in a hospital, and he was at once attracted to the beautiful young girl.

"Amnesia can take a long time to clear up," he explained. "In Jenny's case it took nearly three months."

Jenny looked down at me again.

"When I did remember, Jimmy urged me to go to New Scotland Yard at once and tell them everything. And when he

477

said I was well enough, he flew in with me."

"But Jenny," I whispered, "Jenny, darling, I kept seeing you from the time Ralph left me and I got the British Consul's cable. You were in that ghastly orphanage pinafore with your hair in braids. And you kept coming, in flashes, all the way from Somerset, and then here, at the castello—all the time, except for these last few awful days. And you kept saying that when you wanted help, you wouldn't ask anybody but me!"

Dr. Norman—Jimmy, as instinct told me I must call him from now on—looked at me with great kindness. "Jenny's tremendous link to you, Ruth, connected your mind with her on the subconscious plane. All along, since first encountering Hamilton, her real self was in rebellion. He'd tempted her by telling her about the Ellerman emeralds. In her secret soul, she knew it was wrong. When her conscious mind lay meshed in that self-protective amnesia, her subconscious, recollecting that old pact she'd made with you, winged out on the mental plane and made vital contact with you. In the Greek hospital, she spoke your name, so many times, and in such a tone of laboured anguish."

"So she was sending me messages!" I said, inexpressibly moved. "She—she drew me, deliberately, to the island, so that I could find the green cat and put things right."

"I don't remember what happened when I was in that state of amnesia," Jenny confessed. "But Jimmy's right in that the second I remembered everything, I knew immediately that you and Lars were in terrible danger. That must have been when the extrasensory part of me stopped communicating with you."

Jenny grinned and touched my shoulder chidingly. "Ruth, you silly, I never thought you'd suspect poor old Lars!"

Of all the countenances ringing around me then, the one upon which I found the most understanding was the serious, detached, but very compassionate face of Dr. James Norman.

"We phoned the Mendip cottage, Ruth," Jenny went on. "But there were new tenants there. Then, someone in the village post office remembered that you were believed to have gone to Majorca, and the gentleman to Canada. That creature, Ralph!" and then, smiling, looked from Lars to me, then back to the man she so lovingly called Jimmy.

"Ruth?"
It was just before noon the following day. Jenny and her doctor had disappeared somewhere in the grounds. I had last caught sight of them sauntering deep into the heart of the pine forest fringing the shore, the lovely green woodland that no longer held any terrors for me.

Marie was missing, in a more permanent sense. Lars told me he had no intention of searching for her, and the police said that to charge her with any definite crime would be very difficult.

Ian Hamilton and the Gertaes were on their way to England with the detectives, where Max Gertae would be duly charged with the crime of murder against Rosalie Saunders. Elsa and Ian would go to trial as his accessories, for the attempted murder of Jenny Midnight, and attempted robbery.

The Ellerman emeralds were also on their way to London. Their ownership, we'd all been astounded to learn, was known to New Scotland Yard!

"After the Rosalie Saunders case had been on the files for more than a year," the Chief-Superintendent told Lars, "this gentleman, who wishes his anonymity to be preserved . . ."

Lars nodded, but his eyes were hard.

". . . Privately informed us that he'd lost them. He named no names."

"Very noble, I'm sure," said Lars.

"Yes, sir. I understand your feelings. We had no real clue there was any connection between these gems and the Rosalie Saunders case. Then a veteran detective at the Yard remembered there was the ghost of a whisper our gentleman was one of Rosalie's 'friends.' He kept quiet during the trial, so the police knew nothing about the Emeralds ever having been in Rosalie's hands. But a sneak thief in Wandsworth, when he was dying, in delirium spoke of Rosalie Saunders. Apparently, her maid's husband told the sneak thief Rosalie was hiding the emeralds. We had no evidence against any of those concerned in the old trial. Then, young Miss Midnight and Dr. James Norman turned up at the Yard with their tale, and the pieces began to fall into place."

A glance passed between the two men.

"And myself? And Jenny Midnight?" said Lars.

"No charges. So far as New Scotland Yard and our client's understanding goes he lost the gems and now has them back again."

He half-turned, and with a very gentle smile, put a hand on Lars' shoulder.

"Unlucky gems they're supposed to be, aren't they, sir? But maybe they'll turn out to have brought you another kind of fortune. Just one last word, though. If either you, or any of your friends, thinks of taking the law into their own hands in the future, think again, and ring us up at New Scotland Yard. You'll find we're really quite human, sir."

The officer said nothing further but, like Jimmy Norman's, his eyes were eloquent enough.

One other thing bothered me—that desecrated grave in the English cementario in Genova. With some difficulty, I made my feelings plain.

"We'll put that right, don't you

worry, Miss Foundling," the Chief-Superintendent said. "I reckon you weren't quite rational in your actions at that time, what with seeing the ghost, as you thought, of your friend."

"And I shall see that financial and other compensation is made," Lars assured me.

But there were still a few personal loose ends that I wanted cleared up. Always the logician, the girl with the tidy mind, I wanted to be sure there was a rational explanation for everything.

But where, in what I called logic and reason, did the answer lie to a mind that, on a bed of sickness, across thousands of miles of land and ocean, could so effectively reach out and find another mind in love and warning?

Jenny had bitterly reproached herself for falling victim to temptation to buy herself some of that luxury and wealth we'd both been starved for in childhood and youth.

But I was no better. Because of Ralph, I'd started holding most men in contempt. And the one man I did trust turned out to be my enemy.

"Lars," I said, now that we were alone,

"why did you and Felipe go out so much in that motorboat?"

"I found a scarf of Jenny's floating out in the bay. Felipe dragged it in with the hook. I was already suspicious. Max Gertae wouldn't let me view Jenny's remains and I couldn't prove anything. Soon afterwards you came. Felipe shared my confidences, but mistrusted you. We searched, thinking the sea might offer other clues."

His face was gray. All on his own, keeping silent out of consideration for me, Lars had tried to tackle the horror that had invaded the castello, obstinately, but courageously, shackled by his own legacy from the past and his remorseful, ambivalent love for Rosalie, his sister.

"One more confession, Lars."

I told him how I'd found the tunnel up through the promontory, and the other iron-studded door, and what I'd feared might lie behind it. Lars laughed, it wasn't a pleasant sound.

"So you thought I'd got her bricked up behind that second door! Well, I knew you were busy turning me into some sort of ogre, but not quite such a fearsome one as that. No wonder you couldn't bear to let me come near you."

And he explained that, years ago, there'd been a fall of rock behind the seaward door, making the passage to the dungeons dangerous. It was bricked up now, and there was no access.

The great room was very silent. Pine scent and sea tang drifted in with the aroma of late roses. I looked at Lars. The clove carnation was missing from his lapel, as it had been for days now.

"Well, Ruth?" said Lars harshly. "Are you going to stay over there by those windows forever?"

We were married at Christmas. Our honeymoon was spent in England, with Dr. James Norman and Jenny, who was now his wife. They'd bought an old grey farmhouse up in the Cotswolds. Jenny vowed she'd do no more roaming, and was utterly content to settle down and be a doctor's wife. She had found the love and security she'd been seeking all her life.

"I've let you go now, Ruth darling," she told me one day when we were alone together. "Not because I don't need you.

In our very special sense we shall always need one other. But we've each found the other halves of ourselves."

Yes, that questing for love and fulfillment was over. If Jenny had walked through the valley of the shadow to find it, so had I, and so also, in his own way, had Lars. And if none of us had ever set foot on the island, our lives must all have been immeasurably different. Jenny and I should have been questing still . . .

In the spring, Lars and I came back to the castello. The almond tress were out in a froth of cream and green. The windmills turned under a soft, blue sky. The brown and white goats climbed the meadows above the rocky promontories, the tinkle of their bells mingling with the music of the sea. And I heard that haunting, natural melody, always for me, elemental and mysterious, the true song of Majorca, the shushing, languorous murmur of the high pines.

I turned to Lars as Felipe drove the car towards the iron gates. Beyond I glimpsed the castello, no more the haunted, evil place a search for earthly treasure had made of it; no grim fortress whose dungeons housed sinister and terrible secrets, but a place my husband and I would make into our home.

From the castello I had drawn out two prizes. Lars' love, of course, was the first, coming paramount in my scale of values. I had no illusions there. With his temperament, his stormy and clouded past, and my own inexperience, our married life would never be easy. I was sure, however, it would be satisfying.

The other gift destiny had given me at the castello was self-knowledge. Here, I'd had to work my own magic. Not till I was tested did I find my true self; till then, I had been only half-alive.

But if, without the fight, there could have been no victory, it was love's ancient alchemy which brought me, in every personal sense, my treasure, which now I reckoned beyond all human price.

GUIDE
TO THE COLOUR CODING
OF
ULVERSCROFT BOOKS

Many of our readers have written to us expressing their appreciation for the way in which our colour coding has assisted them in selecting the Ulverscroft books of their choice. To remind everyone of our colour coding—this is as follows:

BLACK COVERS
Mysteries

★

BLUE COVERS
Romances

★

RED COVERS
Adventure Suspense and General Fiction

★

ORANGE COVERS
Westerns

★

GREEN COVERS
Non-Fiction